A Secret Seduction

KIM LAWRENCE
ELIZABETH LANE
WENDY S. MARCUS

MILLS & BOON

First Published in Great Britain 2017
By Mills & Boon, an imprint of HarperCollins*Publishers*
1 London Bridge Street, London, SE1 9GF

A SECRET SEDUCTION © 2017 Harlequin Books S. A.

A Secret Until Now, *A Sinful Seduction* and *Secrets Of A Shy Socialite* were first published in Great Britain by Harlequin (UK) Limited.

A Secret Until Now © 2014 Kim Lawrence
A Sinful Seduction © 2014 Elizabeth Lane
Secrets Of A Shy Socialite © 2013 Wendy S. Marcus

ISBN:978-0-263-929584

05-0417

A SECRET UNTIL NOW

BY
KIM LAWRENCE

Though lacking much authentic Welsh blood—she comes from English/Irish stock—**Kim Lawrence** was born and brought up in North Wales. She returned there when she married and her sons were both born on Anglesey, an island off the coast. Though not isolated, Anglesey is a little off the beaten track, but lively Dublin, which Kim loves, is only a short ferry-ride away.

Today they live on the farm her husband was brought up on. Welsh is the first language of many people in this area, and Kim's husband and sons are all bilingual—she is having a lot of fun, not to mention a few headaches, trying to learn the language!

With small children, the unsocial hours of nursing didn't look attractive so, encouraged by a husband who thinks she can do anything she sets her mind to, Kim tried her hand at writing. Always a keen Mills & Boon reader, it seemed natural for her to write a romance novel—now she can't imagine doing anything else.

She is a keen gardener and cook and enjoys running—often on the beach, as living on an island the sea is never very far away. She is usually accompanied by her Jack Russell, Sprout—don't ask. . .it's a long story!

For my dad, Roy,
who was always proud of his writer daughter.

PROLOGUE

London, Summer 2008, a hotel

ANGEL'S EYES HAD adjusted to the dark but from where she was lying the illuminated display of the bedside clock was hidden from her view, blocked by his shoulder. But the thin finger of light that was shining into the room through the chink in the blackout curtains suggested that it was morning.

'The morning after the night before!'

She gave a soft shaken sigh and allowed her glance to drift around the unfamiliar room, the generic but luxurious five-star hotel furnishings familiar, especially to someone who had slept in dozens of similar suites; someone who had imagined at one point that everybody ordered their supper from room service.

Since she'd had the choice Angel had avoided rooms like this as they depressed her. Depressed... Smiling at the past tense, she raised herself slowly up on one elbow. This room was different not because it boasted a special view or had a sumptuously comfortable bed. What was different was that she was not alone.

She froze when the man on the bed beside her murmured in his sleep and her attention immediately returned to him—it had never really left him. She gulped as he threw a hand above his head, the action causing the muscles in his beautiful back to ripple in a way that made her stomach flip over. She couldn't see his face but his breathing remained deep and regular.

Should she wake him up?

The bruised-looking half-moons underneath his spectacular eyes suggested he probably needed his sleep. She'd noticed them the moment she'd looked at him, but then she had noticed pretty much everything about him. Angel had never considered herself a particularly observant person but crazily one glance had indelibly printed his face into her memory.

Mind you, it was a pretty special face, not made any less special by the lines of fatigue etched around his wide, sensual mouth or the dark shadows beneath those totally spectacular eyes. There was a weary cynicism reflected in those electric-blue depths and also in that first instant anger.

He had been furious with her, but it wasn't the incandescent anger that had made her legs feel hollow or even her dramatic brush with death or that he had saved her life. It was him, everything about him. He projected an aura of raw maleness that had a cataclysmic impact on her, like someone thrown in the deep end who from that first moment was treading water, barely able to breathe, throat tight with emotion as if she were submerged by a massive wave of lust.

It wasn't until much later that she had recognised this as a crossroad moment. She didn't see a fork in the road; there was no definable instant when she made a conscious decision. Her universe had narrowed into this total stranger, and she had known with utter and total conviction that she had to be with him. She wanted him and then she had seen in his eyes he wanted her too.

What else mattered?

Did I really just think that?

What else mattered? The defence of the greedy, absurdly needy and just plain stupid! Angel, who was utterly confident she was none of those things, was conscious that this particular inner dialogue was one it would have been more sensible to have had before, not *after*... After she had broken the habit of a lifetime and thrown caution, baby, bath water and the entire package out of the window!

The previous night there had been no inner dialogue, not even any inhibition-lowering alcohol in her bloodstream, no excuses. The words of a novel she had read years before popped into Angel's head. Although at the time they had made her put the gothic romance to one side with a snort of amused disdain, now she couldn't shake them. 'I felt a deep craving, an ache in my body and soul that I had never imagined possible.'

The remembered words no longer made her snigger and translate with a roll of her eyes—*yes, he's hot!*

Which the man in bed beside her was and then some, but Angel had met hot men before, and she had been amused by their macho posturing. She was in charge of her life and she liked it that way. History was littered with countless examples of strong women who had disastrous personal lives, but she was not going to be one of them.

Admittedly the macho men she was able to view with lofty disdain had not just saved her life, but Angel knew what she was feeling hadn't anything to do with gratitude. Beyond this certainty she wasn't sure of anything much. Her life and her belief system had been turned upside down. She had no idea at all why this was happening but she was not going to fight it. In any case, that would have been as futile as fighting the colour of her eyes or her blood type; it just was…and it was exciting!

'*Dio*, you're so beautiful.' Her husky whisper was soft and tinged with awe as she reached out a hand to touch his dark head, allowing her fingers to slide lightly over the sleek short tufts of hair. Her own hair was often called black but his was two shades darker and her skin, though a warm natural olive, looked almost winter pale against his deeply tanned, vibrant-toned, bronzed flesh. It was a contrast that had fascinated her when she'd first seen their limbs entwined—not just skin tone, but the tactile differences of his hard to her soft, his hair-roughened virility to her feminine smoothness. She wanted to touch, taste…

Angel couldn't understand how she felt so wide awake. Why she wasn't tired. She hadn't slept all night, but her senses weren't dulled by exhaustion. Instead they were racing and her body was humming with an almost painful sensory overload.

Languid pleasure twitched the corners of her full, wide mouth up as she lifted her arms above her head, stretching with feline grace, feeling muscles she hadn't known she had. Who wanted to sleep when it had finally happened? The man of her dreams was real and she had found him!

It was fate!

Her smooth brow knitted into a furrowed web. *Fate* again—this sounded so *not* her. When she had once been accused of not having a romantic bone in her body she had taken it as a compliment. She had never thought she was missing out; she'd never wanted to be that person— the one who fell in love at the drop of a hat and out again equally as easily. That was her mother who, despite the fragile appearance that made men want to protect her, had Teflon-coated emotions.

Angel knew she did not inspire a similar reaction in men and neither did she want to; the thought of not being independent was anathema to her. As a kid she had been saved from a life of loneliness and isolation by two things: a brother and an imagination. Not that she ever, even when she was young, confused her secret fantasy world with real life.

Angel had never expected her fantasies to actually come true.

She stretched out her hand, moving her fingers in the air above the curve of his shoulder, fighting the compulsion to touch him, to tug the sheet that was lying low across his hips farther down. She was amazed that she could have these thoughts and feel no sense of embarrassment. It had been the same when she had undressed for him—it had just felt right and heart-stoppingly exciting.

No fantasy had ever matched the fascination she felt for his body. Her stomach muscles quivered in hot, hungry anticipation of exploring every inch of his hard, lean body again.

'Totally beautiful,' she whispered again, staring at the man sharing her bed.

His name was Alex. When he'd asked she'd told him her name was Angelina, but that nobody ever called her that. Apparently when she was born her father had said she looked like a little angel and it had stuck.

She tensed when, as if in response to her voice, he murmured in his sleep before rolling over onto his back, one arm flung over his head, his long fingers brushing the headboard.

Angel felt a strong sensual kick of excitement low and deep in her belly as she stared, the rapt expression on her face a fusion of awe and hunger. She swallowed past the emotional thickening that made her throat ache. He was the most beautiful thing she had ever seen or imagined.

In the half-light that now filled the room his warm olive-toned skin gleamed like gold, its texture like oiled satin. A tactile tingle passed through her fingertips. Perfect might have seemed like an overused term but he was. The length of his legs was balanced by broad shoulders and a deeply muscled chest dusted with dark body hair that narrowed into a directional arrow across his flat belly ridged with muscle. There wasn't an ounce of excess flesh on his lean body to disguise the musculature that had the perfection of an anatomical diagram. But Alex was no diagram. He was a warm, living, earthly male, and he was sharing her bed.

A dazed smile flickered across her face as she felt all the muscles in her abdomen tighten. Last night had been perfect—perfect, but not in the way she had expected. There had been hardly any pain and no embarrassment.

Angel has still failed to grasp the concept of moderation. There is no middle ground—she is all or nothing.

The words on her report card came back to her.

Her form teacher had been referring to her academic record littered with As and Fs, not to sex, but there had been no middle ground last night either. Angel had held nothing back; she had given him everything without reservation.

'I know this is bad timing, but there's a problem.'

The words had been music to Alex's ears. 'Tell me.'

They had and he had acted. Crisis management was something he excelled at—it was a simple matter of focusing, shutting out all distractions and focusing.

He had gone straight from the funeral to his office, where he'd pretty much lived for the past month. He'd

washed, eaten and slept—or at least snatched a few minutes on the sofa—there. It made sense, and it suited him.
He had nothing to go home to any longer.

Then the crisis was over and Alex had been unable
to think of any reason not to go home, where he had, if
anything, less sleep. He did go to bed but by the small
hours he was up again, which was why it felt strange
and disorientating to wake up after a deep sleep and
find light shining through the blinds of…not his room…
Where the hell?

He blinked and focused on the beautiful face of the
most incredible-looking woman. She was sitting there
looking down at him wearing nothing but a mane of
glossy dark hair that lay like a silky curtain over her
breasts—breasts that had filled his hands perfectly and
tasted—

It all came rushing back.

Hell!

'Good morning.'

His body reacted to the slumberous promise in her
smile, but, ignoring the urgent messages it was sending
and the desire that heated his blood, gritted his teeth and
swung his legs over the side of the bed. Guilt rising like
a toxic tide to clog his throat, he sat, eyes closed, with
his rigid back to her. This was about damage limitation
and not repeating a mistake no matter how tempting it
might seem.

She was sinful temptation given a throaty voice and
a perfect body, but this had been his mistake, not hers,
and it was his responsibility to end it.

'I thought you'd never wake up.'

His spine tensed at the touch of her fingers on his
skin. He wiped his face of all emotion as he turned back
to face her.

'You should have woken me. I hope I haven't made you late for anything…?'

'Late…?' she quavered.

He stood up and looked around for his clothes. 'Can I get you a taxi?'

'I…I don't understand… I thought we'd…' Her voice trailed away. He was looking at her so coldly.

'Look, last night was… Actually it was fantastic but I'm not available.'

Available? Angel still didn't get it.

He felt the guilt tighten in his gut but he had no desire to prolong this scene. He'd made a massive mistake, end of story. A post-mortem was not going to change anything.

'I thought—'

He cut across her. 'Last night was just sex.'

He was speaking slowly as if he were explaining something to a child or a moron. The coldness in his blue eyes as much as his words confused Angel.

'But last night…'

'Like I said, last night was great, but it was a mistake.' A great big mistake, but a man learned by his mistakes and he didn't give in to the temptation to repeat them.

She began to feel sick as she watched him fight his way into his shirt, then he was pulling on his trousers. She responded automatically to pick up the object that fell out of the pocket and landed with a metallic twang on the floor just in front of her toes. She bent to pick it up; her fingers closed around a ring.

'Yours?'

He was meticulously careful not to touch her fingers as he took it from her outstretched hand.

'You're married?'

For a moment he thought of telling the truth, saying

that he had been, but no longer, that the ring was in his pocket because friends kept telling him it was time to move on. Alex doubted this was what they'd had in mind.

Then he realised how much easier and less painful a lie would be. It wouldn't ease the guilt that was like a living thing in his gut, but it would make this scene less messy and allow her to say when regaling her friends later that *the bastard was married*.

'I'm sorry.'

Her incredible green eyes flared hot as she rose majestically to her feet and delivered a contemptuous 'You disgusting loser!' followed up by a backhanded slap that made him blink. He opened his watering eyes in time to see her vanish into the bathroom, the door locked audibly behind her.

Angel ran, hand clamped to her mouth, across the room, just making it to the loo before she was violently sick.

By the time she returned to the bedroom he was gone.

Angel found herself hating him with more venom than she thought she was capable of. She hated him even more than her mother's creepy boyfriend, the one who had tried to grope her when she was sixteen. The only person she hated more than Alex was herself. How could she be so stupid? He had treated her like a tramp because that was how she had acted.

By the time she left the hotel room later that morning, her tears had dried and her expression was set. She had decided she would never, ever think of him again, not think of him or last night.

It never happened.

He never existed.

It was a solution.

She could move on.

CHAPTER ONE

'THEY ARE THE second biggest advertising firm in Europe and—'

'There is something in it for you?' Alex, who had been listening to Nico's pitch while he read the small print on a contract, made the silky suggestion without rancour. He liked his big sister's son and why should his favourite, actually his only, nephew be any different from everyone else?

The younger man acknowledged the point with a self-conscious shrug. 'Well, I had heard there might be an internship going...?'

Alex finished reading, wrote his signature on the last page of the document and laid it on top of the done pile before pushing his chair back and stretching his long legs out in front of him. He flexed his shoulders and thought wistfully about the run he had promised himself as a reward for spending the morning at his desk. Not that he begrudged the youngster his time—Nico was a low-maintenance relative, unlike some who looked on him as their own personal bank. He was philosophical about the role but family was important.

'Consider the decks cleared. You have my attention.'

'Good of you.' But not entirely comfortable for him as his uncle Alex's eyes had always reminded Nico of ice chips. It wasn't the colour, although that was an un-nerving pale blue, as his own mother shared the same strangely coloured eyes with her much younger brother. It was the impression he'd had as a kid that those eyes had always been able to see right into his head. He was no longer a kid but he was always painfully honest around his uncle—just in case.

'You know that Dad's offered me a job and I'm grateful,' came the hasty assurance.

Alex voiced the unspoken addendum. 'But?'

'But I'd like to do something that didn't have anything to do with being his son or your nephew.'

'I admire your intentions if not your practicality, and you seem to forget I was born with a silver spoon.'

'And you turned it gold,' the young man said gloomily.

There was no firm on the brink of the financial abyss for Nico to save. Thanks to Alex the shipping empire founded by his Greek great grandfather had recovered from years of mismanagement and had gone from strength to strength to be hailed as one of the success stories of the global recession.

Of course even if it hadn't his uncle would still be fabulously rich as Alex had inherited the Arlov vast oil fortune a few years earlier from the Russian great grand-father that Nico had never met. That was when Alex had delegated the day-to-day running of the shipping busi-ness to his brother-in-law, Nico's father.

'And that is a bad thing?'

'No, of course not, but no one thinks of you as a little rich boy who's never done a day's work in his life.'

A direct quote? Alex wondered, feeling a stab of sym-pathy for his nephew, who was all of the above but also a rather nice kid.

'You don't have anything to prove.' His eyes fell. 'Just

forget it,' he mumbled. 'I knew I was talking out of my...
I guess I knew you wouldn't be up for it. I just wanted
to impress the guy from the advertising firm and you
should have seen his face when I mentioned your island,
Saronia. He lit up like a firework. Pathetic or what.' He
reached out for the tablet he had opened on his uncle's
desk and drew back as Alex withdrew it from his reach.

'You were trying to impress. Why apologise? Unless
your interest is more personal? I am assuming the new
face of this cosmetic firm is not ugly—one of your actress friends perhaps? Are you still dating...?' The name
of the pretty girl from the soap escaped him as he idly
scrolled down the screen that showed the logo of the cosmetics giant that was apparently launching a new perfume.

It was not a world that Alex knew much about. 'A big
thing, is it, a new perfume?'

'Massive,' his nephew assured him. 'They're planning to make a series of ads to promote it using the same
couple, six ads in all, really glossy and high produc-
tion values, like a kind of serial each with a story and a
cliffhanger like a romantic minisoap. They've got a big-
name director and this guy from Hollywood to star in
it—though he must be at least thirty-five.'

Alex fought a smile. 'That old!' Good to know he
had three years to go before he was classed as elderly
by his nephew.

'They want to film the first three in an exotic setting—
sand, sun and palm trees on an island paradise thing.'

'And a connection with the golden age of Hollywood
would not hurt,' Alex inserted. He could see why Saronia would appeal to them as a location.

In its day the island had been the setting for his grandfather's famous parties. Spyros Theakis—a man with a

well-documented taste for starlets—reaping the financial rewards of his successful Greek shipping empire,
had hosted lavish parties attended by all the stars of the
day on his private island. The photos of those legendary
events still surfaced from time to time, as did the tales
of wild parties, torrid affairs and general excess. Most
left out the fact that the mansion had been burnt down
during an electrical storm. By some miracle none of the
guests had been seriously hurt but the place had never
been rebuilt. His grandfather's fortunes, like those of the
island, had gone into decline and the place had become
uninhabited.

Alex had visited out of curiosity when the resort hotel
he had commissioned was being built on the mainland
just a few minutes away by boat. Emma, who had come
with him, had been fascinated by the romance of the
place. They had always planned to build a house there
but the plans had been put on hold when she'd become
ill and had been shelved permanently after the diagnosis.

He had gone back to Saronia for the first time a few
months after her death, camping on the beach for a few
days that had stretched into several weeks. Later that year
he had commissioned a house, not the family house that
he had planned with Emma but a small place, minimal-
ist, no frills—though not the monk's cell his sister had
called it. It was his own retreat; he went there once or
twice a year to recharge his batteries.... God knew there
were few places where he could guarantee there were no
photographers lurking around the corner, no phones, no
news—he was off the grid when he was there.

As much as he admired his nephew's enterprise he
would sooner have invited cameras into his own bathroom than allow a film crew to invade this precious private sanctuary.

'Louise,' the younger man said suddenly as he took a seat on the edge of the big desk. 'She had a really tough upbringing and she thinks I'm…spoilt.'

'This is your soap star?'

Nico nodded.

'And you want to impress her.' Alex, who had been idly scrolling through the tablet, stopped. 'Who is that?' The lack of inflection in his voice might have made those who knew him better wonder…but Nico's attention was on his own troubled love life, not the sudden tension in his uncle's body language.

His nephew bent over, scanning the inverted image that filled the screen. It was a studio shot of an extremely beautiful young woman pouting provocatively at the camera with lips that were glossy and scarlet. Everything about her was provocative, from the swathe of dark wavy hair that fell artistically across one half of her face to the smile in her heavily lidded eyes, a smile that seemed to invite you to share a secret that gleamed in the shimmering emerald depths as she leaned forward displaying a large amount of cleavage in a gold sheath dress that clung like a second skin.

'Angel. She's a model.'

Angel… Angelina? 'A model.'

It did not surprise him. What did surprise him was the instant effect of a face he had last seen six years ago…. An incident that had not been his finest hour, but one he had consigned to the past. The instant surge of sexual hunger that tightened in his belly had a very *present* feel to it.

His nephew nodded and looked amazed by his uncle's ignorance. 'You must have seen her in that underwear campaign last year. She was everywhere.'

'I must have missed that one,' he mused, seeing the

beautiful sleek brunette not in underwear…not in anything. He went to stand but, not wanting to draw attention
to the testosterone that had suddenly pooled in his groin,
he sat back down again like some hormonal teenager,
resenting his lack of control—or at least the cause of it.

'Gorgeous, isn't she?' the young man continued, oblivious to any undercurrents in the air. 'All that hair and
those green eyes. They are going to build the campaign
around her. It's a calculated risk, they said, not to choose
a big celebrity to be the new face for a perfume, but they
want to build the campaign around someone who—'

Alex tuned out the explanation of the thinking behind
employing a relative unknown—she was not unknown
to him. Seeing that face, those eyes, remembering the
sleek, sinuous body, the undulating curves, the golden
toned skin, brought that night back so clearly that he
could smell the scent of her shampoo.

Lust slammed through him again like an iron fist.
With it came the guilt…always the guilt. Emma dead how
many weeks…? And he had jumped into bed with the
first available woman. She had led but he had followed.

His lips curled in self-disgust. He had moved on since
then, when he'd felt ready. Not one-night stands, that
was not his thing, but he had enjoyed a series of satisfying relationships with women who enjoyed sex but not
drama, and none had been tainted with guilt. If that required he maintain a certain emotional distance it was a
price worth paying.

'Yes.'

He had no desire to revisit that place of agonising guilt
but to recapture that…? It was not so much a *thing* he
was trying to recapture but an absence that he was trying to fill. He gave his head a tiny shake, aware that he
was guilty of the sin of overanalysing. She had been the

best sex of his life, so why not make a push to sample it and her again?

Nico, who had taken his ringing mobile phone from his pocket intending to turn it off, dropped it. It lay where it had fallen as, jaw slack with shock, he scanned the face of the man who sat behind the big desk, a pointless exercise because he never could read his uncle.

'Whaddaya… Yes…?' he said, unable to believe he was this lucky.

Behind the desk Alex brought his formidable mental control into play and pushed the increasingly erotic images from his head.

He raised one dark brow. 'Yes.'

Nico surged to his feet, radiating the sort of youthful excitement that made Alex, who was all of what, twelve years his senior, feel old. 'Seriously…? This isn't a wind-up… No, you don't—'

Alex quirked a dark brow and suggested, 'Have a sense of humour?'

Maybe the boy was right; maybe he had eradicated that along with his conscience.

A conscience was an inconvenient thing, he thought, seeing the expression in those big eyes. He needed to draw a line under what had happened, and this was an unexpected opportunity to do just that. A girl who adopted a 'jump into bed first and ask questions later' policy should have expected a few surprises, yet innocence was an odd word to use with someone who had been so sexually uninhibited. But for some reason…? Again, he was overthinking this.

Take away the acrid taste of guilt and she remained the best sex he had ever had, and due to pressures of work it had been months since he had enjoyed any sex, which might go some way to explaining the strength of his physical response. He didn't try to justify it. He didn't just need sex, he needed a question mark in his life; he needed highs and lows, not a predictable flat-line monotony.

Wondering where that thought had come from, he was aware he sounded like a man who was not satisfied with his life. He was; of course he was. Alex got to his feet and picked up the jacket he had slung over the back of the chair.

'You going to pick that up?' He nodded towards the phone.

Looking dazed, his nephew nodded. 'What…? Oh, sure…'

'You will keep me up to speed?'

'Me? You want me to… Great, of course… So should I run the details past…?' Though tall and blessed with an athletic build, the younger man was forced to tilt his head back to look up at his uncle who, at six-five, was a couple of inches taller than him, and significantly more than a couple inches broader across the shoulders.

'Me,' Alex said, shrugging on a fine wool jacket that was tailored to fit across his broad shoulders so it fell into place without a crease.

'You really mean this? You'll actually let them film on Saronia?'

He'd made the pitch but in his wildest dreams Nico had never seriously expected it to work. Everyone knew how jealously Alex Arlov protected his privacy, even more so since someone had hacked into his wife's medical records not long before she died. It was after the resulting tear-jerking newspaper article that he had gained the reputation of being ferociously litigious, someone prepared to go after perpetrators who crossed the line in the sand regardless of the cost. Some people suggested that this meant he had something to hide, and pointed out the lives he had ruined by taking legal retribution, but they did so in very small voices and only after taking extensive legal advice!

Nico, who was not averse to seeing his own picture on the pages of celebrity magazines, privately considered that Uncle Alex took it a bit far. The paparazzo who had ended up fully clothed in a swimming pool at his mother's birthday bash last year, camera and all, might have agreed with him.

'With certain restrictions obviously. They stay on the mainland and make the daily commute. I don't want them anywhere near the house. I can leave the details with you?'

'Wow… Yes, absolutely and, thanks, you won't regret this.'

Alex watched the boy bounce from the room oozing enthusiasm and incredulous joy. If Alex had been the type to dwell on the motivations behind his decision he might have spent the next hour doing so with increasing frustration. But he wasn't, so he spent the next hour running instead.

Angel poked her head around the door of the lounge where most of the people involved had congregated. Used to the handful involved in a fashion shoot, she thought there seemed to be an awful lot of them.

'I think I'll go for a walk. Anyone fancy some fresh air?' She was an active person, and being cooped up in the claustrophobic atmosphere of the luxury hotel was getting to her.

Several astonished pairs of eyes turned her way. Someone whose name she had forgotten replied, his tone indulgent, 'It's raining, Angel, honey.'

It never rains in August.

Angel had lost count of the number of times she had heard this statement since they had arrived at the resort, but the fact remained that, despite the lack of precedent, it was raining and it had been for two days solid. In fact, it had been ever since they had arrived at the island paradise, this paradise they had yet to set foot on.

The delay to the photo shoot had caused tempers to fray and the money men to start muttering. For Angel it was two days she could have been at home with her daughter, not hundreds of miles away.

'It's just water.'

Her response drew blank looks. 'But you'll get wet.'

'I need the exercise.'

'I'm just off to the gym,' said India, the actress playing her mother in the ad—though the woman was only ten years older than Angel. 'Come with me.'

'I don't really do the gym thing. I'm allergic to Lycra.'

'Seriously?'

'No, not seriously, India, she's joking,' Rudie, the lighting man, explained.

'Your hair will get wet.' The objection was made by the man responsible for making her hair look perfect. He was still recovering from the shock of discovering that, not only was the waist-length ebony hair all her own, but the glossy colour had never been enhanced or altered.

'It will dry.'

'What's that smell?'

'Me, I'm afraid.' Angel brought her concealed hand out from behind her back. 'I can't resist lashings of onions.'

'Is that a hot dog?'

Angel glanced at the item that was causing the executive from the cosmetic company to look so shocked. The

only person in the room who didn't seem horrified was
the handsome young Greek, Nico. She assumed from his
appearance he was one of the Theakis family who owned
the luxury resort and any number of others around the
world, and probably the shipping line of the same name,
but she wasn't sure what his connection was with the
owner of Saronia who he was representing.

'I really hope so.'

Again the young Greek was the only one to laugh so
she winked at him and murmured, 'Tough crowd to play,'
in a terrible New York drawl.

'But you had a full breakfast.' The critical follow-up
came from the stylist.

Walking in the rain had clearly not been received well,
but she could tell from the general air of disapproval in
the room that eating an actual meal was considered ab-
errant behaviour by those present. But Angel coped with
their disapproval by refusing to recognise it.

The same way she had refused to recognise the broad
hints earlier that she might be better selecting a pot of
low-fat yogurt rather than a full English. She was all for
a peaceful life.

'And it was delicious.' Angel could feel the woman
staring at her as though they expected to see her developing unsightly bulges as she watched.

Her grip on her hot dog tightened as she fought the
urge to say something that would make everyone look
at her with the opposite of their current disdain. It had
taken time, but she had conquered her need to seek approval, recognising late in the day that the one person—
her mother—from whom she wanted that approval was
never going to give it.

Only very occasionally these days did she find that
eager-to-please tendency resurfacing. When it did she

quashed it ruthlessly. Needy was just not a good look, and not the sort of example she wanted to set for her daughter.

She lifted her chin and embraced them all with a brilliant smile. 'Then it's just as well I'm going to go for a walk.'

The figure who had been hiding behind a newspaper lowered it, revealing the lived-in features of a photographer who was more famous than the A-list people who posed for him.

'Relax, guys, our girl here never puts on an ounce. Do you, darling?' His brows lifted as his glance slid down the supple curves of the young woman framed in the doorway. 'Looking particularly lush this morning.... Purely a professional observation, you understand, Angel, luv.'

Alex nodded to a gardener whose eyes widened as he recognised the person who had manoeuvred his way past the ladder he had set up against the trellis.

Alex liked to fly under the radar when he could. He had arrived the previous night in a private jet that had landed at a private airport and had made the short crossing alone in the rain that had been falling ever since. It was, according to the information supplied by his spy in the camp, Nico, playing havoc with the filming schedule.

The rain had just stopped and the dampness underfoot was already being turned to misty vapour by the late-afternoon sun. Someone had forgotten to adjust the sprinkler system, which was adding to the moisture, but a few of the holidaymakers had already begun to venture out of the hotel, including a large family group who were playing a boisterous game of cricket on the beach.

Alex had a few hours to kill before the meet-and-greet cocktail party Nico had arranged later that evening. The young man thought that Alex was making the effort to attend as a favour to him. Alex, whose motivation was far less selfless, had seen no harm in letting his young relative—and by association his older sister—think just that. It was always handy to have a favour in hand with his sibling.

Heading towards the noise on the beach, he made his way down the flower-filled terraces that led to the tree-lined walkway above the beach. Normally at this time of day it would have been dotted with parasols and supine brown bodies, but the weather meant it was almost empty except for the family group in the midst of their raucous ball game.

Alex was conscious of an uncharacteristic impatience as he anticipated the evening ahead. The tall, luscious brunette had been the best sex of his life, and he had felt nothing that had approached that level of carnal passion since. But would the incredible chemistry between them still be there?

Seeing her face had definitely aroused the dormant hunting instincts in him, and, though Alex had no intention of investing emotionally in any relationship, he had normal appetites.

He shook his head and decided he would spend the remainder of the evening running through the details of the extension project with the contractors that would double the size of the spa. He was a firm believer in multitasking; to combine business with pleasure was a pragmatism he was comfortable with, but he was considerably less comfortable with the inescapable scent of obsession attached to moving heaven and earth to engineer a meeting with a one-night stand from six years ago.

Thinking it over did not remove her face from his head. Instead, it was the ball that was hurtling towards him at great speed that did that. It would have hit him had not some sixth sense made him turn his head and, without thinking, he shot out his hand to catch it.

There was a ripple of applause to congratulate this display of lightning reflexes and natural coordination, followed by a chorus of apologies from the beach. He nodded acknowledgment and responded to the light-hearted invitation to join in the fun from the players with a negative motion of his head before he tossed the ball back and continued along the wide boulevard.

'Go deep, go deep!'

Someone was yelling, and he turned his head and saw a figure who was doing her level best to follow the in-struction. It was a figure who... He stopped dead. Alex had imagined the object of his lustful machinations sun-ning herself, maybe topless? Sipping a cocktail or taking advantage of the spa facilities, but not pelting across the sand barefoot in a pair of shorts and a cut-off T-shirt, her hair flying and yelling wildly.

'I've got it!'

Before he had a chance to assimilate this extraordinary turn of events she caught the ball, released an exultant whoop, jumped high in the air and was promptly wrestled to the ground by one of the male players. Alex watched with distaste as they rolled around on the ground, the man's hands seemingly everywhere. It was one of those moments when a man felt the layers of civilisation peel away, and he wasn't aware until he had begun to walk rapidly away that his hands were clenched into fists.

Angel, hot, sweaty and deeply involved in the match, didn't see the throw but she did see the distant figure fling the ball back with an accuracy that caused a sec-ond ripple of applause.

There were millions of tall, dark, athletically built,

handsome men in the world and some of them projected an aura of authority and, well…sex. So over the years she had experienced a few heart-thudding, stomach-clenching moments of shocked recognition only to discover after all the breathless anticipation that as the object of her antipathy got nearer it was not HIM, but a pale imitation who did not possess that level of raw sensuality that she had responded to on a primal level.

But she was a mother now and her primal days were in the past. The chances she would ever meet HIM—she always thought of Jas's father in capital letters—again were remote, and if she ever did it was not likely it would be here, she thought, tearing her eyes from the tall figure. Even though she knew it wasn't HIM, her heart was still racing as she followed the bellowed instruction to go deep from the bowler, a ten-year-old who had a well-developed competitive streak.

When she did catch the ball a few moments later she found herself rugby tackled by the handsome husband of the woman who had invited her to join the game. When she disentangled herself and emerged triumphantly holding the ball aloft the suited figure on the broad walkway who had dredged up memories that were better left undisturbed was gone.

CHAPTER TWO

AT THE END of an exhausting game the friendly family invited her to take afternoon tea with them as they were celebrating the grandparents' diamond anniversary. Refusal, they told her, was not an option, so after nipping back to her bungalow to quickly shower and change she joined them in a private lounge where she ate cakes and no one pointed out the fat content.

It was the first time Angel had enjoyed herself since she had arrived, or even come close to relaxing, though watching one of the grandchildren who was Jasmine's age did make her throat swell with emotion as she wondered what her daughter was doing.

As a result, she ate more cake and stayed longer than she'd intended. So after the lively afternoon the silence and emptiness of her bungalow felt rather depressing. Not that it wasn't a lovely room—actually it was a two-bedroom suite furnished in a very expensive version of rustic, with dark, chunky wooden furniture and floors with splashes of colour provided by the original art displayed on the white walls.

All the bungalows had flower-bedecked private terraces with spa tubs, some with a view of the pool with its mountain backdrop; others, like the one that Angel had been allocated, had a sea view. The sand lapped by the turquoise waves was sugary white and dotted with palms. The storm of the previous day seemed a dim and distant memory this evening.

Before stepping back into her room Angel dusted the sand off the soles of her bare feet. It was not hard to see why the place was popular with honeymooning couples lucky enough to be able to afford the prices the very up-market resort charged. But then paradise didn't come cheap. As gorgeous as it was, the place lacked a vital ingredient that was essential for Angel's paradise.

God, she thought, giving her head a tiny shake before she crossed the room to the side table, her bare feet silent on the wooden floor. Her chest tightened and she felt the sting of tears in her eyes as she picked up the framed photo of Jasmine.

'Here five minutes and homesick already! Your mum is a wimp,' she told the picture of the laughing child before she kissed the glass, swallowed the emotional lump in her throat and with a brisk, 'Pull yourself together, Angel,' she replaced it carefully on the side table.

Then after a last wave to the photo she straightened her shoulders and headed for the open French doors, pausing to slip her feet into a pair of flat sandals as she headed for the bedroom. It had been made very clear that the drinks party was not optional! And she was... She glanced at her wristwatch. Yes, she was running late.

So no time to change.

'Drinks and butter up the rich owner...?' She pursed her lips, staring as she aimed a frown at her reflection in the full-length mirror.

The frown was for the rich owner who would most likely have a monumental ego, and the question was purely rhetorical. The thin cotton dress she was wearing was not by any stretch a cocktail dress. It was little more than an ankle-length cover-up she had chosen earlier, a deep cobalt blue shot with swirls of green. It left her smooth brown shoulders bare, or they would have been if it hadn't been for the straps of her halter bikini.

Angel might move in the world of high fashion but she was no slave to the latest trends. She knew what suited her; she had an individual style and the confidence to carry off anything she wore.

Poise, the scout from the talent agency had called it. It was, he had told her later, the reason he had picked her out from countless pretty girls in the park that day, that and the length of her legs. Her legs *were* quite good, and Angel and the scout were quite good friends these days despite the fact that her brother, witnessing the first encounter, had warned the middle-aged man off in no uncertain terms. Her brother was the only male of her acquaintance who thought her incapable of taking care of herself. Exasperating, but she tolerated it because she knew his intentions were good, though his methods sometimes a bit Neanderthal.

She reached the bow behind her neck and, tongue caught between her teeth, managed to unclip the fastener of her bikini. She gave a grunt as she managed to whip it off without disturbing the dress. Already moving towards the door, she slung the top on the bed as she twitched the neckline, pulling it a few modest centimetres higher over the slopes of her breasts as she glanced in the mirror.

'Or should we add the pearls?' She chuckled to herself before warning her mirror image darkly, 'First signs of madness, Angel.' Snatching up the string of pretty green beads she'd bought at a crazy cheap price from an enterprising trader before a security guard had given him marching orders from the private stretch of beach, she left the bungalow at a trot, looping them around her neck as she went, reflecting it wasn't what you wore, it was the way you wore it. A cliché but true nonetheless.

It was rare that Alex felt the need to rationalise his own actions, and why should he now? Looking at the situation objectively, all he had done was agree to Nico's request. He'd helped out his nephew, which was what families did. Plus, he had business here. It was called multitasking, he told himself.

He was curious, no crime. It wasn't as if he had engineered the situation solely for the purpose of meeting with the woman who had spent the night in his bed six years ago.

Sure you didn't, Alex—you were just passing.

Of course, if he took advantage of a situation that had fallen into his lap, who could blame him?

The last time she had not fallen in his lap, she had jumped!

Alex, who believed contrary to popular belief very few people were capable of learning from past mistakes, was an advocate of living in the present. But as a pulse of hot lust slammed through his body he found his thoughts being dragged back to a moment six years ago, when, driven by the need he'd had then to fill his every waking moment with action, he had left his car and driver stuck in rush-hour traffic and walked instead along a crowded London street.

If he hadn't been…?

She had stepped off the pavement into the moving traffic and he had literally dragged the young woman from underneath the wheels of a bus.

The memory, a moment frozen in time etched on his brain, was so vivid he could smell the exhaust fumes in the air now, hear the tortured squeal of brakes and the cry of a solitary onlooker who, alone among those busily going about their own business, had witnessed the moment of near disaster.

Alex's reaction had been pure reflex, not related in any way to bravery, and his body's response had been equally involuntary when he'd turned the figure around and looked down into the face turned up to him…and carried on looking.

His anger had melted.

She was stunning!

He could remember thinking what a crime it would have been for that face to be marked. A delicate, slightly tip-tilted nose; wide, full, luscious lips; a natural pout even in repose and incredible deep green, heavily lashed, almond-shaped eyes set beneath thick, darkly defined, arched brows, and all that general gorgeousness set against flawless satiny skin that had glowed pale gold in the grey city street.

He'd found himself holding the breathing embodiment of sensuality and his body had responded accordingly and instantaneously.

Fighting the impulse to keep her plastered against his body for longer—there was no way she couldn't have picked up on how hard he was—he'd released her, but retained a steadying hold of her elbows as he'd pushed her a little away. His nostrils had flared as the scent of her shampoo had drifted his way.

She had been breathing hard and blinking in a dazed way. Even in the flat, unattractive boots she'd been wearing she'd been tall for a woman, reaching a little past his shoulder. Her slim but voluptuous curves had made the generic jeans and T-shirt she wore look anything but common.

'Are you all right?'

She'd nodded, sending the magnificent waist-length curtain of hair that shone like polished ebony silk swishing around her face. He'd watched as, head tilted forward, she did a sweep of her feet upwards.

'It's all still there and in one piece,' she'd murmured, sounding dazed. Her voice had had a delicious throaty rasp. 'You really do see your life pass before your eyes.' She'd tilted her head back and looked at him, breathing a soft 'Wow!' as her eyes widened.

He had found himself grinning, amused by her total lack of artifice, then watched in fascination as a visible wave of heat travelled up the long graceful curve of her neck, adding an extra tinge of colour to her smooth cheeks. He could not remember ever encountering a woman who wore her emotions so close to the surface. Yet despite the blush, the glowing, gorgeous young creature had held his gaze steadily.

'I think you saved my life.'

He'd given the faintest of shrugs. 'Do you make a habit of throwing yourself under moving vehicles?'

She'd then been staring as hard at him as he was at her. 'It was a first for me.'

When not breathless, the throaty, sexy quality of her voice had intensified.

He'd felt her trembling. Post-trauma or was she feeling the same clutch of lust he was…?

There'd been more than a hint of provocative challenge in her attitude as she'd lifted her chin and asked, 'Can I… Let me buy you a coffee, to thank you…? It seems the least I can do, unless you're…?'

'Coffee would be good,' he'd heard himself say.

She had expelled a tiny sigh and beamed up at him in undisguised delight, and when he'd kept a guiding hand on one of her elbows she hadn't pulled away. He'd felt her shiver and that time he'd known why.

Alex pushed away the memory; as always it was inextricably and painfully linked in his mind with guilt. On one level he recognised the guilt was irrational. He had no longer been married at that point, hadn't cheated, he'd been free to have sex with a total stranger.

Even when Emma had been alive he could have taken a mistress with her blessing. Alex was not easily shocked but on the first occasion she had brought the subject up he had been—deeply. He'd known she'd had something on her mind and had coaxed her to tell him what was bothering her but he hadn't been prepared for the incendiary suggestion she had made.

'You're a man, you have needs that I can't...and you've been so patient with me, never said that I should have told you about the MS. I wanted to, but it might have been years before it came back or even never.'

'It wouldn't have made any difference if I had known,' he had told her, hoping it was true. Even wondering had felt like a betrayal.

'I know that, Alex, but the fact remains you didn't have the choice. I didn't give you the choice. So if you need to, you know...date other women, that's all right with me. I don't have to know, I don't want to know, so long as you stay with me while I'm— I hate hospitals so much, Alex...'

And there it was, the real fear, that he would send her to some anonymous nursing home. It had cut him to the core to know his wife had been willing to endure infidelities for the security and promise of staying in the home that she had enjoyed furnishing in those first months of marriage. She had enjoyed a lot of things before the disease that had finally killed her resurfaced.

A short year later she had been confined to a wheelchair and eaten up with guilt because she hadn't told him before they'd got married. The constant apologising had been hard to hear and sometimes had made him angry with her. Guilt piled on top of more guilt. It had been a vicious circle.

'This is your home, Emma, our home.' Her hand had felt so small under his, the bones fragile as he'd squeezed. 'There will be no hospitals and no other women, I swear.'

And he had kept his word to the letter if not the spirit. He might have been legally free but in his mind, in his heart, Alex had still been married when he had spent the night with Angelina. Though not once during that night had he thought of Emma. How could he have forgotten, even for a moment? The next morning he hadn't been able to get out of there quickly enough.

If he had encountered the stunning Angel when Emma had still been alive would he have found it so easy to keep his promise? The question wouldn't go away and he would never know the answer, but he was pretty sure that if he had it wouldn't have given him any comfort.

Alex liked to think he was able to forgive weakness in others, but he set higher standards for himself. Though he'd got out of there as fast as he could the morning after, memories of the night before had haunted him. Well, he was about to lay that ghost—literally if things turned out as he intended—to rest.

'Only the star is missing.' His inability to prevent his eyes going to the doorway sent a surge of irritation through Alex. 'Does the lady like to make an entrance?'

Beside him Nico responded defensively to the disdain in his uncle's voice. 'She's really nice.'

The balding executive whom he had directed his sardonic comment to nodded in agreement with his nephew's assessment. 'She certainly doesn't stand on ceremony and the last thing you can accuse her of is being a diva.' He laughed at some private joke and took a sip of the orange juice he was nursing. 'And if she wanted people to notice her she wouldn't need any stunts. With Angel in the room no one else exists.' He drew a line in the air and pronounced with utter confidence, 'End of story.'

Alex recalled Angelina, or Angel as it seemed he must learn to call her, in his room, an anonymous hotel room. For him that night, no one else had existed. He clenched his teeth in an effort to eject the image of her sitting on the bed gloriously naked and utterly unselfconscious, acting as if they had just shared more than lust, acting as if there would be a tomorrow.

Dragging himself into the present, he wondered if the executive's admiration was purely professional. Was the man sleeping with the model? He knew little of the world they occupied but he supposed it would hardly be a revelation if they were.

'Rudie says Angel simply doesn't have a bad angle. The camera loves her,' Nico, the new president of her fan club, informed him.

'And Rudie is?'

'Our lighting man, one of the best.'

The guy was probably in love with her too, Alex thought sourly.

Oh, God, she was the last to arrive. Angel fought the impulse to step back into the shadows, then smiled to herself at the irony that she made her living posing for a camera, having her image stared at by the public, though she genuinely hated being the centre of attention.

She didn't retreat but paused in the doorway, her eyes sweeping the room, the light breeze pulling the silky fluttering fabric of her dress against long legs until Ross spotted her. The photographer grinned, giving a thumbs-up sign, in the process slopping what she knew would be tonic water down his front. People assumed he had a drink problem, and he let them think that. He had once confided to Angel that he simply didn't like the taste of alcohol, but being thought an ex-alcoholic made him seem more interesting.

Angel's spontaneous burst of throaty laughter alerted the others to her presence and she was immediately involved in a lot of luvvie air kissing.

Well, she'd been right about one thing: she was underdressed. The men, with the exception of Ross, were wearing suits and ties and the women cocktail dresses.

'Worth the wait,' he heard someone say and Alex could not disagree.

The late arrival's appearance had sent a rush of scalding heat through his body. Six years ago she had been stunning, possessing a natural grace and sleek sensuality that had been all the more powerful for appearing totally unstudied. She still possessed all those attributes but now she held herself with the confidence that came when a woman knew the power she wielded with her beauty, when she enjoyed it.

Every man in the room was enjoying it.

Alex's enjoyment was tempered by this knowledge and the discomfort that could be traced to the testosterone-fuelled ache in his groin. The intervening years slipped away as his blue eyes made a slow sweep upwards from her bare feet, and the pink-painted toenails—presumably the sandals dangling from her fingers belonged there.

Though it looked as if she could not have made less effort, you had to feel sorry for the women who had spent hours getting ready. Angel had stopped short of appearing in her shorts or arriving with a group of salivating half-dressed holidaymakers in tow, but her outfit was more beach than drinks party. Had she deliberately underdressed in order to stand out from the crowd? he speculated. If so, the effort was unnecessary. As the man had said, she would have stood out in every crowd and he doubted any man in the room could find fault with her choice of outfit.

She brought irresistibly to mind the archetypal image of a Greek goddess in the semisheer column that revealed every sinuous inch of her long, shapely legs from calf to thigh. Bare shoulders gleamed gold above the draped fabric that followed the lines of her full, high breasts and was cinched in beneath by a tie before flowing out in long, soft folds.

The fabric shimmered, Angel shimmered.

As far as he could tell she was wasn't wearing a scrap of make-up. Her face, with the full sexy mouth, cute nose and spectacular dark-lashed eyes, was beautiful, framed against a silken fall of river-straight hair that dropped to her waist.

Luckily, Angel thought, when reliving the moment later that night, she'd had a drink already thrust into her hand when the billionaire who had granted them exclusive use of his private island to film the series of commercials was pointed out to her.

'Now, that's what I call a face.'

If only she'd had some warning, some inkling. But then that was, she supposed, the definition of shock, and it hit Angel like a sudden immersion into icy water. Initially her mind went utterly blank, rejecting what she was seeing. Then the breath froze in her lungs; there was a solid block of ice in her chest. Was this a panic attack? she wondered, feeling like a drowning man going down for the final time as she struggled to mask her feelings, willed her face to stay blank.

She looked away and waited for the pounding throb of her heart to slow. Her first instinct had been to run, but that was not an option given her limbs were not acting as though they belonged to her, except for her hand, the one with the glass in it, which managed to find her mouth.

She swallowed the contents in one gulp, her eyes darting from side to side like a trapped animal. There was no place to hide and he was coming her way. Without looking, she could sense his approach.

How was she acting so normally?

She even managed to say something to Sandy, the pretty make-up artist who had initially pointed Alex out to her. What it was Angel had no idea, but she must have been funny because the other girl laughed. *That's me, funny Angel, smart Angel, lucky Angel... Scared witless Angel!*

'Are you cold? You're shivering.' The other girl sounded worried.

Angel swallowed and made herself respond to Sandy's concerned question, forcing the words past the constriction in her throat.

'No, I'm not cold.' And she wasn't. The warm glow in her stomach, the combination of champagne and brandy in the cocktail, had begun to seep into her bloodstream. 'That's Alex Arlov?' Her voice sounded as though it were coming from a long way off. Her head was still spinning as she struggled to take on board the identity of her one-night stand, the father of her child.

Sandy misinterpreted the cause of Angel's stunned expression. 'I know, he looks even better in the flesh, doesn't he? You could cut yourself on those cheekbones.'

The other woman seemed to take it for granted that

Angel recognised the billionaire by sight. And Angel did know the name, of course—who didn't? She could even have recited a potted bio of the man, not because she found money sexy or shared the popular fascination with people who had amassed a great deal of it, but because, and here the irony was so black a short, hard cough of laughter escaped her clenched teeth, her brother had tried in his oh-so-not-subtle way to set her up with the man!

The two men had met while both were driving ridiculously fast cars around a racing circuit for fun. Her brother's excuse was it had once been his day job; the other guy, as far as she had been able to tell at the time, had been there because he enjoyed pushing the limits and he could afford the sort of toys that only very rich men could.

The two men appeared to have bonded over a mutual love of speed and obviously wives had not come into the conversation or Cesare would not have tried to set her up with the man. Her brother had been oblivious, of course, to the fact they were discussing the father of her child, and the man her overprotective sibling had, on more than one occasion, expressed a desire to dismember slowly. Angel's response had been firm but dismissive. For Cesare, the habit of watching out for his little sister was deeply engrained.

'I'm not interested in dating a Russian oligarch, even one who drives well in wet conditions,' she'd said.

Her brother had grinned at the retort but protested. 'Not dating—I was simply suggesting we invite him up for the weekend some time. I think you two would get on. He'd get your sense of humour and, let's face it, that puts him in the minority. And he's only half Russian; his father died before he was born and his mother fell out with his family and moved back home. There was a grandfather in Russia, hence the Russian oil, but as his mother was half Greek he was brought up by that side of his family, and actually he's taken British citizenship.'

'Fine, invite him, whatever you like,' Angel had responded, making a mental note to be away any weekend her brother tried to play matchmaker. 'But I think one adrenaline junkie is enough in any family.'

And it had been left at that.

It was her own adrenaline levels that presented the most immediate problem now. Light-headed to the point where she saw black dots dancing, and with her heart thudding like a metronome-driven sledgehammer against her ribs, it was taking a conscious effort to act with anything approaching normality. The muscles in her cheeks burned with the effort of keeping her smile pasted on as she absently licked the crystals of sugar deposited on her lips by the decorated rim of her now-empty glass. She watched him approach…nearer and nearer…

Her galloping paranoia saw something predatory about his long-legged, straight-backed stride. When he got within a few feet of them her stomach went into a steep dive. In other circumstances she would have been riveted, not by fear, but by admiration. Alex Arlov carried himself like a natural athlete, every action screaming fluidity and grace, but also the arrogance that came when someone knew they were at the top of the food chain. Oh, and he could throw a decent pass too; she knew now he had to have been the man she had seen at the beach.

Angel was seized by an irrational certainty that if she took her eyes off him for even a second she would lose her nerve and just bolt…or faint, which would be a first. There had been a close call in the early months of her pregnancy when she hadn't yet realised why she couldn't stand the smell of coffee. She inhaled and closed the door on those thoughts.

By the time Alex had reached them—seconds? Who knew? It was all a blur—Angel had lost the rictus grin of fear and had her face composed into a mask of polite indifference. Bone-deep indifference, though her grip on her composure was not even a cell deep. But who cared as long as she didn't make a fool of herself by giving in to the need to tell him exactly what she thought of him?

The indulgence of venting her real feelings, though tempting, would not exactly improve the situation. Angel knew exactly what she would say. She'd had nearly six years to figure it out, which didn't make her some pathetic creature who'd been unable to move on, or someone who had spent the past six years thinking about him.

She had a life that she loved and he had no place in it. At least that was the way it had worked this morning…. Now he wasn't an unidentifiable figure; he was here and real and present. She had always dreaded the future conversation with Jasmine that began with, 'Sorry, I don't know who your dad is,' but when she thought of naming Alex Arlov as the man in question it suddenly became not such a terrible prospect.

He might not even recognise her…? No such luck, not the way this day was going, she thought, swallowing the bubble of hysterical laughter as she grabbed another drink.

But if he didn't, if he had forgotten she existed the moment he had left the room, would it be so bad to keep him in ignorance? Well, yes, it would be, Angel thought to herself. You could stretch moral ambiguity just so far but it would make life a lot simpler…. She shook her head, unable to deal with the fallout, the deeper implications now. Not falling down was tough enough, she thought, struggling to focus on her contempt and not her near nervous collapse.

Maybe she focused too hard because as his eyes brushed her face for a split second she thought she saw a flicker of shock in those ice-blue depths, but then it was gone and so was his attention.

Angel experienced a weird sense of anticlimax and thought, *Was that it?* Sandy, the recipient of a smile of practised charm, lit up when he spoke to her in the deep gravelly drawl Angel recalled so well. She winced to hear the make-up artist respond with a high girlish giggle, but she couldn't judge. Especially as someone who had gasped *wow* the first time she had seen him was in no position to judge anyone.

The memory made her cringe. Easy hardly covered how very eager she had been to be seduced. She'd been so convinced that she was feeling some deep spiritual connection that he hadn't had to lift a finger to seduce her.

While Alex's attention was on Sandy and she had pulled back from the brink of total panic, Angel took the opportunity to study him. She wasn't the only one—most of the women in the room were checking him out.

The interest was no mystery—the aura of masculinity that had taken her breath away that first time was still intact, was presumably an integral part of him. He was the sort of man whose testosterone entered the room ahead of him, and, to Angel's intense fury and eternal shame, even after being a victim of it she was still not immune to its effects.

The difference was she was not about to equate her physical response to his blatant sexuality with anything but hormones. The shameful heat between her thighs had nothing to do with love at first sight. She was almost too embarrassed to acknowledge she had ever been naive enough to believe that such a thing existed.

At almost twenty and just starting her art college course, Angel knew she had acquired a reputation for being sophisticated among her fellow students. She never could work out how or why, but the label had stuck.

'You're so independent,' a homesick friend had once remarked enviously. 'And you can talk to anyone.'

Well, Angel was certainly independent. Arriving home for the school holidays to find a cheque and a note from her mother to explain that she'd been invited to spend the week at a villa in Switzerland made a person independent. And ten schools in eight years made it essential that she could talk to people, though it had been hard on her grades and near impossible to cultivate long-term friendships.

Given her reputation, it was ironic that, unlike most of her contemporaries, at twenty, Angel's experience of the opposite sex had been limited. Her sexual experience had been pretty much nil. Angel's problem had not been low self-esteem or issues about her body or that she was a prude. No, much worse, Angel had been a closet romantic!

The fact was none of the men she had met up to that point had come close to the idealised lover she had imagined was out there waiting for her. And when she'd met the man who looked and acted like her fantasy lover he had turned out to be a lying, cheating rat!

Even though beside her Sandy was still talking, Alex was now staring at Angel. Presumably he thought that money and power negated the need for common courtesy. He probably— The contemptuous observation was not completed because he had her hand in his.... How had that happened?

Myriad half-formed, disconnected thoughts flitted through her head as she stared at his hand, noting with a tightening in her chest that he still didn't wear a wedding band. His brown hands were strong, the fingers long and tapering. Her weirdly heightened senses could make out the slight calluses on his palms. The more she tried not to think about them gliding over her skin, touching her, the more space the images took up in her head.

She squeezed her eyes closed.

Her loss of control could only have lasted a fraction of a second but it felt like a lot longer. When, a moment later, she was able to meet his eyes, what she saw there answered one question—he remembered.

She didn't fall apart. Instead she manufactured a frown as if she were struggling to place him and then widened her eyes and nodded as though she had retrieved the memory she was searching for.

She rewarded herself with the faintest of smiles.

'Alex Arlov.' He tipped his sleek head and to her intense relief released her hand. *How could I ever not have seen how arrogant he is?* She grabbed a napkin from a passing tray and wiped it against the heel of her hand.

'The name seems familiar...' She gnawed lightly on her full lower lip, pretending to search her memory before producing a bright smile and pausing to stretch the moment, hoping like hell he was worrying she was going to out him. If it weren't for Jas she would, and to hell with people knowing what a total fool she was.

But he didn't look concerned, just vaguely amused, as he elevated one dark brow. 'That happens to me all the time—an instantly forgettable face.'

And so full of yourself, she wanted to scream as she smiled back, unable to repress a shudder as she looked directly into his ice-blue dark-framed eyes.

She willed herself to relax. Let it go, she told herself, life moves on. He's just a landmark moment, not a threat.

Her life had moved on, and, if time hadn't completely healed the wounds, it had allowed her to see things from a different perspective. She had made a mistake, but that mistake had given her Jasmine; this man had given her a gift and he didn't know. Jas didn't know either, didn't know who her father was and one day... Did she have to tell him?

'Are you enjoying island life, Miss...?' He arched a brow and studied her. Her features had lost some of their youthful softness, revealing the truly lovely bone structure of her face. She was, he recognised, one of those women who would only improve with age, perfect bone structure compensating for the slight blurring of features as the years passed.

Angel could see his mouth moving, a mouth that was a miracle of stern sensuality, a mouth she had dreamed of. But all she could hear was, *You're married.* Pride had been the only thing that day that had prevented her from crumbling when she had heard him speak the words that had crushed her, words that had turned what she had thought was beautiful into something nasty and sordid.

She blinked and struggled to focus as he repeated himself. Paul, the advertising executive who had followed Alex across the room, caught the question and said, 'We're all on first-name terms here—aren't we, Angel?'

Reminded of a puppy dog eager to please, she flicked a glance his way. She felt sorry for the man, but not as sorry as she felt for herself.... This was a nightmare.

Breathe, she told herself. *You've coped with worse.*

Such as once she had got back to her room in the university residence, when she had locked the door and stood under a shower for forty minutes but still hadn't been able to wash off that feeling of self-disgust, shame and the bitterness of disillusion.

Finally she had stopped indulging in the orgy of misery and given herself a stern talking-to.

'What are you going to do, Angel? Stay in here for ever?' Wiping the steam off the mirror, she had glared at her tear-stained face. 'Your problem is you're a dreamer, a stupid dreamer. You wanted deep and meaningful, you wanted to wait, you wanted the first time to be with someone who made you feel special. Well, you didn't get the prince—you didn't even get the frog!' She quite liked frogs. 'So what? Big deal, just suck it up, Urquart.'

It had been good advice then and it still was.

Her chin lifted. 'Angel Urquart, and I'm not actually here to enjoy myself, just to work.' She failed to inject any warmth or animation into her voice, but she managed to deliver the comment with composure. *You're doing well, Angel,* she told herself as she clenched her fingers tight, driving her nails into the softness of her palms.

Now he wasn't touching her she was able to channel some cool of her own. The cool only went skin deep but that didn't matter. What mattered was showing the cheating, lying bastard that there was nothing he could do to hurt her; she had suffered the infection and built up a natural immunity.

'I hope you'll find a little time in your schedule to enjoy what we have to offer, Angelina.'

The predatory gleam in his heavy-lidded eyes shouldn't have shocked her and definitely shouldn't have produced a hot ache at the juncture of her thighs but it did both.

Why surprise? she asked herself. *You jumped into bed with him after five seconds six years ago. Why wouldn't he file you under the heading marked convenient, easy, or most likely both, since you've clearly fulfilled both from his point of view?*

Pushing away the wave of shame, she embraced the anger coursing through her veins. Smiling, she shook back her dark hair and adopted a dumb expression.

'It's Angel, and I'm not actually big on multitasking.' She was confident she could crush his expectations. She might even enjoy doing so. 'You have a beautiful home.'

A home, a wife and to her knowledge at least one child, her child. But for all she knew there could be more, possibly a dozen children…? Did Jasmine have half-sisters, half-brothers…? Not a possibility Angel had considered before, and not one she wanted to consider now!

'This isn't my home. It's a hotel, Miss Urquart.' He paused, the line between his dark brows deepening as he scanned her face. She had gone pale, her full pink lips were blanched of colour and she looked as though she was about to pass out.

'Are you feeling all right?' She heard him ask with more irritation than concern. The rushing sound in her ears made her think of the ocean, which along with a couple of continents was what she needed to put between this man and her before she felt all right. But failing that… She snatched a glass from the tray of a passing waiter, but didn't hold on to it for long.

'I don't think that's a good idea, do you?'

Her green eyes fluttered wide and she stared with utter astonishment as in a seamless motion he tipped the contents of the untouched glass he had taken from her fingers into a flower arrangement. Her jaw dropped as she felt her temper fizz. This man was totally unbelievable!

'What do you think you're doing?' The words didn't deliver the verbal punch she had intended. Instead her voice had a breathy, vulnerable quality. Teeth clenched, she continued to glare up at him, dabbing her tongue to the beads of sweat that clustered along her upper lip. She rubbed a hand across her forearm and found her skin was moist but cold.

He did not enter the debate but, after subjecting her to a narrow-eyed scrutiny, concluded with an air of resignation, 'You need some fresh air.' When he had contemplated her horizontal, a dead faint and ambulances had not entered the picture. So much for a little light flirtation. Alex preferred the woman in his bed to be sober and fully conscious!

He kept telling her what she needed—that night he had known what she'd needed before she had, and he had given it to her. She stiffened as she felt a hand in the middle of her back.

'What do you think you're doing?'

'You are repeating yourself and, in reply… Excuse me…' The small group parted like the sea in response to his soft-voiced request. 'I am saving you from yourself.'

You're six years too late for that, she thought, deciding that struggling to evade him would just draw people's attention. As it was she was conscious in the periphery of her vision of a few curious looks as they moved towards the door.

Outside he spoke to a hovering member of staff and a chair appeared. He pressed her down into it. 'Better?'

She nodded and turned her face to the sea breeze. 'It was a bit warm in there.' Actually it was warmer outside but she no longer felt as if the room were closing in on her. Once her head stopped spinning and the tightness in her chest eased she would be fine. 'Thank you. Don't let me keep you from your guests.'

CHAPTER THREE

'YOU ARE BEING irritatingly childish.'

This lofty condemnation brought her head up with a jerk…mistake! Angel closed her eyes and waited for the world to stop spinning, opening them a moment later when she found a glass placed at her lips. She responded to the terse instruction to drink; the alternative would have been choking because he did not have what could be termed a gentle bedside manner!

She turned her head away and mumbled, 'Enough.'

'You are welcome.' He watched as she dabbed the back of her hand to the excess moisture on her lips and his focus slipped as the memory surfaced of them softening and parting beneath his. The muscles in his angular jaw tensed and the sinews in his neck stood out as he forcibly ejected the memory, but not before he heard the throaty sound of her plea—*please*…!

That husky plea had been all it had taken to silence the voice in his head, the one that had been telling him he ought not to be doing this.

He had done it and he wanted to, needed to, again. The struggle then like now had been to keep his passion on a leash. Something about this woman seemed to tap directly into his primal instincts.

'What happened in there?'

My past came back to bite me. 'Other than you over-reacting,' she accused him, not willing to admit how close she had come to passing out in public. 'I've told you it w—'

His cold eyes narrowed with irritation as he cut across her impatiently. 'It wasn't the heat.'

She narrowed her eyes and fixed him with a glare. Anyone with an ounce of sensitivity would have tact-fully gone along with the heat excuse and not pried and prodded. 'Do we have to have a post-mortem? I got a bit light-headed. It happens. Now I feel much better. I'll have an early night.'

Perhaps the problem was that she had had too many early nights... The thought did not improve his frame of mind. While he was not looking for a long-running thing—there seemed little point waiting for boredom to set in, as it always did—he did like exclusivity.

He was not a possessive man but sharing was a deal breaker.

'It does not happen for no reason.'

Angel started to feel guilty as he continued to scruti-nise her face as though he would find the answer there.

'Will you stop looking at me like that?' she husked. 'You're making me feel like a criminal. I haven't bro-ken any law.'

'Are you sure?'

'I think I'd have remembered.'

'Have you taken anything?'

Still taking breaths of fresh air to clear the muzzi-ness in her head, she flashed him a confused look, then, as his meaning suddenly dawned on her, lost all colour. The heat returned in a searing wave of outrage until her smooth cheeks glowed.

And the insults just kept coming!

'You're accusing me of being a…a…a…junkie!' And then he had the cheek to look astonished when she got upset. This man really was outrageous, she fumed.

He felt relief. Her outrage might be a case of the lady protested too much but his instincts told him otherwise. 'No need to overreact.'

She clenched her teeth. The pat-you-on-the-head, patronising quality of his drawled response made her want to scream.

'I'm simply excluding possibilities before I call a doctor.'

Her eyes widened this time in horror. 'I do not need a doctor and I'm not overreacting. I'm reacting to you insulting me, interrogating me…'

'Insult…?' he drawled, his ebony brows lifting at the suggestion. 'It is not exactly unknown in the world you work in for people to…dabble.'

Her mouth twisted into a scornful smile. 'Now, that's what I admire—a man who isn't afraid to generalise or judge from his secure position of moral superiority.'

Alex blinked. She had claws and a mouth on her, this woman—a million miles from the two-dimensional sexy purring kitten of his memory. A slow, contemplative smile spread across his lean, hard face. These changes didn't make her any less attractive, just more of a challenge.

And he had always liked a challenge, or he had once. Recently he had gone for the easy option way too often, as it came with the lack of emotional commitment that was essential to him. To commit yourself to someone and risk losing them, risk losing part of yourself… A man who invited such a thing more than once was to his mind insane.

'You are clearly feeling better. Actually I was thinking prescription drugs. They can react badly when combined with alcohol.' He tilted his head in the direction of the room they had just exited. 'And you were knocking it back a bit in there.'

So not only was she some sort of junkie, he was also calling her a lush!

'Thanks for the advice.' Her green eyes glowed with contempt, aimed partly at herself. This hypocritical self-righteous creep was the man she'd waited for? She gave a short bitter laugh. Had she really been that young and stupid?

'For the record, being a model doesn't mean I'm part of some seedy subculture. I'm used to people making assumptions—the odd male who thinks that because I've advertised underwear I have no problem with being looked at as though I'm a piece of meat on a slab...' She left a significant pause and had the pleasure of seeing a muscle in his lean cheek clench. 'Not one of the perks of the job,' she conceded. 'However, you have taken insults to a new low. For the record, if I want advice on the clean life I wouldn't come to you, Mr Arlov. You're a...a... Not a nice man.' *Not nice? You're so hard core, Angel.* 'You're a rodent!'

As she finished on a breathless note of quivering contempt a memory surfaced as strong as it was unbidden: the ferociously strong lines of his face relaxed in sleep, the long eyelashes softening the angle of his carved cheekbones. Not vulnerable and not soft but more... She had never been able to put a name to the quivering sensation in the pit of her stomach. No more could she now, though she felt it again.

Alex's nostrils flared as he sucked in an outraged breath. He liked feisty but there were limits. 'And you base this opinion on what?'

'That you're a rodent?' She was already regretting the rather limp animal analogy. If there was an animal she would have likened him to it would have been a wolf, with its piercing eyes, sleek, lean body and dangerous bearing. An illicit little shiver slipped slowly like a cold finger down her spine.

'I've always thought rats got a bad press, but not nice? I'm hurt,' he mocked. Alex could live without being thought nice.

'Rodent works for me, but what would you call a married man who sleeps around? For the record, and to save you the effort, these days it takes more than being told someone *needs* me to get me into bed!'

Even if the person saying the words had a voice that was sin itself.

Six years was a long time and people change but this…! 'Thanks for the heads up,' he murmured, adding without missing a beat, 'What does it take?'

She shook her head, playing dumb because it was on the tip of her tongue to admit not much. It was true, and she was ashamed she had recognised him as her moral Achilles the second he had touched her. It had shocked her so deeply it had triggered the… Whatever it had been, Angel remained reluctant to assign a name to what had happened. She was perfectly willing to accept that panic attacks existed; they simply didn't happen to her.

'What does it take to get you into bed these days?' Whatever it was it would definitely be worth the effort. He had not been this hungry for a woman in a long time—if ever.

'I'm curious—do you work at being offensive or are you naturally gifted that way?'

'You didn't answer my question. On second thought,

don't. Let me get there by myself. It will be more satisfying than being fed the answer.'

The colour flew to her face. The effects of his purred remark on other parts of her anatomy were too mortifying to think about. 'You're not getting anywhere with me.'

'Oh, well, you know what they say—it's all about the journey not the destination…' A saying that had always struck Alex as particularly ridiculous, never more so than in this context. He had every intention of reaching, enjoying and extracting every atom of pleasure from his destination. The anticipation of sinking into her warm body and losing himself was strong enough to taste.

She shot him a look of utter disdain. 'Do you ever listen to anything anyone says?'

He elevated a dark brow and gave a slow smile. Without a word he hooked his hand behind her head and dragged her face up to his. The action was deceptive, the kiss druggingly deep, his tongue sliding between her parted lips while his firm mouth fitted perfectly over hers. Angel registered the heat that was everywhere; she heard the almost feral low moan but didn't connect the sound with herself.

When it stopped and she managed to prise her heavy eyelids open she found herself looking up into a pair of blazing cosmic-blue eyes. So dizzy she staggered, she gave a choked gasp of horror and stepped backwards, once, twice and amazingly stayed on her feet.

'The truth?'

As if she were emerging from a nightmare—one she had shamefully fully cooperated with and not struggled to escape—Angel fixed her blazing eyes on his face, swallowed a bolus of acrid self-disgust and wiped her hand across her pumped-up plump lips. Where was her self-respect? Where was her pride? When this man touched her she stopped being… She stopped being herself and became someone that scared her, someone whose actions she couldn't predict.

She took a deep restorative breath; she would not fall apart. Yes, he'd like to… But no way. He was acting as if it was no big deal and so could she. It was just a pity the message of defiance had not reached her trembling limbs or core temperature.

'You,' she contended contemptuously, 'wouldn't know the truth if it bit you!' Rich coming from someone who wasn't telling him he had a daughter, or couldn't admit she wouldn't fight too hard if he decided to kiss her again. She lowered her eyes over the shamed acknowledgment and heard his throaty chuckle.

'The truth is I'm more into body language.' Especially when the body in question was as lush and perfectly formed as hers. 'Words can lie…whereas there are some things that you can't hide….'

Her head came up with a guilty jerk. 'I'm not trying to hide anything.' The moment the words left her lips she knew silence would have been more convincing.

'For instance, your pupils have expanded so much there is just a thin ring of colour left.' Her eyes were the purest green he had ever seen flecked with tiny pinpoints of swirling gold. 'You really are a very good kisser.'

So long as his observations did not drop below neck level she could deal. 'Kissing is not hard.' It was the knowing when not to that was hard. 'It's a…a…reflex,' she flung back.

His ebony brows lifted. 'I've never heard it called that before.'

Hating the smugness in his voice, she snapped. 'You think you know body language? Well, study this,' she invited, pointing to her own face, pale now and set into a cold mask. 'I was ill in that room because I saw you and was reminded of an episode in my life I'm not too proud of, in fact I'm deeply ashamed of.'

'That's your problem, not mine.' Shame and guilt were not to his mind something to be yelled about. They were things you lived with; they were the price you paid for mistakes.

Angel drew in a deep shuddering breath and revealed the ultimate unforgivable crime that she laid at his door. 'You turned me into the other woman.' Her voice dropped to an emotional whisper as she realised. 'You turned me into the person I never wanted to be—my mother!'

Alex's jaw clenched but his anger almost immediately faded. He was very good at reading body language but it did not require his talent to interpret the expression in her emerald eyes as shock.

So Angel had mother issues? That was not his problem, and he had no interest in helping her work her way through them. He refused to recognise an uncharacteristic urge to draw out more details, an urge that directly contradicted his determined lack of interest.

Six years, Angel, but you got there in the end. How could she not have seen it before? *'Madre di Dio!'* she mocked softly, then gave a little laugh.

The throaty exclamation distracted him. 'Italian?'

She blinked as it took her a few moments to return from wherever she had gone. 'Half.' She didn't elaborate. It seemed, Angel thought grimly, that she had done too much show and tell already!

Economy of detail was something Alex appreciated in his lovers, actively encouraged, but even he liked a whole sentence.

Well, at least the Latin connection explained the golden glowing looks, and possibly the temper too, though if he said so she would probably not waste the opportunity to accuse him of generalising.

'I've heard of people rewriting history but this is the first time I've seen it firsthand. You're acting as though you were some passive victim. The way I recall it you were an equal and active participant, so the outraged-virgin act is a bit over the top.' Although amazingly she retained the ability to blush like one—the colour that washed over her cheeks deepened the pale gold of her skin with a rosy sheen. 'This can't be the first time you've bumped into an old one-night stand?'

Her eyes slid from his as she swallowed the insult, though she doubted he had intended it as such. He wasn't making a moral judgement. That was just who he thought she was. It was easier to let him continue to hold that opinion than tell him the truth.

What would be his reaction, she wondered, if she came out with, 'You're the only man I've ever slept with'? She almost laughed at the image of his imagined incredulity. Or worse, he might ask her the question she'd asked herself a thousand times—why him?

How could she begin to explain to him something she didn't even understand herself?

She made herself look at him and felt her insides shudder as their eyes connected. 'One like you.'

In case he decided to construe her comment as a compliment she added coldly, 'One who made me feel... cheap.' Feeling this was an admission too far, she dodged his gaze and missed the expression that flickered across his lean face. When she raised her eyes his face was stone. 'I may just be a model, which clearly in your eyes makes me a pill-popping bimbo—' she took a deep breath and made a conscious effort to control her indignation '—but I don't sleep with married men!'

Her shrill accusations might not have touched him but this last quiet comment did. 'I'm not married now.'

Was that meant to make her feel better? Or was it a lie to get her into bed? Angel told herself she didn't want to know; all she wanted was to get out of here and away from him.

'Now, why doesn't that surprise me?' she drawled. 'I really hope she took you for a lot of money...' His bank balance was probably the only vulnerable area he had, she thought bitterly.

'She's dead.'

The blunt pronouncement drew a gasp from Angel, who immediately felt like a total bitch. So this was what it felt like to have the rug pulled out from under your feet.

During the ensuing silence the mortified colour flew to her cheeks and then receded. What was she meant to say that didn't sound trite and insincere?

'Oh!'

Before she had said anything more the uniformed employee who had brought her the chair reappeared, this time carrying a tray with a cafetière and coffee cups, and at a nod from Alex he placed it on the table.

The young man spoke in Greek and Alex Arlov responded in the same language.

Questions flying around in her head, Angel watched as he poured the coffee and pushed one her way without asking. Had he loved his wife?

His expression wasn't giving any clues and in her book a man who loved his wife was not unfaithful. *But that's just me, the idealist,* she thought with a wry grimace.

'Do you want sugar?'

Angel, who hadn't been aware she'd been stirring the coffee, put the spoon down with a clatter in the saucer and shook her head. 'No, I don't take it.'

He had slept around, but she supposed that some men did and some women put up with infidelity or didn't know. It was weird to her— Actually, no, it was utterly abhorrent, but marriage meant different things to different people.

'I'm sorry, I didn't know about your wife or I wouldn't have said…what I did.' Then, aware that her comment might come across as hypocritical, she added, 'Even if it is true.'

Had the poor woman lived her life in ignorant bliss, or turned a blind eye, or had she known and cared and suffered the humiliation…? Angel didn't know which scenario was worse.

She tore her eyes from his handsome patrician profile and thought how hellish it must be to be married to a man that other women lusted after. That was one hell she was never going to know about.

Marriage to any man was not on the cards for her. These days, when it was easy to live together—and even easier to drift apart—it seemed to Angel that desire to raise a family was one of the main reasons that couples made their relationship official.

For her there would be no more children. There had been a time when the knowledge had made her sad… angry…filled with a 'why me?' self-pity, but now she had reached a stage of why not me? She had accepted it, and could not imagine a man or a circumstance that would make her walk down the aisle.

She had not discounted the possibility in the future of a man, someone nice who Jasmine liked, someone who didn't make any demands. She could live without head-banging sex but a hug would be nice, and stability. She could remember craving boring stability when she was a child and envying her friends who had complained about the boredom of the things she had longed for.

The expressions scudding like clouds across her face made him wonder what thoughts were responsible for putting that pensive look in her eyes. Then, catching himself wondering, he experienced a flash of irritation.

It seemed a good moment to remind himself that he wanted to bed her, not know how her mind worked.

'I seem to have put a damper on the conversation.'

Her green eyes lifted from the contemplation of the untouched swirling liquid. 'Sorry if I'm not amusing you.' Presumably, she brooded, he was one of those men who expected women to tie themselves into knots being interesting and amusing. 'And we were not having a conversation.' Her eyes lowered towards her coffee and lifted again suddenly. It was as if her resolve not to show any interest broke at the last moment. 'Was it… Your wife… Did she… Did it happen recently?'

'No, it didn't.'

When he offered no further information Angel took a sip of the coffee and looked at him over the rim of her cup. 'It must be hard bringing up children alone…?' she murmured, trying hard not to look like someone who had a stake in his response.

Was Jasmine an only child or did she have half siblings? The brother or sister that Angel had always felt vaguely guilty for not supplying. Siblings looked out for one another when things got tough. If she vanished… Angel gave herself a sharp internal shake. Nothing was going to happen to her, and if it did she had things organised. But a father had not featured in those arrangements.

Of course, if it turned out he had his own family he might not be interested in pursuing a relationship with Jasmine anyway. His loss, though from a selfish point of view it would make life simpler. She felt a stab of guilt. This wasn't about simple, this was about what was best for Jasmine, and if that involved allowing her father to be part of her life she would move heaven and earth to make it happen. He was right; she was no innocent victim. If she hadn't thrown herself at him the way she had none of this would have happened.

She pressed her fingers to her temples. Her head felt as if it would explode with all the unanswered questions swirling round in it, and there were not going to be any of the answers she wanted until she told him.

'We didn't have any children.'

They had planned to have a family but not immediately. Of course, it had seemed as if they would have all the time in the world, then all too soon they had had none. A blessing, Emma, struggling to come to terms with the rapid progress of her illness, had said, but as her denial had turned to deep depression she had become angry and blamed him for... Well, pretty much everything, until it had reached the point when she had turned her head to the wall when he walked into the room.

The doctors had sympathised and called it transference. His wife, they said, was transferring all the guilt she felt for concealing her illness when they married onto to him, and as they had predicted the phase passed. But to his way of thinking what followed was harder. Emma had been consumed with guilt. The precious time they'd had left together had been dominated by it.

Angel lowered her eyes but not before he glimpsed the moisture lingering there and her expression. He reacted to the sympathy he loathed using a tried-and-tested method to kill off the pity that made his skin crawl.

'Turn down the empathy, Angel. I'm not a candidate for a sympathy shag,' he drawled.

Her appalled eyes flew to his face, suddenly minus their emotional moisture. 'You are a candidate for a kick,' she retorted, adding in a conversational tone, 'You really can be vile.' She was almost immediately hit by a wave of remorse, so added, 'I am genuinely sorry about your wife.'

'But I'm vile—a rodent, yes, I get that.' The tension vanishing from his manner along with her sympathy, he produced a mocking grin. 'I'm enjoying living down to your expectations of me. Relax,' he advised, 'I do not require a shoulder to cry on.' Though a warm breast to lay his head against would not be rejected. The one in question rose and fell revealing a glitter of something shiny in the deep valley.

'I was not about to offer one.' Offering anything to the only man you had ever fantasised about lying naked beneath was something to be actively avoided. She swallowed hard and dropped her gaze, wishing she had not thought about being naked. 'And I have no expectations.'

'But some curiosity.' The speculation was pretty much proved when she couldn't meet his eyes. 'Don't feel bad. Everyone wants to ask. Few do—death is one of those subjects that people tiptoe around. Emma died of MS, an aggressive form she had been ill with for some time.'

Angel could only marvel that he could sound so detached while revealing this tragic sequence of events. For all the emotion he was displaying he could have been recounting the story of a stranger's life.

'It was lucky we had no children.' He sketched a sardonic smile. 'Now your turn…?'

She got that he rejected sympathy—hard not to—but she felt it anyway, a strong surge of empathy that she couldn't repress. She would have felt the same for anyone in his situation; the difference was she hadn't spent the past six years hating anyone. Not to do so, even briefly, felt odd…uncomfortable, and required some major mental readjustment.

'One.' She couldn't pretend that Jasmine didn't exist.

He stiffened. 'In most countries that is all a person can have at one time.' The joke, it seemed, was on him. Why the hell hadn't she just told him she was married up front?

Why didn't you consider the possibility, Alex?

Her bewildered-sounding response cut across his inner dialogue. 'One…?'

'You're not wearing a ring,' he clenched out, feeling cheated.

Anchoring her hair against a sudden flurry of wind, she followed the direction of his gaze and drew the hand down to look at it, turning it over as she blew away the errant raven strands that immediately plastered themselves across her face. She was of the school of thought that said less was more when it came to jewellery and she rarely wore rings when working. Her hand went to her neck where she wore her father's signet ring on a chain. Her brother had inherited a Scottish estate complete with castle, and she, being a woman, had got only the ring. She didn't resent it half as much as her brother felt guilty about it.

'Why should I…?' She stopped as the penny dropped. 'God, not a husband! I have a child, a daughter.'

This was only slightly less astonishing to him than her having a husband. His eyes went to the fingers that were rubbing the chain she wore around her neck. Through her fingers he recognised the disc he had initially taken for a pendant nestled between her breasts as a ring.

'You have a baby?' His eyes drifted down her slim body and he felt a kick of lust that made his strong-boned features clench.

Hard not to recognise this as the perfect opportunity to speak. *So why aren't you, Angel?*

We have a baby. It didn't matter how hard she tried, Angel couldn't visualise his reaction to this bombshell.

'She's hardly a baby.' Her expression softened. Jasmine had been a lovely baby, though it might have been easier to enjoy her loveliness if she had ever slept. The first eighteen months had passed in a blur of sleep deprivation.

'But she must be young, and you're a single parent...?' Did the ring have some significance? A token from the father?

Angel instantly prickled with antagonism; her chin went up. She was pretty secure when it came to her parenting skills, able to shrug off and smile her way through well-meaning advice, but when the source of the criticism was the absent father of her daughter it turned out she couldn't.

'Yes, I am, and I really don't think my childcare arrangements are your concern,' she tossed back, realising as she spoke that this situation might change very soon. When he knew he might think that he should have a say. The idea appalled her.

Blinking at the level of belligerence in her attitude, he made a pacifying gesture with his hands. Her eyes followed the gesture—he had lovely hands.

'I am hardly an expert on the subject.'

He watched as her hunched shoulders flattened. He could almost feel her willing the tension away. Her tense smile was a clear effort and she avoided his eyes. 'That doesn't stop most people offering advice.'

'Is her father involved?'

Angel couldn't look at him. Lucky thing she was sitting down because her knees were shaking. 'No.'

'I imagine it can't be easy…?'

He imagined right, but Angel would not have it any other way. The sleepless nights were more than compensated for in a million other ways. 'I make it work.'

'I'm sure you do.'

Again, she couldn't take his comment at face value. 'And no, I'm not naive enough to think a single working parent can have it all, but I don't want it all.'

From this defiant statement he read that she wanted it but couldn't have it. The idea that the father was unavailable, most likely married, seemed a real contender. Funny how some women were drawn to unavailable men…. Was she one of them?

'We all want some things more than others.' And at that moment all he wanted, wanted so much he could taste it, was this provoking, dark-haired, green-eyed witch. His innate ability to distance himself from a situation had failed him completely—he wanted her under him, he wanted to be inside her and he knew he wasn't going to have a moment's peace until he had achieved this desire.

The expression in his eyes stopped her asking what it was he wanted more than other things. The expression in his blue eyes was explicit enough to cause a head-on collision between a fist of some unidentifiable emotion and her solar plexus.

She got to her feet. 'Well, thanks for the coffee and the little chat but I'm fine now.'

'I'll walk you back to your bungalow.'

A cold fist of fear tightened in her belly as Angel realised that she wanted to say yes. When she recognised how much she wanted to say yes the fist tightened even more.

She tossed back her hair and made her voice cold.

'That will be quite unnecessary and I'm not going back to my bungalow. I'm going back to the party.' A room full of people no longer seemed a bad thing; she didn't want to be alone with her thoughts.

'If it makes you feel any better, Emma, my wife, died several weeks before we slept together.'

The words stopped her in her tracks. She shook her head. Was she being slow…? 'You expect that to make me feel better?'

He had, but it was fairly obvious he had been wrong. 'I thought you had a right to know.' The comment had not sounded so lame or pompous in his head.

'But not before I spent six years worrying that I'd turned into my mother. Why on earth did you say you were married?'

'I didn't say, you assumed.'

'And you didn't put me right. Why… Oh, you… Oh…' Comprehension flickered into her eyes. 'It was the quickest way to get rid of me…?'

'I have a distaste of scenes.'

She sucked in a deep breath through flared nostrils. Hearing the beat of helicopter blades somewhere in the distance she could only hope that they were here to whisk him away. 'I'm going back into the party—your party, so I can't stop you coming too, but if you pester me so help me I'll report you to the hotel management for harassment and I don't care who it upsets!'

Not him, if his expression was any indicator. 'I can speak for the management when I say that we take all complaints very seriously.'

'We?' She shook her head. 'This hotel is part of the Theakis group.' Her frown deepened as his firm lips twitched. 'What is so funny? Don't you believe I would?'

'Oh, I believe you would follow through with any rash

threat you make. But before you do I should explain that my grandfather was Spyros Theakis, Angelina. I *am* the Theakis group and speaking in that role I can assure you we take all such complaints very seriously.'

The realisation hit Angel like a stone. Having deflated her, he strode off in the opposite direction without another word or backwards glance.

CHAPTER FOUR

ANGEL STAYED AT the party for another hour but by the time she reached her room her headache had become a full-blown migraine. At least it meant she wasn't going to lie awake going over the events of this evening. Instead, she was going to lie awake waiting for the medication, which she always carried with her, to kick in, willing herself not to throw up while she tried to ignore the vice crushing her skull and the metronome inside it.

Wow, it was a win-win situation!

She did throw up. In fact she spent half the night with her head in the toilet. It had been after four when she had finally crawled back to bed and fallen asleep, a fact that resulted in her spending an age in Make-up—or maybe that was normal for film? Angel didn't have a clue and as she stepped out in front of the camera she was very conscious of her inexperience.

She told herself that no one wanted her to fail, but she could imagine a few people might be amused if she did. As it was, she didn't mess up. Apparently the first full morning's filming had gone well, though to Angel the progress had seemed torturously slow.

She said as much to her co-star, if that was the right description of the actor who was to play opposite her in the soap-style series of adverts.

'Take up knitting like me, darling,' he advised.

'How long do you think we have for lunch?'

'In my humble opinion...' he began.

Angel couldn't not smile. In her opinion Clive didn't have a humble bone in his body.

'All right, not so humble.' He might not do humble, but he did have a sense of humour. 'We have finished for the day.'

It turned out he was right.

Angel had already checked it out so she knew that the narrow strait of water that separated the private island from the hotel beach was safe. So when she declined a seat on the boat in favour of swimming the short distance her co-star responded in much the same way he had when he'd found her reading a book.

'For pleasure?'

Angel, who knew he had a post-grad degree, suspected he was never off duty, always playing his part as the pretty-but-dim public school boy that most of his well-paid Hollywood roles had involved him playing.

The deep turquoise water was warm and Angel, who was a strong swimmer, was a couple hundred yards from the beach when she stopped and began to tread water, watching the people on the beach before flipping onto her back to float lazily.

It was the angry metallic buzz sound of the Jet Ski that made her lift her head. If she hadn't she wouldn't have seen the kid who had obviously drifted out farther than he intended on an inflatable toy, and she watched in horror as he fell off into the path of the Jet Ski.

Two things became immediately obvious. One, he couldn't swim very well and two, the driver of the Jet Ski couldn't see him.

Her yelled warning alerted the people on the shore, several of whom entered the water shouting, but the Jet

Ski rider remained oblivious and she was a hell of a lot closer than anyone else.

With a pounding front crawl that left her breathless, Angel managed to get to the child and make sure he stayed afloat. But it became harder to stay that way when the boy let go of the inflatable and transferred his hold to her neck, gripping tightly. Pulled under without a chance to fill her lungs, she surfaced a few moments later with the kid latched on like a limpet only to see the Jet Ski heading right for them.

At the last moment she pushed the kid's face into her shoulder and closed her eyes, not perhaps the most practical response, but it worked to the extent that they were still alive when she opened them. Though this was, it turned out, less to do with her closed eyes and more to do with the Jet Ski rider seeing them at the last moment.

He swerved and didn't quite miss them. But her shoulder only took a glancing blow, which she barely noticed, as at this point she was busy struggling to stay afloat. The kid was half strangling her with his grip, and the close encounter with the Jet Ski had seriously freaked him out so he had begun kicking out wildly with his legs.

The relief when a speedboat pulled up alongside and someone hauled him up out of her arms was intense.

'Thank you so much.' Her grateful waterlogged smile faded slightly when she saw the owner of the hand she had grabbed gratefully on to, his face a dark shadow against the sun shining directly into her eyes. But there was no mistaking his identity.

She landed in the boat in a staggeringly inelegant, breathless heap and crawled onto a bench seat.

'You're all right?'

'Fine,' she lied, finding herself nodding meekly in response to his stern, 'Don't move.' As if she could have if she'd wanted to!

* * *

Alex didn't trust himself to respond to this patent lie and maintained his silence on the way back to shore, choosing not to compete with the boy, who was now bawling in his ear very loudly.

'I want my mum.'

'She is welcome to you.'

Angel gasped. 'Don't be so mean. Can't you see that the poor thing is upset?'

He was upset! Alex was pretty sure that watching her swim directly into the path of that Jet Ski had taken six months off his life. Angel, on the evidence so far, was not destined to make it to thirty!

'I can *hear* that he's upset,' Alex retorted grimly, holding the kid with one hand and steering the boat with the other. He flashed her a look of irritation and snarled, 'Will you sit still? Because if you fall out, so help me I'll let you drown. In all my life I have never witnessed such a reckless, suicidal, stupid action!' he raged. 'Every time I see you, you are trying to kill yourself!'

Before she could defend herself against this unjust attack he cut the engine and the people who had waded out into the shallows were there, arms outstretched, to deliver the boy to his mother.

A young man wearing the logo of the hotel on his polo shirt and a label that identified him as a lifeguard on his cap climbed into the boat and, after speaking to Alex, took the wheel.

Alex himself peeled off his own shirt, dived neatly into the water from the far side of the boat and vanished under it before appearing on the shore side where the water reached his waist.

Hair slicked wetly back, looking like some impossibly perfect front cover of a men's health magazine, he squinted up at Angel, water streaming down his brown face. 'Do you want someone to take you to the marina or...?' He held out a hand.

She treated his offer of assistance from the boat with a look of cold disdain, though as she lowered herself into the water the pain in her shoulder made her wish she had swallowed her pride.

He didn't turn back once to see if she was managing so it became a matter of pride that she stay on her feet even though a delayed reaction to the drama was beginning to set in.

When she reached the shore slightly distant from the group around the child and his family, she watched Alex in action. He took charge, of course he did—it was clearly second nature to him. He was just one of those individuals people naturally turned to in times of crisis and he was good, she had to admit, as she watched him soothe, calm and casually issue instructions.

It was curious that the father of the child who had up until that moment held it together broke down and started weeping, almost as if Alex's competence gave him permission to fall apart. At that point his wife stopped crying and began berating their son, who had been on the point of enjoying all the attention.

'If it hadn't been for that lady.... She's a heroine.'

Someone clapped and someone else picked it up, then with a chain-reaction effect the ripple spread and everyone was clapping.

Angel, whose entire attention had been focused on Alex—she might even have had her mouth open—became belatedly aware of people looking in her general direction, and looked around expecting to see the heroine referred to until the penny dropped.... *Oh, God!*

With heaven-sent timing the shaken driver of the Jet

Ski chose this moment to wade ashore and, taking advantage of the distraction afforded by his appearance, Angel headed for the rocky area that shielded the main beach from the smaller, quieter cove at the far end. She gave a quick furtive look over her shoulder before she waded through the water and then down onto the beach the other side of the rocky outcrop.

The small cove was empty, and with a sigh of relief Angel flopped down onto the sand, her closed eyelids filtering out some of the brutal midday sun. It wasn't until she stretched out that she realised she wasn't only shaking on the inside but on the outside too, fine tremors that shook her entire body.

She lay still and waited for it to pass, nursing her head, which, still tender from the previous night, had begun to throb gently. Great, she needed that like a… Actually a hole in the head might relieve the pressure she could feel building.

Alex was probably the only one who had seen her slip away. He was definitely the only one to follow her. The idea of her acting like some sort of injured animal, crawling away to lick its wounds, made him furious. The woman had the self-preservation instincts of a lemming.

He clambered over the rocks, not around them, to reach the empty cove. There was a very good reason it was empty at this time of day. The water Angel had waded through was already waist deep and in another ten minutes it would be cut off from the bigger beach. Swimming around or a trek through the pine-forested strip that edged the sand were the only ways back to the hotel, a fact that was written in red letters a mile high on signs along the beach.

When he spotted her stretched out on the sand he hit the ground running, then stopped as he saw her chest lift, her breasts pushing against the black fabric of her bikini top.

At the best of times—which this was not—Alex was not well schooled in compassionate concern; he lacked the finesse and the patience. Yet as he reached the spot where she lay and looked down at her he felt his anger slip away. In his head he saw her face when she had realised the applause was for her. Many people dreamed of earning such plaudits, of being hailed a hero, but she had looked…stunned, horrified. It would have been the prefect punishment to have drawn her in to take a curtain bow, but the hunted expression on her face as she had slipped away had made him repress the malicious impulse.

Lying there, she managed to simultaneously look as sexy as hell and damned, throat-achingly vulnerable.

'Are you all right?' Concern added a layer of gravel to his deep voice.

She didn't leap out of her skin, but only because she had felt his shadow blocking the sun a fraction of a second before he spoke. Still stinging from his unfair comments in the boat, she imagined the expression of impatience on his lean face. In her head she could see him glancing at his watch, thinking, *That bloody woman again!*

She raised herself onto her elbows but didn't lift her gaze. 'I'm fine,' she said, arching her foot to rub the sand off one foot with the red-painted toes of the other.

His eyes on the top of her dark head, he wondered how she managed to make the assurance sound much the same as *go away*—it was a talent. He was sorely tempted to do just that. If she was so determined to put herself in a hospital, who was he to stop her?

Unaware that he had chosen that moment to drop

gracefully into a squatting position beside her, Angel started to sit upright. The near collision of their heads drew a tiny gasp of alarm from her throat. Rocking back on his heels, he remained, from Angel's point of view, far too close!

He still didn't have his shirt on, and he made her think of a particularly sexy pirate. How embarrassing that she couldn't stop staring at his chest; her eyes were welded there.

'I'm fine,' she croaked, thinking this comment had rarely in her life been less true.

'You're working on the theory that if you say it more than once it makes it so.' He didn't sound amused; he sounded exasperated.

'It *is* so.' Teeth pressing into the pink softness of her full lower lip, she finally managed to drag her eyes upwards and discovered that he wasn't looking impatient or even angry. He was looking worried and concerned, and instead of being mollified by the discovery she was thrown into an instant state of heart-pounding confusion. With Alex it seemed a condition she spent about ninety per cent of her time in.

From the tangled muddle of emotions lodged like a heavy stone in her chest, anger and resentment dissolved. Without them she felt oddly defenceless; she didn't know how to deal with his concern. *Who are you kidding, Angel? You don't know how to deal with him full stop!* The man was the father of her child and he was a total stranger—a pulse-racingly disturbing total stranger.

Well, one solution would be to get to know him, she thought. He's right here. Stop snarling and start talking. Was picking fights with him a way that she had subconsciously adopted to delay the moment she told him about

Jasmine? She tried to push the idea away but it lingered...
as did the scent of his soap in her nostrils.

'I really am all right. I was just escaping the fuss....
How about the boy?'

'He doesn't seem any the worse for the experience,'
Alex commented drily. 'He was posing for photos when
I left.... What's wrong?'

'Nothing.'

'You winced.'

She expelled an exasperated sigh of surrender and
snapped. 'My head hurts. It's nothing.' Compared to last
night it was true. She turned her head, giving a little grunt
of relief when she saw that the skin on her shoulder was
not broken. It was sore, though.

Growing irritation made his jaw clench again. She had
managed to make it sound as if it were his fault.

'Let me see.'

She turned her head away. 'No, I didn't hit it. I just
have a headache.'

'Headaches don't leave bruises.' His long brown fingers, their touch delicate but firm, pushed aside the sat-
urated strands of hair from her forehead, causing her
eyes to fly wide and green to his face, the frantic fluttering sensation that began in the pit of her stomach and
spread hot and dangerously fast making her pull away
while she could.

The subsequent jolt caused her bruised shoulder to
ache.

'Leave me alone.'

The words mocked Alex even as her belligerent emerald eyes taunted him.

Leave her alone!

That's your problem, Alex thought grimly. *You can't.*
Six years ago he hadn't been able to and he still

couldn't. From the moment he had seen her he had wanted her and that hunger had not decreased. If anything it had grown and it didn't matter how aggravating, how sheer bloody minded she was, no negative was negative enough to make him any less hot for her.

Around this woman his self-control was zero. Even the fact she had just been involved in an accident didn't save her from his lust. No, lust he could cope with, but this ability she had to draw emotional responses from him was something he was not willing to recognise, let alone deal with.

'You're bloody lucky all you have is a headache!'

The fresh blast of disapproval hurt but at least it enabled her to throw off the weird feeling of vulnerability.

'Do you have to yell?' She framed a pained furrow between her darkly defined brows. 'I'm not deaf.' Or needy, she reminded herself.

His jaw tightened and the memory of her putting herself between the blades of the Jet Ski and the child resurfaced to increase his rage. 'Do you ever think about the consequences of your actions?'

It was the consequences of both their actions that she had been living with for six years. 'I accept them,' she told him quietly. 'How about you?' Well, she was going to find out the answer to that one very soon.

He ignored the wry interjection and barely registered her sudden look of panic. 'We are not talking about me. I'm talking about your publicity-seeking stunt.'

Her temper fizzed. 'A stunt! You think I arranged that?'

Alex didn't, but the thought had flashed through his mind. 'No, I don't think you've got the brains….' he admitted, an edge of weariness entering his voice as he added, 'Do you ever think before you leap or jump?'

She fixed him with an evil-eyed stare. 'You're right, I didn't think. Story of my life!' She sniffed. 'If I had thought, do you think I'd have wasted my virginity on a selfish, lying bastard who let me think he was married just to get out the door?'

She closed her eyes to blot out the expression stamped on his face. The man didn't just look shocked, he looked as though someone had aimed a loaded revolver at him and pulled the trigger.

The words didn't just hang in the air, they vibrated, the volume growing with each beat of her heart. Unfortunately, there was no way she could retrieve them because, true to form, she'd done it again. She'd blurted out the truth at the worst moment imaginable. *Way to go, Angel, out to personally disprove the old adage that wisdom came with age.*

CHAPTER FIVE

'YOU'RE TRYING TO tell me… No… No, you were not a virgin!' Even as Alex voiced the denial his brain was making connections that he couldn't believe he hadn't seen before.

''Course not. What can I say? I have a sick sense of humour.'

Angel's eyes were closed, squeezed tight like a little kid who thought the action made her invisible.

'You were.' He dragged a hand through his hair and got to his feet, walking several steps away before stalking back to stand over her. 'You were a virgin, and you acted like a damned…'

'Damned what?' she challenged, getting to her feet.

He just looked at her and shook his head, groaning. *'Theos!'*

She shrugged, wrapping her arms around herself, cold despite the afternoon heat. Shock, she speculated, viewing the tremors that were shaking her body with a weird objectivity. The genie was out of the bottle, the truth was out there and she couldn't get it back, so she did the only thing possible—she downplayed it like mad!

'Let's not make a big deal of it. A girl's got to lose it some time.'

'You think this is a subject for cheap jokes? It *was* a

big deal. It *is* a big deal—to me and it should be to you.'
He hadn't even been Emma's first lover, and it had not
been important to him. For some men perhaps there was
an appeal in teaching a novice the ropes, but it was a responsibility that he would have actively avoided had the
opportunity ever arisen. It hadn't—or so he had thought.

'I'm sorry if my ability to laugh at ancient history of-
fends you, but it was a long time ago and life moves on.'
And it also occasionally threw some surprises, and the
surprise today was the strength of Alex's reaction to the
news. He was still pale beneath his tan. 'There has to be
a first time for everyone—it's the second time that can
be more problematic.' She cleared her throat and, regretting the reference to her nonexistent sex life, hurriedly
tacked on a laughing, 'Even you.'

She lifted her eyes to his face and her smile faded. It
was impossible to imagine Alex being young and inexperienced, his face smooth, his eyes without cynicism.

'Why the hell didn't you tell me?' he blasted.

His indignation continued to strike her as pretty per-
verse. 'I don't recall conversation being very high on the
agenda.' She forced the words past the tight constriction
in her throat. 'Would it have made any difference if I'd
told you?'

Alex opened his mouth and closed it again. It was a
good question and he'd have liked to think it would, but
on that day he had not been thinking with his brain.

'I resent being made to feel like some sort of bloody
predator.'

He resented! 'Well, I'm *so* sorry I've made you feel
a victim, but I guess it's a responsibility I'll have to live
with.'

The saccharine insincerity dripping from her sarcastic retort brought a defining flash of colour to the knife-edged contours of his carved cheekbones.

'Did you set out that day with the intention of—?' He bit down on the question, but not soon enough to stop Angel's eyes sparking afresh with anger.

'Sure,' she drawled, disguising her hurt with a sarcastic tone. 'I engineered the whole thing.'

A muscle alongside his mouth clenched as their eyes connected, sizzling blue on flashing green. 'You can't leave anything, can you?' he charged. *Like the fact you acted like a total irresponsible bastard, Alex?* 'I know it wasn't your fault,' he gritted through clenched teeth. 'It was my bloody…' He stopped abruptly. 'You said the *second* time was the problem.' He shook his head, not following the crazy idea to its equally crazy conclusion.

'Did I?' she said, thinking did this man miss nothing? She adopted a sweetly insincere smile and hid behind the truth. 'Oh, yes, you've guessed it. You spoiled me for any other man, Alex.'

Responding to her mockery with a curt, unsmiling, 'Except for the father of your child,' he extended a hand to her.

Staring at the hand, not the man she nodded. 'Oh, yes, there is him.' And there was Jasmine.

And Jasmine's father.

Oh, God! She knew the delay with coming clean was not making things better, quite the opposite, in fact. With a sigh she dropped her head into her hands and began to scrub her eyes with the heels of her palms. She felt a surge of despairing disgust as she asked herself where was the woman who never avoided an awkward issue but met it head on?

As she tilted her head to look at him her hair fell back, revealing the beginning of a bruise on her temple. Staring at the discoloration, Alex felt his stomach muscles lurch and tighten with an emotion as strong as his previous anger and totally inexplicable.... Only a madman would feel protective towards this provocative witch with her smart mouth and her combative attitude.

He was not a madman. It was *her* sanity that was the issue here; *her* insane behaviour was what he was here to challenge, although the conversation had drifted somewhat. *Time to refocus, Alex,* he thought.

'That was a crazy thing you did.' Also brave; the private concession was made reluctantly. It was hard not to admire this woman's fearlessness—at least from a distance. For those close to her it must make life hell, he thought grimly. 'You could have killed yourself....'

He closed his eyes, seeing the scene again and experiencing the same awful sense of helplessness. The memory remained like an icy fist in his chest as he glared at her and spelt out the fact she seemed incapable of grasping. 'You could be dead.'

'I can't die. I have Jasmine,' she asserted confidently. It was a simple fact. Jasmine would have been without a mother and that couldn't happen.... It nearly had!

Like a tower of cards her confidence slipped away. Oh, God, he was right. She was a mother—she couldn't go around leaping in without thinking.

'I'm a terrible mother!'

Hearing the anguished wail and seeing the tears rolling silently down her cheeks cut through the righteous anger that gripped him like a hot blade through butter. He was unable and unwilling to identify the emotion that tightened in his chest as tenderness, but he dropped back down beside her. His time when he touched her she did not pull away as though he were poison. Instead she leaned into him, melted into him softly, shaking her head on his chest.

One moment he was fighting the urge to throttle her, the next he was fighting an equally primal desire to comfort her. His emotions did one of those three-hundred-and-sixty-degree shifts that seemed to happen around her.

'What if—?'

'You have lived to tell the tale. There is no point in what ifs. So how old is she, your daughter... Jasmine?' He spoke not out of genuine interest but a need to distract her. At the same time he ran a soothing hand over her wet hair, lifting it off her neck; the texture of her warm, damp skin beneath fascinated him.

'She's started school. Well, she had.'

'Had?'

'She was off a term as she wasn't well, but she's having some home tutoring and she'll soon catch up. She's smart.'

The audible pride in her muffled response caused his hand to still, though the dark strands of her wet hair remained coiled around his fingers. It was difficult for him to see her as a mother but, he thought to himself, *You don't have the exclusive on family feeling, Alex.*

'She's better now?' he asked, giving her time to regain control.

Angel nodded into his chest. 'I took some time off but this opportunity was too good—' He felt her stiffen before she pulled away from him. Tucking her hair behind her ears, she regarded him with a defiance that was echoed in her addition. 'I suppose you don't think mothers should work?'

She clearly expected his judgement. *And why not, Alex? You've done little else but judge so far.*

Quick to judge and slow to forgive. The words of his

mother, a sad observation that he had lived to understand the meaning of but that had meant little to him when she'd spoken them soon after his half-sister had appeared like a disruptive whirlwind in their lives.

'I know nothing of the pressures of being a mother... or a parent.' His brow creased as he admitted, 'I still struggle to think of you as one.'

'A mother or an actual person, not a body that looks good in a bikini?' Before he could respond to the bitter accusation she added wearily, 'Being a mother is one job where experience is not a prerequisite.'

'There's nothing on your website that mentioned you have a daughter. Is that a professional thing?'

'You're not the only one who likes their privacy.' She blinked her sooty lashes over wide emerald eyes as her voice dropped an astonished husky octave. 'You looked me up?'

'I was curious.'

So was she, and maybe it was the hint of evasiveness in his manner but she suddenly heard herself asking the question that she'd heard many people voice, but that as yet had no satisfactory answer. Everyone had theories but nobody could really understand why they were being allowed access to the private island.

'Why *are* you giving us access to Saronia?' The moment the words left her lips she regretted them, but it was too late to back off. 'They say you've refused royal requests.' Why would a man who'd refused honeymooning royals open his doors—or at least a restricted area of his shoreline—to them?

'Do they?'

She narrowed her eyes. 'You know they do.'

'So what is your theory?'

She lifted a hand to shade her eyes. It was a bit late in

the day to make out that she hadn't thought about it, but she tried anyway. 'I don't have one, but if I had to guess I'd go with those who think it's a bored, rich man's whim, unless you really are thinking of expanding into cosmetics?' Apparently the rumour had gone viral.

'Are you asking for insider information?'

'Hardly. The rumour has already sent the firm's shares through the ceiling. Even we mere models have been known to read the financial pages,' she observed, quite pleased to have surprised him. Her smug grin vanished as he hitched a brow and, holding her eyes with his, touched the sole of her foot with his finger. The light, barely there contact made her stomach dissolve and her toes curl of their own volition.

'Has no one suggested that it is because I wanted to have you at my mercy?'

She fought against the seductive quality of his deep voice, hating that he was mocking her. 'Now, that really would make me feel special.'

He shrugged and grinned. 'No mystery. My nephew asked me to further his career.'

'And you're a very nice uncle who does favours for your nephew?'

'It has been known, but I am an *adequate* uncle. It isn't hard—Nico is a nice kid, and it pays to keep on the right side of my sister, Adriana.'

'Do you have much family?' she asked, thinking to herself, *You have one more than you think.*

'My parents died some time ago in a car accident. I have two sisters…. There is Adriana—she's ten years older than me.' His mobile lips twisted into a half smile as he surprised her by confiding, 'I was an afterthought.'

'This is Nico's mother?'

He tipped his head in acknowledgment. 'Her husband,

Gus, was an international lawyer based in Geneva, but now he runs the Greek operation. They have just the one son.'

'You said you had *two* sisters?'

There was a long pause.

'Lizzie is your age.'

Lizzie did not strike Angel as a very Greek or Russian name. 'I thought you said you were the youngest?'

'Lizzie is my half-sister, the result of an affair— actually a one-night stand.' The small shocked sound that escaped her throat awoke him to the fact that he had just revealed more private details in the past thirty seconds than he had in the past... Actually ever. 'The details are not important.' Just the sort of thing that blew a family apart. 'As I said, she is my half-sister, the baby of the family.'

'And you resent her existence?'

The speculation drew a heavy frown and a flash of anger. 'Nobody in the world could resent Lizzie.' Except his mother, who could have but had not.

The softening in his expression when he spoke of his half-sister could not have been feigned. It could be envied, though she was dismayed to discover she did not envy this girl who brought the warmth to his eyes. One thing Angel did not want to be was his sister!

'So your parents' marriage broke down.' Angel, who knew how that felt, was sympathetic.

Being taken away from the only home she had ever known and the father she had adored at age eight had been a trauma that had stayed with Angel. In her youthful eyes it had seemed as if she was being punished. What other explanation could there be? Her feelings had alternated between guilt for some unknown sin she must have committed and anger at her father for sending her away.

She had been acting up during one of their short visits to their father when her big brother had sat her down and spelled a few facts out.

'You can act like a spoilt brat and ruin our time here or you can enjoy it. This isn't Dad's fault or mine or yours.'

'But Mum doesn't want us!'

'Sure.' Her brother had held the fists that were punching him in sheer frustration and explained quietly, 'But she doesn't want Dad to have us more than she doesn't want us. Do you get it, kiddo?'

Angel had, sort of, in her childish way. 'I think I hate her, Cesare.' She had whispered the confession because she knew this was a bad thing.

Cesare hadn't said she was bad; he had simply shrugged and retorted, 'Why bother? She's not worth it. Just remember when we're old enough she can't keep us and then we can live where we like.'

'Here at the castle with Dad?'

'Sure,' her brother had agreed, handing her a tissue and advising her to wash her face and brush her hair because she looked like a banshee.

'My father betrayed my mother, she forgave him, there was no divorce.' Angel sighed a sad smile, curving her lips as she dragged her thoughts back to the present. They had gone back to the Scottish castle of their childhoods but there had been no Dad. He had died and Cesare had inherited the ailing highland estate along with responsibility for its debts.

'You were lucky.'

His astonished stare fastened on her face as he sneered, 'How do you figure that one?'

'Divorce is not a good thing and a mother who forgives is…' Head tilted a little to one side, she studied his face. 'But you didn't, did you?'

'What?'

'Forgive him.' He was quick to hide it but Angel saw the shock move at the back of his eyes, followed by a cold, closed look.

'It was not my place to forgive.' And now it was too late to tell the father he had idolised that he understood the weakness… How could he not when he was staring at his own in the face? 'Though, yes, with the arrogance of youth I did judge. Having indulged in a one-night stand, I am in the classic glass-house-stone-throwing position.'

There was a delicious dark irony that he had blamed his father for not taking responsibility for the consequences of his actions…. Unprotected sex—how stupid is that? He heard the scornful words of his younger self and they still had the power to make him flinch.

The only reason he had not found himself in a similar situation was not down to higher moral standards or even basic common sense, but pure luck!

'So it isn't normal— You…you don't—' She broke off, flushing.

'Sleep with women I have just met? Actually no. Though I can understand why you made that assumption given how we met. That makes you unique on two levels—my only virgin and my only one-night stand,' he remarked bleakly. 'How about you?'

'I thought you'd already decided that a model is an easy lay.'

He winced and frowned at the crudity while uneasily accepting its factual accuracy. 'I was not enquiring about your sexual history.'

'Oh, I see, you just want to know the *real* me?' She widened her eyes. 'Where do I begin? My political views or my favourite author? Let's see, I'm a Pisces, I drink too much coffee and my favourite colour is green….'

'Do you always make a joke when things get too personal?'

Shocked that he had recognised the self-defence mechanism so easily, she shook her head in an angry negative motion, but before she could follow up with a firm denial he asked a question that, even though she knew was inspired by idle curiosity not suspicion, almost tipped her over into outright panic.

'Where is she, your daughter, now?'

Not here, thank goodness.... Angel shuddered to imagine how she would have reacted if fate had thrown this man in her path when Jas had been with her.

'At home, in Scotland, with Ce...' She stopped, remembering that he knew Cesare and not wanting him to make the link between her and her brother until she was ready. 'I always know she's safe with him.'

The mention of the other man and the perceptible loosening of the tension in her body language when she mentioned him caused muscles along Alex's taut jaw to clench.

He rarely found himself taken by surprise but he was. Having established that the father was not involved in the upbringing of the child, it had not occurred to him to question whether another man was. And considering he was a man who was justifiably famed for factoring in all possibilities when he approached a project, in retrospect it seemed astonishing that he had not foreseen any other outcome, when engineering a situation where their paths would cross, other than them falling into bed together. He had not been willing to contemplate failure.

It had genuinely not once crossed his mind that Angel might be with someone. He struggled to readjust to these facts.

While he recognised it was totally irrational, he could not shake the feeling of being cheated.

So what did you expect, Alex—that she'd spent the past six years waiting for you to reappear? The glaring immaturity of his reaction annoyed him, and, continuing in the immature mindset, he found himself blaming her for the situation.

His slightly narrowed eyes went to her left hand, but the long tapering fingers were bare of everything but sand. To leave a child with someone implied a great deal of trust but there was no ring. He half closed his eyes but he could still see her fingers on his skin. He inhaled and fought his way through a rush of hot lust...*a virgin*!

He still could not get his head round the fact that the best sex in his life had been with a virgin! Everything was successfully conspiring to up his guilt levels: the wife he had watched suffer barely in the ground and he had jumped into bed with a green-eyed witch...then that temptress had turned out not to be a siren but a virgin! Effectively making him feel like some sort of predatory sleaze. What was it they said—ignorance was no excuse in the eyes of the law?

It was certainly no excuse in his eyes.

He had been staring so long at her hands that Angel had to fight an impulse to hide them. Instead she dug them into the sand before rubbing them against her thighs and dragging them through her wet hair.

'You're with someone?'

This was good, he told himself. It was always good to focus on a known quantity. A partner meant there was no chance of becoming involved once more with her. That was one line in the sand he did not cross.... *Unlike virginity, Alex?*

'Does the child's father mind her being brought up by another man?'

'Would you?' she countered.

He thought about it—but not for long as it was a no-brainer. 'Yes, I would.' Little Lizzie—not so little these days—had spent the first few years of her life farmed out to relatives and friends before her father had claimed her and given her the home that had always been hers by rights. To allow that to happen to a child of his…?

It would never happen! His child would not suffer an identity crisis. She would always know where she belonged, she would always feel safe, loved and secure.

The instant response sent a flurry of panic through Angel. She brought her lashes down in a concealing sweep to hide her response. Exhaling a slow, measured, calming breath, she told herself there was no way he could know—and he didn't.

She looked up. There was no shocked realisation, not even a shade of suspicion in his bright eyes.

'I am bringing my daughter up alone.'

'So you make the calls and your boyfriend of the moment acts as a childminder, providing he has no problem with your work taking you away from your family?' It amazed him that any man trusted her enough to let her out of his sight, let alone halfway across the globe.

An energising rush of anger surged through her body as, with lush lips compressed in an angry rose-tinted line, she retorted, 'I would never ever farm my daughter out!'

'Why do you constantly assume I'm judging you?'

'And you're not?' she flung back.

'Or do you judge yourself?' he speculated.

'And for the record there's nothing wrong with a man being the carer.'

He arched a brow. 'Did I say there was?'

'You implied it,' she contended. '*If* I had a boyfriend who wanted to stay at home and look after Jas I'd consider myself lucky.' But she'd refuse. Angel would never allow her child to become fond of someone who could vanish. 'And I don't enjoy being away from Jas.' She swallowed, her voice thickening with emotion she couldn't hide as she added, 'But it won't always be this way. I've given myself five years to make enough to start my own—' She stopped and thought, *You are telling him this why, Angel?*

Out of this information one detail jumped out at Alex. '*If*... You do not have a boyfriend?'

'Why? Are you thinking of applying for the vacancy?' As jokes went this one fell pretty flat. Did the man even have a sense of humour? 'That was a joke. My brother is good at helping out with Jas.'

'You have a brother?'

'We share...' She paused and lowered her gaze from his interrogative stare. She felt disinclined to explain the circumstances that had led her to be living in a wing of the highland castle that her brother had inherited. She had tried to replicate for her daughter the idyllic childhood there that had been snatched away from her and Angel was not about to let anyone tear it away from Jasmine.

'He was available to take care of Jasmine.'

She took a step away from him towards the rocks, taking care to avoid the tideline of broken shells and seaweed that was coarse underfoot. 'Look, I'd better be getting back.'

'Not that way.'

She looked at the hand on her arm, feeling a worrying disinclination to break the contact.

'You can't get back along the beach at high tide.' His hand fell away, leaving Angel conscious of the tingling imprint. 'It is nearly high tide.'

Absently rubbing the spot where his fingers had been, she fought another tide—this time one of rising dismay. Alone on a beach she could have coped—she was resourceful and it appealed to her spirit of adventure—but she wasn't alone!

'We're trapped?'

'Another instalment in your dramatic life.' For a split second he was tempted to say they were trapped, but he stifled the impulse. 'Relax, there's a path through the trees.' He pointed to the pines that lined the beach. 'Slightly longer, but quite well marked. Come on, I'll show you.'

Side by side but not touching, they walked towards the tree-shaded area. The pine needles underfoot crunched as they walked beneath the fragrant canopy. In the softer light the bruise on her forehead was much more evident.

'I think you've escaped a black eye.'

'It's my shoulder that I'll feel tomorrow.' She rotated her shoulder, feeling the stiffness that was bound to get worse before it got better. Her hand went to her head, which she dismissed with a casual, 'I bruise easily.' She stopped, her eyes widening as she turned to him, and she grimaced as she realised the implications of his comment. 'There's a bruise? You can see it?'

He nodded, picking up the concern in her voice and wondering why she was bothered about something she had previously shrugged off.

'Terrific!' Wincing slightly, she traced the slightly raised outline on her temple with her finger. It was not vanity or the pain that gathered her brows into a worried straight line above her tip-tilted nose, but the prospect of what the women in Make-up would say when they saw her, and the horror would likely not be limited to them.

The last thing she needed as the new girl was people questioning her professional attitude.

'It's not *that* bad.'

She slung him a gloomy look and continued to walk. 'It is *that* bad if you have lights and a camera pointed at your face. There's only so much even the best make-up and lighting can disguise.'

And even less could she disguise her growing feeling of confusion around him. Life had been simpler before she'd had any insight into the man who had for six years been the focus of her anger. Not a shiny, perfect hero— although he did have a habit of being in the right place to snatch her from the jaws of, if not death, definitely discomfort—but not, it turned out, a serial seducer. He was a man with a family and a history that had left him with his share of emotional scars and even, it seemed, the odd moral value.

Struggling to lift his eyes from the long, sinuous curves of her sleek brown body, his gaze drawn to the tiny slice of paler skin where her bikini bottom had slipped down over the angle of her hip bone, he shrugged.

'Can they not film around your scenes?'

Angel laughed. She could not imagine that this would be the response from the team when she appeared looking this way. 'This is an advert, not a blockbuster. I'm in all the scenes and, as they keep telling me, time is money.'

'No, time is a luxury.'

They had reached the point where the trees thinned and the hotel came into view.

'A luxury I don't have.' She expelled a deep sigh. 'Ah, well, I'd better face the music.' She turned to him. 'I might not have said it. In fact, I know I didn't, but thank you for fishing me out of the drink. I really am grateful.'

He looked down at her with an odd expression. 'I do not want your thanks—I want this!'

Without warning, he bent his head and covered her mouth with his. A primitive thrill shot through her and she moaned into his mouth, responding to the hunger of his lips, melting against him as she was carried along on a dizzy tide of raw need. Not fighting it, not questioning, just sinking into all the warm darkness that only he seemed able to tap into and going with it. The relief... the release, it was incredible! She had stopped being the person she tried so hard to be and let herself be the person she was—with him.... *Why him?*

As abruptly as it had begun, it ended.

They stood there staring at each other. Angel saw wariness in his blue eyes then, with a muttered imprecation, he turned away.

She remained where she was, her eyes wide, her hand to her mouth as he stalked away back along the path they had just walked along.

CHAPTER SIX

AFTER HER FACE had been viewed from all angles and all light conditions by all interested parties, including the dermatologist who had been shipped in when Clive had developed a spot, it was decided that the situation was not as bad as originally feared. In three days' time the swelling would be gone and the bruises that make-up didn't disguise could be airbrushed away.

Three days was not long enough to fly home and see Jas, but long enough to miss her like hell. With nothing to fill her day, Angel found sheer boredom set in very quickly. Sunbathing on a beach might be many people's idea of bliss, but Angel had never been good at sitting still doing nothing.

With no other suggestions after she had been banned from doing anything that might injure her and delay the schedule further, she ended up armed with a pair of knitting needles, a ball of bright blue wool and instructions from Clive, who assured her a child could do it. He predicted she'd be amazed at how relaxing it was so she sat beneath a palm tree and set about being creative.

Half an hour later, her teeth aching with tension, she grabbed the tangled lot and flung it across the beach. She knew she was acting like a spoiled child, if you discounted the adult expletive that accompanied the action.

She knew it wasn't the minor frustration that made her want to yell and stamp her feet, it was everything that had gone before and what was to come. Her teeth ached with the tension that was tying her body in knots. Not thinking was exhausting. If she could have rid herself of the decisions she had to make in the same way she had that damned wool—the colour reminded her of his eyes—she might have been able to enjoy a moment's peace.

Before the voice, the prickling on the back of her neck had warned her she wasn't alone. Even so, she flinched when he spoke.

'It's an instant fine for littering here.'

How long had he been watching her?

She turned her head in the direction of the mocking drawl but sat rigidly, watching as he gathered up her rejected knitting and walked back towards her. It was just her luck. Miles of beach and he had to walk along the stretch that she had chosen. Ashamed of the ache of longing that made her throat dry, she followed his progress across the sand.

Alex was in no hurry, but as he got closer her heart rate became more erratic. Pressing a hand to her chest, she lowered her gaze and trained her eyes on his bare feet. It seemed a relatively safe part of his anatomy to focus on until, unable to stop herself, she lifted her gaze up over his hair-roughened calves and muscular thighs. The khaki shorts he wore were belted low over his narrow hips and his short-sleeved shirt hung open, revealing his lean ribbed brown torso.

'So are you here to arrest me?' She extended her hands, wrists crossed for imaginary cuffs. 'I'll come quietly.'

'Now that I find hard to believe.' The idea of her giving up without a fight brought a grim smile to his face as he dropped her knitting needles onto her lap. 'Actually I'm here to save you.'

The comment drew a sardonic laugh from Angel. The only thing she needed saving from was standing right there, sending her entire nervous system into a state of chaos, with his long, greyhound-lean limbs, oozing sex from every perfect pore.

'From death by boredom.'

'Who says I'm bored?'

He reached down and picked off a fibre of bright blue wool that clung to his shorts. He arched a sardonic brow and let the fibre blow away. 'You're bored.' And unless he was totally out in his assessment, as eaten up with burning frustration as he was.

Bored...much worse, thought Angel. She was hopelessly aroused—just looking at him made her nerve endings tingle. She pressed a hand across her middle to ease the heavy dragging sensation low in her pelvis. There was no place to hide except behind the big floppy hat she wore and the sunglasses that hid her eyes from him.

She produced a scowl. 'Isn't that littering or are you a special case?'

His white teeth flashed. 'I like to think so.'

She stroked a restless hand up and down her smooth calf. 'I'm not good at sitting still.' Catching the direction of his gaze, she stopped stroking and pushed her sunglasses back up on her nose.

The admission did not come as a surprise. She was not exactly what could be termed a restful woman: stubborn, aggressive, confrontational... As he mentally made a list of her less desirable qualities his eyes followed her hand to her face. All that was visible was her firm, rounded chin and her mouth, and there was nothing at all restful about those plump, luscious lips. An unfocused glaze drifted into his eyes as he struggled and failed to suppress the memory of those lips parting beneath his.

The silence stretched and he stood there looming over her like a statue until she could bear it no more.

'I think you're the one that's bored.' She aimed for cool and haughty but achieved something more akin to sulky.

In response he flopped down on the sand beside her, intensifying her cowardly impulse to run. His shoulder was an inch from hers. If she could have figured out a way of widening that gap without being obvious she would have.

Maybe what people said was right: that you could run but you couldn't hide…? On the other hand you could try, at least when it came to examining your own feelings.

Angel jammed the tangled mess from her lap into the massive holdall, managing to jab one of the needles into her leg. 'Ouch!'

'Been for a swim?' He could see the outline of her bikini under the thin thigh-length cover-up she wore.

'I'm not allowed. In fact I'm banned from pretty much everything apart from breathing and I'm in everybody's bad books.'

'They can't blame you for saving a kid's life.'

'Why not?' she countered. 'You did…and saving his life is a bit of an exaggeration.' She jammed her unread paperback on top of the knitting and clicked the clasp of the big raffia bag closed.

'Ever modest.' And ever a temptation. He stared at her mouth, wanting to slide his tongue between those beautiful, provocative lips. The need was so strong that for the space of several heartbeats he lost track of his real objective.

She sniffed and pushed her sunglasses up the bridge of her nose, flashing a small, tense smile. 'That's me…

it's just a shame I'm not the creative type.' She nodded at the bag.

He adopted an expression of innocent surprise. 'Really? I thought you went to art school.'

'I didn't finish the course—' Her expression tensed as she flashed a suspicious look his way. 'How did you know that?' she demanded, whisking her knees up to her chin and wrapping her arms protectively around her calves.

He shrugged casually. 'Someone must have mentioned it.'

Or something, namely the bio in the short report provided by the people who normally did background checks on prospective employees for him, a report that concerned specifically the months prior to the birth of Angelina Urquart's daughter...and most importantly that date.

It had been 3:00 a.m. when the seed of the idea had first entered his head. It had spent the next hour insidiously burrowing in, taking root while he had spent that period by turns becoming totally convinced he was right and equally totally convinced that the idea was a combined product of his overactive imagination, sexual frustration and sleep deprivation.

He needed to know—he needed to know at what point a nightmare became a premonition and for that he needed information. Alex had not bothered to work out time differences. He would not have used a firm who were not available on a twenty-four-hour basis and the person whose direct line he rang sounded alert and helpful—he expected nothing less.

They could not supply the information he really desired, but what they could supply and did was information that could confirm that it was possible.

The details that popped into his email box at 5:00 a.m. gave the bare facts he had requested: Angelina Urquart had given birth to a daughter eight months to the day after they had spent the night together.

He could be a father. Statistically speaking it was probable he was guilty of the crime that he had found it so easy to condemn his father for.

That it was possible to have a child, be a father and not know... He could have walked past his own daughter in the street and not guessed who she was. The idea utterly appalled him, but did fatherhood?

Running normally cleared his head. Facing the idea of being a father while covered in sweat and breathing hard, it still remained totally shocking but not the nightmare he had expected it to be. Was he feeling what his own father had the day that Lizzie's aunt had turned up with the child and a stack of letters that the child's dead mother had written but never sent, to dramatically inform the stunned man in front of a room full of party guests that it was his turn now to take responsibility for the child he had fathered?

At least he had some privacy to get his head around the concept and his big reveal would be at a time and place of his own choosing...if there was a reveal. After all, the question mark remained.

If he was right, why hadn't Angel told him? Did she ever plan to tell him? As he felt his anger mount the sense of loss he experienced, thinking of the years he had missed and would never get back, made it tough to see the situation from her point of view...but he was trying.

She came across as confident, but how much of that was window dressing? Six years younger, alone and presumably scared out of her wits at finding herself pregnant, had she tried to find him? Thoughts of her in that state of mind increased the guilt that gnawed away at him like acid. On one level he recognised that she wouldn't have known where to start to look for him, and in that case he knew that she hadn't set out to deprive him of parenthood. But on another level, he wondered if she hadn't been secretly relieved. Her opinion of him was so bad that she probably thought he would make a catastrophic parent.

His jaw clenched. For a man who rarely found himself not in a position of control to be forced to recognise that his position as an unmarried father gave him precious few rights, let alone control, was tough for Alex.

He was going to be part of his child's life no matter what it took…. The thought of another man thinking access to Angel's bed gave him the right to become a father to her child was a situation that he could not contemplate.

'So why didn't you complete your course?'

The question was casual but something in the way he was looking at her made her uneasy. Angel dodged his gaze and shrugged. Maybe she was getting paranoid but Angel responded to the alarm bells. 'I had some distractions.'

A baby.

His baby?

It had been several hours now since he had faced the possibility; the emotional impact had felt like a ten-tonne truck landing on his chest. Three hours to run, pace, speculate and plan…the weight remained but his brain was now clearer. The solution was there and he would do whatever it took to get the information.

Information that was stored in one place—her beautiful little head.

Not for nothing had the business world named him the perfect poker player. There were no 'tells' to even hint at an agenda behind his casual invitation. 'And how about now?'

She shook her head and gave a shrug of incomprehension.

'Could you do with some distraction?'

She clamped her lips tight over an outraged gasp. 'Well, no one could accuse you of subtlety, could they? Thanks for the offer but no, thanks.'

He gave a throaty laugh. 'Actually I wasn't propositioning you. Don't be embarrassed.'

She stuck her chin out. Embarrassed did not cover the toe-curling mortification that made her want to literally bury her head in the sand. Anything was preferable to seeing his smug face. 'This,' she gritted, circling her face with a finger, 'is relief.'

He took her chin between his thumb and forefinger and with the other hand pushed her shades up into her hair. The action was casual, confident, as though he had the right to touch her. *You're not doing much to disabuse him of this massive misapprehension, are you, Angel, just sitting there like some sort of mesmerised rabbit?* she thought to herself. When she ought to be... What...?

'No, this is beautiful....' he husked.

Trying to kick-start her brain felt like wading through warm syrup. *This is not me.... Why does he make me act this way? Why do I let him do this to me?*

Because you like it?

The crazy thought almost made her laugh. She pulled her sunglasses down again.

'I'd love to discuss your idea but—'

Angel dug her fingernails into her palms, focusing on the pain to help her fight her way to control. She turned her head and his hand fell away.

Digging her heels into the sand, she said, 'It wasn't an

idea.' Her voice sounded very small, the scornful laugh
weak— Well, actually, pathetically unconvincing.

'Don't sulk,' he said, drawing an outraged gasp. 'Obviously I want to have sex with you.'

He delivered this piece of information in a manner
she associated more with ordering a pizza than propositioning. The violent lurch in her chest was possibly,
Angel mused, her heart stopping. Despite the possibility of her imminent expiration she somehow—it was a
miracle—kept her expression blank. Thank goodness
for sunglasses.

'I get that a lot.'

Not a lie, but she'd never felt in danger of requiring
CPR before. Or…best to treat the comment as a joke—
the alternative was not something she felt equipped to
cope with.

She saw something flash in his eyes—anger?

'I'm sure you do,' he countered smoothly, 'but on this
occasion I was thinking more along the lines of lunch.'

Lunch with Alex Arlov? Now, that was a crazy idea.

Or was it? Wasn't this an opportunity to get to know
Jas's father in the nonbiblical sense? She still needed to
decide if he was a man she wanted to be involved in her
daughter's life. For that judgement she had to put her
personal feelings aside.

And what were her personal feelings?

She gave her head a tiny shake and pulled her hat more
firmly down on her dark hair, glad that he could not hear
her thoughts or, thanks to the tinted lenses, see her confusion. Normally someone who had a head-on approach
to life, she had been skirting around that question since
he had reappeared in her life.

And with good reason. Feelings… It sounded so simple but how was she meant to analyse something so, so…

visceral? It was easier to accept it. What was the point of delving deeper? At its most basic, she was attracted to him, but that hardly made her special. She had seen the way women looked at him…all women. He was a man who inspired lust and around him she dropped several IQ points; her brain just didn't function at full capacity. In fact sometimes it just didn't function full stop!

Well, they were welcome to him, she told herself. At least she had the maturity now to be able to differentiate between lust and deeper, more profound emotions.

Tell that to your nervous system!

'Eating is not one of the things you are barred from doing, is it?' He unscrewed the bottle of water he had been carrying. Halfway to his mouth he paused and extended it towards her. 'Want some?'

'No, thank you,' she responded, primly polite.

'Is it?' he said, wiping his mouth with his hand.

She started guiltily—her eyes had been riveted on the muscles working in his brown throat as he swallowed. 'What?'

'They haven't banned you from eating?'

'That depends on the calorie count. They are worried about my hips.' She was regretting the flippant remark even before she had finished speaking, but managed not to make the moment any worse by successfully resisting the impulse to tug the spangled, jewel-bright fabric of her cover-up lower over her hips. As his head tilted to one side his eyes slid over her sleek, smooth curves, lingering on the supposed problem area.

After a nerve-shredding moment his gaze lifted, his expression blank, but the glow in his eyes made her stomach flip. 'Yes, I can see you must need to be careful,' he delivered in a deadpan tone, thinking that he had never met a woman who so totally encapsulated all things erotic and sensual.

Wide and indignant, her eyes flew to his face. A moment later her tension fell away and she was laughing in response to the gleam in his blue eyes. Then the gleam changed, became not amused, and she looked away quickly, her heart thudding, her mouth dry.

'How would you like it if I drew attention to your flaws?' He didn't have any—at least not physical ones.

'You brought your hips into this discussion,' he reminded her. 'Not that I'm complaining, and if you're going to tell me you have any self-esteem issues don't waste your breath.'

His heavy-lidded glance moved from her lips, sweeping downwards over the length of her sinuous, sleek, leggy frame. No woman could be as unselfconscious in bed as Angel had been if she was not happy in her own skin. She had taken pleasure from her own body as much as she had from his, and he had never known a woman to display such fascination with his body before or since.

Without warning a piercing stab of pure lust sliced through him, raising the level of his arousal painfully as he allowed the door in his head to open a crack for the memories to push through, not in a controlled way but in one hot, steamy rush. His brilliant eyes darkened and glazed with licking flames as he saw...felt...her hands gliding over his skin, the moisture of her tongue.

Her lovemaking had been as generous as her cushiony soft lips... It had never crossed his mind for a split second that she had been a virgin, not even when she had been so tight when he had entered. There had been that shocked little cry, but he had taken that as a compliment.

Maybe you didn't want to know, Alex?

The sudden audible crack of his finger joints made

Angel's questioning gaze shift from his extended fingers to his face. The golden skin was pulled taut across his magnificent bones; his angular jaw was tensed; his eyes remained hidden by the luxuriant sweep of his preposterously long eyelashes.

She could see the tension in the rigidity of his powerful shoulders as he reached down and took her hand.

'You shouldn't be sitting here in the midday sun.'

She didn't react to his impatient tone; she reacted to an unacknowledged desire to make contact and to the fizz of electricity through her body that made her head buzz as she allowed him to pull her to her feet.

When she pulled her fingers free they continued to tingle. She held her hand against her chest and struggled to take control of her breathing…and then found she was virtually panting! Acting like some sort of sexually deprived bimbo was sending out all the wrong messages.

Or, more worryingly, the right ones!

Her laughter was as uninhibited as her lovemaking had been in his thoughts.

'I will personally guarantee your physical safety.' He arched a brow and held out a hand towards her. 'I have said something that amuses you?'

She looked at the hand and thought, *You don't make me feel safe. A lot of other things, but not safe.*

'I don't require a bodyguard.'

Their glances connected and suddenly the fizz between them made it hard for her to breathe.

'How about a charming companion and lunch?'

'Really?' She made a pantomime of looking around. 'Where would I find one of those?' she asked, before adding almost shyly, 'Lunch would be good.'

When her desperate attempt at humour did not produce even a half smile Angel huffed a sigh. 'I am hungry,' she admitted, thinking, *Where is the harm?* And she was doing this for Jas. She wasn't looking for a soulmate, but that was no reason to deprive her daughter of a dad. Though that did depend on the dad.... And how was she meant to judge if he was good enough for Jas if she ran away every time she saw him?

What sort of man was he?

Oh, she'd read the stuff on the internet and knew about the wealth, the enigmatic reputation that had resulted in some wild speculation, and she took all that with a pinch of salt, but the man did come across as a mass of contradictions.

They walked in silence along the path that led from the beach through sweet-scented pine trees. Once or twice she looked up at the tall man walking beside her and he seemed lost in thought and showed no inclination to engage her in conversation. This suited Angel, who made no attempt to break the stalemate, though, as she mockingly told herself, in order to get to know him she might have to speak at some point.

As they reached the place where the path entered the hotel's gardens Alex took a left turn instead and opened a gate marked Private that had always previously been locked.

'Where are we going?' She had her answer as they rounded the bend and a small cove came into view. It was empty but for the motor launch moored off the rocks.

'For lunch. Careful, the rocks are slippery.'

'I thought we were going to the hotel.'

'We're not.' He did not elaborate.

'I can see that,' she returned, ignoring his hand. She was making a point, a trivial one perhaps, but it felt important to emphasise the fact that she could cope alone. Or was she simply prepared to fall rather than risk experiencing the electrical surge that occurred whenever she touched him?

With a frown she pushed the intrusive suggestion away and, with one hand out to balance, the other holding the heavy swathe of her hair out of her eyes, she inched her way cautiously down the rocks, aware that landing on her bottom would prove both painful and humiliating.

Her refusal to accept a helping hand, literally, brought a small ironic twist to his lips. The action encapsulated the woman: stubborn, reckless and damned irritating. But he conceded as he watched her from the vantage point of the boat that she really was the most incredibly graceful and alluring creature he had ever seen.

There were very few people who could make slipping and slithering look elegant, but she was one of them. His jaw clenched as he restrained himself from flying to her rescue after a particularly spectacular lurch.... If she fell and broke her beautiful neck it would serve her right.

This was no path, thought Angel, more a free climb, and the appeal of clinging to a rock face with nothing to harness you for pleasure passed Angel by. She decided it was a case of practicality over pride, but a few feet from the end of the rocky path she did not refuse the hand he reached out. She'd made her point and it was quite a leap into the boat.

He had made it look easy, of course.

'Thank you.'

His ironic grin broadened as he clasped her hand, then vanished as she landed. The momentum of her landing sent her crashing into his body and the flash of heat that slid down his front caused his smile to fade. His heavy eyelids lowered, hiding the hard, hungry look in them, as his hands on her elbows pushed her away and he directed a cool, 'Steady!' to the top of her head.

Concealing the fact that all his instincts were telling him to grab that gorgeous behind and mould her to him came at a price, in the form of the pain in his groin and the slick of sweat that lay like a fine sheen over the surface of his skin. Despite appearances and the Northern blood running in his veins, he was immune to the heat, but the same could not be said of a soft warm female, at least not when it came in the dangerous form of Angel Urquart.

'We're eating on Saronia?' she speculated, experiencing mixed feelings about this journey into the unknown. The caution was sensible, the excitement was not!

'Don't you like surprises?'

'Only some of them.'

'Come on, Angel,' he urged, mocking her with his electric-blue eyes. 'Live dangerously.'

Angel looked away, remembering what had happened the last time she had lived dangerously. Now she was a mother who was going to provide her daughter with what she had craved as a child: a calm, nurturing environment to grow up in. Combustible relationships were not on the agenda and there was no escaping the fact that sparks flew every time she came within the same square mile as Alex.

Unlike yesterday, she was in a position to actually appreciate the wind-in-your-face experience of cutting through the water in the fast speedboat. She sat back, knowing the journey would not last long, though it turned out to be a little longer than she anticipated. Instead of mooring where the film crew were dropped off, he continued on, following the coastline.

The filming had all taken place at the side of the island that faced the mainland. They had been requested not to leave the immediate area so she had never seen this side of the island, and she immediately saw how different it was—much greener and more lush.

He cut the engine and brought the boat expertly up to the edge of the small wooden pier.

'There used to be a road from the other side of the island but it fell into disrepair. The only access now is by water or helipad.'

It turned out there was no road this side either. The stony, near-vertical route he drove the open-topped four-wheel drive along barely deserved to be called a track. Halfway up the hill Angel, who was hanging onto the overhead strap, turned her head and yelled, 'If you're going to drive like this, you might at least put two hands on the steering wheel.'

He threw her a lazy smile. 'You're a back-seat driver.'

Angel didn't respond. They had just topped the crest of the hill and she was staring at the scene revealed in front of her. The pristine sand was as silver white as the Hebrides, the long waving grass behind it dotted with wild flowers, and set in the middle of the green rippling carpet was a white marquee and pitched under it was set a long table. Two figures were unloading items from the four-wheel drive vehicle parked close by.

'If I'd known I would have dressed.'

She half expected the couple who were unloading food to wait on them, but they drove away after a quick word with Alex. As she watched them vanish and responded to the light touch between her shoulder blades that made her conscious of every prickling inch of her skin she realised just how alone they were.

She gave a laugh to cover her nerves and approached the shaded table covered with a white cloth laid with silver and crystal.

'This is your idea of a picnic?' It might be some peo-

ple's idea of a seduction scene. Discounting the possibility and the flip of excitement low in her pelvis, she was
sure that he wouldn't have gone to this much trouble for
nothing. The question remained—a lot of effort, but why?

'I don't like sand in my food.'

'You could always concrete over the beach.'

'An idea, but I have to think about my eco credentials.'

'Especially as they're so profitable.'

The muttered response drew a thin smile from him.
'You are, as always, eager to assign the worst possible
motives to my actions.'

She opened her mouth to deny this charge and closed
it again, her eyes sliding from his as she mumbled, 'I
can be a cynic.'

'If you're interested in all things eco you might like
to look around my house sometime.'

Following the direction of his gesture, she frowned,
seeing only a grassy hill above the high-tide mark, but
then a glint of light reflected off glass caught her attention.

'Goodness!'

'Yes, it's easy to miss at first, isn't it?' The architects
had fulfilled their brief and made the structure blend in
with the landscape, but they had gone one step further—
they had made it part of the landscape.

Excavated into the hillside, his sanctuary with its turf
roof and no manufactured walls was invisible from most
angles, but the clever design meant that every room was
flooded with light from the massive glass panels that
faced the sea.

'You live there?' It was not the power statement that
she had assumed any home of his would be.

'I stay there occasionally. It suits my needs, but it is

not equipped for entertaining, hence...' He gestured to the table.

'Won't you sit down?' He pulled out one of the chairs and, feeling both awkward and anxious, she took her seat.

The first fifteen minutes did not give her any insight into him as a person. His conversational skills were as she had expected but he managed to avoid any personal questions, instead turning them back on her. It was deeply frustrating.

'You do not care for seafood?'

Angel, who had been pushing her food around her plate, set her fork down and decided the best approach was a direct one.

'Why did you ask me here? Not to talk about the food, I'm sure.' Nibbling on her lower lip, she caught hold of one of the crystals that weighed down the cloth, rolling it between her fingers.

'Why did you come?' he countered.

She set her elbows on the table and stared across at him. 'Do you always respond to a question with another question?'

His brows knitted as he forked a large prawn into his mouth. 'I am resisting the temptation to say pot, kettle, black.'

'Not very well,' she inserted sourly.

'The answer to your question is, yes, I do, when the answer interests me.'

'I was bored and hungry.'

'You haven't eaten much.'

'I'm watching my weight.'

'Do you ever worry about your part in the message that the media sends out to young girls?' His tone was deceptively casual but the eyes that met hers were anything but.

'Message?'

'The pressure to achieve an impossible level of perfection, like the women they see in the magazines. The message that equates beauty with happiness. Of course, I was forgetting you have a daughter of your own. I'm sure you are well aware of the pressures facing young women.'

She stiffened, her heart beating fast as she twisted the linen napkin between her fingers. He knew, somehow he knew! Or he thought he knew....

'Jasmine is not a woman. She's a child.'

'True, but they grow up so quickly and I believe that anorexia sufferers are getting younger and younger.'

She shook her head, angry now, and got to her feet. Looking down at him lessened the feeling of being a mouse being toyed with by a large feline. 'Why are you suddenly so interested in my daughter?'

He laid his own napkin down with slow deliberation, holding her eyes as he got to his feet. 'Because I had this idea... It's crazy, but in my experience those are the ones that it pays not to ignore. So I did a little research and a few surprising things came up, like the fact that your daughter was born eight months to the day after we spent the night together and there was no one before.'

'Or after.' *Did I really say that?*

He didn't react, but she could feel the emotions rolling off him.

Angel didn't blink; she didn't breathe. She shrugged and struggled to hold on to her manufactured calm.

'So you want to know if you're Jasmine's father? Couldn't you just have come out and asked? Did it really require all this elaborate stage-managing?'

'It occurred to me that you might be waiting for the right moment to tell me...?' He had really tried hard to think of this from her point of view but her expression

was not saying she appreciated the effort. He had been
her only lover.... Only... He experienced a stab of sheer
primitive possessive satisfaction, and breathed out, letting the air escape in a slow, measured sigh.

'I thought I'd provide it.... I thought if you were relaxed—'

'You thought you'd get me drunk,' she countered,
pointing to the second bottle in the ice bucket. 'And trick
me into saying things!'

The comment hit a raw nerve. First she threw his consideration back in his face, now she tried to make herself
the victim. 'I shouldn't have to trick you into anything. If
I've got a bloody child I have a right to know.... I have
a right to know her!' It was the first time she had heard
him use Russian but she was guessing she wouldn't find
the translation of what he snarled in any phrase book.

As angry now as he was, she heaved in a taut, angry
breath of her own. What did he know? Parenthood wasn't
a right—it was a privilege!

'Rights? You have no rights! You see Jasmine only if
I say so, and I don't. I came here wanting to find out if
you were the sort of person I want in Jasmine's life, the
sort of person who would be good for her to know. Well,
now I do know, and you're not. I wouldn't have you near
my daughter...for...for...anything! You're a manipulative
bastard who treats people like chess pieces... You're the
last father I'd choose for my daughter.'

Breathing hard like duelists, they stood either end of
the table facing one another, firing angry words, not bullets, though the words could inflict considerable damage and once they were out there they were impossible
to retract.

Even though she was still furious Angel was already
beginning to regret the things she had said.

He leaned forward, his hands flat on the table, and fixed her with an icy blue arctic stare. When he spoke it was in a voice that was several decibels lower than the hot words shouted in the heat of the moment. Cold, considered and chosen to inflict the maximum level of fear.

Angel was seeing the man that made powerful men tremble with fear.

'You have picked the wrong man to challenge. You will not keep my daughter from me. Attempt to prevent me seeing her and it will be me you come begging to for visitation rights. If you have a skeleton… If you have a bone fragment in your cupboard I will find it and my lawyers will use it.' He hardened his heart against her pale, stricken expression and added, 'You started this, but I will finish it. That much is a promise.'

Without another word he walked away.

Angel didn't react. She just stood there, frozen. She roused only at the sound of an engine and she turned in time to see him vanishing in a cloud of dust.

He had driven away, leaving her stranded.

Not quite able to believe the situation she found herself in, she looked from the dust cloud to the food and wine spread out and with a laugh she slumped down into the chair.

'At least I won't starve.'

She was still sitting there twenty minutes later when one of the men who had earlier been laying out the food appeared. If he found the situation strange nothing in his manner suggested it as he framed his meticulously polite question.

'Are you ready to return to the mainland?'

She was ready to kiss the feet of her rescuer but she was much more circumspect in her icy state, and responded to the respectful enquiry with a nod and a smile.

CHAPTER SEVEN

ALEX PULLED THE car over after a mile, leaning his elbows across the steering wheel. He thought he knew every inch of the island but he struggled to get his bearings as he pushed his head back into the padded headrest and looked up through the open roof at the trees that blocked out the sun.

'Well, that worked out well, Alex.'

He'd had it all planned. While he had rejected all Angel's charges at the time, had she been so wrong?

Driving like a lunatic, while satisfying, was not going to solve anything. He had blown it; he had acted while the emotive impact of discovering he was a father was still fresh. When she hadn't said what he'd wanted to hear he had launched into attack mode and made a tough situation ten times worse.

Back at the bungalow the only thing she wanted to do was... Actually there were two things she wanted to do: throw herself on the bed and weep, and break something. The first she didn't do because she was due to have her prearranged chat via the internet with her daughter in less than half an hour, and the second... Well, she was supposedly a grown-up and grown-ups did not throw their rattles out of the pram, unless of course the supposed grown-up was Alex Arlov!

Things hadn't gone his way and he'd simply gone off in a strop. Admittedly, a pretty magnificently broody strop, but the fact remained that she had refused to play by his rules so he'd walked away, issuing threats that had made her blood turn to ice. Not to mention that they revealed what a truly ruthless man lurked beneath the urbane exterior.

Would he adopt the same sort of parenting style? When the going got tough would he opt out?

Her hands balled into clawed fists at her side as she paced the room. The man made her so mad! She took a deep breath and reminded herself that this was not about her or her feelings, or, for that matter, Alex. It was about Jas and she was not going to run the risk of laying her precious girl open to hurt or rejection.

It was after her chat with Jas that Angel did cry—tears of regret more than anger. Her little girl was so lovely. She deserved a father, someone who would take her as she was, and not weigh her down with unrealistic expectations. Did Alex even know what having a child involved? Or would Jas just be another possession to him?

Had he meant those threats?

Should she get legal advice? The thought of anyone trying to take away her daughter… She shuddered as she recalled his lethally soft-voiced threat, aimed with dagger-like accuracy to inflict the maximum fear and panic.

She wouldn't panic; she would fight!

The last thing she felt like later that evening was being sociable, but Angel knew that her no-show would be construed as standoffishness by the others so she was forced to sit around the big table and smile her way through the evening. She responded good-naturedly to the teasing about her heroics until she realised why the ad-agency man who had been the most vocal in his exasperation after the resulting delay now seemed quite jovial about the subject.

She expressed her relief to Clive, who was sitting beside her. 'I'm glad he's calmed down.'

'Of course he's calmed down, darling—all that free publicity!'

Angel shook her head. 'Publicity?'

'Seriously?' The slightly tipsy Hollywood actor scanned her face for signs of irony, then, finding none, laughed hilariously, causing someone at the opposite end of the table to request being let into the joke.

'It turns out that our Angel is one of life's innocents. She doesn't know that someone recorded the whole hero thing on their phone and uploaded it onto the web.' He turned back to Angel and explained with a touch of envy he didn't quite disguise, 'You have gone viral. All that free publicity is better than sex as far as our Jake is concerned, and the only thing the world loves more than a heroine is a heroine that looks like you do in a bikini.'

The other man raised a glass at the charge.

'Oh, God, no!'

Her genuine horror made Carl laugh even more. 'Of course, there are some theories the whole thing was staged. Don't you just love conspiracy theories?'

'No.' She huffed out an exasperated sigh. Clive's blend of superficial charm and malicious humour was beginning to pall. Compared to Alex's far more abrasive, abrupt and in your face— God, why was she even thinking about Alex, let alone using him as a measure of male perfection? She couldn't think of anything less perfect. She closed down the inner dialogue with a resounding snap and produced a clear, focused smile. Nobody could accuse her of being obsessed. 'I don't, but I believe in respecting a person's right to privacy.'

The actor gave a shaky smile, clearly in two minds. Was she being serious…? 'Ever thought you were in the wrong line of work, darling?'

'Frequently,' she admitted, permitting herself a dry laugh before she turned her attention to Sandy on her right. Her present career was a means to an end, something she had fallen into rather than planned. She had given herself five years, and if at that point she had not made enough money to set herself up with the fashion-design label she had mapped out in her head then she would walk away with no regrets and possibly more than a little relief.

Angel made it through the meal, avoided the copious free-flowing wine, but not even her sweet tooth gave her the appetite to make it through the pudding course. Pleading tiredness, which was not a lie, she made her excuses early and during her walk back to her bungalow found fifty messages when it occurred to her to check her phone!

She only replied to the two from her brother. It took even longer than she had anticipated to calm and reassure him, and she agreed with his decision not to keep Jas up to speed with her mother's newfound fame. In the back of her mind she wondered if being an internet heroine would be a plus or a minus if the fight got to court?

Her brother hadn't laid a guilt trip on her; it wasn't his style. But even so, Angel was feeling pretty much a failure as a mother by the time she reached her bungalow and searched for the swipe card for the door.

'It's not locked. Anyone could have walked in.'

Angel yelped and spun around as the tall figure

emerged from the shadows. Even without the moon-light that illuminated his face, revealing the strong syb-aritic slashing angles and spine-tinglingly strong bones, it would have been impossible to mistake the identity of the person who was lurking there.

'And did you?' She managed to project a level of cool she knew she didn't have a hope of sustaining for long. The sound of his voice had begun a chain reaction that she had no control over; his physical presence made the feelings that were surging unchecked through her body even more urgent and mortifyingly obvious.

How could you hate someone and want them at the same time?

She crossed a hand over her chest, unable to restrain a wince when it brushed the shamelessly engorged nip-ples she was attempting to hide. Her heart was in her throat, the dull, thunderous clamour echoing in her ears drowning out the more peaceful sound of the waves as she lifted her chin to an imperious angle and repeated her accusation.

'Well, did you?'

'I thought I'd wait to be invited.'

'Then you'll have a hell of a long wait.' A predictable response and, she realised, shamefully untrue. Where this man was concerned, instead of locking doors she had a terrible tendency to fling them wide open and drag him in!

He didn't react to the belligerent challenge. Instead his narrowed eyes followed the hand she wiped across her face. 'You're shaking.'

Acutely conscious of the unblinking blue stare, she responded to the note of accusation in his voice with a resentful, 'Probably because the last person who jumped out from behind a bush as I was trying to open my door now has a restraining order against him.'

The mocking smile vanished from his face. 'A restraining order?' A relationship turned sour, violent…? His hand clenched. 'Who was… Is this man?'

Angel, already regretting she had mentioned the incident, shrugged. 'Just a sad man. He was harmless really.'

A nerve clenched in his cheek as Alex stared at her in stunned disbelief. She sounded so calm, so casual!

'So harmless you took out a restraining order against him.' His sardonic statement was shot through with audible anger, the same anger that made his blue eyes burn as he focused on it instead of the sick lurch in the pit of his belly as he imagined her defenceless, vulnerable and at the mercy of some crazed lunatic. Yet today he had ripped into her himself, issuing every kind of threat he could think of…trying to hurt her.

'It turned out all he was carrying was a bracelet.'

'What did you think he was carrying?'

'A knife,' she admitted, adding with an embarrassed grimace, 'What can I say? I watch too many cop shows on telly.'

'You thought I was a knife-wielding maniac?'

She moved her head in a negative motion. 'You surprised me, that's all. And he didn't have a knife and he wasn't really a maniac, though obviously not entirely right in the head.' She accompanied the explanation with an illustrative tap on her own head, thinking as she did so that perhaps she was in no position to throw stones.

After all, sane did not exactly describe her own reaction when she had seen him as being that of someone in full possession of all her mental faculties. Her stomach muscles were still quivering. She had spent the best part of the evening calling him every name under the sun, inside her head of course, but the moment she had seen him her throat had thickened and her traitorous heart had started to thud.

'A person who serves you coffee and decides your smile means you are soulmates has issues. Obviously if I'd realised it was just another of his presents I wouldn't have hit him over the head with the plant pot, though maybe it was a good thing I did,' she mused. 'Because the plant pot actually proved a lot more effective than a police warning and he decided that I was not his soulmate after all.'

'Plant pot?' he echoed, struggling to wade through this information.

'It was the only thing there.'

The note of apology drew a choked sound from his throat and he realised it was impossible to judge Angel by the other women he knew. She was clearly a creature who acted on instinct.

Combine that sort of reckless impetuosity with youth and a passionate nature and it wasn't hard to see how she had ended up pregnant. But then the mystery was how he had been the first. He still struggled to get his head around that knowledge.

Alex had no excuse, which was why he was here and he couldn't allow himself to be distracted.

'The things you said this afternoon… You were right. You were not telling me anything I don't already know…. I just wasn't ready to hear it.' She watched as he dragged his hand through his dark hair, which, she noticed, was already tousled. He was still wearing the same clothes he had been in earlier that day, though they were a lot more creased, and for the first time since that night six years ago she was seeing his jaw shadowed with dark stubble.

'From me?' She anticipated a savage rebuttal and got instead a thoroughly and totally disarming tip of his head.

'This is your call and I will abide by your decision. The threats I made were…selfish. I'm sorry, you were right. You have every reason to hate me. I slept with you, I took no precautions, it was thoughtless, I've never…' He just stopped himself producing the classic 'I've never done it before' line. After all, why should she believe it? Actions, he reminded himself, spoke louder than words. 'I want to make things right.'

Angel was shaken by the depth of self-loathing in his voice, but she forced a laugh and framed her ironic rebuttal in a voice as cold as she could make it. 'You want Jasmine.'

The goad made the lines bracketing his mouth tighten but he managed to hide his frustration, well aware that once already today he had barged in like the proverbial china-shop bull, issuing threats when he should have been asking questions, building bridges.

'It's true, I want to be a father to my child. But you were right—I'm in no position to call the shots.'

Not being in a position to call the shots, as he termed it, had to be a new experience for him. But Angel was not totally trusting of this new Alex, and she refused to be lulled into a false sense of security. She would not lower her defences just yet.

'That's a pretty big U-turn for someone who was talking custody battles not a few hours ago.'

'I told you about Lizzie…'

'Your half-sister?'

He nodded. 'She was ten before she knew who her father was, before she knew *she* was wanted…. I want Jasmine to know she is wanted.'

The soft addition sliced through her determined stance

of wary hostility. There was no question of his sincerity. 'She does!' Angel rushed to protest earnestly. 'I know what it feels like to think you're nothing but a nuisance.' Feeling awkward at the admission, she dodged his glance and added, 'I've never let Jas think for one second she isn't wanted and loved.'

'I'm sure you're a great mother, but that isn't the issue.'

He thinks I'm a great mother? 'What is the issue, Alex?' It was pretty obvious that the superficial similarities had dredged up some old issues for him. 'This isn't about your relationship with your father. You can't allow the things that happened in the past to colour the present.'

He emitted a laugh of disbelief. 'So it's purely accidental that your mothering style is the complete opposite of your own mother's? That's not a criticism, it's a fact. It's what people do. We try to avoid our parents' mistakes. Some of us fail....' He gave a snort of self-disgust. 'Talk about history repeating itself.'

'That's not true! The situations are totally different,' she protested.

'In as much as Lizzie's mother chose not to tell my father she was pregnant because she knew he was married. You didn't even know my name. My dad had always been my hero. He made a real effort with me, maybe to compensate for the fact he'd been estranged from his own father. We did everything together, then afterwards... It was never the same between us. I didn't hold back. I let him know I despised him. I never lost an opportunity to twist the knife. Pretty ironic considering that I ended up emulating him.'

'But you didn't!' she exclaimed. 'You're not—!'

His blue eyes lifted and Angel could see that they blazed with self-contempt in the half-light. 'Married...?

My wife had been dead weeks! Tell me how that makes me any better?'

The pain in his voice made her wince. 'People do things when they're grieving that they wouldn't do normally.'

A sound of astonishment escaped his lips as he moved towards her out of the shadows. 'You're trying to excuse what I did…?' He swallowed, the muscles in his brown throat visibly working as he finished on a note of raw incredulity, '*You* of all people!'

'You're not being fair on yourself, Alex. You loved your wife, you were hurting, grieving… You had been for a long time….'

'I knew it was going to happen.'

'And is that meant to make it easier? For goodness' sake, Alex, cut yourself some slack.' She registered his startled expression but didn't let it faze her or allow him the space to protest. Some things needed saying, especially when they were so obvious, and he was too close to it. 'You were there when your wife needed you, weren't you?'

'I think so…. Yes, I was, but I couldn't…'

'I know that's hard, but you tried and you did your best. And when she was gone you did something out of character, not because you loved her any less, but because you wanted to stop…thinking.' She shook her head sadly. 'I don't know what your wife was like, but I'm willing to bet she would have understood what you did and not considered it any sort of betrayal. I wouldn't, if it had been me.'

She was displaying a generosity of spirit that made him feel humble. 'I think you are a better person than me.'

'I wish I was. You lost yourself in one night of sex and I…I…' She choked with a bitter laugh. 'I was kind of in love with the idea of being in love. Relax,' she added, seeing his expression. 'I have grown up.'

'Being a single parent will do that to a person.' She might have relieved some of his guilt over that night but not over the repercussions. 'I want my child to know she is wanted, Angel.' He doubted very much he could be as good a father as Angel was a mother, but he would try.

'So why didn't you just say so instead of... It's obvious your sister had a tough time, but Jasmine knows she is wanted, Alex.'

'She doesn't know she is wanted by me.'

The words made her heart give a heavy thud of empathy. In the fast-falling dark she struggled to read his expression. Now his figure was little more than a dark outline, backlit by the moonlight reflected off the silvered ocean surface.

'You wanted me to listen.... Angel, I'm listening. I want to help, I want to be involved. Is that selfish? I don't know....' He took a deep breath, a soft sibilant hiss escaping through his teeth before he said quietly, 'No threats.'

'I wasn't threatened.' Not true—she had been. But not nearly as much as she would have been had she not had the security and the confidence of a brother with all the ruthlessness and resources to face Alex on equal terms. To fight on her behalf, should she ask him.

'I need to be part of her life...whatever it takes.'

Angel's restless covetous glance was drawn and then lingered on the sculpted contours of his wide, sensual mouth.

There was a big difference, she reminded herself, between wanting and needing. She needed to rediscover that mouth about as much as she needed a boil on her nose, but, God, she wanted it so much it hurt.

Angling her chin defiantly, she cleared her throat.

'I suppose you think all you have to do is kiss me and I'll agree to pretty much anything?' she challenged. 'Your problem is you think you're irresistible!' she tacked on, realising as she spoke that she was halfway to believing he was!

Maybe more than half, she thought. She recalibrated as she lost the ability to move, actually to breathe, as he surged towards her, taking the shallow steps of the bungalow veranda two at a time. He was at her side before she had an inkling of his intentions and then it was too late to stop him.... Did she actually want to?

He framed her face between his big hands. His stare had a soul-piercing intensity and she couldn't look away, afraid that a blink might break this spell.

'Kiss…?' The flash of his white grin was predatory as he bent his head and kissed her slowly, extending the erotic pleasure, taking his time as he slid his tongue deep between her parted lips, tasting her. There were no words to describe the sweet, hot ache between her thighs.

Angel was left gasping, open mouthed, for air when his head finally lifted. She felt his hands at her waist supporting her; her knees sagged; her legs felt as though they belonged to someone else.

'I'm planning to do more than kiss you, Angel,' he rasped, the promise making her tremble in anticipation. Still holding her eyes, he ran his tongue across the plump, trembling outline of her lower lip before tugging it gently with his teeth and asking, 'You have a problem with that?'

His problem is he thinks he's God's gift!

My problem is he's right.

In her head Angel saw herself pushing him away, defusing the situation with a few well-chosen words interspersed with the odd acid barb.

Outside her head, she was melting into him, pushing

her aching breasts up hard against his chest, absorbing his heartbeat, his heat and the sheer maleness of him. She drew his head down so she could take the initiative and move her lips slowly across his, sampling the texture, breathing in his scent as, with eyes half-closed, she whispered into his mouth, 'No problem.'

His eyes flared and the primal incandescence made the breath in her lungs catch and burn. She stood trembling and passive, her heart thudding like a drum as he pushed his fingers deep into her lush hair so that they cradled her skull, dragging her head back to expose the long line of her throat.

Her eyelids squeezed tightly shut as he pressed his mouth to the pulse at the base of her throat. Her deep sigh became a long moan, the sound slipping past her clenched teeth as his tongue and lips progressed up her neck until he reached her mouth again. By this time her skin was slicked with a layer of moisture and she was panting short, shallow gasps as if she had just run a marathon.

Alex was breathing hard too as he brought his face in close. His nose grazing hers, she wrapped her arms around his neck, conscious of the rasp of each laboured inhalation. He was close enough for her to see the faint pinpoint marks left by sutures running either side of the thin white scar that was almost hidden by his hairline. His forehead was creased in a frown of intense concentration as he stared into her upturned features; the skin of his own face was drawn tight, pushing against the perfect bones, emphasising each individual plane and angle. He was breathtakingly beautiful, but it was the raw, rampant hunger stamped on his face that sent a fresh, explosive surge of sheer need coursing through Angel's body.

Struggling to articulate what she was feeling, simultaneously frightened and helplessly excited by the desire roaring like an out-of-control forest fire, in a voice that was hers, yet not hers, she whispered, 'I need this. I need you.'

Not her voice, but it was definitely his mouth that came crashing down on hers. Her body arched as she kissed him back, responding to the pressure with a wild frenzy of need that drew a deep, throaty moan from Alex.

'Hell, I don't have… We need to be careful.'

'No, it's fine. I'm on the pill.'

'Thank God!'

Still kissing frantically, they stumbled backwards. Angel was dimly aware of the sound of the door closing behind them a split second before she lost her footing and stumbled. Before she fell she was in his arms, swept quite literally off her feet, and being carried, a novel experience for a woman who was five-ten in her bare feet! A woman who had never before wanted to feel weak or helpless and out of control… That so wasn't her.

In the bedroom he rested one knee on the bed before he sat her down in the middle of the soft downy quilt. She rested there looking dazed and so beautiful that the box he had locked his feelings away in cracked wide open.

'You're beautiful,' he said, looking into the luminous, passion-glazed eyes lifted to his. He touched the side of her soft cheek with his thumb and felt her shiver. Her eyes drifted closed as she turned her head and, catching his wrist, pressed her lips to his palm.

The speed with which she had gone from hating him to feeling his pain and then wanting him more than oxygen was disorientating. Actually it was scary. 'This is me, not the airbrushed version.'

The warning drew an amused grunt. Alex abandoned the pretence he was in control as a wave of emotion moved through him. Instead he decided to enjoy it…and her.

'I have seen you naked before.'

Her eyes opened as he rose to his feet. She grabbed the front of his shirt and, falling backwards, pulled him with her.

She felt rather than heard his throaty chuckle as he raised himself on one arm and warned in a voice thickened by passion, 'I'll crush you.'

Still holding his shirt, she tugged—hard—smiling as pressure caused buttons to fly in all directions across the room. Hands flat on the delicious, warm golden skin of his chest, she leaned up to kiss him, tugging at the flesh of his lip with her teeth as she whispered, 'I'm kind of hoping you will.' The torrent of need he had awoken in her was elemental, out of control… *She* was out of control. The raw passion left no room in her head for any thought. She was driven, focused on one thing: to lose herself in him, to be totally consumed by his raw power.

Kneeling over her now, he didn't take his eyes off her face as he fought his way out of his shirt before flinging it across the room.

Her skin was so sensitised that even a light shiver made her conscious of every point of contact between her and her clothes. They felt heavy; she felt too hot.… She tugged at the neckline of her dress and tried to smooth the fabric bunched around her middle, barely able to breathe now as her eyes drifted hungrily over his naked torso and her quivering stomach muscles cramped. The heat crackling under her skin burned as she absorbed the details. He was utterly perfect: lean, hard, gold-toned skin gleamed with a slick of sweat; his broad chest had power and strength and was marked by whorls of dark hair and sharply defined with slabs of muscle; his belly was washboard flat and bisected by a directional arrow of dark hair. Her chest lifted in a deep, voluptuous sigh of appreciation.

The shirt long gone, moving quickly and urgently, Alex reached for the buckle on the narrow belt that was threaded through the waistband of the linen trousers he was wearing. But Angel was there before him, driven by an all-consuming need to feel him, see him, her fingers shaking but surprisingly nimble as they unclipped the belt.

Before she could follow through with the action, he took her hands and lifted them high above her head. He kissed her with slow, erotic thoroughness before he took hold of the thin top she wore and, taking the hem, lifted it over her head.

She was wearing a tiny pair of panties and a bra that was little more than a couple of triangles of lace in a matching pink.

Alex gave a low appreciative growl in his throat and reached for the catch on her bra.

The underwear was gone before her head hit the pillow and he was bending over her, stroking her, his hands moving down her sides and over her ribcage and up to cup the quivering flesh of her breasts. Her body arched up to meet him, her arms wrapping themselves around his neck, as she struggled to anchor her aching core to him, all the while pressing increasingly ardent kisses to the strong brown column of his neck.

Angel squeezed her eyes closed and sank her fingers into the deep lush pelt of his hair, extracting and relishing every individual sensation, but somehow it wasn't enough.

She wanted more; she needed more.

Maybe if she said it?

'I know.' His breath was moist and hot on her cheek, on her neck then her breast, and the air left her lungs in one open-mouthed gasp. His hands were moving up over her ribcage as his tongue traced the outline of her areola, before drawing the engorged peaks into his mouth first one, then the other.

In a fever of need she only distantly registered him sliding her panties down over her hips, gasping but not resisting as he parted her legs. She moaned low in her throat, pushing against his hand as he slid his fingers between her legs, parting the swollen and incredibly sensitive folds, making her pant and gasp as he rhythmically stroked the swollen flesh. Her gasps turned to deep feral moans as he touched the tight nub at her core and her body lifted off the bed.

'You like that?'

She nodded. It made her dizzy to look into his burning eyes but she knew that the trust required to let him touch her went way beyond the merely physical. She had a connection with this man who was the father of her child, and that made it neither shocking nor shameful.

She lifted her head and kissed him back hungrily, no longer even attempting to retain control. She didn't want control; she wanted wild and elemental. She wanted Alex, wanted to be devoured, absorbed, to become one with him.

'I want you too!'

Had she spoken out loud?

'Hell, I haven't been able to think straight,' he groaned, 'since I saw that photo of you.' Holding her eyes with his as they lay side by side, he took her hand and curled her fingers around his hard, smooth shaft. 'That's how much I want you, Angel,' he slurred thickly.

He felt so good, and his half-closed eyes gleamed feverishly bright as she touched him. His expression turned raw and predatory and aroused her more than she had imagined possible.

Her lips parted as he lowered his mouth to hers, the deep, probing kiss draining her, sending her deeper and deeper into a vortex of sensation. As he moved over her she reached down and guided him into her, holding his gaze until that last moment when he slid thick and hard inside her.

Her eyes squeezed closed as every cell of her being focused on the feeling. She heard herself gasp.

'Oh, please!' As they began to move together his hands anchored her hips to the bed and she wrapped her long thighs tightly around him. Breathless, Angel moved with him, her sweat-slicked skin gliding and sliding against his. Their gasps and cries merged into one as their bodies came together, until she gave herself up to the firestorm of wild sensation that rocked her body.

As she began to float back down to earth Angel felt light. The secret burdens she had carried all her life were gone. She had slain her demons, she wasn't her mother—she loved him.

She lay in the dark, appreciating what had happened to her, not being afraid of it any more than she was afraid of her own heartbeat. He was as much a part of her as that. That he didn't feel the same way, that he couldn't, made her sad, but it also made her determined to extract every last atom of pleasure from the moment.

There were more moments during the night, less urgent, less bruisingly raw perhaps, but each one more shatteringly sensual than the last.

Angel woke feeling cold. The sheet was crumpled on the floor and Alex was lying on the other side of the bed.

He woke as she shuffled across the bed and shivered as she pushed closer to the warmth of his body. Streaks of light had appeared along the wide horizon where the sea met the sky. It would soon be morning and what then...?

She shivered again and felt her chest tighten with an emotion she identified as loneliness. How crazy. She wasn't alone—she had Jas. A sigh hissed from her lips.

'Are you cold?'

'I'm fine,' she said, her voice muffled against his shoulders. He threw his arm across her and it lay big and heavy and reassuring across her shoulders. She liked the feel of his hair-roughened thigh against her smooth leg.

Don't get to like it too much, Angel, the voice in her head advised. Turning a deaf ear to that voice, she focused on the fingers that were moving in slow, lazy, circular movements across her belly.

Then the hand stilled and she sensed the tension in his body. 'What is that?'

She shivered, this time with pleasure as the heel of his hand rested on the sensitive mound of her pubic bone, though he ran his thumb along the thin white line not quite obscured by the soft fuzz of curls at the apex of her long legs.

'Complications during labour. I had an emergency C-section.'

He felt as if a hand had reached into his chest. So much had happened to her that he was responsible for and he'd been totally oblivious.

'You could have died?' Guilt rose like bile in his throat. What had he been doing at the time? Driving a fast car? Signing off on a deal and congratulating himself? Enjoying technically perfect sex with a beautiful woman...?

There had been nothing technical about last night.

Raw, explosive, elemental—yes; as addictive as a narcotic—definitely! He knew now why he had gone to such
lengths to bring her back into his life. He'd been trying
to recapture this feeling, this emotional connection that
only a single one-night stand had given him.

'If I'd been living in a Third World country possibly,
but I wasn't. It was all routine.' And scary as hell.

He didn't believe a word of it. He had taken her innocence and got her pregnant. *A prince among men, that's
you,* Alex told himself.

'You were alone?'

She shook her head.

'Your mother was with you?'

The suggestion drew a chortle of laughter from Angel.

'I thought maybe having a baby would have brought
you together.'

Her hands curled over his. Drawing his fingers to
her lips, she kissed them, then his mouth. Some breathless moment later she admitted with a laugh, 'Being old
enough to be a grandmother is a crime my mother has
still not forgiven me for. I'm not even sure what country
she was in when I gave birth. She bores easily.'

He said a word that sounded vicious.

'Will you teach me to swear in Russian? That sounds
really satisfying.'

'If you teach me to make love in Italian, *cara.*'

'It works for me.'

'Tell me you weren't alone when you gave birth.'

'I wasn't,' she said, hearing the guilt in his request.
'My friend, Clara.' Who despite her very good intentions
had spent the first few hours of Angel's forty-eight-hour
labour flirting with a young doctor, and when things had
started happening had fainted away gracefully. While
the labour had gone disastrously wrong, Clara was

being diagnosed with concussion and even got admitted overnight. Angel had been her maid of honour when her friend had married the handsome young obstetrician six months later.

'And my brother flew back from Dubai as soon as he got the news I was in labour. Jas arrived a month early, so he was there to hold her before I came around.' According to the midwives he had worn a trench in the floor walking up and down, waiting for her to recover from the anaesthetic.

That should have been me. The thought surfaced, the strength of it taking him by surprise. He should have held his baby, and now he never would. His loss, not hers. It was obvious that Angel put her child above all else.

She omitted a few details from her potted history, such as that she'd come around in a high-dependency unit, or that her first recollection when she had surfaced from the anaesthetic had been hearing her forceful sibling who had no doubt bullied the information out of the doctor asking him if he was sure she would never be able to have children in the future.

'Is there no hope? IVF…?'

'Not impossible but extremely unlikely,' had been the medic's response. 'Would you like me to tell the father…? Or will you…?'

'If I ever find the scum who did this to her I'll do better than that! I'll make sure he doesn't do this to any other woman! Is she awake yet?'

Angel, who had closed her eyes and pretended to be unconscious, had almost immediately drifted back into a drug-induced slumber.

But when she'd woken she had remembered the conversation she had overheard, which had helped when Cesare had broken the news to her later; she had been able to make it easier for him by responding calmly as she'd told him honestly that she was fine. When she'd been discharged a few days later everyone had considered her to be coping remarkably well, though Angel had been unable to dispel the feeling that they were waiting for her to fall apart.

When they'd realised she wasn't going to—it had taken a while—it had been a relief that everyone had stopped walking on eggshells around her and she could get on with looking after her baby. She had happily left the anger to her brother, who had deduced with no help or confirmation from her that the father was married.

She had genuinely believed she was all right until that morning six months down the line when she had been folding away the clothes that Jasmine had outgrown, smoothing the fabric of a hand-knitted, exquisite, tiny newborn cardigan that it was hard to believe her robust bouncing daughter had ever fitted into. The reality had hit her with no warning.... Why was she storing the tiny garment so carefully in layers of tissue and lavender bags for the future? There would be no brother or sister to wear it.

No more babies.

The tears had begun to leak from her eyes, silently at first, then had come the muffled sobs and finally the awful wrenching wails. A lot later she had dried her eyes and the next day had delivered all the baby clothes to the local charity shop, reminding herself sternly that she had a precious child and many people were not that lucky.

She had not thought of it since, but now she realised that she had needed to cry, needed to mourn a future that was lost, she thought sadly. But she had done her mourning and moved on; now she was getting on with her life.

Had Alex? Was he still mourning the future with his wife that had been denied him?

'Was your wife ill a long time?'

She felt him stiffen a moment before he rolled away from her. 'Yes.'

'I know mourning is a very personal process.' She reached out to stroke his back before taking a deep breath and beginning tentatively, 'My friend had grief counselling when her—'

'I don't need a grief counselor. I have you. You were right—I have been eaten with guilt because I buried my grief in anonymous sex. I'm not proud of it but you helped me see...I have moved on, Angel. The question is,' he said quietly, 'have you?'

In the space of a heartbeat Angel experienced the disorientating sensation of a total role reversal. One second she was feeling supportive and understanding, the next she was the one being asked to face her demons, and it was too soon.

CHAPTER EIGHT

ANGEL HAD LAIN with her eyes closed, pretending to be asleep, as she heard him getting dressed. But when she heard Alex moving around in the other room she got up. She didn't want him to leave without doing something to close the distance that had opened up between them.

Belting her robe, she walked quietly into the adjoining room. Alex, who hadn't heard her, was holding the photo of Jasmine in the silver frame. It was the expression she saw etched on his face in the brief moment before he realised she was there that swung it—the longing mixed with pain that vanished the moment he knew he was not alone.

Swallowing the lump of emotion in her throat and ignoring the small voice in her head that told her she'd live to regret opening this door, she responded to his cautious good morning with, 'You can see Jas.'

He went rigid for a moment, his face a total blank, then he smiled and tipped his head. 'Good.'

'If you agree that when and how to tell her who you are is my call.'

Slowly he nodded. 'That seems fair.'

Angel expelled a deep sigh and hoped like hell once more that this was going to work out.... She had to make it work. 'Right, I'll make arrangements. Another thing

I think that—no!' She backed away shaking her head, one arm extended as if to fend him off as he approached, the gleam in his eyes sending her nervous system into meltdown. 'Don't!'

His fingers that had moved to loosen the knot on her robe stopped; he was frustrated but not alarmed. He bent his head towards her. 'What's wrong?'

Wrong, yes, she thought, that was the right word. He'd been the wrong man at the wrong time for all the wrong reasons.

'I can't.'

The furrow on his brow smoothed. 'You have an early call? That's a pity,' he murmured, thinking it was a disaster! Unable to stop himself, he dropped his eyes to the thrusting profile of her nipples. He had never wanted a woman as much as he did Angel. It was a struggle to present a casual attitude about this delay when every cell in his body was pumped and primed to peel back the layer of silk and explore the even silkier delights beneath.

'I don't have an early call. I mean… What I mean…' She stopped, squeezed her eyes closed and groaned. 'Don't look at me like that,' she pleaded.

'Like what?'

His display of innocence drew a growl of frustration from Angel. 'Like you're…'

'Thinking about making love to you…?'

When wasn't he?

His eyes narrowed as he struggled to contain a flicker of shock. Sex no longer came with a big guilt trip. It had become a normal part of his life again, but it was not something that occupied his thoughts exclusively. Or it hadn't been until Angel had come back into his life.

This frank translation made her flush and press a hand to her heaving chest.

'I can't focus!' she choked. 'I'm trying to tell you we can't…ever do…' she jerked her head in the direction of the open bedroom door where the tumbled bedclothes were visible '…that.'

'That?'

She lifted her chin and responded to his taunt with an unintentionally loud reply. 'Sex. That's part of the deal. If you want to be part of Jas's life then we have to get our act together.' She expelled a breath. It was over with; she had said it. This was the point where the tension was meant to flow from her body. She had told herself she'd feel better once she got this over with, but she didn't.

'You just lost me.'

She struggled to preserve her calmness, aware in the face of this pretence of ignorance that with his steel-trap mind he got the point half an hour before most people. 'A child needs continuity…security.'

What she did not need was a constant stream of 'uncles' at the breakfast table; she did not need slammed doors, raised voices, dramas played out at volume at all hours of the day and night; she did not need spurned lovers who turned nasty or even the ones that turned pathetic.

'You expect me to argue with that?'

'I put Jas's needs ahead of my own,' she said quietly.

There might not be a definitive rule book that told you how to be a good mother—Angel had discovered everyone had to work it out for themselves, and there were times when she frankly got it wrong and worried about just how much mothering skills were down to genes—but at least she knew how not to be a bad mother, or at least an uninterested one.

Growing up, she would have settled for her mother remembering once in a while that she had children! Her beautiful and erratic parent had lived her life exactly as she had wanted and her children had been the ones who had done the adapting.

'And you need me.'

The smug insertion proved to Angel that they were still not on the same page. 'This isn't about your ego,' she flared, tightening the belt on her robe, thus unwittingly causing the neckline to gape.

Jaw clenched, Alex dragged his gaze off the heaving contours of her bosom and the effort made his tone abrupt.

'Then what is it…?' He stopped as the penny belatedly dropped. He could see where this was going.

'You mean you want to get married?'

The cynic in him was not surprised. It was not the first time a woman had looked at him as prospective husband material. He was normally alert to the subtle signs that signalled attempts to manoeuvre him into matrimony, but he hadn't seen this one coming. For some reason, neither could he summon up his well-rehearsed smile, the one that softened his harsh response.

And none of the women he had let down gently had been the mother of his child.

His eyes narrowed. That made a difference. And now that he thought of it, was it such a bad idea from a purely practical point of view? Of course he was old-fashioned enough to prefer to be the one making the proposal, but Angel's horrified exclamation suddenly cut into his stream of thought.

'M-marry? Of course not!'

The unmitigated horror in her voice was reflected on her face. It seemed he could always rely on Angel to deliver a kick to his ego.

'That would be ridiculous.' She gave a laugh, wincing

when her effort to convince him she was neither crazy nor an idiot made her sound both. 'I'm not wife material, believe me.'

'What, parents getting married?' His jaw clenched as he resisted the childish impulse to inform her that there were more than a few women who would not consider the idea of being his bride a nightmare. 'Hell, yes, you're right, crazy...that would never catch on,' he drawled, swinging away from her, his feet silent on the floor as he stalked towards the window. He reminded her of a caged tiger on a short leash as he traversed the room.

'Please, this is not a joke,' she reproached to his retreating back.

He spun back, spearing the fingers of both hands deep into his hair as he rocked back on his heels. 'Sorry.'

Her eyes narrowed. 'Thanks for that sincerity.'

'I'm sincere—sincerely tired of this ridiculous discussion.' His sarcasm made Angel clench her teeth. 'Just tell me what is bothering—'

'My pretty little head?' she jumped in, glaring.

A spasm of irritation crossed his patrician features. 'You are not pretty.'

Angel was not particularly mad about her looks. Given the choice she would have chosen blonde and petite, but she had no body-image issues and she was well aware that she was considered by most people to be more than averagely attractive, so it made it all the more crazy that the comment hurt. 'So I'm ugly!' She could not believe this childish response was coming from her own mouth.

'No, you are beautiful,' he countered. Midglare his eyes broke contact with Angel's and slid to the photo. 'So is she. She looks so like you....'

The husky observation successfully refocused Angel's attention. 'She has a much sweeter temperament.'

'Maybe she takes after her father...?'

Alex Arlov, sweet? Any other time the two words in the same sentence would have had her in hysterics but Angel didn't crack a smile.

She made an effort to channel calm. 'I can't have an affair with you, Alex.'

Even if she could have stomached the idea of sex without an emotional commitment it wouldn't have worked. She simply lost all sense of perspective when it came to Alex. She could never maintain any sort of simple sexual relationship with the way he made her feel.

She had never understood women who would risk everything for a man. She didn't want to understand, but what she did know was that if such a man existed Alex Arlov was the living, breathing embodiment of it.

'Who's saying I want an affair?'

She flinched at the growled rebuttal and, lifting her chin, defiantly murmured, 'My mistake.' Presumably an affair was too formal a footing for what he had in mind. 'As a matter of interest, what did you have in mind?' She arched a delicate brow and suggested in a sardonic drawl, 'Friends with benefits?'

'We are not friends.'

'Thank you for reminding me.'

A look of regret slid across his lean face. 'I didn't mean it that way.... I just...' He dragged a hand through his dark, tousled hair. 'I just... You're driving me crazy.'

There's a lot of it around, Angel thought grimly. 'Don't worry, I appreciate bluntness,' she said instead. Hopefully he could take it as well as dish it out. 'I can't have sex with you at all. We need to keep our relationship uncomplicated for Jasmine.'

He struggled to follow her logic and realised there was none. 'How is us sleeping together bad for Jasmine?'

'I want my daughter to learn about relationships based on mutual respect and—'

'Our daughter.'

The correction made her grate her teeth. 'For five years she's been my daughter, Alex.'

'And you resent the fact it has to change,' he flung.

The suggestion that this was a *fait accompli* annoyed her. He was failing to recognise that she was the one making an effort.

'I'm an example to my daughter. I don't want her to think casual sex is all she can have. I watched my mother sleep her way around the fashionable spots of Europe. I had her boyfriends drift in and out of my life and I don't want that sort of instability for Jasmine.'

'So you *are* holding out for marriage.' He seized on this evidence triumphantly.

'I'm holding out for a relationship based on more than lust,' she countered. 'One that is…safe.'

His heavy-lidded gaze slid over her sleek, sensuous curves and the fist of desire in his belly tightened. 'Safe!' he spat in disgust. 'And what is so terrible about lust? Lust is not a bad place to start….' he commented in a deep throaty drawl that made the surface of her skin tingle.

The deep, drowning blue of his eyes made her dizzy and it was an effort to break the contact. 'Only if both participants want the same thing.'

'I thought I gave you what you wanted.'

His inability to see what she was saying drew a frustrated grunt from Angel.

'My mother changed her lovers the way some women change their shoes. I know what it feels like to grow fond of someone and have them vanish or to hear arguments when you're trying to go to sleep, to have a sleazy boyfriend of your mother's make a pass at you.' She saw the outrage flare in his eyes and added quickly, 'Only once and my brother walked in.'

'So how is the fact your mother was a lousy parent relevant?'

'I know what bad parenting is.'

'And good parenting involves being some sort of born-again virgin? I'm curious—are you planning on not having any sex or is it just sex with me that will emotionally scar our daughter?'

'You're deliberately twisting things.'

'So untwist things and tell me you're not saying I can either be part of my daughter's life or sleep with you?'

'It is not an either-or situation, Alex.'

He exhaled a frustrated hiss through his teeth. 'What is it, then?' Without waiting for her to respond, he shook his head and, drawing a sharp line in the air with his hand, said, 'You know, I really don't want to hear, because none of it is true. You know what I think? I think this isn't about Jasmine, it's about you. You're using her as an excuse because underneath that facade you're scared. What of? Becoming your mother?'

'Of course not,' she answered too quickly.

'From what you've told me you are the exact opposite of your mother.'

'This isn't about my mother. It's about us.... You.'

'You're scared of me?' A look of shock chased across his lean face. 'It never occurred to me you were... Why would you be?' His eyes narrowed as her eyes slid from his, shifting to a point over his shoulder. It was a telling gesture.

'Of course not.' It was true, she wasn't afraid of Alex, but she was afraid of the way he made her feel. The emotional impact of meeting him again had felt like having a tourniquet removed from a deadened limb and the abrupt resumption of circulation and feeling had been agonising. But as hard as she'd tried she couldn't reapply the tourniquet to her emotions.

She loved him and he was going to break her heart. It was as inevitable as night following day. But it wasn't the broken heart precisely that she was avoiding—it was Jasmine witnessing it breaking, seeing the slow disintegration of the relationship and thinking, as Angel had, that that was all there was to look forward to in life.

'We all have issues in our childhood....'

The insensitive attempt at amateur psychology brought her resentful gaze back to his face. A second was all it took for him to capture and hold her.

'What made you so scared of enjoying a normal healthy sex life?'

'I'm not afraid,' she replied, hiding her discomfiture behind a cool mask.

'Did your father cheat on your mother?' he speculated.

'My dad adored my mother even after she walked out on their marriage and took us with her, then did her level best to forget we existed.' In a small corner of her head a voice was saying, 'Too much information, Angel!' but she couldn't stem the flow of revelations. 'And in answer to your question, I'm not scared, I'm determined—determined that my daughter will always be my first priority.'

She gave a weary sigh. 'It's simply the way I want it to be. Don't you see?' she appealed to him. 'This,' she said, moving her hand in an illustrative sweep from her chest to him and back again, 'is exactly the situation I want to avoid.'

'This is a situation that you have engineered,' he countered grimly. 'You've created a self-fulfilling prophesy. Do you even know how unrealistic you're being? Do you really think you're going to find some guy you'll never fight with? You'd be bored within a week,' he predicted.

'I'm not looking for a guy. This is just the way it's going to be, take it or leave it.'

It was the torment in her green eyes that made him hold his tongue—that and the realisation that she genuinely believed all the rubbish she was spouting. Her logic was totally crazy but he recognised this might not be the time to point it out. This was the time for a tactical retreat...but he would be back.

Alex closed the door behind him as he left, which should have made her happy. It was what she wanted, but as she picked up the phone to arrange Jasmine's trip over to meet her father happiness was not the emotion that was uppermost in her mind. She might never have sex again, and that was reason enough to feel depressed.

She had had the most gorgeous man in the universe ask her to be with him, and she had sent him away! More significantly, he had gone without even putting up much of a fight.... Probably, she thought gloomily, he'd been secretly relieved.

But she'd done the right thing, almost definitely she'd done the right thing. They'd made a great child, but living together... No, she had made the right decision... totally!

Wasn't the right thing meant to make you feel good?

She didn't feel good; she felt like someone who had just slammed the doors of paradise shut and stayed on the wrong side, which was mad because paradise was a

cool, calm place of serenity. Serene and Alex… No, she
had made the right decision, hadn't she…?

She lifted her chin and took a deep breath. *For God's
sake, Angel, you've made your bed and now you have to
lie in it…alone.*

Things happened faster than Angel had anticipated. The
young woman who was standing in for her nanny was
available to accompany Jasmine on the next flight, and
she seemed eager to. So it was less than twenty-four
hours later that she was thanking her for accompanying
Jasmine on the journey and saying goodbye, leaving her
to wait for her return flight.

Jasmine, strapped into the seat beside her, was so excited she chatted constantly all the way from the airport,
unable to keep still in the seat. When they reached the
bungalow she was visibly flagging.

'You like your bedroom?' Angel asked as the little girl
did her umpteenth circuit of the room.

'Love it loads,' she said, taking a seat on the bed,
watching while Angel unpacked her small suitcase. Jasmine began to swing her legs metronome style, her heels
hitting the wooden frame with a regular dull thud.

'These shorts are too tight,' she remarked as Angel
took out a blue denim pair with cute ducks on the patch
pockets. 'But we didn't have any time to buy some more.'

'Don't worry, we'll buy you some new ones. There
you go—all done,' Angel said as she put the last T-shirt
in the drawer and closed it. 'How about a nap?'

The little girl looked offended. 'I'm not a baby, and I
want to go in the water. You promised.'

Angel sighed. Like an elephant, her daughter never
forgot. 'Everyone has naps in the afternoon in warm
countries.'

'Even grown-ups?'

Angel nodded. 'Absolutely.'

'So you're going to take a nap too…with me?'

The logic was inescapable, and Angel, knowing a rash promise once made was hard to escape, dodged the issue.

'Why don't you change into your swimsuit and we'll have a swim first?' She floated the idea, knowing what the response would be. Watching her daughter leap up and down like a crazy thing on the bed made her realise how quiet her life was without Jas in it, how much emptier.

This was her. This was what she wanted, but did Alex, with his billionaire jet-setting lifestyle, have a clue what he was asking for?

Having left Jas to change into her swimsuit, Angel changed into her own one-piece—a black halter that she double tied at the neck. The last time she had been wearing it in a public pool, Jas had thought it funny to unfasten the bow and Angel had found herself in a very embarrassing topless situation.

He was nervous.

Alex gave a self-derisive smile. He was nervous of meeting a five-year-old child! Maybe nervous was not the best word to describe the combination of excitement, anticipation and trepidation in his gut. Carrying the gift—it had been a novel, actually a unique, experience for Alex to pick out a gift personally and not delegate the task to his excellent PA—he walked along the beach towards Angel's bungalow. He was a few hundred yards away when he heard the sound of laughter.

He did not consciously follow the sound but he ended up on the shore, oblivious to the waves lapping over his leather shoes, watching the two playing a game that involved much splashing and lots of noise. The first glimpse of his daughter was as Angel lifted her high out of the water, a wriggling laughing figure whose high-pitched chuckle he could hear above Angel's husky contralto tone.

There were few perfect moments in life, the really golden ones that stayed with you until the end. Alex had read somewhere that witnessing the birth of your child was considered by many to be one of them. He had not been there for the birth of his child so in some ways this was it: perfect. She was perfect.

'Who is that man, Mummy?'

Angel, who had just surfaced from the water and was kneeling, turned her head and saw him. Her stomach flipped. She had never associated the word lonely with Alex Arlov but standing there he looked... She swallowed the boulder lodged in her aching throat and slowly got to her feet.

'That's my friend.' She extended her hand to Jasmine. 'Shall we go say hello?'

Alex remembered a friend who had described how unreal it had felt to take his newborn home from hospital for the first time. He had spoken of the shock of overnight becoming, not a couple, but a family.

Times that by a million, Alex thought, and you might get somewhere near the complex swirl of emotions he was feeling.

He wasn't seeing a new baby. His daughter was not a blank slate; she was a fully formed little person with a store of experiences that he knew nothing about, a personality. Was she scared of the dark? He resented that he didn't know, but he was going to find out, and the only way to do that was to be a family.

Alex believed that only fools rushed headlong into important decisions, and allowing emotions to become involved was just so obviously a massive mistake that it did not even warrant debate. It turned out there were exceptions to this rule and standing on the beach he discovered one. He made the most important decision in his life without a second's debate or hesitation.

He was going to marry Angel and they were going to be a family. It would happen.

CHAPTER NINE

JASMINE ACCEPTED THE explanation without question. 'Does he want to play with us?'

Angel shook her head. 'I don't think so, sweetheart, and I think maybe we've had enough now too.' She took her daughter's hand and they waded out of the shallows and onto the beach where Alex, his dark hair fluttering slightly in the breeze, was standing looking gorgeous. This was obviously a given, but he was also incongruous in this setting in a tailored pale grey suit. The top button of his white silk shirt open and his tie hanging loose around his neck were the only minor concessions to the sun beating down.

His appearance was not lost on Jasmine.

'Your shoes are wet. It's really stupid to wear shoes on the beach.' She wriggled her own bare toes in the wet sand and directed her critical gaze to the rest of him. She didn't seem impressed by what she was seeing. 'Or a suit. It's not p-pract...?'

She looked to her mother, who automatically supplied the word, 'Practical,' before adding, 'Don't be rude, Jas.'

Alex stepped back out of the shallow water, barely giving his handmade Italian-leather shoes a glance. His daughter had a Scottish accent; the highland lilt was unmistakable. It brought home forcibly the extent of his ignorance. He didn't even know where she had lived her five years. He had assumed London, but clearly he couldn't have been more wrong.

'She's right. My outfit is not beach appropriate.' His outfit was appropriate for the discussion of oil leases. If the change of venue had been considered unusual by the oil executives who had expected to be in London, they had not said so when he had met the fleet of helicopters personally. 'But I've been working, and you, I see, have been swimming.'

'I can't swim yet. Mum has tried to teach me but I'm not a natural.'

Her sigh and serious expression drew a smile from Alex. While he did not know a lot about five-year-olds it seemed to him as a not-totally-objective observer that his daughter was pretty advanced for her age, and she not only looked startlingly like her mother but she was also not afraid of speaking her mind.

'Perhaps I could teach you?'

He turned his head towards Angel to gauge her reaction to his suggestion. She was bending forward to pick up a towel from the sand, a wet swathe of her hair concealing her face.

'Mummy?'

Angel dropped the towel around her shoulders. 'That's very kind.' The little girl skipped ahead.

'So do you mind?'

'That's not the point. You made it impossible for me to say no, and I don't appreciate that. Don't manipulate me, Alex.'

'It wasn't intentional. She didn't look to be afraid of the water.'

Angel laughed. 'Jas isn't afraid of anything. That's the problem—she has very little sense of danger. I don't want to make her scared but it's a hard balance…. She's not afraid of water. It's the cold—she hates it. I first tried to teach her at home when she was a toddler—we have the white sand and the clear seas, but the water is not warm at any time of the year and she is a warm-blooded little creature. She loves the sun.'

'So I see. The accent came as a surprise—charming, but a surprise.'

'I don't even notice she has an accent. We have an apartment in the castle….' She saw Alex's expression and added a quick explanatory footnote, 'My brother inherited the estate when our dad died—beautiful, remote and a lot of rain. Isn't it every little girl's dream to live in a castle?'

'Is it?'

'I was happy there when I was her age.'

'You have no accent.'

Her smile faded. 'No, I lost it and my roots, but Jasmine won't.'

'Roots are less about places and more about people.'

'There speaks someone who didn't grow up in a series of hotel rooms.'

'You said she had been ill? Was it serious?'

'It took a while to diagnose, a thing with her hip. It required a lot of bed rest and that was tough. They thought she might be left with a limp but she's fine. Are you all right, Alex?'

He tore his eyes off the playing child and nodded. 'Fine.' As fine as any man could be when he knew the woman he loved had faced all those things alone.

'Are you sure?'

He nodded. 'I should have been there.'

The burning intensity of his gaze made her look away. 'You're here now.'

'Yes, I am.'

They caught up with Jasmine, who, to Angel's maternal eyes, was showing visible signs of flagging. 'Want a carry, sweetheart?'

'No, I'm okay. What's that?' She stared curiously at the parcel in Alex's hand.

He withdrew the book from behind his back. 'A book. I thought you might like it. It's about a princess who marries a handsome prince after he saves her from a dragon.' A far simpler time when all a man had to do to prove himself was slay the odd dragon. Life was much more complicated these days.

'I already have a book about a princess. She rescues the prince and she hates pink.'

A lot more complicated—he couldn't even impress a five-year-old. 'It seems,' Alex said in a soft rueful aside to Angel as she took the book from him, 'that I am not politically correct enough.'

They had reached the steps to the bungalow and Angel opened the book. 'Look, Jas, this book has such lovely pictures, really beautiful.' How crazy that she wanted to save his feelings. He was trying so hard that it made her heart ache to watch him.

'Are there any cats in it?'

'I'm not sure,' Alex admitted.

'I like cats. Thank you very much.'

He inclined his head. 'You are most welcome, Jasmine.'

She allowed herself to be led up the steps to the veranda, where she jumped directly onto a bench. 'I could look at the pictures now.'

'Nice try. We had a deal. A swim and then a nap.'

With a show of reluctance she got up.

'Say goodnight to Alex.'

'Goodnight, Mr Alex.'

'Goodnight, Jasmine.'

'There's a bottle of wine open in the fridge if you want some. I won't be long…if you want to wait.'

'I want…'

He stood up when Angel walked back into the living room a few minutes later and pulled out a chair for her, wincing as it scraped on the wooden floor. 'Sorry.'

'Don't worry. Nothing will wake her now.'

'She's quite a character. You have done a good job.'

Angel felt herself blush with pleasure at the compliment. 'I've had a lot of help….'

'You have a nanny?'

Her chin lifted defensively. 'Luckily.'

He watched, one brow raised, as she ignored the wine he had poured and filled her coffee cup from a Thermos jug. 'It was not a criticism.'

'My brother is great and my normal nanny is sporting a leg plaster. Her really great stand-in flew over with Jas and then back.'

'So what does your brother do—?' He broke off, frowning. 'Is that a good idea?' She looked at him over the rim of her cup. 'You do know you're displaying all the classic signs of caffeine overload?'

'Am I?'

'You're jumpy as hell, you can't sit still… Look,' he broke off to say as the cup she had put back down on the table rattled. 'You're trembling and I bet your heart is racing and you're dizzy? Am I right?'

Oh, he was right. 'And that's because I drink too much coffee?' A man with a mind like a steel trap, but it turned out he didn't know everything. She was beginning to think that where she was concerned he knew nothing!

'If you're not careful…'

She gave a sputtering laugh and drew his frowning disapproval.

'This isn't funny, Angel.'

'Oh, I know it's not, believe me,' she said, looking at his mouth hard enough to memorise it. She picked up a magazine from the table and wafted her face with it. 'But don't worry, I know my limitations with coffee.' It was her limitations with Alex that were her problem. Her internal red light just failed to activate with him.

'You've met him, I think.'

He watched as she topped up her coffee cup. 'Who?'

'My brother. I believe you played with cars together. Cesare…?'

A look of utter astonishment spread across his face. 'You are Cesare Urquart's sister?' Meeting someone with a public persona in the flesh could, Alex knew, be disappointing when that person fell far short of your mental image. But that hadn't been the case when he had met the ex-racing driver whose career he had followed. He had liked the man and the feeling seemed to have been reciprocated.

She nodded.

'Does he know about me?' Alex asked, imagining his own reaction if the situation was reversed and he discovered the identity of the man who had got his young and beautiful sister pregnant.

'Not yet.'

'I'm assuming there will be no place to run,' he observed sardonically.

She flicked him a glance, resenting the fact he could look amused when she was genuinely worried about what her brother would do. Wade in all guns blazing probably.

'That settles it,' Alex said. 'I'll have to marry you.'

She struggled to match his flippancy. 'You really

know how to sell the idea. Of course I'll marry you. Name the day.'

'Tomorrow, unless you want a big wedding?'

The joke was beginning to grow tired. 'Very funny.'

'Why would you think I'm joking?'

She turned to him with an astonished stare. 'Because if you weren't that would make you insane.'

'It is insane to think a child is better brought up within the confines of a marriage?'

'We're not talking about Jasmine.'

'Yes, we are, Jasmine and us. You won't be my lover, so be my wife.'

Feeling the panic begin to build, she pressed a hand to her tight chest. 'There is no us.'

A spasm of impatience moved across his lean face. 'Don't be ridiculous. I'm the father of your child and I'm the only man you've ever slept with. That adds up to a big fat us.'

'It doesn't add up to marriage.'

'I'm not talking a paper marriage, if that is what is bothering you. Not a sterile, convenient—' He saw her flinch and stopped. 'What have I said?'

Pale as paper, she shook her head. 'Too much.'

He shrugged and forced himself to stifle his impatience. He had given her enough to think about, planted the idea, now it would grow.

He allowed himself one final parting shot.

'You don't want Jasmine to be an only child, do you?'

She was glad he couldn't see her face, or the tears that began to slide down her cheeks. She was grateful to him; she needed that. For a moment there she had started to let herself think that the crazy things he said were possible.

CHAPTER TEN

THE MOMENT ALEX walked into the hotel foyer, a trail of assistants behind him, he realised that something was wrong—it did not take a genius to work this out.

The area was crowded, some people talking, others gawking, and in the middle of them was Angel, white faced, wild eyed and she was shouting.

'What is wrong with you people? I don't want to sit down. I don't want to fill in a form. I've told you I can't find my daughter. My little girl, she was there and now she isn't. I need help, not tea!'

The shrill words stopped Alex in his tracks. He felt a cold hand close around his heart, then a moment later he was surging forward and the crowd was parting.

'Angel.'

She spun around; her expression when she saw him would stay with him for ever. 'Thank God, Alex, it's Jas, she's—'

He laid his hands on her shoulders and held her eyes with his. 'I heard. Just tell me what happened.'

Angel expelled a deep shuddering sigh and focused on his eyes, trying to block out the rest of the room and the white noise of panic in her head. 'We were walking back after lunch.' She gave another deep sigh and shook her head.

'Look at me, Angel.'

She responded to the firm voice, taking comfort from the calm in it. 'She'd spent the morning at the shoot with me watching. We had lunch, yes, I already said that, and...I really should get back outside.'

'In a moment.'

'I saw Nico, he asked me about... I don't remember. I only turned away for a moment, really only a moment, and when I turned around she was gone, vanished!'

'And when was this?'

'A couple of... I don't know, just now.' She clutched her head and struggled to think straight, fighting her way through the panic.

'Fine. Show me where you last saw her.'

The next few minutes were a blur for Angel, who retraced her steps and repeated the sequence of events for what seemed like the thousandth time, then sat and watched, feeling helpless and more scared than she had imagined possible, while Alex divided up the volunteers into teams and gave them areas to cover.

'She can't have gone far, and ten teams can cover a lot of ground. We will find her.'

She caught his arm. 'I want to go too.'

'No, I need you and Nico to stay here in case she makes her own way back, and everyone has Nico's number.' Nico held up his phone. 'He's the contact so you'll be the first to know.'

'You're afraid you'll find something bad—that's why you don't want me to go!' she accused shrilly.

Alex took her by the shoulders. 'You can't think that way, Angel, and you're not going to fall apart. You're strong. Look at me, Angel.' Her wild restive gaze settled on his face. 'We are going to find her.'

She swallowed and took a deep shuddering breath. 'I'm not strong, Alex.'

He gave the most tender smile she had ever seen and touched her face. 'You are as tough as old boots.'

Then he was gone.

Nico's phone rang exactly ten minutes later, the longest ten minutes of her life.

Still holding his daughter's hand, Alex dropped into a squatting position beside her and pointed towards Angel, who was belting across the sand with Nico and several staff trailing in her wake. 'There's your mummy!'

As Angel reached them he released Jasmine's hand and, rising to his feet, took a step back as Angel, panting, tears streaming down her face, dropped down on her knees and grabbed Jasmine, hugging so tightly the little girl protested and wriggled to escape.

'Sorry…sorry…' Angel pushed her back, one hand patting her own mouth to hold back the sobs that struggled to escape from her throat as her anxious green eyes scanned her daughter's face. 'You're all right?' She lifted her eyes to the tall figure who stood over them both. 'She's a-all right? Oh, God, my teeth won't stop chattering.'

To witness the emotion she was leaking from every pore was making his throat ache. 'She's fine,' Alex promised huskily. 'She's just had a little adventure, haven't you, Jasmine? And none the worse for it, excepting a few scratches.'

'I was very, very brave.' She looked to Alex for confirmation of this proud boast and he tipped his head gravely.

'Just like your mother.'

Angel, shaking with the force of her relief, impelled to touch Jasmine every other second just to prove she was real, was not feeling brave. She was still fighting the nightmarish images in her head. As her distress began to communicate itself to the little girl the proud smile vanished and her lip began to tremble. 'Mummy...?'

'Don't do that again...ever...promise me.!'

Jasmine's face crumbled. 'You weren't there!' she wailed.

The words pierced Angel's heart. 'Don't cry, darling....' Angel sniffed, hugging her daughter's rigid body. 'It's all right now.' She stroked her daughter's head and Jasmine's arms went round her neck. Carrying her, Angel rose awkwardly to her feet and over the top of Jasmine's head she smiled at Alex and mouthed 'thank you'.

Cool focus and the ability to empty his mind of everything but what he needed to do had got Alex through this, had kept his darkest imaginings at bay. All it took was the gratitude in her shining eyes and those self-imposed barriers crumbled. He tipped his head, his own smile giving not a hint of the rush of powerful emotions locked tight in his chest, the primal need to protect the two women in his life from all the dangers that lurked out there.

He moved to stand protectively beside them and kissed the top of the curly head pressed to Angel's shoulder and said quietly, 'Will you be all right?'

Angel felt her face drop. 'You're not coming with us?' Hearing the wobble in her voice, she pinned on a weak smile in an effort to retrieve the situation, and she struggled to display some of the self-reliance she prided herself on.

All in all it was a pathetic effort.

His fingers tightened on the bones of her shoulder; his hand felt heavy, reassuring. Angel closed her eyes, sucked in a deep breath, before throwing her head back to meet his eyes.

'I'll be fine,' she pronounced, thinking, *Don't get used to leaning on him, Angel. He won't always be there.*

'I won't be long. I just want to make sure that this section of beach is fenced off by the morning. We don't want this happening again.' He sketched a bleak but determined smile and beckoned his nephew over. 'Nico will see you back to the bungalow and wait until I get back.'

Nico nodded. 'Of course.'

Jasmine raised her head. 'I want my kitten back.'

Angel arched a questioning brow and angled a glance up at Alex. 'Your kitten, darling?'

'She saw a stray cat and it looks like she followed it through the hole in the fence, crawled through after it. The cat led her back to her litter of feral kittens and Jasmine decided she wanted to take one home.' He skimmed over the struggle he had had to convince her that this was not a good idea. His daughter had, it seemed, inherited her mother's stubborn disposition as well as an underdeveloped sense of danger.

Life for a man in a household with two such females was not to be envied, but it was what Alex had discovered he wanted for himself, what he would do anything to achieve.

'Hence the scratches.'

'Scratches?'

He took one small grubby hand, turned it over, and Angel saw the scratches on the chubby wrist and arm. They looked red and angry. 'Hold on...' He pulled his mobile phone out and glanced at the message on the screen. 'Mark Lomas.'

Recognising the name of a man whom she had exchanged the odd good morning with during the week, Angel felt a stab of resentment that Alex should consider taking a message from a guest a priority at such a moment.

He gave a nod of satisfaction as he slid the phone back into his breast pocket. 'Mark should be there by the time you get to the bungalow.'

'Why?'

He felt a stab of anxiety as he studied her face more closely. Angel remained dramatically pale, her skin the colour of wax, her eyes dark emerald bruises nestled among the pallor.

He wanted to urge her to sit down before she fell down and give him Jasmine, but he knew it would be a futile exercise. Angel was holding on to her daughter as if she would never let go and would definitely resist any efforts he made to lighten her burden.

His jaw tightened—a burden she had been carrying alone for too long because of him.

'I thought you might have spoken the other night. He's in the next bungalow to you. A doctor…?'

'I might have.'

'He's coordinating the medical backup on the charity race,' he explained, referring to the charity Ironman event that was currently causing a buzz in the hotel.

'I sent a text when I found Jasmine and explained the situation. I thought he could take a look at her, clean up those scratches and do what is necessary. He asked if her tetanus is up to date. I didn't know.' His jaw clenched as he looked away. He would know…next time. Not that he wanted there to be a next time, but there would be other times…other crises, and he would have the knowledge a father should.

'She's covered.' She kissed her daughter's tear-stained cheek and realised that she herself probably didn't look any better.

'Shall I take her?' Nico offered.

Angel shook her head and held on to her baby. Life would be so much simpler if she could never let go, could keep her safe from the big bad world for ever. She heard people say that the hardest part of parenting was letting go, but it wasn't until now that she knew what that really meant.

With Nico by her side she walked away from Alex, thinking that it felt wrong to be doing so. What was so important that he couldn't come with them? She wanted to tell him he should be with them but didn't—he ought to know.

They reached the bungalow two minutes ahead of the doctor, who arrived apologising for his tardiness, wearing shorts and little else but a reassuring air of calm competence.

As Alex had predicted he cleaned the scratches, applied some antiseptic and managed to distract Jasmine while he gave her a shot of broad-spectrum antibiotic. He advised Angel to keep an eye on the scratches as cats' scratches, he explained, were more prone to infection than dogs', and told her to contact him if she had any concerns at all.

Angel had managed to adopt Alex's what-an-adventure-you've-had tack with Jasmine, who was displaying a youthful resilience that Angel envied. After having a bath and a sandwich or two from the tray that had arrived at the room Jasmine had barely been able to keep her eyes open. She was asleep before her head hit the pillow.

Going back to the living room, Angel persuaded a reluctant Nico that he didn't need to stay.

'Are you sure?'

'Totally. I'm just going to take a shower and head for bed myself.'

Finally alone, she checked on Jasmine before she padded over to the shower, leaving all the interconnecting doors open so that she would hear should Jasmine wake. She didn't, of course, but Angel spent more time stepping out wet to check for some imaginary sound than she did washing off the sand and grime.

Not bothering to dry her hair, she squeezed out the excess water and brushed it back off her face with her fingers. It fell in a heavy rope-like twist down her back. Pulling on the silk robe hung behind the door, she belted it and hurried back to Jasmine's room to double check, her heart suddenly pumping double-time as she stepped into the room.

Angel felt the panic leave her with a soft whoosh. Her daughter hadn't moved since she'd last looked, which was probably all of five minutes ago. It wasn't as if she had expected Jas to have vanished.... Her knees shook a little as she made an effort to gather her composure.

Walking back into the adjoining room, she started on hearing a knock on the door. It wouldn't be Alex—he wouldn't have knocked and maybe he wouldn't even come. Nico would have reported that they were all right. Why should he come?

Because I want him to!

Pull yourself together, Angel. Since when did you need a shoulder to cry on? Impatient with herself, she went to the door where a smiling maid in the dark blue hotel uniform stood holding a tray.

'The coffee you ordered, miss.'

Did I?

Angel thanked the girl and didn't pursue the forgetfulness. Amnesia registered pretty low down in the day's events, so Angel asked the maid to put the tray down on the coffee table.

Two reviving cups later Angel was standing on the veranda when she saw him.

She watched him approach, shading her eyes against the glare of the setting sun that threw pink fingers of light across the silver water. He was too far away for her to make out anything, but his silhouette and his long-legged elegant stride were unmistakable, the way he moved as distinctive as a fingerprint.

Post-caffeine hit she was thinking more clearly, and as she squared her shoulders she knew what he had come to say. Not the words precisely, but definitely the sentiment of the things he would not say in front of Jasmine. And she wasn't going to fight him on it. He was here to blame her, call her a terrible mother and he was right. She had no defence against the truth any more than she had defence left against her feelings for him.

She loved him.

It had taken her long enough to work it out. When it came to personal relationships she was a blank page. Unlike her, Alex knew about relationships. He'd been in love enough to get married, enough to be devastated when he lost the love of his life, enough to sleep with the first... Well, maybe not the first woman he met but probably the first one who had begged him to take her to bed.

One night of escaping his nightmares, seeking oblivion in mindless sex and who could blame him? It would take a harsh critic to judge him for that but he had clearly judged himself and struggled to wipe the shameful memory from his mind. Marry him.... Yeah, sure, they really were the foundations of a great relationship!

Obviously she knew that Alex was physically attracted to her, and his devotion to Jasmine was not in question.

But Angel knew that wasn't enough. Easy thing to say now when she was clear headed, but in his presence—and certainly in his arms—she rarely felt that way.

Then keep out of his arms, Angel!

Alex slowed and paused, one hand on the wooden balustrade, coming to a dead halt at the bottom of the shallow flight of wooden steps. The sight of her standing there stole his breath away, the same way she had stolen his heart.

She had every reason to hate him but her generous heart had let him in. She'd given him a second chance, and of course he understood she was wary of trusting him, but if it took him the rest of his life he would convince her.

Her heart started to thud heavily, the echo loud in her ears as he mounted the steps. She could feel the acid taste of self-recrimination in her mouth. He could not possibly blame her more than she did herself.

And she'd lectured him on the responsibilities of being a parent! It was on her watch that this had happened. It didn't matter how many times she went over it in her head, she still couldn't figure out how it had happened; her attention had only been distracted for a moment—and that had been enough.

The blue pedal pushers and white shirt were gone. She now wore a black silk kimono emblazoned with humming birds that ended midcalf to reveal her endless golden legs. His eyes slid hungrily down her body, over the soft, sinuous, sexy curves, and he swallowed, losing his focus as his body surged lustfully. When his gaze settled back on her face her slicked-back hair revealed her face as a perfect oval.

'Is she asleep?'

Angel nodded, lifted her chin and launched into a preemptive apology. 'I know it was my fault, totally and—'

He touched a finger to her lips. 'You talk so much rubbish.'

Angel had steeled herself for his accusations; she was totally prepared for his anger. She could have taken that, but what she had no protection from was the incredible tenderness in his face, the concern in his blue eyes and the caressing warmth in his vibrant voice as he took her by the shoulders and looked down into her face, not judging her but offering her support.

'Sorry I was so late but I wanted to be there when the police arrived and explain the situation. And I didn't want to leave until we'd checked the perimeter fence for holes, a classic case of after the horse has bolted, I know, but—' He stopped. 'Here's me babbling and you…you poor baby, you look like hell.'

Her lip quivered. 'I… For God's sake, don't be nice to me, Alex!'

Ignoring her plea, he slid his arms slid around her back. 'Come here.'

Her face crumpled and she stepped into him, feeling his arms close around her as the tears began to flow.

She almost choked on her shame and sense of inadequacy as she struggled to communicate her guilt to him. 'It was all my fault. I—'

'Don't be ridiculous,' he condemned roughly as he passed a hand over her slick wet hair. 'You can't watch a child every second. Even I know that.'

Her teary face lifted. 'I can and I will,' she flashed fiercely, fighting against every instinct she had as she pulled away, dabbing her wet face with her hands and sniffing.

Who'd have thought a sniff could be sexy…? Not Alex,

but with Angel there had always been a steep learning curve. Fighting against the temptation to haul her back into his arms, he took a couple deep breaths to conquer and beat the dangerous need into submission. She was shattered physically and emotionally; this was not the time.

'So what did Mark say? You didn't mind me calling him? I just thought it would be less traumatic than a trip to the hospital. I explained about her hip.'

'He was great with her and she's fine. Just superficial scratches and she was very thirsty. He gave her an antibiotic jab to be on the safe side.' Angel's eyes darkened as she shuddered and whispered, 'When I think what could have happened.'

'Don't!'

She closed her mouth over the smart 'easy for you to say' retort, realising with a stab of remorse that it wasn't easy for him. If she still needed it she'd had ample proof today that Alex loved his daughter deeply. Today he had been a rock.

'It is a totally pointless exercise to torture yourself this way.'

She exhaled a long shuddering sigh. 'You're right.'

Some of the gravity left his face as he gave a crooked half smile. 'I am?'

She didn't smile back. 'I don't know how I'll ever thank you for what you did today.'

Alex shook his head, embarrassed by her shining-eyed gratitude. He did not want her gratitude—he wanted her. 'There is nothing to thank me for.'

Her green eyes widened in protest. 'If you hadn't found her before it got dark it could have been hours before she was discovered and anything could have happened.' There were a lot worse things out there than kittens.

He touched her chin, drawing her face round to his as his fingers moved to frame the side of her face. 'You weren't going to do that, remember...?' She nodded, her throat too thick with emotion to speak. 'I was only doing what a dad is meant to and, let's face it,' he added bleakly, 'I have some time to make up for.'

The regret in his voice brought a lump to her throat. No matter what pain it cost her it was worth it for Jasmine to have her father in her life.

'Can I see her?'

Her reply was husked with emotion. 'Of course. You don't have to ask.'

'Since when?'

She gave an uncomfortable half shrug. 'I know I've been defensive and suspicious. It's hard for me to—'

He filled in the blank. *Trust.* And he had played a big part in any trust issues Angel might have.

A strange expression flickered across his face. Taking her totally by surprise, he leaned down and kissed her mouth softly. 'I'll hold you to that promise.'

Balling her hand into a fist to stop it going to her trembling lips, she went with him, but paused at the bedroom door and let him go inside alone.

When he dragged himself away from the sleeping child—it still seemed a total stunning miracle that he had had anything to do with her creation—Alex found Angel outside on the veranda. Night had fallen and the white fairy lights wrapped around the branches in the trees had sparked into life, their glow lending the scene a twinkling other-worldly quality.

'It's a beautiful evening....'

Angel turned and she looked so magnificent that for

a moment he couldn't breathe. He stopped midsentence and, loosing a low growl of frustration, he dragged a frustrated hand through his hair.

'This is ridiculous!' His dark brows drew together in a straight, uncompromising line above his hawkish, masterful nose. 'I have so much to say and I'm discussing the weather with you, as if we've just met in the street!'

From where she was standing Angel could feel the waves of emotion rolling off him. She shook her head urgently. 'No, Alex!' She knew what he was going to say—today could only have convinced him more that his duty was to marry her. Everyone thought she was cool and capable and it was an opinion she liked to encourage. Sometimes even she fell for the act, but today had outed her as a spineless, needy wimp who, when the going got tough, fell apart.

'I can't marry you, Alex.'

Aware of how fragile she was, he struggled to control his impatience but he knew it was a battle he was losing.

Pale but composed now, she took a step backwards, widening the gap between them, but not the growing tension. As she continued to hold his gaze she explained the situation in a distant expressionless voice.

'Marriage,' she explained carefully, 'isn't meant to be a penance.'

His eyes darkened with outrage at the suggestion. He started forward and then stopped himself. 'You think marriage to me would be a penance?'

'Oh, God, no!' She took a deep breath and waited for the urgent need to walk into his arms to pass. 'Marriage to you would be...' She stopped, lowered her gaze, thinking, *Too little too late, Angel.*

Way too late. She had been standing there, not wearing

her heart on her sleeve, but instead painted like a neon sign across her face!

Still, she mused darkly, she was not telling him anything he didn't already know.

She made herself meet his eyes. 'I know you think it's your duty to marry me.' Feeling the pressure of a future without Alex, a future where she waved goodbye as he drove off with Jasmine for the weekend pressing in on her, heavy and dark, she struggled to maintain eye contact as she told him bluntly. 'I'm not what you need.'

'What I need!' he grated through clenched teeth before swearing in several languages. To hell with this not being the right time, to hell with her being fragile. He had to challenge her blind, wilful stupidity. 'You know nothing, Angel Urquart, but I do. I know that you love me, so why the hell don't you stop putting us both through hell and admit it?'

'Love has got nothing to do with it,' she flared back. 'And don't you dare yell at me. And even if it did...' She shook her head and said firmly, 'There are very good reasons why I can't marry you.'

'Name one,' he challenged, looking unimpressed.

'Well, you don't love me.' Hard words to say without sounding terribly vulnerable and needy but Angel liked to think she pulled it off. 'You don't even like me most of the time....' Taking a moment to flick the damp tail of her hair over one shoulder, she left ample room for him to jump in, but he didn't. He just stood there being unhelpful and looking so gorgeous that she wanted to weep.

'You make me laugh, when you're not making me yell.'

She slung him a reproachful look. Did he have any idea how hard this was for her? 'You think that you should marry me because of Jasmine. I know you mean well…!'

His lips curled in dismissive scorn. 'I am not some misguided do-gooder!' He took a purposeful step towards her. 'I am a man who wants you, and I intend to have you….'

This outrageously arrogant pronouncement should have made her do many things: laugh scornfully, realise what a lucky escape she'd had, but no. Where on that list of responses came a surge of heavy, hot, toe-curling excitement?

His confidence was total, impregnable. The gleam in his dark eyes as they looked down into her face was hungry.

The urge to melt into him, to lift her face to receive the kiss she could almost taste, was so compelling that resisting it drew a tiny moan from her lips. His silence seemed to be willing her to make that move.

'You know you want me, so why are you fighting it?'

'Yes, I want you.'

The admission upped the tension several more notches. His eyes glowed an incandescent, dizzying blue. The combustible quality that was always there just beneath the surface was no longer buried beneath a veneer of sophistication but right there in her face.

'But you're not talking about wanting, you're talking about marriage. I can't marry you, Alex.'

'I keep hearing that—'

She was unable to retreat any more as the back of her legs had made contact with the small rail that ran around the veranda. She held up her hand, more in hope than any real expectation it would stop his advance, and if he touched her she'd…!

'I can't marry you,' she blurted, 'because I can't have

any more children.' His reaction to this information was hard to read because he didn't display any reaction at all.

She had been quiet too when they'd told her the details. She'd thought the overstretched professionals had been relieved when she hadn't broken down, and they had spoken of her healthy attitude.

'Do you understand what I'm saying?'

He tilted his head to one side and surveyed her through narrowed eyes. He didn't buy her supernatural composure for one second. He could feel the pain she was struggling to hide as sharply as if it had been his own. He fought the urge to haul her into his arms and tell her everything was going to be all right. He needed facts.

'How about you tell me what you're saying?'

She responded to the quiet request with a minimal shrug. 'I told you that I needed a Caesarean when Jas was born.' He nodded. 'I might have implied that it was straightforward.'

He hefted out a deep sigh. 'And it wasn't.'

Her shadowed gaze flickered upwards. Remote was the word that came to mind when she tried to read his expression. 'I lost a lot of blood,' she admitted. 'And, well, technical stuff aside, the long and short of it is the chances of me conceiving again are pretty remote.'

He heard her out in silence, his expression growing colder the longer she spoke. 'You could have died— something that slipped your mind, I suppose.'

She was not surprised he was angry. 'Childbirth is very safe these days and my life was never in any real danger. It's not something I think about too often. I have Jasmine, I don't need... It's a closed chapter for me and I didn't see how it could affect us. I mean, how was I to know that you were so ridiculously old-fashioned? I wasn't expecting you to propose.'

'I really don't see… If what you're saying is true…'

Her spine stiffened. 'If!' she ground out tautly. 'Why would I lie?' Did he think she got a kick out of revealing intimate medical details?

'Get down off that high horse, Angel. I'm just trying to make sense of you taking the contraceptive pill unless you were just saying…'

'Oh… I am on the pill, the doctors advised it. Although the chances of me getting pregnant are pretty much the same as winning the lottery, it still is technically possible.' With further tests he had said he could be more precise but Angel, who had had enough of being poked and prodded, had refused.

'Why am I getting the impression that you are giving me only half the story?'

The consultant's final comments came back to her.

'I cannot emphasise how important it would be for you to seek medical advice immediately, *immediately*, Miss Urquart should you even suspect you might be pregnant.'

'If I did by some miracle get pregnant I'd need to be monitored.'

Under his tan Alex paled. 'By that you mean it would be dangerous for you to have a baby…as in life-threateningly dangerous?'

'That,' she said, dodging his gaze, 'is an overstatement. If it did happen—'

'No!'

She gulped at his tone. 'Yes, I know, like I said, the likelihood of it happening is a bit like winning the lottery.'

'I mean you will not try.' His hands landed on her shoulders and she could feel the tremors running through him. 'Not now, not ever, will you put your life at risk that way.' It would be just like Angel to pull some stupid stunt like that. 'Do you hear me? Ever!'

Hard not to hear him, not that he was yelling. His voice had dropped to a low bass rumble, the way she'd noticed it did when he was particularly annoyed, but there was nothing wrong with his projection.

His blazing blue eyes burnt into her as he groaned and slid his big hands down her back. She could feel his fingers, warm through the fabric, as they came to rest on her hips, his thumbs on the indent of her waist. 'I've only just found you again. Do you think I'd run the risk of losing you? It would be selfish—Jasmine needs her mother, she needs you.... I need you, Angel. There was a time when I thought about you as my weakness...now I know you are my strength.'

Tears of emotion filled her eyes, spilling like crystal drops down her cheeks. 'You need a woman who can give you everything. You need to wait. I know it might seem impossible now,' she told him gently, 'but one day you'll love someone the way you did Emma. Imagine how awful it would be if, when that time came, you were tied to me. You need love in a marriage, Alex, and you deserve it. And you deserve babies with that person. I've seen you with Jasmine. You'll want a family of your own one day and I can't give it you.'

'You stupid woman.'

She blinked.

'You really are a stupid woman!' The insult was delivered in a voice that held so much love that her eyes filled. 'You already have given me a family—you have given me Jasmine. You and Jasmine are all the family I want or need, my bolshy, belligerent, beautiful Angelina, my very own Angel. I love you.'

She swallowed and covered the bottom half of her face with her hands. 'But I'm not…'

'You're not second best.'

Her eyes widened at this display of perception. 'I loved Emma,' he agreed quietly. 'And I was glad I was there for her, but we barely had a relationship before I became her carer. We were never really a couple. I think if things had been different we could have been happy but you… you…' He touched her cheek, wonder shining in the incandescent blue of his eyes as he bent to kiss her lips. 'You are my soulmate.'

Joy exploded through her. 'I love you, Alex.'

At the words the tension drained from him and he smiled. Taking her hand, holding her eyes with his, he placed it palm flat against his chest, against the beat of his heart. 'If life took you away from me, it would break. I would break,' he told her in a voice thick and throbbing with the strength of his emotions.

Tears of joy seeping from her eyes, Angel took his hand and kissed the palm lovingly while she looked up at him, vision blurred with tears of joy. 'I won't let you break, Alex,' she promised huskily.

He brushed the tears lovingly away from her face with his thumb. 'Marry me, my Angel.'

'What are you doing tomorrow?'

His grin blazed as he bent his head to claim her lips. 'Becoming the luckiest man on the planet!'

EPILOGUE

'DADDY!'

It was a title he never tired of hearing. 'Yes, Miss Jasmine?'

'Can we go now?'

'Homework done?'

Jumping up and down impatiently, Jasmine nodded vigorously. 'I've been ready for hours.'

Alex shrugged. 'Don't look at me—so have I. We're waiting for your mother. Blame her.'

'Blame me for what this time?' Angel asked, walking into the room.

'Keeping us waiting,' Jasmine supplied.

'What's the hurry? The snow isn't going to melt anytime soon.' It had been one of the longest winters on record.

'It might! The sun is shining and I want to show Daddy my snowman. He doesn't believe it's taller than him... nearly taller than him.'

'Well, I'm sorry, but getting this one ready is not a five-minute job.' Angel looked down at the bundle in her arms who was barely visible beneath the layers he was cocooned in. His eyes were closed; his dark lashes lay like a fan across his cheeks. Looking at him it was hard to believe he had kept them awake half the night.

Amazing to think now that when she'd first discovered she was pregnant she had really thought it might split them apart. It was the thing they had both agreed on: no more children. But it had happened anyway, her little miracle, and in the end it had drawn them closer than ever.

She had been more worried about telling Alex than about the pregnancy itself, and she would never forget the look on his face when she had told him. She had never thought to see her big, bold, impossibly brave husband scared, but he had been. She never saw that look again, but she knew the fear was there and the memory of the terror in his eyes would stay with her for ever. Now though, when she thought of it, she was able to see it beside the expression on his face when he had held his newborn son for the first time.

But Alex had been there for her every step of the way. She didn't think she could have made it through those months with her sanity intact; his wildly overprotective instincts had been in overdrive.

But if ever she became impatient with him when he wrapped her in cotton wool, Angel had reminded herself of that look.

Appearing at her elbow, Alex twitched aside a fold of blue blanket to reveal his son's face. 'His first trip out.'

'Are you sure he'll be warm enough?'

Alex's rich warm laughter rang out. 'In that lot he's more likely to suffer heat exhaustion.'

It still didn't seem real to Alex that he had a son, and, while he loved little Theo more than life itself, the pregnancy itself had been the worst months of his entire life.

The fear of losing Angel had never left him for a single instant. He had felt as though he were walking around with a stone in his chest. He had tried to hide his fears, for Jasmine's sake he had struggled to maintain an illusion at least of a normal family life, but the strain had been immense.

Angel had been amazing. She had sailed through the pregnancy serenely; despite two stays in hospital and intense monitoring she had never once complained.

His wife was truly amazing. He kissed her, a long and lingering kiss that brought a flush to her lovely cheeks.

'What was that for?'

'A man has to take what he can when he can.'

The reminder of the previous afternoon when they had not used the time to catch up with lost sleep but with lost lovemaking brought a deepened flush to her cheeks and a sparkle to her eyes.

'Can I push Theo?' Jasmine asked. 'I'll be very, *very* careful.'

'We'll take turns,' Alex decided as he took control of the pram and zipped up the protective covering, then in a soft aside to his wife added, 'My turn on top later, I think.'

'Marriage is all about give and take.'

And she had married a man who gave a whole lot more than he ever took!

* * * * *

A SINFUL
SEDUCTION

BY
ELIZABETH LANE

Elizabeth Lane has lived and traveled in many parts of the world, including Europe, Latin America and the Far East, but her heart remains in the American West, where she was born and raised. Her idea of heaven is hiking a mountain trail on a clear autumn day. She also enjoys music, animals and dancing. You can learn more about Elizabeth by visiting her website, www.elizabethlaneauthor.com.

For Pat, my wonderful sister
who loves Africa

One

San Francisco, California, February 11

The headline on Page 2 slammed Cal Jeffords in the face.

Two Years Later
Exec's Widow, Foundation Cash
Are Both Still Missing

Swearing like a longshoreman, Cal crumpled the morning paper in his fist. The last thing he needed was a reminder that today was the second anniversary of his best friend and business partner's suicide. And he didn't need that grainy file photo to help him remember Nick and his wife, Megan, with her movie-star beauty, her designer clothes, her multimillion-dollar showplace of a home and her appalling lack of human decency that let her steal from a charity and then leave her husband to carry the blame.

With a grunt of frustration, he crammed the newspaper into the waste basket.

He had no doubt that the whole ugly mess was Megan's fault. But the questions that still haunted him two years later were *how* and *why?* Had Megan coerced Nick into complying? Had the demands of their lavish lifestyle driven Nick Rafferty to embezzle millions from J-COR's charity foundation? Or had Megan embezzled the money herself and forced her husband to take the blame? She'd had plenty of opportunities to siphon off the cash her fundraisers brought in. He'd even found evidence that she had.

But Cal would never know for sure. The day after the scandal went public, he'd found Nick slumped over his desk, his hand still clutching the pistol that had ended his life. After the private funeral, Megan had vanished. The stolen money, meant to ease the suffering of third-world refugees, was never recovered.

It didn't take a genius to make the connection.

Too restless to sit, Cal unfolded his athletic frame and prowled to the window that spanned the outer wall. His office, on the twenty-eighth floor of the J-COR building, commanded a sweeping view of the Bay and the bridge that spanned the choppy, gray water. Beyond the Golden Gate, the stormy Pacific stretched as far as the eye could see.

Megan was out there somewhere. Cal could feel it, like a sickness in his bones. He could picture her in some faraway land, living like a maharani on the millions stolen from his foundation.

It wasn't so much the missing cash itself that troubled him—although the loss had cut into the foundation's resources. It was the sheer crassness of taking money earmarked for food, clean water and medical treatment in places rife with human misery. That Megan hadn't seen fit to make amends at any point after her husband's death made the crime even more despicable.

She could have returned the money, no questions asked. Even if she was innocent, as she'd claimed to be, she could have stayed around to help him locate it. Instead, she'd simply run, further cementing Cal's certainty of her guilt. She wouldn't have run if she didn't have something to hide. And the woman was damned good at hiding her trail. Not one of the investigators he'd hired had been able to track her down.

But Cal wasn't a man to give up. Someday he would find her. And when he did, one way or another, Megan Rafferty would pay.

"Mr. Jeffords."

Cal turned at the sound of his name. His receptionist stood in the office doorway. "Harlan Crandall's outside, asking to see you. Do you have time for him now, or should I schedule an appointment?"

"Send him in." Crandall was the latest in the string of private investigators Cal had hired to search for Megan. A short, balding man with an unassuming manner, he'd shown no more promise than the others. But now he'd come by unannounced, asking for an audience. Maybe he had something to report.

Cal seated himself as Crandall entered, wearing a rumpled brown suit and clutching a battered canvas briefcase.

"Sit down, Mr. Crandall." Cal motioned to the chair on the far side of the desk. "Do you have any news for me?"

"That depends." Crandall plopped the briefcase onto the desk, opened the flap and drew out a manila folder. "You hired me to look for Mrs. Rafferty. Do you happen to know her maiden name?"

"Of course, and so should you. It's Cardston. Megan Cardston."

Crandall nodded, adjusting his wire-rimmed glasses on his nose. "In that case, I may have something to tell you. My sources have tracked down a Megan Cardston who appears to fit the physical description of the woman you're looking for. She's working as a volunteer nurse for your foundation."

Cal's reflexes jerked. "That's impossible," he growled. "It's got to be a coincidence—just another woman with the same name and body type."

"Maybe so. You can decide for yourself after you've looked over this documentation." Crandall thrust the folder across the desk.

Cal opened the folder. It contained several photocopied pages that looked like travel requests and personnel rosters. But what caught his eye was a single, blurry black-and-white photograph.

Staring at the image, he tried to picture Megan as he'd last seen her—long platinum hair sculpted into a twist, diamond earrings, flawless makeup. Even at her husband's funeral, she'd managed to look like a Hollywood screen goddess, except for her pain-shot eyes.

The woman in the photo appeared thinner and slightly older. She was wearing sunglasses and a khaki shirt. Her light brown hair was short and windblown, her face bare of makeup. There was nothing behind her but sky.

Cal studied the firm jawline, the aristocratic nose and ripe, sensual lips. He willed himself to ignore the quiver of certainty that passed through his body. Megan's face was seared into his memory. Even with her eyes hidden, the woman in the picture had the same look. And Megan, he recalled, had worked as a surgical nurse before marrying Nick. But was this image really the woman who'd eluded him for two long years? There was only one way to be sure.

"Where was this picture taken?" he demanded. "Where's this woman now?"

Crandall slid the briefcase off the desk and closed it with a snap and a single word.

"Africa."

Arusha, Tanzania, February 26

Megan gripped the birth-slicked infant and delivered a stinging fingertip blow to its tiny buttocks.

Nothing happened.

She slapped the baby harder, her lips moving in a wordless plea. There was a beat of silence, then, suddenly, a gasping wail, as beautiful as any sound she'd ever heard. Megan's knees slackened in relief. The delivery had been hellish, a breech birth coming after a long night of labor. That mother and baby were both alive could only be counted as a miracle.

Passing the baby to the young aide, she mopped her brow with the sleeve of her smock, then reached over to do the same for the baby's mother. The air was warm and sticky. Light from a single bulb flickered on whitewashed walls. Drawn by the glow, insects beat against the screened windows.

As Megan leaned over her, the woman's eyelids fluttered open. *"Asante sana,"* she whispered in Swahili, the lingua franca of East Africa. *Thank you.*

"Karibu sana." Megan's deft hands wound a cotton string, knotted it tight and severed the cord. With luck, this baby would grow up healthy, spared the swollen belly and scarecrow limbs of the children she'd labored so desperately to save in Darfur, the most brutally ravaged region of Sudan, where a cruel dictator had used his mercenaries to decimate the African tribal population.

Megan had spent the past eleven months working with the J-COR Foundation's medical branch in the Sudanese refugee camps. Two weeks ago, on the brink of physical and emotional collapse, she'd been ordered to a less taxing post for recovery. Compared with the camps, this clinic, on the ramshackle fringe of a pleasant Tanzanian town, was a luxury resort.

But she would go back as soon as she was strong enough. She'd spent too many years feeling purposeless and adrift. Now that she'd found focus in her life, she was determined to finally make the most of her skills and training. She should be where she was needed most. And she was sorely needed in Darfur.

By the time the afterbirth came, the aide had sponged the baby boy clean and swaddled him in cotton flannel. The mother's eager hands reached out to draw him against her breast. Megan took a moment to raise the sheet and check the gauze packing. So far, everything looked all right. She stripped off her smock and her latex gloves. "I'm going to get some rest," she told the aide. "Watch her. Too much blood, you come and wake me."

The young African nurse-in-training nodded. She could be counted on to do her job.

Not until she was soaping her hands at the outside faucet did Megan realize how weary she was. It was as if the last of her strength had trickled down her legs and drained into the hard-packed earth. Straightening, she massaged her lower back with her fingers.

Beyond the clinic's corrugated roof, the moon glimmered like a lost shilling through the purple crown of a flowering jacaranda. Its low angle told her the time was well past midnight, with precious few hours left for sleep. All too soon, first light would trigger a cacophony of bird calls, signaling the start of a new day. At least she'd ended the day well—with a successful delivery and a healthy new life. The sense of accomplishment was strong.

Tired as she was, Megan knew she had no right to complain. This was the life she'd chosen. By now her old life—the clothes and jewelry, the cars, the house, the charity events she'd hosted to raise money for Nick and Cal's foundation—seemed little more than a dream. A dream that had ended with a headline and a gunshot.

She'd tried not to dwell on that nightmare week. But one image was chiseled into her memory—Cal's stricken face, the look of cold contempt in his glacial gray eyes, and the final words he'd spoken to her.

"You're going to answer for this, Megan. I'll hold you accountable and make you pay if it's the last thing I do."

Megan hadn't embezzled a cent, hadn't even known about the missing money till the scandal had surfaced. But Cal would never believe that. He'd trusted Nick to the very last.

Seeing Cal's look and hearing his words, Megan had realized she had no recourse except to run far and fast, to someplace where Cal would never find her.

That, or be trapped with no way to save her own soul.

But all that was in the past, she reminded herself as she flexed her aching shoulders and mounted the porch of the brick bungalow that served as quarters for the volunteers. She was a different person now, with a life that gave her the deepest satisfaction she had ever known.

If only she could put an end to the nightmares....

As the sleek Gulfstream jet skimmed the Horn of Africa, Cal reopened the folder Harlan Crandall had given him. Clever fellow, that Crandall. He alone had thought to look in the last place Megan would logically choose to hide—the volunteer ranks of the very foundation she had robbed.

The photocopied paperwork gave him a summary of her postings—Zimbabwe, Somalia and, for most of the past year, Sudan. Megan had taken the roughest assignments in the program—evidently by her own choice. What was she thinking? And if the woman in the photo was really Nick's glamorous widow, what in hell's name had she done with the money? She'd stolen enough to live in luxury for decades. Luxury even more ostentatious than the lifestyle her husband had given her.

Cal couldn't repress a sigh as he thought of the expensive trappings Nick had lavished on his wife. He'd always wanted her to have nothing but the best. His taste might have been over-the-top, but Cal had always been certain that Nick's intentions were good, just as they had been back when the two had become friends in high school.

They'd graduated from the same college, Cal with an engineering degree and Nick with a marketing major. When Cal had come up with a design for a lightweight modular shelter that could be erected swiftly in the wake of a natural disaster or used at construction and recreation sites, it had made sense for the two friends to go into business together. J-COR had made them both wealthy. But they'd agreed that money wasn't enough. After providing shelters for stricken people around the world, it had been Cal's idea to set up a foundation. He'd handled the logistics end. Nick had managed the finances and fund-raising.

Within a few years the foundation had expanded to include food and medical services. By then Nick was married to Megan, a nurse he'd met at a fund-raiser. Cal had been best man at their wedding. But even then he hadn't quite trusted her. She was too beautiful. Too gracious.

Too private. Beneath that polished surface he'd glimpsed something elusive; something hidden.

Her cool distance was a striking contrast to Nick's natural openness and warmth—particularly given the way Nick clearly doted on her. He had showered his bride with gifts—a multimillion-dollar house, a Ferrari, a diamond-and-emerald necklace and more. Megan had responded by using her new position in society to supposedly "help" the foundation. The charity events they'd hosted for wealthy donors at their home had raised generous amounts for the foundation. But of course, those events had done much more to line Megan's pockets. Three years later, after a routine tax audit, the whole house of cards had come tumbling down. The rest of the story was tabloid fodder.

Cal studied the photograph, which looked as if it had been snapped at a distance and enlarged for his benefit. Megan—if that's who it really was—may not have even known it was being taken. She was gazing to her left, the light glinting on her sunglasses—expensive sunglasses. Cal noticed the side logo for the first time. He remembered her wearing that brand, maybe that very pair. His mouth tightened as the certainty slid into place. Megan hadn't quite abandoned her high-end tastes.

It was a piece of luck that she'd been sent to Arusha. Finding her in Sudan could have involved a grueling search. But Arusha, a bustling tourist and safari center, had its own international airport. The company jet was headed there now, and he knew how to find the clinic. He'd been there before. If he so chose, he could round her up with the help of some hired muscle and have her on the plane within a couple of hours.

And then what? Tempting as the idea was, Cal knew it wasn't practical to kidnap her in a foreign country without a legal warrant. Besides, would it do any good if he could?

Megan was smart. She'd know that despite her signature on the checks that had never made it to the foundation's coffers, he had no solid proof she'd kept the money. If she stuck to her original story, that she'd had no knowledge of the theft and knew nothing about the missing funds, he'd be nowhere.

He didn't have grounds or authority to arrest her; and it wasn't in him to threaten her with physical harm. His only hope of getting at the truth, Cal realized, was to win her trust. He wasn't optimistic enough to think he could make her confess. She was too smart to openly admit to her crimes. But if he got close to her, she might let something slip—drop a tiny clue, innocent on its own, that could lead Crandall to the location of the hidden accounts.

That could take time. But he hadn't come this far to go home without answers. If that meant wining and dining the lady and telling her a few pretty lies, so be it.

The slight dip in the angle of the cabin told him the plane was starting its descent. If the weather was clear, he might get a look at the massive cone of Kilimanjaro. But that was not to be. Clouds were gathering off the right wing, hiding the view of the fabled mountain. Lightning chained across the distant sky. The seasonal rains had begun. If this kept up, which it likely would, they'd be landing in an African downpour.

Fastening his seat belt, Cal settled back to watch the storm approach. The plane shuddered as lightning snaked over its metal skin. Rain spattered the windows, the sound of it recalling another time, a rainy night three years ago in San Francisco.

It had been the night of the company Christmas party, held downtown at the Hilton. At about eleven o'clock Cal had bumped into Megan coming out of the hallway that led to the restrooms. Her face was white, her mouth damp, as if she'd just splashed it with water. Cal had stopped to ask if she was all right.

She'd laughed. "I'm fine, Cal. Just a little bit…pregnant."

"Can I get you anything?" he'd asked, surprised that Nick hadn't told him.

"No, thanks. Since Nick has to stay, I'm going to have him call me a cab. No more late-night parties for this girl."

She'd hurried away, leaving Cal to reflect that in all the time he'd known her, this was the first time he'd seen Megan look truly happy.

Was she happy now? He tried to picture her working in a refugee camp—the heat, the flies, the poverty, the sickness.… What was she doing here? What had she done with the money? The questions tormented him—and only one person could give him the answers.

Megan sank onto a bench outside the clinic, sheltered from the rain by the overhanging roof. The day had been hectic, as usual. The new mother and her baby were gone, carted off by her womenfolk early that morning. Her departure had been followed by a flood of patients with ailments ranging from impetigo to malaria. Megan had even assisted while the resident Tanzanian doctor stitched up and vaccinated a boy who'd been foolish enough to tease a young baboon.

Now it was twilight and the clinic was closed. The doctor and the aide had gone home to their families in town. Megan was alone in the walled compound that included the clinic building, a generator and washhouse, a lavatory and a two-room bungalow with a kitchen for volunteers like her. The utilitarian brick structures were softened by the flowering shrubs and trees that flourished in Arusha's rich volcanic soil. The tulip tree that shaded the clinic had ended its blooming cycle. Rain washed the fallen petals in a crimson cascade off the eave, like tears of blood.

Closing her eyes, Megan inhaled the sweet dampness. She'd yearned for rain in the parched Sudan, where the dusty air was rank with the odors of human misery. Going back wouldn't be easy. But the need was too great for her not to return. The need of the refugees for care and treatment—and her own need to make a difference.

She was about to get up and brave the downpour when she heard the clang of the gate bell—an improvised iron cowbell on a chain. Rising, she hesitated. If someone had an emergency she could hardly turn them away. But she was here alone. Outside that gate there could be thugs intent on breaking into the clinic for drugs, cash or mischief.

The bell jangled again. Megan sprinted through the rain to the bungalow, found the .38 Smith & Wesson she kept under her pillow and thrust it into the pocket of her loose khakis. Grabbing a plastic poncho from its hook by the door, she tossed it over her head as she hurried toward the sheet-iron gate. The key was in the rusty padlock that anchored the chain between the gate's welded handles.

"Jina lako nani?" she demanded in her phrase-book Swahili. She'd asked for the person's name, which was the best she could manage.

There was a beat of silence. Then a gravely, masculine voice rang through the rainy darkness. "Megan? Is that you?"

Megan's knees crumpled like wet sand. She sagged against the gate, her cold hands fumbling with the key. Cal's was the last voice she wanted to hear. But hiding from him would only make her look like a fool.

"Megan?" His voice had taken on a more strident tone, demanding an answer. But her throat was too tight to speak. She should have known that Cal wouldn't give up looking until he found her—even if he had to travel half-way around the world.

The lock fell open, allowing the heavy chain to slide free. Megan stepped back as the gate swung inward and Cal strode into the courtyard. Dressed in a tan Burberry raincoat, he seemed even taller than she remembered, his gray eyes even colder behind the rain that dripped off the brim of his hat.

She knew what he wanted. After two years, Cal was still looking for answers. Now that he'd found her, he would hammer her mercilessly with questions about Nick's death and the whereabouts of the stolen money.

But she had no answers to give him.

How could she persuade Cal Jeffords to see the truth and leave her in peace?

Two

Cal's eyes took in the cheap plastic poncho and the tired face beneath the hood. Something in his chest jerked tight. It was Megan, all right. But not the Megan he remembered.

"Hello, Cal." Her voice was rich and husky. "I see you haven't changed much."

"But you have." He turned and fastened the gate behind him. "Aren't you at least going to invite me out of the rain?"

She glanced toward the bungalow. "I can make you some coffee. But there's not much else. I haven't had time to shop…" Her voice trailed off as she led him through the downpour to the sheltered porch. Rain clattered on the corrugated tin roof above their heads.

"Actually I have a taxi waiting outside," he said. "I was hoping I could take you to dinner at the hotel."

Her eyes widened. She seemed nervous, he thought.

But then, she had plenty to hide. "That's kind of you, but there's no one else here. I need to stay—"

He laid a hand on her shoulder. She quivered like a fawn at his touch but didn't try to pull away. "It's all right," he said. "I spoke with Dr. Musa on the phone. It's fine with him if you leave for a couple of hours. In fact, he said you could use a nice meal. His houseboy's on the way over now, to watch the place while we're gone."

"Well, since it's all arranged..." Her voice trailed off.

"Dr. Musa also mentioned that you're doing a great job here." That part was true, but Cal made a point of saying it to flatter her.

She shrugged, a slight motion. The old Megan would have lapped up the praise like a satisfied cat. This thin-drawn stranger seemed uncomfortable with it. "I've just finished cleaning up in the clinic. I'll need to wash and change." She managed a strained laugh. "These days it doesn't take long."

"Fine. I'll open the gate for the cab."

As Cal slogged back across the compound, he spared a moment to be grateful that he'd thought to bring a pair of waterproof hiking boots before his thoughts returned to his encounter with the woman he'd come to find. Meeting Megan tonight was like meeting her for the first time. He was puzzled and intrigued, but still determined to get to the bottom of the money question. If this new Megan tried to play on his sympathy—and she likely would—it wasn't going to work. So help him, whatever it took, he was going to nail her to the wall.

Minutes after the cab pulled up to the bungalow, Benjamin, Dr. Musa's strapping young servant, arrived. Megan emerged from her room wearing a white blouse, fresh khaki slacks and a black twill jacket. A corner of the folded plastic poncho stuck out of her beat-up brown

leather purse—Gucci, he noticed the brand. Some things
at least hadn't changed.

Giving Benjamin her pistol, she thanked him with a
smile and a few words. Cal lifted a side of his raincoat like
a wing to shelter her as they descended the porch steps
and climbed into the cab. Her face was damp, her hair
finger-combed. She hadn't taken more than ten minutes
to freshen up and change, but it had worked. She looked
damned classy.

"When did you get in?" she asked him, making small
talk.

"Plane landed a couple of hours ago. I registered at the
Arusha Hotel, cleaned up and headed for the clinic."

She'd been looking straight ahead, but now she turned
toward him with a frown. "Is something wrong, Cal? A
crisis back home?"

He managed a wry laugh. "Not that I know of. I could
say I was just passing through and decided to stop by..."
He saw the flash of skepticism in her caramel-colored eyes.
"But you wouldn't believe me, would you?"

"No." A smile tugged a corner of her luscious mouth.
The sort of mouth made for kissing. Though he had never
warmed to her personally, he'd never denied that she was
an attractive and desirable woman. When was the last time
she'd been kissed? he caught himself wondering. But never
mind that. He was here for just one reason. Although, if
getting to the truth involved kissing her, he wouldn't complain.

"I know you better than that, Cal. I left you with a lot of
questions. But if you're here to charm the answers out of
me, you could've saved yourself a trip. Nothing's changed.
I don't know anything about where you could find the
money. I'm assuming Nick spent it—which, I suppose,
makes me guilty by association. But if you're looking for

a big stash under my mattress or in some Dubai bank account, all I can do is wish you luck."

It was like her to be direct, Cal thought. That trait, at least, hadn't changed. "Why don't we table that subject for now. I'm more interested in why you left and what you've been doing for the past two years."

"Of course you are." Something glimmered in her eyes before she glanced away. The cab's windshield wipers swished and thumped in the stillness. Rain streamed down the windows. "For the price of a good steak, I suppose I can come up with a few good stories—entertaining, if nothing else."

"You never disappoint." Cal kept his voice as neutral as his comment. He had yet to pin down this new Megan. The inner steel she'd always possessed gleamed below a surface so fragile that he sensed she might shatter at a touch.

He knew she'd been sent here for rest and recovery. Nothing in the documents he'd seen explained why, but Dr. Musa, the tall, British-trained Chagga who ran the clinic, had expressed his concern about her health and state of mind to Cal over the phone. Cal needed to learn more. But right now, he was still taking in her presence.

He recalled the perfume she used to wear. The fancy French name of it eluded him, but he'd always found it mildly arousing. There was no trace of that scent now. If she smelled like anything at all, it was the medicinal soap used in the clinic. But strangely, her nearness in the cab was having the same effect on him as that perfume used to have back then.

Things were different now. Back in San Francisco she'd been his best friend's wife. Megan had been widowed for two years, and if there was anyone else in her life, there was no mention of it in Crandall's report. As long as the end justified the means, bedding her would be a long-denied pleasure. A little pillow talk could go a long way in loosening secrets.

If nothing else, it would be damned delicious fun.

Megan had spent little time outside the clinic since her arrival, so the remodeled nineteenth-century Arusha Hotel was new to her. Catering to wealthy tourists, it featured a lobby decorated in rich creams and browns with wing-back chairs and dark leather sofas, a bar and a restaurant with an international menu. Through the glass doors at the rear of the lobby, she glimpsed a large outdoor swimming pool, deserted tonight except for the rain that whipped the water to a froth.

Cal's big hand rested beneath her elbow as he ushered her toward the restaurant. Megan was of average height, but she felt small next to him. He was almost six-three, broad-shouldered and athletic, with a hard-charging manner that defied anyone to stand in his way. John Wayne in an Armani suit—that was how she would have described him back in the day. Even tonight, in travel-creased khakis, he looked imposing. John Wayne in the old movie *Hatari* came to mind—maybe because it was also the name of the hotel bar. She'd always found Nick's best friend over-bearing. But there'd been times when she'd wished her husband was more like him.

She wasn't surprised that he'd found her. Once he set his mind, Cal Jeffords could be as fiercely determined as a pit bull. And he'd come too far to leave without getting something to make his trip worthwhile. She'd told him the truth about the money. But he hadn't even pretended to believe her. Her signature on the donation checks she'd endorsed and given to Nick to deposit had convinced him she was guilty. Megan's instincts told her he had a plan to wear her down and make her pay. It would do her no good to fight. Cal was as much a force of nature as the storm raging outside. All she could do was wait for it to pass.

Sitting at their quiet table, she allowed him to order for her—filet mignon with mushrooms, fresh organic vegetables and a vintage Merlot. She could feel his gaze on her as the white-gloved waiter filled their wine goblets and set a basket of fresh hot bread between the lighted candlesticks.

"Eat up," Cal said, raising his glass. "You need to put some meat on those lovely bones."

Megan broke off a corner of the bread and nibbled at the crust. "I know I've lost weight. But it's painful to fill your plate when people around you are starving."

His slate gray eyes narrowed. "Is that what this is all about—this life change of yours? Guilt?"

She shrugged. "When I was married to Nick, I thought I had it all—the big house, the cars, the parties…" She took a sip of the wine. The sweet tingle burned down her throat. "When it all fell apart, and I learned that my lifestyle was literally taking food out of people's mouths, it sickened me. So, yes, you can call it guilt. Call it whatever you want. Does it matter? I don't regret the choice I made."

A muscle twitched in his cheek, betraying a surge of tightly reined anger. "The choice to run away without telling me? Without telling anybody?"

"Yes." She met his eyes with her own level gaze. "Nick left a god-awful mess behind. If I hadn't run, I'd still be back in San Francisco trying to clean it up."

"I know. I had to clean up most of it myself."

"There wasn't much I could do to help. The house was mortgaged to the rafters—something I didn't know until the bank called me after Nick's death. I told them to go ahead and take it. And the cars were in Nick's name, not mine. I'm assuming your company took those, along with the art and the furniture. I boxed up my clothes and shoes for Goodwill and pawned my jewelry for travel money—cash only. I knew my credit cards could be traced."

"By me?"

"Yes. But also by the reporters who kept hounding me and the police who seemed to think I'd have a different answer the fiftieth time they asked a question than I did the first."

"If you'd stayed, I could have made things easier for both of us, Megan."

"How could I take that chance? I knew the questions from the police, from the press and from you wouldn't stop. But, so help me, Cal, I didn't have any answers. It was easier to just vanish. I was half hoping you'd believe I'd died. In a way, I had."

The waiter had reappeared with their dinners. Megan half expected Cal to start grilling her about the missing funds, but he only glanced toward her plate in an unspoken order to eat her meal.

The steak was surprisingly tender, but Megan's anxiety had robbed her of appetite. She took small bites, glancing across the table like a mouse nibbling the cheese in a baited trap. Her eyes studied Cal's craggy face, trying to catch some nuance of expression. Was he about to trip the spring?

He'd aged subtly in the past two years. The shadows had darkened around his deep-set eyes, and his sandy hair was lightly brushed with gray. Nick's betrayal and suicide had wounded him, too, she realized. Like her, Cal was dealing with the pain in his own way.

"I was just wondering," he said. "When you joined that first project in Zimbabwe, was the director aware of who you were?"

"No. He was a local, and Zimbabwe's a long way from San Francisco. My passport was still in my maiden name, so that was the name I used. I showed up, described my nursing training and offered my help at the AIDS clinic. They needed a nurse too badly to ask many questions."

"And the transfers?"

"Once I got on the permanent volunteer roster, I could go pretty much where I wanted. Early on I was nervous about staying in one place too long. I moved around a lot. After a while it didn't seem to matter."

"And in Darfur? What happened there?"

The question shook her. Something too vague to be called a memory twisted inside, silent and cold like the coils of a snake. Megan willed herself not to feel it.

"You were there for eleven months," he persisted. "They sent you here for recovery. Something must have gotten to you."

She shrugged, her unease growing as she stared down at the weave of the bright brown-and-yellow tablecloth. "It's nothing. I just need rest, that's all. I'll be ready to go back in a couple of weeks."

"That's not what Dr. Musa told me. He says you have panic attacks. And you won't talk about what happened."

Megan's anxiety exploded in outrage. "He had no right to tell you that. And you had no right to ask him."

"My foundation's paying his salary. That gives me the right." Cal's leaden gray eyes drilled her like bullets. "Dr. Musa thinks you have post-traumatic stress. Whatever happened out there, Megan, you're not going back until you deal with it. So you might as well tell me now."

He was pushing too hard, backing her against an invisible wall. The dark coils twisted and tightened inside her. Sensing what was about to happen, she willed herself to lay down her fork. It clattered onto her plate. "I don't remember, all right?" Her voice emerged thin and raw. "It doesn't matter. I just need some time to myself and I'll be

fine. And now, if you don't mind, I need to get back to…
the clinic."

Her voice broke on the last words. As her self-control
began to crumble, she rose, flung her linen napkin onto
the table, caught up her purse and walked swiftly out of the
restaurant. There had to be a ladies' room close by, where
she could shut herself in a stall and huddle until her heart
stopped thundering. Experience had taught her to recognize the symptoms of a panic attack. But short of doping
herself with tranquilizers, she had little control over the
rush of irrational terror that flooded her body.

She reached the lobby and glanced around for the rest-
room sign. The desk clerk was busy. No matter, she could
find it by herself. But where was it? She could hear her
heart, pounding in her ears.

Where was it?

Caught off guard, Cal stared after her for an instant.
Then he shoved out his chair, stood and strode after her.
She hadn't made it far. He found her in the lobby, her
wide-eyed gaze darting this way and that like a cornered
animal's.

Without a word, he caught her shoulders, forcing her to
turn inward against his chest. She resisted, but feebly, her
body shaking. "Leave me alone," she muttered. "I'm fine."

"You're not fine. Come on." He guided her forcefully
through the lobby and out the back door to the patio. Sheltered by the overhanging roof, they stood veiled by a curtain of rain. Her body was rigid in his arms. He could feel
her heart pounding against his chest, feel the slight pressure of her breasts. She'd stopped fighting him, but the
trembling continued. Her breath came in muted gasps.
Her fists balled the fabric of his shirt.

He might not be the most sensitive guy in the world, but even he could tell that the woman was terrified.

What had she been through? Cal had visited the Sudan refugee camps—a hell of human misery if ever there was one. Tens of thousands of people crammed into tents and makeshift shelters, not enough food, not enough water, open sewers and latrines teeming with disease. Organizations like the United Nations and private, nongovernment charities, known as NGOs, did what they could. But the need was overwhelming. And Megan had spent eleven months there.

He wouldn't have been surprised to find her dispirited and worn down—which she clearly was. But there was something more here. Harsh conditions wouldn't have made her this fearful. Something had happened specifically to her. Something so terrifying that the briefest reminder of it was enough to make her quake.

He was here about the money, he reminded himself. She was guilty as hell, and he couldn't let himself be moved by sympathy. But right now Megan's need for comfort appeared all too real. And besides, hadn't he wanted to get close to her—close enough to learn her secrets? Here was his chance to take that first step.

"It's all right, girl," he muttered against her silky hair. "You're safe here. I've got you."

His hand massaged her back beneath the light jacket. She was bone thin, the back of her bra stretched tight across shoulder blades that jutted like wings. He'd come here to get the truth out of her and see that she was punished for any part she might have played in Nick's suicide. But arriving at that truth would take time and patience. Megan was fragile in body and wounded in spirit. Pushing her too hard could shatter what few reserves she had left.

Not that Cal was a saint. Far from it, as his hardening

arousal bore witness. It might have been an indelicate response to the situation, but it was the only way he knew to reply. His relationships were usually short-lived affairs, with plenty of heat that burned out quickly. With all the time he devoted to J-COR and the foundation, he had little to spare for romantic entanglements. Brief, passionate flings were usually his preference—the sort of relationship shallow enough for every conflict to be solved by taking matters to bed. He had little experience comforting genuine distress, and his body shifted into default mode, wanting to solve the problem by replacing her troubled thoughts—and his own niggling guilt for causing her such distress—with ecstasy for them both.

The desire was there, smoldering where her hips rested against his, igniting the urge to sweep her upstairs to his luxury suite and ravish her till she moaned with pleasure. Maybe that was what the woman needed—a few weeks of rest, good food and good loving to restore her health and build her trust.

But that wasn't going to happen tonight. It was comfort and support she needed now, not some big, horny jerk making moves on her.

Giving himself a mental slap, Cal shifted backward, easing the contact between them. She was calm now. Maybe too calm. "Want to talk about it?" he asked.

She exhaled, pushing away from him. "I'll be fine. Sorry you had to see me like that. I feel like a fool."

"No one's blaming you. I've seen those camps. You've been through eleven months of hell."

"But not like the people who have nowhere else to go. Seeing their children die, their women—"

"You can't dwell on that, Megan."

"I can't forget it. That's why I plan to go back as soon as I'm strong enough."

"That's insane. I could stop you, you know."

"You could try. But if you do, I'll find another way."

The defiance in her gaze stunned him. Back in San Francisco, where he'd known her as a charming hostess and a lovely ornament, he would never have believed she could possess such an iron will. But her will looked to be all she had left. She was like a guttering candle, on the verge of burning out.

"You should go back and finish your dinner," she said. "I've got my rain poncho. I can catch a *matatu* back to the clinic."

"One of those rickety little buses? You'd end up walking for blocks, alone in the rain. I'll take you." Cal wouldn't have minded inviting her upstairs for a hot bath and a chaste, restful night in his suite's second bed—as a simple act of kindness. But she was certain to turn him down. And even if she accepted, he didn't trust himself to behave. For all her devious ways, Megan was an alluring woman, made more so by her surprising strength and the unspoken challenge in her manner. The urge to bury himself between those slim, lovely legs might prove too much to resist.

But an idea had taken root in his thoughts—one so audacious that it surprised even him. First thing tomorrow he would make some calls. What he had in mind might be just the thing to restore her health and win her trust.

Minutes later Megan was huddled beside Cal in the cab's backseat. The rain had stopped, but the night was chilly and the black blazer she'd worn to look presentable was too thin for warmth.

"You're shivering." Cal peeled off his Burberry coat and wrapped it around her shoulders, enfolding her in the heat and manly scent of his body. A thread of panic uncurled inside her. She willed it away.

"We've talked about me all evening," she said, making conversation. "What's new with you?"

"Nothing much, except that I'm here. The company's doing fine. So is the foundation. I've hired a team of professionals to do the fund-raising. But they don't have your elegant touch. I miss you and…Nick."

Megan hadn't missed the beat of hesitation before he spoke her late husband's name. "That time seems like a hundred years ago," she said, then tactfully changed the subject. "Any special lady in your life? As I recall, you always had plenty to choose from."

"Having a special lady requires an investment in time. More time than I can spare."

"Remind yourself of that when you're a grumpy, lonely old man," she teased. "You're what? Forty?"

"Thirty-eight. Don't make me out to be more decrepit than I already am."

"Fine. But one of these days you're going to look back and wish you'd had a family."

"You're a fine one to talk," he countered.

"Well, at least I tried." She remembered telling him about the baby. Had Nick let him know she'd miscarried? Or had her statement made him think of her wedding day, when his best man's toast had congratulated the two of them on the new family they were making together?

His answering silence told Megan she'd pushed the conversation onto painful ground. Cal had been as devastated as she was by Nick's death. Devastated and angry—or at least, there had been anger on *her* part, when she'd learned about the embezzlement. Cal had seemed determined to find some way to clear Nick of any blame…which had meant shoving that blame on her, instead. Now, more than two years and half a world away, she was sitting beside him with his coat wrapped around her. It was as if they'd come full circle. She'd done everything in her power to put the past behind her and find peace. But it was no use. Being with Cal had brought it all back.

Three

Cal had offered Benjamin a cab ride back to Dr. Musa's. The distance wasn't far but by the time they arrived, jet lag from the long flight had caught up with him. He was nodding off every few minutes.

"Won't you come in, sir?" the husky youth asked as he climbed out of the cab. "I can make you tea."

"Another time, thank you. And give my best to the doctor. Tell him I'll ring him up tomorrow."

As the cab headed on to the hotel, splashing through the backstreet ruts, Cal reflected on his evening with Megan. Nothing had been as he'd expected. She was so fragile, and yet so powerfully seductive that he'd been caught off guard. It would have been all too easy to forget that the woman had either stolen or driven his best friend to steal millions from the foundation before killing himself, and that the money was still missing. In the days ahead he'd do well to remember that.

A few evenings out weren't going to break down her resistance. He was going to need more time with her—a lot more time, in a setting calculated to put her at ease. A safari would be perfect—days exploring Africa's beautiful wildlands, and the kind of pampered nights that a first-class safari company could provide.

Tomorrow he would put his scheme into action. First, as a courtesy, he would ask Dr. Musa's permission to take Megan out of the clinic for a couple of weeks. If need be, he could fly in another volunteer to take her place. Arranging a photo safari on short notice shouldn't be a problem. Business tended to slow during the rainy season. Most companies would be eager to accommodate a well-paying client.

Not until everything was in place would he let Megan in on his plan. She might argue. She might even dig in her heels and refuse to go along. But in the end she would go with him. If he had to knock her out and kidnap her, so help him, she would go.

Evenings were long and peaceful on safari, with little to do except eat, drink, rest and talk. As for the nights... But he would let nature take its course. If things went as planned, Megan would soon be stripped of any secrets she was hiding.

But first he wanted to cover all his bases. Tomorrow he would compose an email to Harlan Crandall. If the man was sharp enough to locate Megan, he might also be able to ferret out more details about the last months of Nick's life. He might even be able to locate the missing money.

For now—Cal punctuated the thought with a tired yawn—all he wanted was to go back to the hotel, crawl between the sheets and sleep off his jet lag.

On a cot veiled by mosquito netting, Megan writhed in fitful sleep. Her hellish dreams varied from night to night.

But this one from her time in Darfur dominated them all, replaying as if it had been burned into her brain.

Saida had been just fifteen, a beautiful child with liquid brown eyes and the doelike grace of her people, the Fur. Because she spoke fair English, and because her family was dead, Megan had given her a translating job at the camp infirmary, with an out-of-the-way corner for sleeping. Bright with promise, Saida had one failing. She had fallen in love with a boy named Gamal, and love had made her careless. Checking on the patients late one night, Megan had found Saida's pallet empty. Earlier, the starry-eyed girl had mentioned her trysting place with Gamal, a dry well outside the camp. That had to be where she'd gone.

Leaving the camp at night was forbidden. Beyond the boundaries, bands of rogue Janjaweed mercenaries prowled the desert like wild dogs in search of prey. No one was safe out there. Megan had known that she needed to find the two foolish youngsters and bring them back before the unthinkable happened. Arming herself with a loaded pistol, she'd plunged into the darkness.

Now the dream swirled around her like an evil mist. She was sprinting through pools of shadow, the waning moon a razor edge of light above the naked hills. Behind her lay the camp; ahead she could make out the gnarled trunk of a dead acacia, its limbs clutching the sky like the fingers of an arthritic hand. Beyond the tree lay the well, a dry hole marked by a cairn of stones.

Near the cairn she could see the two young lovers. They were locked in a tender embrace, blind and deaf to everything but each other. A turbaned shadow moved behind them. Then another and another. Raising the pistol, Megan cocked it and aimed. Time slowed as her finger tightened on the trigger.

Before she could fire, a huge, sweaty hand clamped over her mouth. Pain shot up her arm as the pistol was wrenched away. She tried to fight, twisting and scratching, but her captor was a wall of muscle. Powerless to move or cry out, she could only watch in horror as a knife sang out of the darkness and buried itself to the hilt in Gamal's back. He dropped without a sound.

Saida's screams shattered the darkness as the Janjaweed moved in. One of them flung her to the ground. Two others pinned her legs as the circle of men closed around her. Megan heard the sound of ripping cloth. Again Saida screamed. Again and again...

Megan's eyes jerked open. She was shaking violently, her skin drenched in sweat beneath her light cotton pajamas. Her heart slammed in the silence of the room.

Easing her feet to the floor, she brushed aside the mosquito netting, leaned over her knees and buried her face in her hands. The dream always ended the same way. She had no memory of how she'd managed to escape. She only knew that Gamal had been found dead outside the camp the next morning, and Saida had vanished without a trace.

She'd soldiered on, hoping time would help her forget. But even here in Arusha the nightmares were getting worse, not better. Maybe Dr. Musa was right. Maybe she did have post-traumatic stress. But so what if she did? As far as she knew, there was no simple cure for the malady. Otherwise, why would so many combat veterans be suffering from it back in the States?

All she could do was go on as if nothing had happened. If she could control her fears, she could still do some good. One day she might even be able to live a normal life.

But normal in every respect? She shook her head. That would be asking too much.

* * *

Wednesday was vaccination day at the clinic. While the aide managed the paperwork, and Dr. Musa took care of the more urgent cases, Megan spent the hours giving immunizations. Most of her patients, babies and children, had departed squalling. She loved the little ones and was grateful for the chance to help them stay well; but by late afternoon she'd developed a pounding headache.

Taking a break as the stream of people thinned, she gulped down a couple of aspirins. She couldn't help wondering where Cal was. He'd promised to come by the clinic, but she hadn't seen him for two days. Had some emergency come up, or was he just avoiding her?

But why should she care? Cal wanted to stir up memories she would be happy to keep buried. Seeing him again would only sharpen the loss that had dulled over time.

Dared she believe he'd given up on her and left? But that wasn't like Cal. He'd come here seeking satisfaction, and he wouldn't walk away without it. Was it just the money? Or was he looking for some closure in the matter of Nick's death? Either way, he was wasting his time. She had no insight to offer him.

But her conflict over the prospect of spending time with him went deeper than that.

The other night when the calming strength of his arms had temporarily eased her panic, she'd been grateful for his comfort—and troubled by how it made her feel. Cal was a compelling man, and he'd touched her in a way that had sent an unmistakable message. There was a time when she would have found him hard to resist. But when he'd held her so close that his arousal had hardened against her belly, it had been all she could do to keep from pushing him away and running off into the rain. Only when he'd stepped back had she felt safe once more.

Over the past months, it was as if something had died in her. The things she'd witnessed had numbed her to the point where she doubted her ability to respond as a woman.

The issue had come to light a few months ago when a volunteer MSF doctor in one of the camps had invited her for a private supper. He'd been attractive enough, and Megan had harbored no illusions about what to expect. Such things were common enough between volunteers, and though she'd never indulged before, she'd actually looked forward to a few hours of forgetting the wretched conditions outside. But when he'd kissed her, she'd felt little more than a vague unease. She'd tried to behave as if everything was all right; but as his caresses grew more intimate, her discomfort had spiraled into panic. In the end she'd twisted away, plunged out of the tent and fled with his words echoing in her ears— *What the hell's the matter with you? Are you frigid?*

By the next night the doctor had found a more agreeable partner. Megan hadn't attempted intimacy again. She'd hoped it had been a fluke, but her reaction to Cal had confirmed her suspicions.

Her problem hadn't gone away, and most likely wouldn't. If Cal had seduction in mind, the man was in for a letdown. For that, and for every other reason she could think of, it would be best if she never saw him again.

But that was not to be. The next morning, as Megan was eating a breakfast of scrambled eggs and coffee, he roared through the gate in an open jeep that bore the logo of one of the big safari companies. A flock of brown parrots exploded from the tulip tree as he pulled up to the bungalow.

Dr. Musa stepped out of the clinic, grinning as if in on some secret joke.

Cal vaulted out of the jeep. "Pack your things, Megan," he ordered. "You're coming with me—now."

"Have you lost your mind, Cal Jeffords?" She faced him on the porch steps, her arms folded across her chest. "What gives you the right to come in here and order me around as if I were six years old?"

His eyes narrowed, glinting like granite over a sharklike smirk. "I'm the head of the J-COR Foundation and you're a volunteer. Right now I'm volunteering you to come with me on safari for ten days. I've already cleared it with Dr. Musa." He glanced toward the doctor, who nodded. "Your replacement's flying in this afternoon, so the clinic won't be shorthanded. Everything's been arranged."

"And I have no say in any of this?"

"Dr. Musa agrees with me that your work here isn't giving you enough rest. You need a real break. That's what I'm offering you."

"Offering? Does that mean I can refuse?"

"Not if you're smart." He stood his ground at the foot of the steps, his slate eyes level with hers.

"What if I say no? Will you haul me off by force?"

"If I have to." He didn't even blink, and she knew with absolute certainty that he wasn't bluffing. Once the man made up his mind, there'd be no moving him.

Not that the idea of a safari seemed so bad. It might even speed her recovery. But how was she going to survive ten days with Cal? Scrambling for a shred of control, she squared her jaw.

"Fine, I'll go with you on one condition. If I'm fit and rested by the end of the safari, I want to be sent back to Darfur."

One dark eyebrow twitched. "Are you sure that's a good idea?"

"Is it a good idea for any of those poor people who have nowhere else to go? It's where I'm most urgently needed.

And without that goal, I can't justify wasting ten days on a...vacation."

He scowled, then slowly nodded. "All right. But while we're on safari, you're on orders to relax and have a good time. That's the best medicine you can give yourself if you want to recover. And as you said yourself, you'll need to be fit and rested to return there."

She took a moment to study him, the jutting chin, the steely gaze. Cal Jeffords wasn't spending precious time and money on a safari just to help her get better. The next ten days would be a contest of wills. She would need to be on her guard the whole time.

"So, do we have a deal?" he demanded.

Megan turned toward the door of the bungalow. Pausing, she glanced back at him—long enough for him to see that she wasn't smiling. "It won't take me long to pack," she said. "The coffee's hot. Have some while you're waiting."

The single-engine Piper Cherokee circled the rim of the Ngorongoro crater, a place designated by *National Geographic* as one of the world's Living Edens. Cal had been here two or three times over the years and knew what to expect. He was more interested in watching Megan, who was seeing it for the first time.

As the pilot banked the plane, she pressed against the window, looking down at the grassy floor of the twelve-mile-wide caldera. "This is amazing," she murmured.

"It's all that's left of an ancient volcano that blew its top." Cal shifted comfortably into the role of guide. "Geologists who've done the math claim it was as big as Kilimanjaro. Can you believe that?"

Megan shook her head. She'd been quiet during the short flight, and Cal hadn't pressed her to talk. There'd be plenty of time for conversation later. He studied her

finely chiseled profile against the glass. Even in sunglasses, with no makeup and wind-tousled hair, she was
a beauty. No wonder Nick had been eager to give her anything she wanted.

"We could've driven here in less than a day," he said.
"But I wanted your first view of the crater to be this one,
from the air."

"It's breathtaking." She kept her gaze fixed on the landscape below. "Why is it so green down there? The rains
have barely started."

"The crater has springs that keep it watered year-round.
The animals living there don't have to migrate during the
dry season."

"Will we see animals today?" Her voice held a childlike
anticipation. Once Megan had resigned herself to going,
she'd flung herself into the spirit of the safari. Despite
his hidden agenda, and his long-nurtured distrust of her,
Cal found himself enjoying, even sharing, her enthusiasm.

"That depends," he replied. "Harris Archibald, our
guide, will be meeting the plane with our vehicle. Where
we go will be mostly up to him. You'll enjoy Harris—at
least, I hope you will. He's a relic of the old days, a real
character. Be prepared—he's missing an arm and he'll tell
you a dozen different stories about how he lost it. I've no
idea which version is true."

He'd been lucky to hire Harris for this outing, Cal reflected. The old man usually guided trophy hunters, and
his talent for it had him in high demand. But when Cal had
called on him in Arusha, Harris had just had a client cancel. He'd been glad for the work, even though shepherd-
ing a photo safari had meant changing the arrangements
he'd already made.

The old rogue swilled liquor, swore like a pirate and
had been through four wives; but when it came to scout-

ing game, he had the instincts of a bloodhound. There was no doubt he'd give Cal his money's worth.

"Will we be sleeping in tents tonight?" Megan asked as the plane veered away from the crater toward the open plain.

"You sound like a little girl on her first camping trip." Cal squelched the impulse to reach out and squeeze her shoulder. She seemed in high spirits this afternoon, but he sensed the frailty beneath her cheerful facade. Or was that an act? He'd have to remember to be on his guard against her. This was a woman used to wrapping men around her little finger.

"Wait and see," he said. "I want you to be surprised."

And she would be, he vowed. By the end of the next ten days, Megan would be well rested, well fed, well ravished and trusting enough to tell him anything.

The plane touched down on an airstrip that was little more than a game trail through the long grass. Cal swung to the ground, then reached up for Megan. Using his hand for balance, she climbed onto the low-mounted wing and jumped lightly to earth.

A cool wind, smelling of rain, teased her hair and ruffled the long grass. Far to the west, sooty clouds boiled over the horizon. Lightning flickered in the distant sky. Megan counted the seconds before the faint growl of thunder reached her ears. The rain was still several miles away, but it appeared to be moving fast. Their personal gear had been unloaded and the plane was turning around to take off ahead of the storm. If no one showed up to meet them, she and Cal would be left in the middle of nowhere with no shelter to protect them from the weather or the wildlife.

But there was no way she'd let Cal know how nervous

she was. Glancing over her shoulder, she flashed him a smile. "So our big adventure begins."

He wasn't fooled by her bravado. "Don't worry, Harris will be here," he said. "The old boy hasn't lost a client yet."

As if his words were prophetic, Megan saw a mottled tan shape approaching in the distance. Lumbering closer, it materialized into a mud-spattered heavy-duty Land Rover with open sides and a canvas top. There were two men in the front seat—a tall African driver and a stockier figure in khakis and a pith helmet.

Waving to the pair in the Land Rover, the pilot gunned his engine. The little plane droned down the makeshift runway, cleared the ground and soared into the darkening sky.

Cal hefted the duffel bags and strode toward the vehicle, where he tossed the gear in the back, keeping hold only of the case he had told Megan held the binoculars and cameras. Once the bags were arranged, he opened the door for Megan to climb into the rear seat. The driver gazed politely ahead, but their aging guide turned around to give Megan a look that could have gotten him slapped if he'd been a generation younger.

The man reminded Megan of an aging Ernest Hemingway, with battered features that would have been handsome in his youth. His bristling eyebrows and scruffy gray beard showed lingering traces of russet. His blue eyes held a secretive twinkle that put Megan at ease.

"I'll be damned, Cal." He spoke with a trace of lower-class British accent. "You told me you were bringing a lady friend, but you didn't tell me how classy she was. Now I'll have to be on my best behavior."

Cal settled himself on the backseat. "Megan, my friend Harris Archibald needs no introduction," he said. "Harris, this is Ms. Megan Cardston."

"It's a pleasure to meet you, Mr. Archibald." Megan extended her hand, then noticed, to her embarrassment, the pinned-up right sleeve of his khaki shirt.

He chuckled and accepted her handshake from the left. "You can call me Harris. I don't hold much with formality."

"But I'm holding you to your remark about being on your best behavior, Harris," Cal said.

"Oh, you needn't worry on that account. I've long since learned my lesson about fooling around with the client's womenfolk. See this?" He nodded toward the stump of his arm, which appeared to have been severed just above the elbow. "Jealous husband with a big gun and a bad aim."

Cal rolled his eyes heavenward. Remembering what he'd told her about Harris's stories, Megan suppressed a smile. "And our driver?" she asked. "Are you going to introduce him?"

Harris looked slightly startled, as if most clients tended to ignore the African staff. "Gideon," he said. "Gideon Mkaba. We'll be in good hands with him."

"*Hujambo,* Gideon." Megan extended her hand over the back of the seat.

"*Sijambo.*" The driver smiled and shook her hand.

"So where are we going, Harris?" Cal broke the beat of awkward silence.

The guide grinned. "Thought you'd never ask! Elephant! Whole bloody herd of 'em down by the riverbed. We were scouting 'em when we saw your plane."

As the engine coughed to a rumbling start, lightning cracked across the sky with a deafening boom. The roiling clouds let loose a gush of water that deluged down on the vehicle's canvas top. Wind blew the rain sideways, dousing the passengers.

"Move it, Gideon!" Harris shouted above the storm. "They won't be there forever!"

"But it's raining!" Megan protested, shivering in her wet clothes.

Twisting in the front seat, Harris shot her a devilish grin. "Excuse me, miss, but the elephants don't bloody care!"

Four

By the time they came within sight of the riverbed, Cal had managed to clamber into the back of the jouncing Land Rover and find Megan's duffel among the gear. Pulling out her rain poncho, he reached over the seat, tugged it past her head and worked it down around her shivering body. It was too late to keep her dry, but at least the plastic sheeting would act as a windbreaker and help keep her warm.

As he moved back to the seat, she looked up at him. Her lips moved in silent thanks. A freshet of tenderness welled inside him. Even a strong woman like Megan needed someone to care about her. Something told him she hadn't had anyone like that in a long time.

But he hadn't come on this trip to feel sorry for her. He couldn't let sympathy—or any other emotion—divert him from his purpose.

"There." On a slight rise above the riverbank, Harris motioned for the driver to stop. The growl of the engine dropped to a low idle. Glancing back at Cal and Megan, the guide touched a finger to his lips and pointed.

At first Cal saw nothing. Then, not fifty yards ahead, a huge, gray silhouette emerged through the sheeting rain. Then another and another.

Cal could feel Megan's hand gripping his arm as the herd ambled toward them on silent feet. Did the tension in her come from awe or worry? He wasn't quite sure what to feel, himself. He knew that most animals in the game parks were accustomed to vehicles. But these elephants were close, and the open Land Rover offered little in the way of protection. He could only hope that Harris knew what he was doing.

Somewhere below them, hidden by the high bank, was the rain-swollen river. Over the rush of water, Cal could hear the elephants. They were vocalizing in low-pitched rumbles, their tone relaxed, almost conversational. Gideon slipped the gearshift into Reverse, ready to back away at the first sign of trouble. Surely, by now, the herd was aware of them. But the elephants continued on, undisturbed.

The leader, most likely an older cow, was within a stone's throw of the vehicle's front grille when she turned aside and disappeared through an opening in the river-bank. The others followed her—adult females, half-grown teenagers and tiny newborn calves trailing like gray ghosts through the rain, down the slope toward the river. Megan's grip tightened. Cal could sense the emotion in her, the fear and the wonder. He resisted the impulse to take her hand. They had just shared an unforgettable moment. He didn't want to risk spoiling it.

The last elephant had made it down the bank to the water. The contented sounds of drinking and splashing drifted up from below. Harris nodded to the driver, who backed up the Land Rover, turned it around and headed back the way they'd come.

"You had me worried, there," Cal admitted. "Any one of those elephants could have charged us."

Harris chuckled. "No need to fret. I know that herd, and I knew they'd be thirsty. They always take the same path down to the river. As long as we didn't bother them, I was pretty sure they wouldn't pay us much heed."

Megan hadn't spoken. "Are you all right?" Cal asked her.

Her voice emerged as a nervous laugh. "Unbelievable," she breathed. "And we forgot to take pictures."

Cal could feel her trembling beneath the poncho, whether from cold or excitement, he couldn't be sure. But her green-flecked caramel eyes were glowing beneath the hood. It had been a good moment with Megan, the elephants and the rain, he mused; maybe the best moment he'd known in a long time. But he couldn't forget what he'd come to do.

Megan had expected that being on safari would involve roughing it in a tent. In her cold, wet condition, the luxury lodge on the outer slope of the Ngorongoro Crater came as a welcome surprise. Less welcome was the discovery that Harris had clearly misread her relationship with Cal. He had reserved just one bungalow for the two of them. With one bed.

"Don't worry. I'll take care of this." Cal stood beside her in the open doorway surveying the elegantly rustic quarters, decorated in native rugs, baskets and tapestries. "While you shower and change for dinner, I'll go talk to the manager. They're bound to have an extra room somewhere."

With the door locked behind him, Megan stripped

down and luxuriated in the hot, tiled shower stocked with lavender-scented soap and shampoo. It wouldn't be a good idea to get used to this, she lectured herself. In the camps, a bucket of cold water was often as good as she could get. Much of the time she'd had to make do with sponge baths, reminding herself that even that was better than most refugees had.

If she could move beyond the panic attacks and the nightmares, Cal had promised to send her back to Darfur. Ten days wasn't much time. But if she could relax and focus on getting well, it might make a difference.

She wanted to go back, needed to. Working among the poor and dispossessed had given her the only real sense of worth she had ever known—something she had craved after her world had collapsed under her feet.

In her naïveté, she hadn't learned about Nick's embezzlement of the charity funds until days before he'd shot himself. Between his death and his funeral, she'd done a world of soul-searching. For years, she'd taken it for granted that her husband was rich, and she'd spent accordingly. But how much of the stolen money had gone to support her extravagant lifestyle? Megan had no way of knowing. She had known, though, that while she couldn't return the money, she could at least make some restitution through her own service.

Cal's cold anger at the funeral and his threat to make her pay had startled her. Until then she hadn't realized that he blamed her for the theft and for his friend's suicide. Knowing that he would find some way to go after her legally and that she had no power to fight him had pushed her decision—she'd had no choice except to run far and fast, where Cal would never think to look for her.

Using her political connections and her knowledge of the J-COR Foundation, she'd managed to expedite the paperwork and lose herself in the ranks of volunteers. What surprised her was the fulfillment she'd found in working with the refugees. They had needed her—and in that need she'd found the hope of redemption.

She was proud of the work she'd done in Arusha, but she could do so much more in Darfur. She had to go back; and she couldn't let Cal stop her.

Megan had put on fresh clothes and was fluffing her short damp hair when she heard a knock on the door. She opened it to find Cal standing on the threshold with his duffel bag.

"No luck," he said. "They've got a big tour group coming in tonight, and everything will be full-up. I even asked about borrowing a cot. Nothing."

"Can you room with Harris?"

"Harris has a single bed in the main lodge. He'll probably come in drunk, and even when he's sober he snores like a steam calliope. I let him know about his mistake—the old rascal just grinned and told me to make the best of it."

He glanced around the bungalow, which, except for the bath, was all one L-shaped room. Near the window, a sofa and two armchairs were grouped around a coffee table. "Sorry. I'll be fine sleeping on the couch. I even have some sheets and an extra mosquito net they gave me at the desk."

Grin and bear it. Megan sighed as her gaze measured his looming height against the modest length of the sofa. "I may be a better fit for the couch myself. But I suppose we can work that out. Come on in. You'll want to clean up before dinner."

While Cal showered, Megan opened the camera bag and went over the instruction manual for the small digital camera Cal had bought her in Arusha. In the background, she could hear the splash and gurgle of running water as he sluiced his body—probably a very impressive body, she conceded. But she'd been married to Nick for five years; and working in the camps, she'd seen more than her share of nudity. If Cal were to walk out of the bathroom stark naked, she would do little more than shrug and look the other way.

The small intimacies of sharing a room didn't bother her. It was Cal's constant, looming presence that would take some getting used to.

The shower had stopped running. The door opened a few inches to let out the steam, but it appeared he was getting dressed in the bathroom. A few minutes later he stepped out, freshly shaven and combed, and dressed in clean jeans and a charcoal-gray sweater that matched his eyes. The clothes should have seemed casual, but something about his presence lent a rugged elegance to whatever he wore. She'd always noticed that.

Megan had done some needed shopping in Arusha before their departure, but she'd bought mostly plain khakis and T-shirts, a fleece jacket and a pair of sturdy boots, which she could take back to Darfur. Her one indulgence had been a colorful but practical jade-green scarf, which she'd knotted at her throat tonight. It was as dressed-up as she was going to get.

She surveyed him from head to toe. "You look like a page out of *GQ*."

He grinned. "And you look like Ingrid Bergman in *For Whom the Bell Tolls*. Shall we go to dinner?"

It was still raining, but there was a good-size umbrella in the room. Stepping out onto the terrace, Cal opened it and sheltered Megan while she locked the door. With rain a streaming curtain around them, they followed the brick walkway across the grounds to the dining room.

The lodge stood on an old coffee plantation, its original German owners exiled by the British, who'd taken over the country at the end of World War I. The trees, the gardens and some of the old buildings had been preserved and beautifully restored. A high brick wall around the property kept out prowling animals. Veiled by rain and twilight, memories of a forgotten world lingered in the shadows. It seemed so distant from any world she'd been used to—in America or in Africa—that it almost felt like a dream. She'd have to remind herself not to get lost in it. This wasn't a fairy tale, she was not a princess and Cal was no Prince Charming. He was a man with an agenda, and she would do well to keep that in mind.

Gideon would be sleeping and eating in the staff quarters; but Harris was waiting at their table in the dining room. Already glowing from the whiskey in his glass, he kept them riotously entertained through the five-course gourmet meal. Megan was grateful for his presence, which saved her from making awkward conversation with Cal. She found herself liking the old rogue, despite his proclivities for strong drink and colorful curses. Even when he flirted outrageously with her, she took it in the good humor it was meant to be.

"Join me in the bar for a nightcap?" He gave her a sly wink as their dessert plates were whisked away. "We might even invite that old sourpuss Cal along if he asks nicely."

"Thanks, but I can barely keep my eyes open now," Megan said, rising. "Of course, I can't speak for Cal. But I'll see you tomorrow morning."

The men had risen with her. "I'll excuse myself, too, Harris," Cal said. "It's been a long day, and I know you'll want to get an early start in the morning."

"Where will we be going?" Megan asked.

"Wait and see," Cal teased. "More fun that way."

"Fine, but can you at least tell me where we are now? I've totally lost my bearings."

"Sure. I've got a map of the country in my bag. That'll give you a better idea."

They stepped outside to discover that the rain had stopped. The clouds had swept away to reveal a dazzling expanse of stars. Water dripped from the trees as they walked back down the path to their bungalow.

"How early does Harris expect us tomorrow?" Megan asked.

"Six, maybe. Early morning's the best time to see animals. He may be up half the night drinking, but don't worry, he'll be there first thing. And we'll be there, too, if we know what's good for us."

"You seem to know Harris pretty well. How did you meet him?"

"Partly luck. A few years ago I took one of our big donors to see some projects in Africa. The man was a hunter and wanted a safari while he was here. Harris was available."

"You hunted with them?"

"I just went along for the ride. Took a few pictures. Harris thought I was a wuss. Probably still does, but we managed to become friends. I've sent him other clients over the years, but after seeing those beautiful animals go down under the gun, I've no desire to hunt anything. Life's too short and too precious."

"I like that about you," Megan said, meaning it. "And I never thanked you for commandeering me on this trip. So far it's been wonderful."

She waited, expecting some kind of response, but Cal was silent. He hadn't brought her along on this trip for pleasure, Megan reminded herself. Or if he had, it was only because he thought that he could get her guard down and pry away her secrets.

Two years ago, Cal had been the one to walk into Nick's

office and find him dead at his desk. A shock like that would leave a lasting scar. If Cal had blamed her, even in part, for his best friend's suicide, the blame would still be there, festering like an infected wound beneath the veneer of charm and affability he was showing her now. Even before Nick's suicide, he'd never approved of her. He must hate her now.

Had he come here to punish her? Maybe she should simply ask him. She doubted he'd tell her the truth. Worse, voicing her suspicions might raise his guard. But at least it would let him know he wasn't fooling her.

"I've been thinking about our sleeping arrangement," she said. "If you try to stretch out on that sofa, you'll hang over the ends and keep us both awake with your tossing and turning. But I'm short enough to fit—not to mention the fact that, after living in the camps, I can sleep anywhere. You're taking the bed. End of discussion."

"Fine," he answered after a beat of silence. "I bow to your common sense. But you get one of the pillows and your first choice of blankets."

"Deal." They'd reached the terrace of their bungalow. She fished in her pocket for the key. "How long will we be staying here? Surely you can tell me that much without spoiling any surprises."

"We'll be using this lodge as our base for the next few days, so you can go ahead and unpack for now. After that... you'll see."

"Sorry, but I've grown accustomed to being in charge of my life."

"For the next nine days, your only responsibility will be to relax. Leave the logistics to Harris. That's what I'm paying him for."

"And what are *you* getting out of this?"

The slight intake of his breath told her that her question

had thrown him. In the silence that followed, she turned the key in the lock and opened the door. Before she could step inside, he touched her arm. "It's early yet. Let's sit outside for a while. If you think you'll be cold, I'll get a blanket."

"Thanks." The overhanging roof had kept the rain off the bench under the window, but the night breeze carried a chill. Megan took a seat, huddling for warmth while Cal went inside and turned on a lamp. He hadn't answered her question, but at least he seemed willing to talk.

Moments later he returned with a light woolen blanket. It was long enough to cover them both as he sat next to her. Megan was acutely conscious of his body heat and the rain-fresh aroma of his skin. She'd always found Cal intimidating, like facing down a lion. There was something about him that shriveled her self-confidence. It had gotten much worse after Nick's death, when he'd begun to treat her as an adversary. But she'd have to put her discomfort aside if she wanted him to deal with her as an equal.

The night was still except for the lightly rustling wind and the drip of water off the leaves and buildings. A night bird called from outside the wall, a shimmering sound that, in Megan, touched a chord of sadness.

"You asked me a question," Cal said.

Her heart stumbled. "I did. You don't owe me anything, Cal. You've no reason to like me, or do me any sort of kindness. For all I know, you still blame me for Nick's death. So why should you invest your time and money in this adventure? That's why I'm asking, what's in it for you?"

He stirred beside her. "Peace of mind, maybe. Or at least some answers. I've never gotten past what happened with Nick, or his death. For years he was my closest friend. I thought I knew him. But it appears I didn't know him at all. I want to move on. But for that, I need to understand

Nick and what motivated him to kill himself. I need to see him through your eyes."

Megan swallowed the ache in her throat. As expected, he hadn't asked her about the money directly. But his words had stirred up some painful emotions. She'd asked for this; but even after two years she wasn't ready to talk about her marriage.

"I don't know if I can help you," she said. "When the theft was discovered and Nick took his own life, I was as shocked as you were."

"So have you been able to move on, Megan?"

Had she? Megan struggled with the question. She'd dealt with Nick's death by running away to a part of the world where tragedy was commonplace. But the past was still there, like an unhealed wound, and now Cal wanted to rip that wound open.

"Maybe we can help each other," he said. "It might do us both good to talk."

"Talk about Nick?" She shook her head. "If that's what you want from me, you've come a long way for nothing. It still hurts too much."

Turning away from her, he fixed his gaze on the night sky. Megan studied his craggy profile, the Roman nose, the determined chin, as she waited to see how he'd respond to her refusal of his request. Cal Jeffords wasn't a man to take no for an answer.

"If talking about Nick's too painful, why don't you tell me about yourself?" he persisted. "I don't know much about your background, except that you were a nurse. Where did you grow up, Megan?"

Even talking about her early life was hard. But Cal wasn't about to let up. "I grew up in Arkansas," she said, "in a little hill town you've never heard of."

He looked at her again, one eyebrow quirked. "I'd never have guessed it. You don't sound like a Southerner."

"I was born in Chicago and lived there till I was six. Then my parents died in a car accident—New Year's Eve, drunk driver, no insurance."

"Sorry. Tough break for a kid."

"My grandmother agreed to take me and raise me up 'in righteousness,' as she was fond of saying. Granny was a good woman, and she meant well, but…"

The words trailed off as Megan remembered the spankings with a hickory rod, meant to drive out the devil, the long passages of scripture learned by rote, the endless hours of sitting on a hard bench in revival meetings while the preacher raged hellfire and damnation.

"I get the picture," Cal said. "And I'm guessing some of that so-called righteousness was a hard pill to swallow right after losing your parents. No kid wants to be told that her parents had to die so they could be in a better place without her. It explains, in part, why you left that all behind so completely."

"Don't try to psychoanalyze me, Cal. I've done enough of that on my own."

"Fine. Go on." He shifted beneath the blanket, his knee brushing hers. Megan sensed a shift in his manner, but she willed herself to ignore it.

"We were so poor that we wore clothes from the church's charity bin. But Granny had inherited her little house and the acre of land it sat on. When I was seventeen, she died of a heart attack and left it to me. I sold the property to pay for college and never looked back."

"And so you became an angel of mercy." His tone was razor-edged. But given the extravagant way she'd lived with Nick, Megan could hardly blame him for being cynical.

"Oh, at first I had some idealistic dreams about what I

could do with a nursing degree," she said. "But by graduation I was broke, and the top-paying job I could find was with one of San Francisco's best-known plastic surgeons."

"I take it the good doctor didn't hire ugly nurses."

"That's not fair!" Megan reined the impulse to slap him. Apparently he'd dropped the pretense of just wanting to know her better. Now he was firmly back into judgmental mode—the way he usually was when he spoke to her, back before Nick's death. Their interactions had been limited, but his tone with her had always made his disdain perfectly clear.

"I was good at my work—very good," she insisted. "But yes, we had to project the right image for the clients—hair, makeup, fitted uniforms, the whole package. And I didn't mind. After years of donated clothes—washed out, shapeless and worn down nearly to rags—I enjoyed having nice things that I could buy new, and money to spend on a hairdresser or a manicurist. I learned a lot from the women who came in for procedures—where to shop, how to dress, where to get my hair done. Some of them were even friendly enough to invite me to their charity galas. That was how I met Nick." She paused, sensing she'd stepped onto dangerous ground. "That's it. You know the rest of the story."

"Yes. Cinderella went to the ball, met her handsome prince and they lived happily ever after…or, whatever the hell really happened."

The anger that flashed through Megan was as instantaneous as torched gasoline. She'd tried to be patient and open with the man. But he'd repaid her with sarcasm and contempt. Twisting on the bench, she faced him with blazing eyes.

"It's my turn to ask the questions, Cal Jeffords!" She flung the words at him. "I didn't steal the money! I didn't

kill Nick! I've done nothing immoral or illegal! What gives
you the right to be my judge and jury? What have I done
to make you hate me so much?"

"Hate you? Damn it, Megan, all I want is to understand what happened—and to understand you! Why do
you make it so hard?"

"You're the one who's making it hard," she flung back
at him. "You didn't come here for a good time. You came
because you wanted something. Why can't you just be
honest with me for a change? What kind of game are you
playing?"

With a muttered curse, he seized her shoulders and
jerked her close. For an instant his eyes burned their anguish into her soul. Then his mouth captured hers in a
brutal, crushing kiss.

Five

The heat of Cal's kiss jolted through Megan like the burn of a bullet. She felt a rush of sensation—too sharply intense for her to decide if it was even pleasurable or not. Then her pulse went crazy as stark panic set in. Wild with senseless fear, she thrashed against him, fists flying at whatever target they could find.

Shoving her to arm's length, he released her and sank against the back of the bench. His face reflected shock—and a few red marks from where her wild blows had connected—but he spoke calmly. "Megan, it's all right. Nobody's going to hurt you."

Something in his voice reached her. She willed herself to clasp her hands in her lap and breathe. She was safe, she told herself firmly. Cal hadn't meant to harm her. The only danger was in her mind.

As the panic ebbed, she began to tremble. Her shoulders sagged. Her head dropped into her open hands. How could she have let this happen?

"Forgive me, Megan. I should have known better." He made no effort to touch her; but when she found the courage to look up, his stricken eyes met hers. With wrenching effort, she found her voice.

"Please…I'll be fine. Just don't do that again," she whispered.

Releasing a long breath, he stood. "Relax. I'll get you something to drink." Stepping inside, he returned a moment later with one of the water bottles from the room and held it out to her. Megan took long sips, letting the cool water calm her. Her senses took in the fresh smell of rain and the musical drone of crickets in the darkness as her heartbeat calmed enough for her to hear past its thudding in her ears.

"Better?" he asked.

She managed to nod. "Getting there. Not quite the reaction you get from most of the ladies you kiss, is it? But I'm in no mood to offer any sort of apology. You were out of line. What were you thinking?"

"I won't even try to answer that question." His chuckle sounded strained. "Is there anything I can get you?"

"Not really. But some time alone to settle my nerves might help."

"Fine. I'll go keep Harris company in the bar. You won't be going anywhere else, will you?"

"Just to bed." The panic attack had drained her. She barely had the energy to speak. "Take the key. With luck I'll be asleep when you get back."

"Got it." His voice was edged with caution. "Rest, now. We've got a long day ahead of us tomorrow. Let's put tonight behind us and make it a good one." He turned to go, then glanced back at her. "I've learned my lesson, Megan. You have my word. I won't frighten you like that again.

You're right that you don't owe me an apology—I owe you one. I'm truly sorry for upsetting you."

Unable to form a response, she looked away and heard his footsteps fade around the corner of the bungalow. Outwardly she was calm enough. But Cal's kiss had set off a maelstrom of inner turmoil. Wrapping herself in the blanket, she struggled to sort out her thoughts.

Cal was experienced enough to read most women. If he'd had any idea she might fight him, he would never have kissed her. Had he picked up on signals she wasn't even aware of sending? Had she actually *wanted* to be kissed? By him, of all people? He was an attractive man, but she could honestly say she'd never imagined him in an intimate context. He'd always seemed so cold toward her—coldly disdainful at first, and then, at Nick's funeral, coldly vengeful.

She recalled, in vivid detail, the white-hot sensation that had flashed through her body as his lips crushed hers. There had been nothing cold about him in that moment. With the last man she'd kissed—the doctor in the camp— she'd felt nothing. With Cal, what she'd felt was a sensual overload so powerful it had terrified her.

What did it mean? Was she healing or getting worse?

What would happen if she let him kiss her again?

Trembling, she hugged her arms against her ribs. For now there was little chance of that. Cal had promised to leave her alone for the rest of the trip. If she was wise, she would hold him to that promise. The boundaries they'd set tonight were meant to keep her safe. Pushing those boundaries would involve more risk than she had the courage to take.

But there was one thing tonight had taught her. Cal wasn't the problem. She was.

Rising, she walked into the bungalow, locked the door and set herself to making her bed on the sofa.

Cal was in no frame of mind to sit around in the bar. His restless pace carried him along the darkened walkways, through the coffee grove and around the inside perimeter of the wall. With each stride, his thoughts churned.

He hadn't planned on kissing Megan. In fact, he'd warned himself not to. But it had happened—and the brief seconds it lasted had only sharpened his appetite for more. Even after her fear-driven response, his body ached with the desire to sweep her into bed and pleasure her torment away.

But never mind his own needs. There were darker forces at work here, and deeper concerns.

Megan's frenzied reaction had opened his eyes to what he should have realized earlier. She wasn't just exhausted from her time in the camps. And she wasn't just traumatized by the things she'd witnessed.

Something had happened to her.

Lack of cell service rendered Cal's mobile device useless here. But the lodge had a bank of antiquated computers with internet available for guests. Sitting in an empty spot, he logged in to his email and checked a few incoming messages, then opened a new window. Taking his time, he composed a message to the director in charge of volunteer records for the J-COR Foundation, requesting a copy of Megan's performance evaluations and medical history for the past two years. The records were supposed to be confidential; but as the foundation's head, he had the power to override that rule.

Megan would be upset if she knew he was meddling. But he needed to get to the root of her fear. Otherwise, how could he hope to understand her, or get her some help? Whatever their past connection, he could tell she was deeply troubled. How could he be so callous as to turn his back and leave her hurting?

He'd come to Africa with one purpose—to track down Megan and get justice for the loss of the money and Nick's death. But he hadn't counted on the complications. He hadn't counted on Megan's fragility or on his own accursed need to rescue the woman. He hadn't counted on becoming emotionally involved.

Now he was scrambling for answers—answers to questions he wouldn't have thought to ask a week ago. And it wasn't in his nature to walk away. He wouldn't rest, he knew, until he'd learned everything he needed to know about her.

Megan heard Cal come in and lock the door; but she pretended to be asleep. As his footsteps paused beside the sofa, she willed herself to keep perfectly still. She knew that he was no threat to her safety. But he might want to talk— and the last thing she'd wanted was to be grilled about what had happened tonight. Cal wasn't her doctor or her therapist. The mess inside her head was her private concern. She would deal with it in her own time, in her own way.

Before long, he was asleep in bed, snoring lightly. She lay awake in the darkness, comforted by the peaceful, masculine sound. Strange, how safe that sound made her feel.

If only she'd felt that way in his arms.

But Cal was a complication she didn't need right now. She was too damaged for any kind of relationship— especially with a man whose past history with her was one big red flag.

She was beginning to drift. The couch wasn't the most comfortable bed, but she'd slept on far worse; and the long day had worn her out. She'd come here to rest, she reminded herself; to relax and do her best to heal…if only she could.

For a time she slumbered quietly. Then, the specter rose from the darkness of sleep once more. Like bones exposed by blowing sand, it emerged, took shape, took on life and substance to become living memory. Once again she heard Saida's cry as her young lover fell. She saw the shadowy forms close around the helpless girl, heard the rough laughter as they flung her to the ground, heard the helpless cries and the sound of tearing cloth. Beyond the dry well, Megan writhed against the sinewy arms that held her, screaming into the greasy palm that clamped her mouth. She could smell the sweat, taste it…

Something jolted Cal awake. He sat up, eyes staring into the darkness. As his senses cleared, he heard muffled whimpers and the sound of thrashing from the couch.

Flinging the covers aside, he switched on a bedside lamp and stumbled out of bed. As he neared Megan, he saw that she'd become tangled in a web of netting and covers. Eyes closed in sleep, she was fighting to get free.

"Megan." He spoke softly, knowing better than to grab her or shake her. "Megan, wake up. You're dreaming."

Clearly in torment, she continued to struggle. Working with care, he pulled away the netting and the twisted sheet and blanket. It seemed to make a difference, ending her frantic writhing—though her expression remained tense and fearful. She sprawled in her cotton pajamas, calmer now as he bent over her. Daring to touch her, he smoothed the damp curls back from her forehead. "It's all right," he murmured. "You're safe. I'm here."

Her eyelids fluttered open. She stared up at him. "Cal?"

"You were dreaming. Do you know where you are?"

He saw the flicker of uncertainty in her eyes. "You're in the bungalow with me," he said. "Everything's all right."

Her breath came in hiccupping, dry sobs. Cal remembered her panic attack in the hotel, when she'd allowed him to draw her close. It had helped her then. But after she'd fought her way out of their kiss, he knew better than to reach out to her without her permission. "Would you like me to hold you?" he asked.

She hesitated, then nodded. Ever so gently he circled her with his arms, pulling her against his chest. She clung to him like a frightened child, her heart still hammering her ribs.

Megan, Megan, what frightened you so? What can I do to help?

This was no time to voice his questions. Maybe the medical report would tell him something. Until then, he could only do his best to comfort her.

The room was chilly. A glance at the clock confirmed that it was too early to get up. But he didn't want to risk leaving her alone on the couch. There was only one thing to do.

"Let me carry you to the bed," he said. "You'll be safe there, even from me, I promise. All right?"

When she didn't answer he lifted her in his arms. Her hands crept onto his shoulders as he carried her across the floor. Parting the mosquito net, he lowered her to the mattress and pulled the covers over her. She was still quivering when he left her to walk around the bed and switch off the lamp.

Could he really climb between the sheets with this woman and keep the promise he'd made to her? He didn't entirely trust himself awake, let alone half-asleep. But there was a precaution he could take.

Lifting the blankets, he slipped under them, leaving

the top sheet as a discreet layer between his body and
Megan's. He couldn't recall ever sharing a woman's bed
without planning to make love to her. But there was a first
time for everything.

She lay curled slightly away from him, but he could feel
her trembling body through the sheet. She couldn't possibly be asleep. "Are you all right?" he asked her.

"I will be."

"Tell me about your dream." Was he pushing her too
fast? He wasn't sure she'd answer, but after a slow, unrav-
eling breath, she spoke.

"There was this young girl who used to help me, when I
was in Darfur. She was just fifteen, a beautiful child. She
left the camp at night to meet a boy. I went after them, but
I was too late."

"They were killed?"

"The boy was killed. The girl was...raped. Afterward
she was never found."

"Janjaweed?"

"Yes."

"And you saw it happen."

"There was nothing I could do."

"I'm sorry, Megan." Acting on instinct, he laid an arm
across her shoulders, on top of the covers. He half expected
her to pull away, but the weight seemed to calm her. She
was no longer trembling. Encouraged, he tightened his
clasp. With a sleepy murmur she snuggled against him,
warm through the sheet. "Go to sleep," he murmured. "No
more bad dreams. I'm here."

She relaxed with a sigh, the cadence of her breath deepening. Wide-awake now, Cal lay holding her in the darkness. He had nothing but admiration for the volunteers
who served in the refugee camps. The work demanded
courage, compassion and the strength to look death in the

face. Until Harlan Crandall's report, he would never have believed Megan capable of such fortitude. But her time in the camps had taken its toll. He'd seen evidence of that toll tonight.

He was familiar with the Janjaweed, of course—mercenaries paid by the Sudanese government for the express purpose of genocide against the black African population. Known as Devil Riders for the horses and camels they rode, they swept down on innocent civilians, killing, robbing and raping. Now that much of the bloody work was done, groups of Janjaweed had turned to banditry, even going so far as to rob the big white U.N. trucks that carried food and supplies to the camps. The refugees had little worth stealing, but if the marauders happened to catch an unguarded woman...

Cal's arm curled protectively around Megan's slumbering body. He could scarcely imagine the bravery it must have taken for her to go after that young girl and boy in the dark of night. At least she'd made it safely back to the camp. Thank heaven for that. Maybe now that she'd talked about the experience, she could begin the healing process.

She stirred, shifted and settled back into sleep. Now he could see the dark outline of her profile, fine-boned and elegant against the white pillowcase. His memory of the pampered ice queen he'd known in San Francisco was fading. This was Megan, as he thought of her now. And it was getting harder to reconcile her with the cold, high-living trophy wife whose extravagance had driven his best friend to suicide.

Cal had seen the checks himself—the generous donations from the charity events Megan oversaw that had never made it into the foundation's bank account. The graceful signature on the back had been Megan's, but they'd gone to a joint account in a different bank—an account in her name and Nick's. The online statements had gone to their home computer, which was registered to Megan. By the time the theft was discovered, the account had been almost empty.

How could he not believe she'd been involved in the theft, or even responsible for it?

Was there more to the story than what he knew? He wanted to believe that Nick was innocent—or that, at worst, he'd crossed the line solely to please his demanding wife. Nick had seemed so proud of her, so anxious to satisfy her every whim. But the woman beside him now didn't seem the type to manipulate her husband into theft—especially since the money had been earmarked for aid to the very same people she'd spent the past two years nursing.

Had Nick's death triggered a change of heart, making her regret her past actions? Had she changed...or had he been wrong about her all along?

Whatever was going on with Megan now, Cal couldn't let himself forget what had happened back in San Francisco. He'd been betrayed by the friend he would have trusted with his life. If he'd mistrusted Nick, how could he let himself believe that Nick's wife was blameless?

He couldn't afford to trust her until he knew the whole truth, no matter how ugly.

Megan woke alone in the bed. The bungalow was dark, but as her confusion cleared she became aware of water running in the bathroom. Beneath the closed door she could see a sliver of light.

Sitting up, she switched on the bedside lamp. Now she remembered the dream, and the aftermath—Cal's comforting voice, his strong arms lifting her off the couch and carrying her across the room to the bed. Amazingly, she'd slept for the rest of the night without nightmares.

She'd just flung back the covers when he stepped out of the bathroom, shaved, combed and dressed. He gave her an easy grin.

"Good morning, sleepyhead. I was about to wake you."

"What time is it?" she asked with a yawn.

"Five-thirty. Harris wants us on the road by six, so get a move on. There'll be coffee and a light breakfast in the lobby."

"Where are we going?" She dropped her feet to the cold tile floor.

"You'll see. It's a surprise."

"A surprise! Why do you and Harris insist on treating me like a five-year-old?"

His laughter followed her into the bathroom as she closed the door with a decisive click. She remembered what he'd said last night. Yes, it was time to put the drama behind her and start the day fresh.

By the time Gideon pulled the Land Rover up to the front of the lodge, Megan had finished her breakfast. The trees were alive with bird calls, and the amethyst sunrise promised clear weather. She looked forward to a day of adventure. Maybe this trip was exactly what she'd needed.

She stole a glance at Cal, where he stood talking with Harris. Her gaze traced the taper of his back from well-muscled shoulders to taut buttocks. By any measure, the man was prime stud material. But last night had proved she wasn't fit for any kind of physical relationship. Maybe she never would be.

At least he seemed to understand that. Since that disastrous kiss, he'd treated her like a kid sister. Even sharing the bed with him had been a chaste experience—perhaps a first for a man like Cal.

She tore her gaze away from his body. Under different conditions, she might not have minded sharing more than a blanket. But something vital in her was broken, shattered by forces she couldn't even name. If she was going to panic again, as she surely would, the last person she wanted it to happen with was Cal Jeffords.

"Ladies aboard!" Harris gave her a wink as he crushed his cigar with his boot heel and swung into the front passenger seat. "And may I add that you're looking right pert this morning, Miss Megan! Are you ready for your surprise?"

"Bring it on!" She tossed her day pack into the vehicle's bed, behind the backseat. It bounced off a basketball-size chunk of broken concrete lying next to the tailgate. "Is that what you plan to throw at anything that attacks us?" she joked.

"That's my wheel block," Harris said. "Believe me, if you get a puncture out there or need to park on a hill, you don't want to have to go looking for a rock. There could be some nasty surprises in that long grass. I've never had to use it—hope I never will. But it pays to be prepared."

Giving him a grin, she climbed into the backseat and spoke to the driver. "Good morning, Gideon. It's nice to have you with us."

"Thank you, miss." His tone was formal, but his expression told her he was pleased with her greeting.

"Let's go." Cal climbed into the backseat with Megan. The air was cool now, but the rising sun promised to be hot. Megan tightened the chin strap on her canvas hat. She was going to need it.

Cal studied Megan as the Land Rover climbed the winding road to the rim of the Ngorongoro Crater. She had just discovered where they were going today, and she was as excited as a child at the circus. Last night he'd feared for her mental state. But seeing her this morning, radiant and laughing, with her jade-green scarf knotted at her throat, was worth every dollar this safari had cost him. If he were meeting her for the first time today, with no past history between them, he could easily see himself falling for her charm.

This must have been the woman Nick saw when he looked at her. For the first time, Cal understood why Nick had fallen so hard and so fast. And Cal could no longer really say that he blamed him.

The thought shook him. Nick had been the type to fall in love easily, but while Cal had known plenty of women, he hadn't fancied himself in head over heels since high school. He'd been too serious, too driven for such frivolous emotion. He'd always felt that it was an advantage he had over Nick. But it didn't feel like too much of an advantage at the moment.

He put the thought out of his head. Megan was a fascinating package, but not what he'd call a candidate for a stable relationship. And he'd be a fool to let desire color his need for justice.

This morning he'd taken a moment to check his email. The medical report hadn't arrived. It might not arrive for days. Meanwhile he had no choice except to be patient—and Cal was not a patient man.

A flock of doves whooshed out of a flowering tree and soared skyward against the sunrise. "Beautiful…" The word was a whisper on Megan's lips. Cal remembered kissing those lips, crushing them with his. And he remembered what had followed. What had thrown her into panic? Was it him?

The Land Rover had crested the top of the crater and

was starting down the graveled road to the vast caldera below.

"Can you see any animals yet?" Cal asked Megan. "Here, take the binoculars."

Looking out the open side of the vehicle, she scanned the landscape below. "All I can see is grass and brush."

"You'll see a lot more when we get to the bottom," Harris said. "Last time I was here I saw a black rhino. Poor buggers will be extinct if the poachers get many more of them. The horns are worth big money. Arabs buy them for dagger handles. And powdered rhino horn's the rich Chinese version of Viagra. Works on the mind if nothing else, I suppose. Not that I've tried it—or needed to." He shot Cal and Megan a mischievous look.

"Are there poachers here in the crater?" Megan asked.

"They've been known to sneak in at night. Rangers have the go-ahead to shoot them on the spot. I'd do the same if I caught the bastards."

"But you guide hunters, don't you Harris?"

"Not here. This place is a national park. The animals here are meant to be protected. And legal hunting's not like poaching. Hunters pay thousands for a license to take one trophy animal. Part of the money goes to fund game management, including protection for animals like our rhino friend. And the cash that goes into the economy encourages the locals to see wild animals as the resource they are. Poaching's like the dark side. It takes all the good away."

"I see something." Cal pointed to a cluster of black dots. "Down there to the right, four o'clock."

Harris nodded. "Cape buffalo. Tough and mean as they come. We can get closer in the vehicle, but don't let them catch you on foot. I learned that lesson the hard way—see this?" He pointed to his empty, pinned-up sleeve. "Biggest bull you ever saw. Damn near killed me."

Lifting an eyebrow, Cal glanced at Megan. She rewarded him with a wink and a sexy smile that kicked his pulse into overdrive. He cursed silently. A few hot nights between the sheets would suit him fine. But with her panic attacks, her shadowed past and her connection to Nick and the stolen money, Megan was the last woman he should get serious with.

He could see it happening, and it made a delicious picture. Sharing some pillow talk with Megan had been his plan all along. But he hadn't planned on becoming emotionally involved. He was walking a fine line, and Lord help him if he stepped over. He could find himself in serious trouble.

Six

Megan gripped her camera, hesitant to raise it and risk triggering a charge. She'd heard how dangerous the huge black Cape buffalo could be. But these seemed accustomed to vehicles. They barely raised their massive heads as the Land Rover passed at a fifty-yard distance. Egrets—fairy white—stalked among their ebony legs, unafraid as they probed for insects in the grass.

"They seem so peaceful," she whispered to Cal. "And look, there's a little black calf—and another!"

"All the more reason to be careful." Cal's low voice was close to her ear. "They're family animals. Very protective."

"We should be seeing more babies." With the buffalo upwind of them, Harris spoke in his normal tone. "Now that the rains have started, there'll be plenty of grass—plenty of meat for the predators, as well. Good time to raise young ones."

Megan gazed ahead to an open plain where dainty

Thomson's gazelles were grazing. The ebony stripes along their sides glimmered in the morning sunlight.

"Do you have children, Harris?" she asked.

"A boy by my second wife. She took him home to England after the divorce. I hear he's a barrister of some sort, but we don't talk."

"I'm sorry."

"That's life, girl. You play the hand you're dealt and make the best of it."

Wise words, Megan thought. She'd been trying to make the best of her own life. But surprises kept throwing her off track. Surprises like Cal Jeffords showing up and turning her world upside down.

"How about you, Gideon?" she asked the driver. "Do you have a family?"

A smile broadened his long face. "Yes, miss. Three fine boys and two girls. They keep my wife very busy."

"I can tell you're very proud of them."

"Yes, miss. Good children are a blessing from God."

Something had spooked the gazelles. Their heads and tails shot up, and they burst into glorious flight, leaping and bounding like winged creatures. Even the little ones, all legs, were fleet enough to keep up with the herd as they vanished over a rise.

Gideon glanced at Harris, who nodded. "Lion, maybe. Come up easy."

Lion. Megan's heart crept into her throat as the Land Rover slowed to a crawl. She'd been in Africa for two years, but there were few, if any, large wild animals left in the places where she'd worked. Outside of a zoo, she'd never seen a lion.

In the open-sided vehicle, they were fully exposed to any creature that might decide to attack them. She'd glimpsed the high-powered rifle Harris kept mounted next to the passenger door, but he didn't seem concerned about having it ready.

She glanced at Cal. Reading her anxiety, he laid a light hand against her back. She moved closer to him. He might not be much use against a lion, but his size and strength made her feel safer.

The Land Rover inched around a bend in the narrow road, and suddenly there they were—two lionesses, sprawled on the grass a mere stone's throw away. The larger one studied the vehicle and its passengers with calm amber eyes. Her huge mouth opened in a disdainful yawn that showed yellowed fangs as long as Megan's fingers.

"Mother and daughter, I'd say," Harris whispered. "Look, the older one's pregnant. Big sister will likely stick around to help raise the cubs. Go ahead and take a picture. They're posing for you."

Megan's hands shook as she centered the pair in her viewfinder and pressed the shutter. The click was startling in the silence, but the lionesses barely glanced toward the sound. Gideon was about to move on when Harris touched his arm. "Hold it," he whispered. "Here comes papa!"

Megan was aware of a stirring, like wind in the long grass. She forgot to breathe as a majestic male lion strolled into view. Regal and unhurried, he seemed more interested in the females than in the Land Rover and the lowly humans inside. There was no need to prove who was king here.

Megan managed a few more shaky photos before Gideon pulled away, leaving the lions in peace. Harris grinned. "Now there's a life for you! The women raise the cubs and bring down the meat. Nothing for the old man to do but fight and make love."

"Not that he has it that easy." Cal's voice was close to

Megan's ear. "He has to defend his territory and his family from gangs of rival males. The stakes are life and death."

"That's a grim thought," Megan said. "Oh, look! Zebras out there in the open! And what's up there, next to the road? Something black!"

"Warthogs," Harris said. "A family of them, rooting for their breakfast."

"And they've got babies!" Megan rose in the seat, aiming her camera and snapping. "Look at them! So tiny and so cute!"

"Again, it's the male's job to protect them." Cal steadied her with a hand at her waist. "He may not be very big, but those tusks can rip a lion's belly, and the lions know it."

She glanced down at him. "Why aren't you taking pictures?"

He gave her his Hollywood grin. "I've got plenty of pictures from other trips. Right now I'm having more fun watching you."

Cal had spoken the truth. Being with Megan today was like being with a little girl at Disneyland. She was so natural and so excited; every minute with her was a delight.

He remembered the glittering ice queen who'd been married to Nick—perfect hair and makeup, runway clothes, the best of everything. Which one was the real her? Was this exuberance a part of her that she'd stifled all those years? If so, then he could almost understand Megan running away to escape the person she'd become.

What if it hadn't been about the money, after all? Today he could almost believe that. But no—he brought himself up short. Megan was as changeable as the wind. He'd be a fool to start trusting her.

Last night he'd watched her fall apart. Today she was behaving as if nothing had happened. Had the panic attack and the nightmare been some kind of performance, staged to gain his sympathy?

But how could that be? How could any person with a shred of honesty be capable of such deception? He couldn't believe that of Megan. But what *could* he believe about her? He had little choice except to wait for the report he'd ordered and hope it would give him some insight.

They stopped to eat bagged lunches on a safely fenced rise with primitive restrooms, picnic tables and a wide vista of the grassland below.

"I still can't believe one of those lions didn't jump right into our laps." Megan took a sip of her bottled water. "What would you do, Harris, if something like that happened?"

"I'd fire into the air and try to scare the bugger away. There'd be no end of trouble if I shot one of those babies in the park. Best way to keep that from happening is to read their body language. If they're looking uneasy, you keep your distance. Those lions we saw back there were as mellow as big pussycats. Otherwise we'd have given them a wide berth."

"Have you ever had an animal charge your vehicle?"

"Just once. White rhino in Tarangire. Made a bloody dent in the door and crushed my arm. That's how this happened." He glanced toward the pinned sleeve. Megan shot Cal a knowing glance, her eyes dancing, her smile a flash of white in her tanned face. He'd thought she was beautiful when she was married to Nick. Today she was spectacular.

The breeze had freshened. Harris squinted toward the far rim of the crater, where black clouds churned above the horizon, ready to stampede across the empty sky.

"We'd best be heading back," Harris said. "But there's plenty of time. We'll take a different road, off the beaten track as they say. Might see something new."

Megan climbed into the backseat and settled next to Cal. The morning had been incredible, but the hours spent in the hot sun and the jouncing, swaying vehicle had taken their toll. As time passed, her energy had begun to flag.

Back in the camps, she'd spent her days working in the infirmary from first light to bedtime, collapsing on her cot and then getting up at dawn to more of the same. Only now that she had the luxury of rest did Megan realize how exhausted she'd become. Even so, she missed being useful. When she got back to the bungalow, she would find some paper and write letters to people she'd known and worked with in the refugee camps. If she could let them know she meant to come back, that would strengthen her own resolve to get strong again.

After she finished the letters, maybe she'd look for some light reading in the lodge gift shop—a thriller or maybe a romance, anything to engage her mind and block the nightmares before she went to sleep.

The distant growl of thunder pulled her back to the present. Cal was watching her, mild concern in his eyes. "I thought you were about to nod off," he said.

"Would you have let me?"

"Only until we saw something you wouldn't want to miss. If you're sleepy, my shoulder makes a good pillow."

For an instant Megan was tempted. But accepting Cal's offer might be courting fate. Bad enough that Cal had witnessed one of her nightmares. She didn't want Harris or Gideon to see them, too. She shook her head. "I'm fine— and I don't want to miss anything."

The sky was getting darker now as fast-moving rain clouds blocked the sun. The Land Rover had cut off onto a side trail and was crossing an open plain dotted with thornbush. A herd of zebras and dark-hued wildebeest grazed in the distance. There were no other vehicles in sight.

"Along here is where I saw the black rhino," Harris said. "If he's still in the neighborhood, we might get lucky. Keep your eyes open."

He'd no sooner spoken than the sky split open as if someone had slashed a giant, water-filled balloon. Thunder roared across the horizon as sheets of gray rain turned the road to a quagmire of flowing mud.

Gideon muttered what Megan assumed to be a curse. Harris, however, was undeterred. "What's a little rain?" he shouted, grinning. "We can't stay here, so nothing to do but keep going!"

The canvas roof kept off the overhead downpour, but water was still blowing in. Megan, who hadn't thought to bring her rain poncho, was already drenched. There had to be a way to roll down the side covers. But she assumed it would involve stopping and having someone get out—impractical now because they'd just come up on another herd of Cape buffalo.

Something—maybe the lightning and thunder—had disturbed the hulking black beasts. More numerous than the first group, they were milling and snorting like range cattle on the verge of a stampede. Megan remembered Harris's words about reading an animal's body language. The signs that she could read from them made it clear that danger was very real.

The others seemed to agree. Gideon was driving as fast as he dared, trying to get past the herd without agitating them further. As the vehicle swayed along the muddy road, Megan found herself shivering, not only with cold but with fear.

Reaching across the seat, Cal circled her with his arm and drew her close. She huddled against his side. There was little warmth to be had, but she found the hard bulk of his body comforting, like a rock to cling to for safety.

What happened next happened fast. A low, dark shape—a warthog—shot across the road, almost under the front wheels. Instinctively, Gideon slammed the brake. The animal streaked away unharmed, but the Land Rover fishtailed in the thick mud and crunched to a stop with one rear wheel resting in a water-filled hole at the roadside.

Gideon revved the engine and tried to pull out—once, then again, rocking forward and back. It was no use. The mud was so slippery that the heavy-duty tires could find no purchase. They spun in place, shooting geysers of mud and water.

For a tension-filled moment nobody spoke. But Megan guessed what the men were thinking. The rain could go on for hours, making the road even worse. Even if they could radio for help, it was doubtful that anyone could get here before the storm let up. If they were going to free the vehicle, somebody would have to brave the buffalo and push from behind.

Since Gideon knew the vehicle best, it made sense for him to stay at the wheel. With one arm, Harris could neither push nor shift and drive efficiently. That left Cal—the huskiest of the men—to climb out into the mud.

The buffalo had turned as one to watch them. Frozen in place for the moment, they were perhaps fifty yards away—a distance that a charging animal could cover in a heartbeat.

Harris lifted the rifle from its bracket next to the door. "I'll cover you," he said. "If the bastards get any closer, I'll fire over their heads, try to scare them off."

Megan read the knowing glance the two men exchanged. If one of the massive bulls were to actually charge, there'd be little chance of stopping it, even if Harris aimed to kill. A single rifle shot, even a lucky one, wouldn't be enough to drop it on the spot. And a wounded Cape buffalo would be a murderous foe.

"Why not scare them off now?" Megan asked.

"Risky," Harris grunted. "Spooking them could make them more aggressive. Safest thing is to keep them calm, if we can."

"What can I do to help?"

"Pray," he snapped, dismissing her.

Harris shouldered the rifle with his left hand, resting the barrel on the door. Megan had wondered briefly whether he could handle a gun with one arm. Evidently he could.

He glanced back at Cal. "Whatever you do, keep your head down and stay close to the vehicle," he said. "If the buffalo see you in the open, you're in trouble. Ready?"

"Ready." Ducking low, Cal climbed into the back of the Land Rover and bellied over the tailgate. Megan's heart crawled into her throat as she watched him go. More than anything she wanted to stop him. Harris had told her to pray, but her mind had lost the words. There was nothing she could do but watch.

She could see the back of Cal's head and shoulders as he braced himself behind the rear bumper. "Hit it," he growled.

Gideon slammed the vehicle into gear and gunned the engine. The wheels inched forward, spattering mud, then the rear sank back into the hole.

Cal muttered a curse. "Can you back it out?"

"I already tried. No good," Gideon said.

"There's a shovel back here. Can we dig out a track?"

"Better not to try," Harris said. "That much activity could set off the buffalo." He was looking not at Cal but at the herd. As lightning crackled across the sky, they were becoming more agitated, stamping, lowing and tossing their heads. The biggest bull of all, with curling horns as broad and thick as the bumper on a truck, had moved front and center. His nostrils flared as he processed the alien odors of motor exhaust and human sweat.

Cal repositioned himself behind the tailgate. "All right. Again."

Once more the engine roared. Cal's shoulder muscles strained like steel cables as he pushed back and upward. The tires spun and spat showers of mud before he gave up and slumped forward. "We need something to brace that wheel." His voice rasped with fatigue. "A rock, maybe to jam in the hole."

A rock! Megan remembered the chunk of concrete she'd seen in the back of the truck. It might work, but Cal couldn't shove it in place while he was pushing. He would need a second pair of hands. Hers.

The buffalo were massing behind their leader. Rain poured down their sleek black sides and dripped off their horns. Megan forced herself to look away and concentrate on her task as she slipped into the back bed of the vehicle and found the concrete. Harris and Gideon were watching the herd. They hadn't noticed her, but Cal did.

"What in hell's name do you think you're doing?" His eyes blazed in his mud-coated face.

She hefted the gray chunk, which was even heavier than it looked. "Hold this," she hissed, passing it to him.

He took it, but when she started to scramble over the tailgate, his gaze narrowed dangerously. "For God's sake, Megan, stay put!" he growled.

"You need me." She dropped to the ground, staying close to the vehicle. Taking the piece of concrete from him, she knelt and set it rough-side-up against the back of the mired wheel. She tried not to think about the buffalo and how close that big bull might be. Rain soaked her hair and streamed down her body, but she no longer felt the chill.

"Tell Gideon to try it again," she said, hoping Cal had one more push left in him. He was a powerful man, but he was only human and the effort would be excruciating.

He positioned himself against the bumper, feet braced, eyes meeting hers through the gray veil of rain. "Be careful," he muttered. "This thing could roll back and crush your hand."

"I'll be fine."

"If there's a charge, roll under the vehicle. That'll be the safest place. Understand?"

She gave him a nod, willing herself not to look toward the buffalo. "Ready."

"Hit it!"

Gideon gunned the motor to a roar. Grunting with the strain, Cal pushed and lifted. Spitting showers of mud, the mired wheel inched forward, leaving just enough space and time for Megan to shove the lump of concrete into the hole.

But would it be enough? As she tumbled backward, out of the way, Cal eased off long enough to let the tire settle onto the solid surface. Gideon was still racing the engine. Now, finding slight purchase, the wheel began straining forward.

"Now!" Cal began pushing with all his might. Scrambling to her feet, Megan flung herself next to him. Her weight was scant, her strength meager, but coupled with his it might be enough to make a difference.

Inch by inch the Land Rover crept forward. Now it was out of the deep mud, moving forward onto the main trail and gaining speed. Harris was whooping like a cowboy on Saturday night.

Hoisting Megan in his arms, Cal dumped her over the tailgate and clambered after her. She sat up and swung her attention back to the buffalo. The bull had burst into a false charge but stopped short, snorting and tossing its horns in what could almost pass as a victory dance at the sight of their retreat.

Bracing her by the shoulders, Cal looked her up and down as if inspecting her for damage. His hat was gone, and he was coated with mud from his hair to his boots. Megan realized she must look the same. "You're all right?" he asked.

She gave him a grin. "Never better. We did it!"

"You crazy woman! You could've been killed!" He caught her close, holding her fiercely against his chest. She was dimly aware of Harris and Gideon in the front seat, but it was as if the two men were far away and nobody was here but Cal. Adrenaline rushed through her body. She felt wonderfully wild and reckless.

"You brave, beautiful fool!" Laughing, he cradled her close, muddy clothes and all. His arms were warm and safe, his laughter like a joyful drug. Carried away, Megan was surprised to find herself wanting to be kissed—really kissed—by him.

But there was no way Cal was going to kiss her. Not after what had happened the last time. If Megan wanted a kiss from him, there was only one thing she could do.

Fueled by euphoria, she hooked his neck with her arm, pulled him down to her and pressed her parted lips to his.

Seven

Megan sensed the shock of Cal's surprise. Her heart shrank as he stiffened against her. But he was quick to recover. With a little growl of laughter, he took charge. His compelling mouth molded to hers with a teasing flick of tongue—playful and, at the same time, so sensual that she experienced a delicious twinge at the apex of her thighs.

The fear was still there, slumbering in the depths of her awareness. But the thrill of Cal's kiss swept her away like a plunge over a waterfall. For a fleeting moment, she savored the sweetness of something she'd believed lost.

Too soon, he ended the contact. "We have an audience," he muttered in her ear.

Megan glanced forward to find Harris turned in his seat, grinning back at them. "I'll be damned," he said with a wink. "I knew you two would come around. All it took was a thunderstorm, a stuck wheel and a herd of buffalo."

"Eyes front, *mzee*," Cal said, using the Swahili term for

an old man. He smiled as he spoke, but Megan sensed that any more kissing would have to wait for a private time.

Riding in the bed of the Land Rover was rough and wet. Cal boosted her over the back of the seat and took his place beside her. His arm circled her shoulders, pulling her against his side to protect her from the worst of the storm.

Megan's heart hammered as she weighed the risky step she'd just taken. Had she turned a corner? Was she really getting better, or had the moment's excitement swept her away?

She yearned to be emotionally well again. To go through life unafraid of intimacy, to make love, even to remarry and have children—that was what she'd wanted all along. But over the past months she'd lost hope. The fear that had frozen some vital part of her—a fear so dark and deeply rooted that she didn't fully understand it herself— still lurked like a monster in its cave, waiting to reach out with its cold tentacles and crush her courage.

Back in America she might have sought professional help. But here what little help there was to be had was focused on treating the trauma of refugees—which was as it should be. And going home would only bring her up against the demons Nick's death had left behind.

For the first time she felt a glimmer of hope. She'd fought her attraction to Cal for as long as she'd known him. Now there was no more reason to fight. Something about his solid strength wrapped her in a sense of safety. His kiss had left her with a delicious buzz. But was it enough? Could she risk more, especially when she knew the reason he'd come here? Could she trust him not to manipulate her, or use her vulnerability against her? He'd been so good to her the previous night, but could she truly trust him? And could she trust herself not to get too invested?

Even if she dared go the distance, she knew better than

to think a fling with Cal would last. He wasn't the sort of man to settle on one woman. Even if he was, his dark suspicions and the painful history they shared would drive them apart. But he was an exciting man—a very sexy man. And she had little doubt he'd be willing to cooperate with her present needs.

Was it time she faced her fear?

The Land Rover crawled upward toward the rim of the crater. The going was treacherous, with rain churning the road to mud; but soon the long drive would be over. Chilled to the bone, Cal looked forward to a hot shower, dry clothes, a gourmet dinner at the lodge—and just maybe something more.

Megan nestled against his side, the contact of their bodies providing the only spot of warmth. As his arm tightened around her shoulders, she glanced up and gave him a quiet smile. She'd been amazing today, braving the buffalo to climb out of the vehicle and brace the wheel. How many women—or men—would have shown that kind of courage?

Her kiss, he suspected, had demanded a different kind of courage. After last night's panicked response, her sweet passion had caught him off guard. Whatever she'd meant by it, he wasn't complaining. But now what?

Clearly Megan was up to something. But he knew better than to push her. Be patient, Cal lectured himself. Let her take the lead; then follow to where they both wanted to go.

Hadn't he meant to seduce her all along? If that was what the woman had in mind, she was playing right into his hands. Get her warm and purring, and maybe she'd open up about what had happened in San Francisco.

It was still raining by the time they topped the crater and made it downhill to the lodge. Gideon pulled up in front to let his weary passengers climb out of the vehicle. Harris headed inside, probably for a warming glass of whiskey at the bar. Cal helped Megan out of the backseat. Chilled, muddy and cramped from sitting in the rain, they made their way down the brick path to their bungalow. They paused to leave their muddy boots on the doorstep for the staff. Then Megan used her key to open the door.

Inside, Cal fished a Tanzanian shilling out of his pocket. "I'll flip you for the first shower."

Meeting his eyes, she took the coin out of his hand. "It's a big shower," she said.

Cal was quick to get her meaning, even though her fingers trembled as she laid the coin on the table. This was her call, he reminded himself. All he had to do was follow her lead. He would have Megan right where he wanted her.

Their clothes were dripping mud. It didn't make sense to shed them anyplace but in the spacious, tiled shower, where they could at least rinse out the worst of the dirt. Megan walked into the bathroom, leaving the door open. Turning on the water, she stepped into the shower and began unfastening her mud-soaked blouse. Her quivering fingers fumbled with the buttons.

"Let me give you a hand." After shedding his leather belt, his watch and his wallet, Cal stepped in beside her and took over the buttons. He heard her breath catch as his knuckle brushed her breast. Slow and easy, he reminded himself. Megan was putting herself out to make this work. The last thing he wanted was to frighten her back into her shell.

Her jade-flecked eyes widened as the front of her blouse fell open to reveal a lacy black bra—perhaps a relic of the old days in San Francisco. The sight of that dark lace against creamy skin triggered an ache of raw need. Cal suppressed a groan as his sex rose and hardened. All he wanted right now was to rip off her wet clothes, sweep her into bed and bury himself inside her.

But haste could ruin everything. Megan was clearly willing to try. But he knew she'd been traumatized, and one wrong move could spoil everything. If he wanted her, he would have to hold back, be patient and let her set the pace.

If he could manage to keep himself under control.

Cal's shirt was open to his chest. Willing herself to stay calm, Megan freed the remaining buttons, down to the waistband of his trousers. There was nothing to be afraid of, she told herself. She'd been married to Nick for five years. Being naked with a man and having sex was nothing new. And she *wanted* this. She needed it. So why was her heart pounding like a jackhammer gone berserk?

She could feel his eyes, those perpetually cold gray eyes that had always seemed to look right through her. Eyes she remembered as contemptuous, especially after Nick's death. If she looked up, what would she see in them now?

Maybe she was making a fool of herself. Why would Cal want to make love to a woman he had every reason to dislike?

But then again, why wouldn't he?

The warm, clean shower spray rinsed their hair and sluiced down their bodies, running brown with African mud before it gurgled down the drain. A shiver of anticipation passed through Megan as Cal pushed her wet blouse off her shoulders. It slid down her arms and dropped to the tiles.

"Look at me, Megan." His voice was husky. His thumb caught the curve of her jaw, tilting her face upward. The eyes she'd remembered as cold burned with raw need.

Her hand moved upward to rest against his cheek. His

skin was warm, the stubble rough against her palm. "Kiss me, Cal," she whispered.

Leaning down, he feathered his lips against hers. The contact passed like a glowing thread of heat through her body, warming her to an aching awareness of how much she needed him. She strained upward to deepen the kiss and felt him respond, his arms pulling her close, his lips nibbling, tasting, moving to her cheeks, her throat and back to her mouth. His hand unhooked her bra and pushed at the waistband of her slacks. The fit was loose enough for them to slide off her hips and drop, along with her panties, to the shower floor. She stood naked in his arms—a trifle self-conscious because she was so thin, but Cal didn't seem to notice—or at least not to mind.

Finding a bar of scented soap, he lathered his hands and then reached for her, his palms slicking the warm suds across her shoulder blades and down the long furrow of her spine. Sweet sensations melted her body like hot fudge flowing over ice cream. Her tension eased out in a long sigh. Almost purring, she arched against the exquisite pressure of his hands. Her eyes closed as his fingers worked their delicious way down to trace the deep V of her lower back, splaying to cradle her buttocks. For a moment he held her that way, cupping her hips against his. Through his wet trousers she could feel the hard ridge of his sex pressing her belly.

A memory glimmered, awakening the cold coils that slumbered inside her. Megan willed herself to block the fear. She wanted to let Cal make love to her. She wanted to believe that she could heal. She wanted *him*.

He lowered his mouth to hers, his kiss gentle and lingering. "I want to touch all of you," he whispered, turning her around so that her back was toward him. His big soapy hands slid over her breasts, caressing them, cupping them in his palms, thumbing the nipples until they ached with yearning. A moan quivered in her throat.

"You're so beautiful, Megan. You were made to be loved." One hand lingered on her breast, and the other slid down to skim her navel, splay on her belly and brush the dark triangle of hair where her thighs joined. She wanted the burst of sensation that his touch would awaken when he explored further. But as his fingers moved lower, a chill passed through her body. The coils of fear shifted and tightened, and she sensed that she was losing the battle to hold them at bay.

Maybe things were happening too fast. If she took more time she might still be all right. Shifting away, she turned to face him.

"You need to clean up, too," she said, forcing a smile as she found the soap. "Let me wash your back."

Ignoring his slightly puzzled expression, she turned him away from her, pulled the mud-soaked shirt off his shoulders and tossed it onto the shower floor.

He had a magnificently sculpted back, broad and tanned and powerful. His smooth skin warmed to her touch. Megan luxuriated in the feel of him, letting her soapy hands glide over his muscular shoulders and down the solid, tapering curve of his spine. Little by little, as she stroked his warm, golden skin, she felt her fear ebbing. It was going to happen, she told herself. All she had to do was relax and let nature do the rest.

Reaching his waistband, she hesitated. With a raw laugh, Cal reached down, yanked open the fly and let his pants and briefs drop around his ankles. "Don't stop now," he said. "I'm enjoying this."

Ignoring a prickle of uneasiness, Megan soaped his taut buttocks. His body was perfect, everything tight and in flawless proportion. Any woman should be thrilled to have him in her bed. Her hands caressed curves and contours, moving forward to skim the ridges of his hip bones. She could feel the tension growing in him, sense the urgency in the harsh cadence of his breath. Her own pulse had begun to race—but was it from desire or from that unknown terror that had given her no peace since the night she'd gone after Saida?

He cleared his throat. "I think my back is clean enough. If you want to wash the rest of me, I'm all yours. Otherwise, just say so and I'll shut off the water and grab us some towels. I look forward to drying you off."

Megan glanced down at her soapy hands. Her heart lurched as she imagined Cal's jutting erection, gleaming like wet marble in her hands. She knew what he wanted. Heaven help her, she wanted it, too. But she could feel the cold dread, as sure and silent as death, rising inside her.

She froze.

"What is it, Megan?" He glanced back at her, his eyes narrowing with concern as he shut off the water. "What's the matter?"

She'd begun to shiver. Her arms clutched her ribs. Tears might have helped, but she hadn't shed them since that awful night in Darfur.

"I'm sorry." She choked out the words. "I thought I could do this, Cal. But I just can't. There's something wrong with me—something I can't control." She stared down at the shower drain, wishing she could just dissolve and flow away.

"You're getting cold." Stepping out onto the mat, he reached for one of the two white terry-cloth robes that hung on the back of the door. Gentleness masked his obvious frustration as he laid it over her trembling shoulders. Slipping her arms into the sleeves, she knotted the sash around her waist. Little by little her racing heart began to calm. By the time she forced herself to look at him, he'd donned the other robe.

"I was hoping this wouldn't happen," she said. "I should've known better. I feel like a fool."

"At least I appreciate your honesty," he said. "I wouldn't want to make love to a woman who wasn't enjoying herself."

"Not even if she *wanted* to enjoy herself?" Megan gripped her sash, yanking it tighter around her waist. "Do you think I want to be this way—flying into a panic whenever I'm faced with intimacy? All I want is to be a normal woman again. So I took a chance. It didn't work. Not even with you."

Not even with you. It was too late to bite back the words. The subtle shift in his expression told her what he'd read into them. He wasn't just another man to her. He was a man who meant something—even if she wasn't completely sure what. Their past together had been so troubled, but the things she admired about him—his strength, his determination, the intensity of his feelings—had made her hope that he could carry some of this burden for her, lighten the load enough to let her heal.

"Come sit down." His hand at the small of her back guided her out of the bathroom and across the bedroom floor to the couch. Sitting, he pulled her down next to him and covered them both with a woolen blanket. Tucking her bare feet under her, she nestled into its warmth. Rain drummed on the tile roof and streamed down the windowpanes.

"You were amazing out there today," he said. "I mean it."

"It was an adventure—and somebody had to help."

He slipped an arm around her shoulders, a friendly gesture, meant to be comforting. "You're a brave woman,

Megan—and strong. I'm just discovering how strong. But something's frightened you badly. When did these panic attacks start?"

"Are you trying to analyze me, Dr. Freud?" She attempted a feeble joke.

"I'm just trying to understand you—maybe even help if I can. When did you become aware that something was wrong?"

"I'm not sure." She wasn't about to describe her fiasco with the doctor. That disastrous date wasn't the source of her problem, just a symptom.

"The incident you dreamed about—going after that young girl and boy, seeing them attacked. When was that?"

She shrugged, uneasy with the question. "Five, maybe six months ago. It's hard to keep track of time there. But I remember it was the dry season."

"Where were you when you saw it happen? If you were afraid to help them—"

"No, I was *trying* to help them. I'd brought a pistol. But before I could use it, somebody grabbed me from behind and took it away. I couldn't move, couldn't scream. I could only watch." Megan felt the fear rising. "Don't ask me to talk about this, Cal. I don't want to."

"Fine." His breath eased out in a long exhalation. "Just one more question. How did you get away?"

The cold coils tightened. "I don't know. Maybe the Janjaweed let me go because I was American. Or maybe somebody came from the camp and scared them off. The next thing I remember, I was waking up in the infirmary."

"You really don't know what happened?"

"I was probably knocked out—or fainted—and somebody found me. That's the only explanation that makes sense." Agitated now, she flung the blanket aside and rose from the couch. "No more questions, Cal. Two innocent young lives were destroyed that night. I'll remember it forever, but that doesn't mean I want to talk about it."

Pulse racing, she strode to the wardrobe where she'd hung her meager supply of clothes and went through the motions of rummaging through the hangers. "Isn't it about dinnertime? I'm starved, and I can hardly wear this bathrobe to the dining room. So please excuse me while I get dressed." She grabbed a set of clothes without really looking at them and glanced back at him. "That debacle in the shower never happened. I never want to hear about it again."

Cal glanced across the table to where Megan was conversing animatedly with Harris. Since he'd grilled her about the incident in the camp, she'd barely spoken to him. Clearly his questions had made her uncomfortable. All the more reason to keep pursuing them, but in a more subtle way.

He'd come to Tanzania to track down the stolen money and learn what he could about her role in Nick's suicide. That goal was still high on his list. But what drove him now was Megan—finding the key to understanding this maddeningly complex woman. He couldn't seem to make the pieces line up in his mind.

She had a fortune tucked away, but chose to work in one of the grimmest refugee camps in the world. She was equally at home in designer brands and mud-stained safari gear. She kissed him as if she couldn't get close enough to him, but froze at the feel of his hands on her body. She was brave but frightened. Passionate but withdrawn. Charming and at ease in this moment with Harris but still the same woman who had trembled with pain and fear barely an hour before.

The more he learned about her, the less he understood.

And the more driven he became to figure her out, find the key to unlock her inner demons and set her free.

Earlier he'd looked forward to making love to her. But even as she undressed him, he'd sensed that she was pushing herself too far. By the time she'd finally crumpled, he'd been prepared to back off. Bedding a terror-struck woman wasn't his idea of a good time—for him or for her.

Not even with you.

Her anguished words came back to him—the words that had told him he was more than just another man to her. She'd wanted him, and only him—the awareness of that made him all the more determined to break through her fear. Whatever it took, he would get to the bottom of what she was dealing with—and make love to her as she was meant to be loved.

A stray thought reminded him that he hadn't checked his email tonight. After dinner he would make his excuses and wander down the hall to the front desk. By now he should have a reply to his request for Megan's file. If it wasn't there, his next request would be less cordial.

By the time they'd finished their tiramisu, Cal was getting restless. It came as a relief when Megan accepted Harris's invitation to have a drink at the bar. Promising to join them later, he strode down the corridor to the front office. The computers were busy with people from the tour group using the antiquated machines, but he managed to find an empty spot and log on to his email.

The file was there, as he'd hoped. But it was a long one, and he didn't want to read it in this crowded room, with people jammed around him, awaiting their turn at the machines. Sending the file to the office printer, he picked up the sheaf of pages and went in search of some privacy.

Two doors down the hall from the dining room was a small library, the shelves stocked with books and out-of-date magazines left behind by past guests. It was furnished with two well-worn leather chairs, both empty. Switching on a lamp, Cal took a seat and began to read.

The first few pages were routine—lists of assignments and duties, along with evaluations, all of them praising her work. He was halfway through the file before he found what he was looking for—her medical history, including a doctor's account of the night Megan had described.

As he read, his fingers gripped the page, crumpling the edges of the paper.

Dear God. Megan…Megan…

Eight

With mounting horror, Cal reread the doctor's account—how searchers had found Megan unconscious outside the camp one morning, bruised and smeared with blood, her clothes ripped away. She'd been eased onto a stretcher and carried back to the infirmary, where an examination confirmed that she'd been raped, most likely multiple times.

For four days she'd lain in a stupor with an IV in her arm. The medications she'd been given were listed in the report—antibiotics along with a light sedative and drugs to prevent pregnancy and sexually transmitted diseases.

The doctor had attempted to make arrangements to have her airlifted to a hospital, but there was no plane readily available. On the fifth day, while they were still awaiting transport, Megan had opened her eyes and sat up. She'd insisted that the flight be canceled and that she be allowed to go back to work. She appeared to have made a full recovery except for one thing—when asked about the incident, she had no memory of anything beyond the attack on the young Sudanese girl.

Heartsick, Cal read the concluding paragraph.

After consulting with other medical staff, I made the decision that, given her emotionally fragile state, it would be a dangerous risk to inform Miss Cardston about the rape. It is my recommendation that she seek counseling at the first opportunity at which time she can be told and deal with the issue. Meanwhile, since she appears to be in good physical condition, and since we need her help, I see no reason why she shouldn't resume her work.

So Megan didn't know.

Cal sank back into the chair, feeling as if his blood had drained out his legs and onto the floor. No wonder she was scared at the thought of physical intimacy. No wonder she was having panic attacks. Her conscious mind had blocked the rape. But her body remembered and reacted with terror.

Lord, he'd done all the wrong things—grilling her with questions that made her feel vulnerable and under attack even when he wasn't touching her, pushing her to have sex with him, thinking he could fix her problems with a good old-fashioned roll in the sack. That Megan had been so willing to try, so desperate to feel normal again, made him feel like an even bigger heel.

The papers had slid off his lap and onto the floor. Cal gathered them up and folded them in half. He wasn't ready to go back to the bar and face Megan—especially in the presence of Harris and his teasing innuendos. And he needed to get the documents out of Megan's sight. It might be prudent to shred or burn them. But going back to them at a later time, when he'd had a chance to calm down, might give him more insight into her state of mind.

For now, he would take them back to the bungalow and hide them in his bag. Maybe the walk from the lodge would help clear his mind—as if anything could. He hadn't meant to get involved in Megan's problems. But he'd brought this mess on himself; and now he was in deep, way over his head.

"Another one?" Harris shot Megan a devilish grin as he signaled the waiter. "It's on Cal's bar tab, and he can bloody well afford it."

Megan shook her head. The man was shameless, but she couldn't help liking him. His outrageous manner, she sensed, hid a genuinely kind heart.

"One banana daiquiri's enough for me," she said. "Too much alcohol gives me a headache. Maybe you should think about cutting back yourself. All that whiskey can't be good for you."

He lifted his freshly refilled glass. The cut crystal reflected glints of flame from the candle on their table. "No lectures, m'dear. An old man like me has few enough pleasures in life—a sunrise over the Serengeti…an occasional drink with a pretty lass…and the taste of a good Scotch on your client's dime. Doesn't quite make up for coming home to an empty bed, but it's close enough." He sipped from the glass, taking time to savor the taste. "Speaking of beds, how are you and Cal getting along in that cozy bungalow?"

Megan felt the heat creep up to the roots of her hair, embarrassed not just by the indelicate question but by the memory of how close they'd come to being *very* cozy— before her panic ruined things. "All right. We've made some…accommodations."

"Right sorry about the mix-up," he said. "When Cal told me he was bringing a lady friend along, I just assumed…"

"You assumed wrong. But it was an honest mistake."

"When I saw that kiss today, I was hoping it wasn't a mistake, after all."

Megan faked a chuckle. "We were just celebrating our safe getaway. Nothing's changed."

"I'll just have to take your word for that, won't I?" He gave her a knowing look. What would he do if he knew the truth? Would he offer her fatherly advice or just shake his head in disbelief? "Speaking of Cal, where do you suppose the lad's run off to? I'm beginning to wonder if he's lost his taste for my company."

"He said something about checking his email." Feeling the need for a break, Megan rose. "Why don't I go and look for him? I shouldn't be long."

Harris rose with her, minding his manners. "I'll be right here. If you don't come back, I'll assume you've found another diversion." The teasing light in his eye gave way to something warmer and more genuine. "Whatever's happening between you two, I can tell he cares for you. Whenever you step into view, you're all that he sees."

Don't. Megan bit back the word. Harris was pulling her strings; that was all. The old man enjoyed stirring up intrigue.

"Take your umbrella with you," he said. "You may want to go outside."

With a murmur of thanks, Megan took the umbrella Cal had left with her and walked down the hall to the front desk. Cal wasn't in the computer alcove, but the clerk told her he'd been there and had printed out a file before leaving.

Glancing around the lodge, she failed to find him. Why hadn't he joined her and Harris in the bar? Had he received some unsettling news? Would she find him in the bungalow packing his bag to leave?

Cal was a busy man, she reminded herself. He had

responsibilities and concerns in the outside world. If he needed to fly home, she'd be a fool to take it personally, or to expect any kind of promise to return. But she would always wonder what might have happened between them if he'd stayed. Would they have found some answers to whatever they were seeking—or only more disappointment?

Megan opened the umbrella and stepped outside to find that the rain had stopped. The clouds had moved on, leaving a glorious panoply of stars in a sky as black as a panther's coat. Closing the umbrella, she hurried down the brick path. Cal was an adult, she reminded herself. There was no need to go looking for him. But a sixth sense whispered that something had changed—something that had stopped him from rejoining her and Harris. She needed to find out what it was.

Cal had hidden the volunteer report between the folds of the map, which he'd zipped into the inner pocket of his duffel. Now, seated on the bench under the window, he pondered what to do next.

Sharing what he'd learned with Megan was out of the question. He was sure that her first reaction, if she learned what he'd done, would be fury at him for accessing her private information. But that much he could live with. It was the reaction that would follow, once she discovered the information in the file itself, that had him more worried. How would it affect her to know she'd been raped?

Would the awareness push her over the edge—or might it be cathartic, even helpful? Either way, he couldn't be the one to tell her. He had no right to make that decision—nor did he want to. He agreed with the doctor who'd written the report. Megan would need professional help to deal with the way she'd been hurt. And here in the wilds of Africa, there was little help of that kind to be had.

So what now? Should he try to get her back to the States? He couldn't imagine she'd be willing to go without knowing why. Should he try to help her himself, maybe get her talking? Lord, he wouldn't know where to begin. In his blundering way, he could make things worse.

For now, he could only behave as if nothing had changed. Megan was a proud woman and she was smart. If he showed pity or an excess of concern toward her, she'd pick up on it. And she'd demand to know what was wrong.

Leaning back on the bench, he closed his eyes and let the memories of the day crumble around him. Warring emotions flailed at him from all sides—worry, rage and frustration. He found himself wishing he could find a wall and punch it till his knuckles bled.

Megan hadn't asked him to come and find her, Cal reminded himself. She hadn't asked him to get involved in her life. But he *was* involved, and now he couldn't just walk away.

For the first time he found himself asking whether Megan had suffered enough. Whether she was guilty or innocent in the embezzlement, surely she'd paid the price for anything she might have done. If she returned to the States, there'd be legal entanglements—the civil suit he'd filed against her after she'd disappeared had been the first and not the last—but he could withdraw his own charges and hire a lawyer to help her with the rest.

But what was he thinking? The money was missing and his best friend was dead. How could he let that go without learning more about what had happened? He still needed answers, still had to understand what kind of person Megan truly was. The report was just the tip of the iceberg. There was still so much he wanted to know.

"Cal?" Her low voice startled him out of his reverie. "What are you doing out here? Is everything all right?"

"Fine," he lied. "I must've dozed off."

"Why didn't you come back to the bar? Harris was concerned about you."

"Sorry. The rain had stopped. I felt like some fresh air. I'll apologize to Harris tomorrow." More lies. Megan deserved better. But if he was going to be around her, lies were something he'd have to get used to.

Coming around the bench, she stood gazing down at him. She looked so fresh and pretty with the stars behind her and the night mist glistening on her hair. *Brave, sweet Megan...how could those bastards have hurt you the way they did?*

"You're sure everything's all right?" she asked. "The desk clerk mentioned you'd printed a file."

"Just business. Something that needed my okay." Another lie.

"When you didn't come back, I was afraid I'd find you packing your bags."

"I wouldn't do that without telling you." That much, at least, was true. "Sit down. It's a nice night, and it's too carly to go in."

She took a seat on the bench, at a stranger's distance. Cal guessed she was still smarting from their near miss in the shower. He ached to cradle her in his arms, but he pushed the urge away, struggling to rebuild the emotional walls that had always kept him strong and centered, thinking clearly. They'd taken a bad blow tonight, and he felt uncomfortably certain that Megan's warm body in his arms would wreck them completely. He had to stay focused and rational, and not lose sight of why he was here.

"Was Harris upset about being abandoned in the bar?" he asked, making small talk.

"I hope not. He told me that as long as the drinks were on your tab, he'd be fine." She shifted her gaze to the stars. "I get the feeling Harris is a better man than he pretends to be."

"You're right. He'd deny it if you asked, but I know for a fact he's paying to educate Gideon's children. And no one works harder to make sure his clients are safe and taken care of. I'd trust the old man with my life—and have."

She gave him a tentative smile. "Somehow that doesn't surprise me. What's the real story behind his losing that arm?"

"I haven't a clue, and I've heard at least a dozen different versions. Part of his white hunter mystique, I suspect. Harris is one of a dying breed. These days, your safari guide is more likely to be African."

"That's as it should be, I suppose. Still, there's that old Hollywood image—John Wayne, Clark Gable…" A visible shiver passed through her body. She'd worn a light jacket to dinner but now the night air was getting chilly.

"Stay put. I'll get a blanket." Rising, Cal strode inside. Tonight Megan seemed relaxed and willing to talk. He very much wanted her to stay that way.

Seconds later he returned with the blanket. She snuggled into one end, leaving the rest for him.

"Better?" Cal pulled his end of the blanket over his chest.

"Better, thanks. The sky's beautiful tonight, isn't it?"

Cal murmured his agreement, suppressing the urge to circle her shoulders with his arm and pull her close.

"I always wanted Nick to take me with him to Africa when he made trips for the foundation. But when I asked him, he told me I wouldn't like it. Can you imagine that?"

"Imagine your not liking it?" Cal shook his head. "Not after seeing you out there today." Back in California, he might have agreed with Nick that his pampered, high-maintenance wife was ill-suited to the wilderness. He knew better now...and suddenly found himself wondering just how well Nick had bothered to get to know his wife.

Her smile flickered in the darkness. "Oh, today was wonderful. But it's not just the wild country and the animals I love. It's the people—like those poor souls in Darfur. They've suffered unthinkable wrongs, lost their homes and their loved ones, seen their women raped and their young boys marched off to be soldiers. But I see so much courage in the camps, so much selflessness—the way they take care of each other and share what little they have. They're the reason I want to go back to that awful place, Cal. The reason I *need* to go back."

Gazing at her, he shook his head. After what had happened to her, how could she even think of going back to Darfur?

"You're quite a woman, Megan." The understatement was deliberate. To say more might reveal too much.

"It's not me. It's them. They showed me the person I was meant to be—the person I'm still trying to become. I know that might sound maudlin to a man like you, but it's the truth."

"A man like me?" Cal quirked an eyebrow, teasing her a little to lighten the mood. "How am I supposed to take that?"

"Oh, not badly, I hope. But you've always struck me as a very pragmatic man, more focused on charging ahead and getting things done than on sentiment."

"A cold-blooded cynic, in other words."

"I didn't say that." Something flashed in her eyes. She looked away, her gaze tracing the path of a falling star. She used to do that back in California—find some excuse to turn away from him whenever they talked. What had she been hiding? Dissatisfaction with her glittering lifestyle? Unhappiness in her personal life? Or...had she been hiding something more sinister, such as her crimes against the organization where she now worked?

As he studied her sharply etched profile, a thread of doubt crept into his mind. Had Megan really changed? Could he take her words at face value, or was she conning him? What if the money was still out there, waiting to be drawn on when she felt safe enough—or when she'd volunteered long enough to salve her guilty conscience?

The report verified everything she'd told him, Cal reminded himself. Her spotless service record was real. The rape was real. But so was the crime that had come before all of that. Someone was responsible for taking the money, and Cal still didn't want to believe it was the friend he would have entrusted with his life.

He didn't realize how long they'd been silent until she spoke.

"Looking back, I don't think Nick knew me at all— maybe because I didn't know myself. I became what I thought he wanted. Not that it made any difference in the end."

Cal shot her a startled glance. Her words matched his own thoughts, but he was surprised to hear her bring it up. She'd seemed firmly against discussing Nick with him earlier. "I thought you and Nick had the perfect marriage," he prompted, testing the waters. "It certainly looked that way."

She gazed up at the sky. "We put on a good show. But we both knew better."

"Would you have stayed with him?"

"You mean, if he hadn't shot himself when the money scandal broke? I've asked myself the same question. I was raised to believe that marriage vows are sacred. But when your partner is cheating and doesn't care how much he hurts you, those vows can seem more like a prison sentence. Maybe if I hadn't lost the baby…" Her voice trailed off.

So Nick had been cheating on her. The discovery tightened a raw knot in the pit of Cal's stomach. He and Nick had been best friends since high school. True blue all the way, or so he'd thought. But if Nick had been faithless to his beautiful wife, what else would he have been capable of?

"What happened with the baby, Megan?" he asked. "Nick never said much, except that you'd lost it."

"That doesn't surprise me. I'd hoped having a baby might make a difference, force him to take our marriage more seriously, but it barely seemed to register with him. As for the miscarriage…" She shrugged. "It was what it was—nothing I could have prevented. At least that's what the doctor said. I've always wanted children. But maybe it isn't in the cards. Especially not now."

Cal studied her profile in the faint light. How could any man have cheated on a woman like Megan? Nick had always been a flirt, quick with compliments and flattery whenever a beautiful woman was involved, even after he was married. Cal had simply chalked it up as part of his friend's personality. He'd never imagined the man would cheat—Nick had given every indication of worshipping his beautiful wife. Had it really all been for show?

There was no denying the aching resignation in Megan's tone. Nick hadn't just indulged in an indiscretion or two—it sounded as if Megan was saying he'd never been faithful at all. Now that Cal thought about it, Nick had always been one to take his commitments lightly. Instead of apologizing for missed meetings or deadlines, he was more likely to brush it off with a shrug and a smile, confident that he could charm his way into forgiveness. The truth of that hurt like hell. But how much more had it hurt Megan?

If things were different between them, Cal thought, he might try to make it up to her—show her how a woman should be treated by a man who claimed to care for her.

But given the past, that wasn't in the cards, either.

Megan wrapped the blanket tighter, taking care to leave enough slack for Cal. The moon had risen above the distant hills. Full and ripe as an August peach from her grandmother's old tree, it flooded the brick terrace with light and etched Cal's craggy face into ridges and shadows. She'd thought she'd managed to put her old life behind her. But being with Cal had brought it all back—and not in a good way.

"Maybe the camps have been an outlet for your mothering instincts," he said.

"Are you trying to analyze me again?" She didn't like being examined, especially by Cal.

"I wouldn't dream of it," he said. "But as long as we're on the subject, wouldn't it be worth getting professional help for those panic attacks and nightmares?"

"Maybe." A prickle of distrust stirred. She faked a chuckle. "If I could find a good witch doctor to rattle the bones."

"You're not going to find help here." He turned on the bench, impaling her with his eyes. "I've glimpsed the pain you're in, Megan. Come home with me and get the therapy you need. I'll do whatever it takes to help you."

Megan lowered her gaze, alarms going off in her head. Of course, she told herself. This was why Cal had come here. He was determined to get her back to the States, where he could go after her legally, maybe even have her arrested. This wasn't the approach she'd expected him to take, but the end result was the same either way.

And she'd actually begun to trust him. What a fool she'd been!

Meeting his eyes again, she shook her head. "Cal, I know you mean well." *A necessary lie.* "But I'm not leaving Africa. If I were to go home, there's a chance I'd never make it back here."

"Not even if I promised to send you?"

"I can't depend on that. Things get in the way. Besides, there's nothing wrong with me that time and hard work won't heal."

"But to go back to the very place where—" He broke off, as if he'd been about to say too much.

"Don't you see? That's exactly what I need to do—go back and deal with what happened. If I can face it, and understand it, it won't have the power to frighten me."

The breath exploded out of him. "Damn it, Megan, if you'd just listen—"

"Stop pushing me, Cal. I'm not a child."

"You're working for my organization. I can order you home for treatment."

"Not if I resign. Believe me, there are plenty of NGOs who'd be happy to have an experienced nurse." She stood, tossing the blanket aside. "I'm too tired to argue any more. If you'll excuse me, I'm going to turn in. Truce, all right?"

"Truce." He rose with a weary sigh. "I'll go and spend some time with Harris. That'll give you a chance to get settled. We'll be off to another early start tomorrow."

"Fine." She opened the door, which was unlocked.

"Megan."

She turned at the sound of her name.

"Take your side of the bed. I promise to be a perfect gentleman."

A gentleman? Is that what he called someone who flew halfway around the world to hound a woman into his idea

of justice? Did he really think she didn't know about the
civil suits waiting to fall on her the minute she reentered
the United States? What kind of gentleman—what kind of
man—was he to do this to her and pretend it was for her
own good? She was angry with herself for even listening
to him, much less beginning to trust him. And that wasn't
even mentioning the way she'd let him kiss her, or the way
she'd started to feel in the shower with him before her fear
had taken over. For a short while, she'd actually thought
that he was the man who could make things better for her.

She stepped into the bungalow and closed the door. If
only she could close the door as easily on her frustrating
feelings toward the man.

Nine

By the time Cal crossed the grounds to the bungalow, the moon had risen above the treetops. A bat flashed past his head, its wings slicing the dark likc scimitars. The haunting cry of an owl shimmered through the night.

He'd spent the better part of two hours with Harris, gently urging him to call it a night and go to bed. The old hunter hadn't looked well tonight—not really sick, but sad and fatigued. At sixty-six, his rough life and hard drinking had begun to catch up with him, and it showed. Cal had been worried enough to stay with him and walk him to his private room in the rear of the lodge. It would be a relief to get him away from this place and out on the Serengeti with no hotel bar to keep him up drinking at night.

The bungalow was dark. Hopefully Megan would be asleep. She'd been tired, too—and prickly, he recalled. He should have known better than to bring up the idea of flying her home for therapy. But she'd given him an opening. He'd seized it and come away with his whiskers singed.

He'd learned where she stood on the question of going home. But he also knew something Megan didn't. She needed serious help—and going back to Darfur without that help could send her spiraling into an emotional abyss.

Unlocking the door, he stepped inside. Moonlight fell between the parted curtains, softening the darkness. Relief lifted his mood as he glanced through the mosquito netting and saw the slight form raising the covers. At least she'd trusted him enough to share the bed. Or maybe she'd wanted him close by to protect her from the lurking monsters in her dreams.

Moving closer, he gazed down at her. She lay curled with her lovely rump toward his side of the bed, sleeping as sweetly as a child. Something tightened around Cal's heart. Whatever phantoms threatened that innocent slumber, he wanted to be there to drive them away. He understood himself, and he knew these protective feelings toward her might not last for long, not when he still had so many questions and doubts. But while Megan was suffering, he couldn't turn his back and walk away from her.

He undressed in the dark. Clad in his skivvies and undershirt, he walked around the bed. He slept raw at home and had planned to do the same on this trip. If he'd foreseen that he'd be sharing a room—and a bed—with a woman he'd resolved to treat like a kid sister, he'd have brought along some pajamas.

He did have a pack of condoms in his bag, which he'd bought at the hotel gift shop in Arusha after making plans to take Megan on safari—and hopefully seduce her. But they were locally made, so he couldn't count on their reliability. Given the present arrangement, maybe that was just as well.

Doing his best not to wake her, he lifted the blanket and slid over the top sheet onto his side of the bed. The mattress wasn't king-size, or even queen-size. It was a double, like the one his grandparents had slept on all their married life. There was no boundary line down the middle, but Megan was definitely taking more than her share of space. Unless he wanted to sleep on the couch, he would have to choose between disturbing her rest to move her over or spooning around her. The latter struck him as the more appealing choice.

Easing deeper into the bed, he curved his body around hers and pulled the blankets up to his shoulders. Head on the pillow, he closed his eyes. It was late, and he was tired. With any luck he'd go right to sleep.

But something told him it wasn't going to be that easy. Megan's warmth crept around him, seeping into his senses. She smelled of the lavender soap from the shower. It was the same soap he'd used, but on her woman's skin the innocent aroma, coupled with the memory of that shower, was sensual enough to rock his libido. The notion that he mustn't touch her, mustn't have her, heated his blood like torched gasoline. He bit back a groan as his sex rose and hardened. Only the thin sheet between their bodies kept his male impulses in check.

It was going to be a long night.

Megan stirred and opened her eyes. Except for a shaft of moonlight falling through the window, the room was dark. She'd gone to bed alone. But the sound of breathing and the manly warmth radiating against her back told her she was alone no longer. Sometime in the night Cal had joined her.

As she drifted into wakefulness, she became aware of her curled position in the bed. Moving in her sleep, she'd left Cal with little more than the far edge of the mattress.

Instead of pushing her out of the way, she realized, he'd done his best to sleep around her.

Despite the awkwardness between them, she would have to give him credit for being a gentleman in this respect, at least. True to his word, he hadn't laid a hand on her. But he'd stayed close, and even in her sleep, something about his presence had made her feel safe and peaceful. Maybe that was why the dreams hadn't come tonight.

Stretching full length, she rolled toward her own side of the mattress. Looking back, she could see Cal. He lay awake with one arm propping his head. Had he been watching over her?

"Hello," she whispered. "Did I wake you?"

He shook his head. "Any bad dreams?"

"No. But I don't always have them. When did you come in?"

"A couple of hours ago. You were sleeping like a kitten."

"All over the bed! No wonder you're still awake. You should've booted me back where I belong."

His chuckle warmed her. "You looked so contented, I didn't have the heart."

"There's plenty of room for you now," she said. "Go ahead and stretch out. I won't bite you."

"I won't touch that comment." The bed creaked slightly as he eased onto his back and straightened his legs. "Ah… that's better," he breathed.

"Now get some sleep," she ordered. "And don't let me crowd you again."

Another chuckle was followed by silence, as if he'd bitten back a too-clever retort.

They lay side by side, modestly clad and separated by a thin layer of muslin sheet that might as well have been a brick wall. There was something Victorian about the arrangement, like two strangers sharing a bed in a nineteenth-century inn. Megan knew that Cal had come up with this silliness to ease her fear. But no barrier could hide the intense masculinity exuded by the man next to her.

Even when she was married to Nick, Cal's presence had given her a rush of heightened awareness. She'd willed herself to ignore the sensation, but he was so powerful, so decisive and rugged that he fluttered the pulse of every female who came within range. Next to him, even the glib and charming Nick had seemed shallow and insubstantial. Cal was like the lion they'd seen in the crater—fierce, majestic and completely sure of himself. She'd be foolish to trust him—he was every bit as dangerous as the lion. But she couldn't deny her attraction to him.

Cal had never had any shortage of women. And he was doubtless an accomplished lover. She remembered the touch of his big hands in the shower, how he'd caressed her naked breasts until she'd ached for more. He'd awakened feelings she thought she'd lost forever. She'd *wanted* him—and she'd desperately needed the release he could give her.

So why had she stopped him? What gave her fear such uncontrollable power? If only she could understand that much, she might be on her way to healing.

"Are you all right, Megan?" His throaty whisper stirred the darkness.

"Aren't you supposed to be asleep?"

"Aren't you?" He paused, then turned toward her, shifting onto his side. "Feel like talking?"

Talking? Megan could guess what that meant. He was preparing to back her into a corner and grill her again, maybe about Nick and the money, or about her time in Darfur, or even what had happened in the shower that afternoon. Why did *she* always have to be the one answering questions?

"I've done enough talking," she said. "I'd rather listen for a change. Tell me about yourself."

"Not much to tell. My story's pretty dull compared with yours. Nick must've told you most of it."

"Not really. Just that the two of you were friends in high school and decided to start J-COR after college. But I don't want to talk about Nick. Where did you grow up?"

"Fresno. White house. Picket fence. Barbecue in the backyard. Station wagon in the driveway. How does it sound so far? Are you getting sleepy?"

"Don't count on it." She shifted deeper under the covers, her hip brushing his through the sheet. The contact triggered a subtle ache—a yearning to snuggle against his side and lie cloaked in his warmth. She battled temptation, telling herself that any move on her part would only confuse the man, leading him to assume she wanted more.

Maybe she *did* want more. But a second failure on her part would be frustrating for him and scathingly humiliating for her. Better to leave well enough alone. She sighed, willing herself to remain where she lay. "Go on," she urged him. "I'm listening."

Cal's words could have painted a pretty picture of his childhood home. It would have been a true picture, as far as the description went. But that would mean leaving out the screaming, cursing fights that raged between his parents within the walls of that home. Those fights had driven him out of the house to wander the streets at all hours, afraid of what he'd see if he came back too soon.

Sharing that part of his life was painful. But Megan had been open with him about her past. He owed her as much.

"My mother left us when I was eleven," he said. "My father made sure I knew she'd run off with another man—

one who'd told her he didn't want a snot-nosed kid like me tagging along."

"You were an only child?"

"Yes, fortunately."

"And your mother never came back?"

"We got word years later that she'd died of cancer. By then I was in high school. I can't say I blamed her for leaving—my dad was pretty rough on her, and it may have been her only way out. But the fact that she didn't even tell me goodbye or write me a letter…that part was hard to take."

"Oh, Cal…"

His jaw tightened. If there was one thing he couldn't stand it was pity from a woman—especially *this* woman.

"No need to be sorry," he said, cutting her off before she could shovel on more sympathy. "I got through it fine. My dad sold cars and hung out with his drinking buddies. I took after-school jobs—mowing lawns, bagging groceries, lifeguarding at the pool. The work kept me in spending money and out of trouble. I earned my own car, bought my own clothes and still managed to do pretty well in school. Even dated a few girls and played a little football."

"And that was when you met Nick."

"Yeah. You know the rest." They'd shared a table in study hall and, for some reason he couldn't even remember, they'd hit it off. The big, scrappy kid from the wrong side of town and the handsome, smooth-talking boy who seemed to have everything—two doting parents, an imposing brick home and a black Trans Am to drive to school. They'd formed an alliance that had lasted until two years ago, when a single gunshot had ended it all.

Remembering that part still hurt like hell.

Megan stirred beside him, warm and soft and fragrant. "I know you cared about him, Cal," she said. "I cared about him, too. Nick had some wonderful qualities. But he hurt us both. I've done my best to forgive him and move on. I hope you have, too."

Cal's throat went painfully tight. He had no words—and even if he had, he wouldn't have been able to speak. All he could do was hook her with his arm and draw her close while raw emotions surged through his body. It wasn't a lustful gesture, just one of simple human need, and she seemed to know it. Her head settled into the hollow of his shoulder. Her breath eased as she fitted her body to his side. It felt good holding her like this, even with nothing else in the plan. Little by little he could feel the tension flowing out of him.

Turning his head, he brushed a kiss across her hairline. "Go to sleep, Megan," he whispered.

She didn't reply, but her nearness said enough. Lord, but she was sweet. Almost sweet enough to make him forget their shared past. But some wrongs were too grievous to put aside. For him, there could be no forgiving and no moving on until he knew the full story behind Nick's death, the stolen money and Megan's part in it all.

Megan lay still, lulled by the steady beat of Cal's heart. His skin was warm through the thin fabric of his undershirt. She closed her eyes, feeling the gentle rise and fall of his chest against her cheek.

Tonight he'd shared some surprising secrets—things that not even Nick had told her about his friend. Surely Nick had known Cal's background; but maybe he hadn't expected her to be interested. Sadly, now that she thought of it, there were a lot of things she and Nick hadn't talked about.

She tried to picture Cal as a lonely, unwanted young boy, abandoned by his mother and probably ignored by his father. No wonder he'd developed a cold manner and a cynical attitude. No wonder he'd never trusted any woman enough to develop a serious relationship.

The only person Cal seemed to have trusted was Nick. And in the end, even Nick had betrayed him. His anguish would have been as deep as her own—different, yes, but just as painful and just as lasting.

Cal's revelation gave her new understanding and an unexpected sense of peace—like a gift. She wasn't alone in her pain. In his own way, Cal was suffering, too; and he was looking for answers. Why else would he have come all this way to find her?

She was beginning to drift. Most nights she dreaded sleep and the nightmares it brought. But tonight she felt safe. Cal was here to protect her and calm her fears. For now that was enough.

Was she getting better?

But it was too soon to ask that question. The past three days had been intoxicatingly normal, with drives into the crater and along the river where the elephants came to drink. They'd seen crocodiles, great, lumbering hippos and more lions, a pride of them with cubs. They'd scouted a tree where a leopard had hung its kill and, after some searching, managed to spot the beautiful, mottled cat sprawled along a high limb.

Megan had filled her camera's memory card with photos and her head with stunning images that would stay with her the rest of her life. But did that really mean she was getting better?

She felt vital and restored; and the nightmares had yet to return. But it wasn't as if she could spend the rest of her life on safari. How would she hold up in the world she'd left behind—especially in Darfur?

As for Cal, they'd managed a cautious truce. He treated
her like a friend and kept his distance both in and out of
bed. If it wasn't everything she wanted—and there were
times when she ached for more—at least she felt safe with
him.

His touch on her arm tugged her back to the present.
They were driving the crater today, on the narrow track
where they'd been mired in the rain. Gideon had slowed
the Land Rover to a crawl. A hundred yards ahead, a hulking dark shape moved through a screen of thornbush. Cal's
lips moved, forming the words *black rhino*.

They'd cut the distance by half when the rhino burst
out of the bush, coming straight toward them. The beast
was immense—not tall like an elephant, but massive—
long-bodied and as sleekly powerful as an old-time steam
locomotive. The horn on its nose was as long as Megan's
arm and looked to be spindle-sharp at the tip.

Megan forgot to breathe as the rhino paused, ears and
nostrils twitching. Her hand crept into Cal's as Gideon
idled the engine. They were close—too close. Rhinos were
known to be short-tempered, and this one was capable
of wrecking the vehicle and trampling or tossing anyone
who couldn't get away. Harris had drawn and cocked the
rifle—not to shoot the precious beast but more likely to
try to scare it if the need arose.

The rhino snorted and tossed its enormous head. The
small brown birds roosting on its back flapped upward,
chattering an alarm—not a good sign.

At a touch from Harris, Gideon eased the Land Rover
into Reverse and began slowly backing away. A bead of
sweat trickled down the side of the driver's face. No one in
the vehicle moved or spoke as the wheels inched backward.

Snorting again, the rhino lowered its head. Sunlight
glinted on the deadly black horn. Megan's grip tightened

around Cal's hand. His body tensed, moving slightly in front of her.

But the rhino must have calculated that the intruders weren't worth bothering with. Changing course, the huge beast turned aside and trotted into the scrub. Gideon gunned the vehicle backward, stopping only once they were safely out of range. Pulling the hand brake, he sagged over the wheel. Harris uncocked the rifle, breaking the silence with a laugh. "Well, hell, I said I wanted to show you a black rhino, didn't I?"

"That you did." Cal's arm went around Megan's shoulders, squeezing her fiercely tight. Megan managed a nervous chuckle.

"I don't suppose I can talk you into going back, can I?" she joked. "I forgot to take pictures."

Still giddy from the rush of their close call, they headed out of the crater. Sullen clouds were rumbling over the rim, and nobody wanted to be caught in the rain again. Tomorrow they'd be leaving Ngorongoro for a tent camp on the vast Serengeti grassland to the north. What remained of the afternoon would be set aside for resting, washing and packing up for a predawn start.

By dinnertime Megan had her things well organized. She'd enjoyed the lodge but she was ready for a change of scene. Over plates of coq au vin and rice pilaf, Harris described what she could expect to see.

"We'll be there for the big game migration that happens every year with the rains. Nothing like it on earth. Wildebeest, zebra and more—oceans of them—marching south to new grass. Bloody picnic for the meat-eaters that tag along. Not a pretty sight for a lady, but I shouldn't worry about you. After all, you've been in Darfur."

Cal glanced toward her. She caught the dark flicker in his eyes before he looked away. Was he thinking about the nightmares and panic attacks she'd come on safari to escape—details he'd agreed not to share with Harris? Was he worried about how she'd react to the more violent aspects of the migration?

It would be like Cal to worry. That was one thing Megan had learned about him on this outing—that he paid attention to everyone around him and seemed to feel responsible for their well-being. That included her—sometimes to her annoyance.

They finished their dessert. Then, as had become custom, Megan rose, excused herself and went back to the bungalow to shower and relax while Cal stayed to keep Harris company. Not only did the arrangement give her some needed private time, but it helped ensure that Harris would make it back to his room without drinking too much. Cal had voiced his concern for the old hunter, and Megan had agreed that Harris shouldn't be left alone at night in the bar.

After showering and dressing in her pajamas and robe, she curled up on the couch with the afghan and a paperback murder mystery she'd borrowed from the lodge's library. The book had looked promising, but the story wasn't holding her attention. She'd already guessed how it would end, and a peek at the last page proved her right.

Setting the book on the coffee table, she leaned back into the cushions and tried to imagine what the next few days would be like. She knew about the migration and had even seen video footage of it on PBS's *Nature*. But being there, actually seeing it, would be a thrill to remember.

The more she thought about it, the more she wished she'd asked Harris more questions. How soon would they get to the Serengeti? What would they see on the way?

Maybe it would help to look at a map. Cal had a map,

she remembered now. He'd mentioned that he kept it in his bag.

Crossing the room, she found the packed duffel where he'd left it on the floor of the wardrobe. Her fingers probed inside and felt the stiffness of paper in the inner pocket. Unzipping the pocket, she lifted out the folded map, which felt thicker than she'd expected.

As she unfolded the map, a sheaf of printed papers dropped out and scattered on the tiles. Bending to gather them up, Megan noticed a name at the top of one page.

Her name.

Ten

Roiling clouds blackened the night sky, hiding the moon and stars. Lightning sheeted across the horizon, followed seconds later by the subtle roar of distant thunder. Walking the brick path back to the bungalow, Cal was grateful that Harris had decided to turn in early. Otherwise he'd be running a gauntlet through the coming downpour.

As it was, he took his time. Today, under the equatorial sun, the humid air had felt like a thick flannel blanket. Tonight the breeze was cool, the air sweet in his lungs. The day had been a good one, crowned by the close brush with the rare black rhino. When Megan's hand had crept into his, he'd felt the connection of electric fear and excitement that coursed through both their bodies. In that breathless moment when the beast was threatening to charge, his foremost thought had been keeping her safe.

Was he falling for the woman? But that would be the craziest thing he could do. Megan was an emotional wreck.

And whether she did or didn't have anything to do with the stolen money, their past history didn't bode well for any kind of relationship.

But things weren't that simple. As attracted as he'd been to her beauty, he was even more drawn to her now that he'd seen her courage, her kindness and her magnificent spirit. Lying next to her in the night, separated by nothing but that damnable sheet, he'd burned with wanting her. It had been all he could do to keep from ripping away the thin muslin, seizing her in his arms and burying his swollen sex in that deep, hot wetness he craved like a drowning man craves air.

But that would be the most despicable—and damaging—thing he could do.

Reaching the porch of the bungalow, he fished for his key. The curtain was drawn, but the glow of a single lamp shone through the fabric. Would he find her awake, maybe reading that paperback she'd found in the lodge? That might not be so bad, he mused. This would be their last night in the bungalow—maybe their last chance for some relaxing, private talk.

After a polite knock to announce his presence, he turned the key and opened the door.

Megan was seated on the couch, wrapped in the afghan. Her back was ramrod straight, her fists clenched in her lap. The rigid expression on her face made it clear that something terrible had happened. Cal's heart dropped as he saw the papers laid out on the coffee table.

He stifled a groan. "Megan—"

Her look stopped him from saying more—raw eyes, filled with shock and a kind of frozen rage.

"How long have you known?" Her hoarse whisper rose from a well of pain.

Cal forced his mouth to form words. "Not long. A few

days. I can imagine what you think, but I was looking for a way to help you."

"Help me?" She flung the words at him. "By going behind my back? This was private information. You had no right!"

"That's where you're wrong. As the head of the foundation, I have the right to see volunteer records."

She glared at him in helpless fury. Cal stood his ground, hoping that a cool facade might help keep her calm. But he didn't feel cool. Heaven help him, what had he done to this woman?

"So why didn't you tell me?" Megan was beginning to crumble. "How long did you plan to keep it to yourself that I'd been...*raped?*" She choked on the last word.

Cal ached to gather her into his arms. But he knew better than to try. She was too angry to welcome comfort, especially from him. "You saw the report," he said. "The doctor didn't think you were ready to be told. Not without professional help."

"The doctor was *wrong!*" She was on her feet, eyes blazing. "He was wrong, and so were you! I'm not a child! I *needed* to know! How could I heal without understanding what happened to me?"

"I'm sorry. I deferred to the doctor's judgment. I didn't feel I had the background to make any other call." Lord, he sounded so detached. She probably thought he was the world's coldest bastard.

"You should have told me, anyway." The afghan had slipped off her shoulders. She let it fall to the floor. "It would have been a kindness to tell me, Cal. Instead, you let me make a fool of myself. That time in the shower— did you know then?"

"No. If I had, things would never have gone that far."

He took another step toward her. "Sit down, and talk to me, Megan."

"Why should I? You went behind my back. You kept a secret from me—a terrible secret—"

Her fists came up to flail impotently at his chest. He stood like a pillar, letting the harmless blows glance off him. He deserved her anger for the way he'd let her down. The last thing he'd wanted to do was to hurt her again— and yet, that was exactly what he'd done.

As her strength ebbed, she began to quiver. Her shoulders slumped. She buried her face in her palms. Sobs shook her thin frame. Cal had always prided himself on his ability to manage a crisis. But trying to reason with Megan had only made things worse. Now he had run out of things to say. There was only one thing left to do.

Without another word, he wrapped her in his arms and held her tight.

Outside, the storm had broken. Lightning crashed across the sky, flickering through the curtains as the thunder roared overhead. Rain battered the windowpanes and drummed on the roof, like an echo of the emotions that churned through Megan's body.

Pressed against Cal, she had no will to pull away. She was still furious, but she needed the solid anchor of his strength. Tonight, as she'd waited for him to come back from the lodge, she'd struggled to remember what had happened on that tragic night. The details of the brutal assault on Saida had haunted her dreams for months. But she had no recollection of the same thing happening to her.

Had she been unconscious at the time, or had her mind mercifully blocked the memory? And what of the physical signs of assault? She supposed that thanks to the swift treatment she received, and the four days she spent in a daze, the worst of the injuries had time to heal before she came back to full awareness. If only the mental and emotional damage were as easily fixed.

She had to accept that the rape had been real. Given the medical evidence and her state of mind, nothing else made sense. But the truth was still sinking in, too much truth for her ravaged psyche to process. It was as if she was tumbling through a black void with no bottom and nothing of substance to hold on to.

Except Cal.

"It's all right, Megan." His lips brushed her hair as he whispered phrases meant to comfort her. "You'll be fine, girl. You're safe."

Liar, she thought. It wasn't all right—and maybe she would never feel safe again. But she was grateful for the arms that held her, supporting and protecting her. Megan pressed her face into Cal's shirt. The fabric was wet and salty with her tears—real tears. For the first time since that awful night, she was *crying.*

"Go ahead and cry," Cal murmured. "You don't have to be strong all the time. Let it go. I'm here."

She sagged against him, drained by her furious outburst. Cal hadn't meant to hurt her, she reminded herself. He'd only wanted to help. And here, in this remote place, he was all the help she had.

Her knees were threatening to buckle. As if sensing what she needed, Cal swept her up in his arms and carried her to the bed. Throwing back the covers, he laid her on the sheet and tucked the quilt over her, tenderly as if he were tucking in a frightened child.

"Do you want me to go?" he asked.

"No. I need you to stay."

She heard the sound of his boots hitting the floor before he stretched out beside her on top of the quilts. For the first few minutes they lay still, listening to the sounds of the storm. Cal didn't speak, but his weight on the bed and the deep, even cadence of his breathing surrounded her with a sense of peace.

"I still don't remember," she said. "I've no reason to doubt what happened, but the memory isn't there."

"Maybe you're lucky," he said.

"In Darfur, in the camps, I knew so many girls and women who'd been raped by the Janjaweed. It was a form of warfare, a way to shame them and humiliate their families." She turned onto her side, spooning her hips against him. His breath eased out as he laid an arm across her shoulders.

"I used to wonder how they could bear the horror of it," she said. "But somehow they did. They survived and moved on with their lives because they had no choice. They showed so much courage. How can I expect any less of myself? I need to move on, too—and now that I know what happened to me, I will."

"I know you will," he said softly. "You're a strong woman, Megan."

"They're the strong ones. They remember everything—and they don't have a safe place to go to keep it from happening again."

Cal didn't reply, but his arm tightened around her, drawing her closer. The light pressure of her hips set off a rush of sensual warmth. The reaction was nothing she hadn't felt before with Cal. But the fact that it was still there was a surprising comfort. She snuggled closer, feeling his breath quicken in response. The tingling heat spread, flowing into the core of her body to become a subtly throbbing pulse of desire.

She wanted him—with an urgent hunger she'd feared

she would never feel again. But the risk was a fearful one. Another failure would be devastating.

"Cal?" She turned to face him. He was watching her, his silvery eyes tender and questioning. Lifting her hand, she traced a fingertip along his cheek, feeling the soft burn of whisker stubble. "Cal, would you make love to me?"

For what seemed like forever, he didn't reply, didn't even stir. Only a subtle flicker in his eyes betrayed that he'd even heard the question. What if he was about to refuse? The embarrassment would kill her.

One eyebrow quirked. "Are you sure about this?" he asked.

"Yes…" The word barely made it past her trembling lips.

"Then I have a suggestion. Why don't *you* make love to *me?*"

She stared at him, searching his face in the lamplight. Slowly his reasons dawned on her. Let her take control, set the pace, back off if she became uncomfortable. It would be the furthest possible thing from the hellish rape that was locked in her memory.

Did she have the courage to try?

Rising onto her elbows, she leaned over and kissed him—softly at first, letting her lips feather over his, then deepening the contact. As her tongue brushed along the sensitive inner surface of his lower lip, she felt the quiver of his response. She could sense the strain as he willed himself to lie still.

Her mouth nibbled a trail down his throat, tasting the sweet saltiness of his skin. Her caresses barely skimmed the edge of intimacy, but her heart was racing. She could stop anytime, Megan reminded herself. But she didn't want to. All she wanted was Cal, his arms around her and his naked body warming hers.

Tossing her robe aside, she knelt over him. Her fingers, clumsy with haste, fumbled with the buttons of his khaki shirt. So many buttons…

"Let me." He sat up, swung his feet to the floor and in a few easy moves stripped down to his tan silk briefs. With his back toward her, he opened the drawer in the night-stand and withdrew a small packet. The lamplight cast his splendid torso in bronze. The sight of him, and the aware-ness of what was in the packet, kicked Megan's pulse to a thundering gallop. She yanked at the buttons that held her modest pajama top in place.

When he turned around, she was kneeling on the bed, bare to the hips. The way his face lit did wonders to calm her jittery nerves. It told her that he thought she was beau-tiful, and that he wanted her—something she desperately needed to believe.

Hiding the packet under the pillow, he raised the covers and slipped into bed. His heavy-lidded eyes smiled up at her in the shadows. "I can't wait to have you pleasure me," he murmured huskily. "Now, where did we leave off?"

As the storm beat against the bungalow, she stretched out alongside him, aching to touch him, smell him, taste him—every part of him. She wanted to feel alive again—to feel the thrill pulsing through her body and the hot blood coursing through her veins. She wanted to feel joy—with this man.

His mouth was cool and tasted faintly of the single-malt Scotch he'd drunk with Harris. Her tongue darted to meet his in a playful pantomime of what was meant to come. Her bare nipples grazed his chest, lingering until she broke off the kiss and nipped her way down over his collarbone.

As if playing a game with rules, he kept his hands at his sides; but other parts of him were fully responsive. He moaned as her lips closed around his aureole, tongue circling the tiny nub, coaxing it to heat and swell. His flesh was salty after the day in the hot sun, his pungent sweat deliciously male. Even this…it was heaven. She couldn't get enough of him.

As his hips arched against her, she could feel his sex, jutting along her thigh. She shifted, legs parting, pelvis tilting to bring her throbbing center into contact with that rock-solid ridge. Even through layers of fabric she could feel every inch of him. She thrust harder, hungry need spiraling through her body until the gentle press of his hand on her hip stayed her.

"You naughty girl…" he growled. "Do you have any idea what you're doing to me?"

"Yes, and I'm about to do more." The sense of power was intoxicating. Giddy with her newfound courage, she shed her pajama bottoms and panties and slid her hand beneath the waistband of his straining silk briefs. Her pulse leaped as her fingers brushed, then clasped his naked erection. To her touch, he felt as big as a stallion, as hard as a hickory log and as smooth as velvet. A purr of sheer pleasure vibrated in his throat as she stroked him, intensifying her confidence and her desire.

She loved the feeling of him in her hand, but she sensed she was pushing him to his limit. And her own sweet hunger was growing more urgent. She could feel the pulsing of her own need, the slickness of moisture all but dripping from between her thighs. She'd expected to be fearful, or at least hesitant; but all she could think of was how much she wanted him inside her.

Stripping his silk briefs down his legs, she tossed them aside and reached for the condom he'd hidden under the pillow. Slipping it over his firm erection was done in seconds. Cal's lust-glazed eyes held a glint of amusement as he watched her cloak him.

"Are you all right with this, Megan?" he whispered.

She flashed him a grin. "I've never been more all right in my life."

A slow smile spread across his face. "That's good, because you're driving me crazy. I want to be inside you so much I can't stand it."

And that was enough, she thought. No pretty lies about being in love with her. No useless flattery. Nothing was settled between them except that he wanted her. And she wanted him.

Straddling his hips, she found the center of her slickness and lowered herself down the length of his shaft. He filled her, so deep that, as she settled onto him, she could feel his manly heat pulsing through her whole body.

As she began to move, he responded with a groan. Unable to keep still, his hands came into play, clasping her hips as he drove upward into her, thrusting deeper and deeper. Where their bodies joined, shimmering bursts of pleasure ignited inside her. She came, clenching around him as the climax washed over her in waves, leaving her deliciously spent.

"Don't stop," he urged, thrusting again. She matched her motion to his. This time she rode a rocket into the stars, reeling and gasping as his release mounted. He came with her, exploding with a grunt, followed by a long outward breath and a low chuckle of satisfaction.

Still feeling spasms in the depths of her body, Megan sagged over him. She was utterly spent, but she had never felt more free. Only time would tell whether the nightmares would return. But with Cal's help, she had broken the barrier of fear. He had given her hope—and so much more.

Tears of relief and gratitude welled as she leaned forward and brushed a kiss across his smiling lips. "Thank you," she whispered.

* * *

As early dawn crept through the curtains, Cal lay spooned against Megan's sweet nakedness, his hand resting on her hip. The even cadence of her breathing told him she was still fast asleep.

They'd made love again in the night, this time in the more traditional way. Cal had feared that having a man on top of her might awaken her bad memories, but his worries had been unfounded. The second time had been every bit as wonderful and revealing as the first.

She shifted against him, settling her lovely bum deeper into the curve of his body. With a sigh, he tightened an arm around her. He'd enjoyed her beauty and relished her passion. But what moved him most was her trust. That a woman who'd been through hell would give herself to him as Megan had, with nothing held back, stirred emotions Cal had never known he possessed. It was as if he'd been handed a magnificent gift he didn't deserve. He felt unworthy, humbled, overwhelmed.

With Megan he'd ventured to a place where he'd never been with a woman—and it scared the hell out of him.

After last night, the thought of letting her go was more than he could stand. He wanted to protect her from the ugliness in the world. He wanted to heal her pain and see her smile every day—maybe for a long time to come. But questions swarmed at him. What about the past? What about her determination to return to Darfur? And what if he were to find evidence that Megan had embezzled the missing money?

As long as doubt existed on any front, he'd be a fool to trust her. He'd trusted his mother. He'd trusted Nick—trust that he was now beginning to question. The last thing he needed was another betrayal from a person he cared about.

Pulling her closer, he filled his senses with the soft lavender fragrance of her hair. For now, at least, he would be here, giving her the support she needed to heal. As long as she was willing, he would enjoy every minute of their lovemaking.

But he would keep his emotions under tight rein; and he would remember why he'd come to Africa in the first place. No one, not even Megan, would ever deceive him again.

Eleven

Megan woke to the sound of the shower running. For a moment she lay still while her mind processed the realities of her new, changed world. Last night, she'd learned the shocking truth about the rape in Darfur. And later on, when she and Cal had made love, she'd responded with newfound passion. It was as if a dam had burst, forever changing the landscape of her life.

She stretched her naked body in the bed, relishing the aches and twinges she hadn't felt in so very long. She felt like a whole woman again, and she had Cal to thank for it.

Not that she believed she was healed. The brutality she'd experienced would haunt her for the rest of her days. At some point she might remember everything. Even if she didn't, she might need therapy. But she'd turned a corner. She believed and accepted what had happened; and she no longer felt paralyzed by the fears that had taken over her life.

The shower had stopped running. Facing Cal would be one more new reality. Last night they'd become lovers. But what about today? Where would they go from here?

She had no illusions about love. Not with Cal. To a man like him, sex was just sex. And if she allowed herself to want more, she'd only get her heart broken.

But on safari, she couldn't simply get dressed and leave. The two of them would be together twenty-four/seven for most of the next week. Things could become awkward between them. As for the future...but even if she wanted something with him, and even if she could somehow convince him to agree, what kind of future could she expect, given the baggage from their shared pasts?

She was sitting up, reaching for her robe, when the bathroom door opened and Cal stepped out. He was naked except for the white towel that wrapped his hips, his splendid torso gleaming with moisture. Tossing the towel aside, he strode toward the wardrobe and then glanced back at her with a friendly grin. "Rise and shine. Harris wants us out front in thirty minutes."

So it would be business as usual—and that was fine, Megan told herself. Clutching her robe to her chest, she fled toward the bathroom. After flashing in and out of the shower, she finger-combed her hair and slathered her face, neck, arms and hands with sunscreen. By the time she emerged from the bathroom, Cal had dressed and gone out, leaving his packed duffel next to the door, probably for the staff to pick up.

The message was clear. He was keeping his distance.

Had she said or done something wrong? Had last night's performance failed to meet his expectations? Or was he just making it clear that he didn't want to get entangled? Fine, she would follow his example and behave as if nothing had happened between them.

Willing herself to ignore the sting, she finished dressing, closed her duffel and made a last-minute sweep of the bungalow to make sure nothing had been left behind. That done, she parked her bag next to Cal's and opened the front door.

Cal stood on the porch, a grin on his face and a cup of coffee in each hand. "We've got a few minutes," he said. "After last night, I thought we might need this to wake up."

Megan's heart rose like a helium birthday balloon as he put the cups on the outdoor table and turned to pull her into his arms. His kiss was sweet and tender, lingering just long enough. Exactly what she needed this morning. "You're amazing," he whispered in her ear.

"You're pretty amazing yourself," she countered, playfully rubbing her head against his chin.

Letting her go, he retrieved the cups and handed her one. Together they stood on the porch, cradling the warm cups between their palms and watching the African sunrise flame across the sky. It was one of those moments made all the more perfect, Megan thought, because it couldn't last.

"Will you be all right today?" Cal asked her.

"I'll be fine." She took a sip of the hot, rich Tanzanian brew. "But I'd just as soon not share this situation with Harris. He'd have far too much fun with it."

"Agreed." He punctuated the word with a chuckle. "I'll be on my best behavior today. Just so you won't be surprised, we'll be sharing a single tent with two cots for the next few nights."

"Fine. Something tells me I don't really want to be alone in a tent on the Serengeti. I have visions of some hungry hyena wandering in to munch on my leg. You can be there to chase him away."

"I'll confess that wasn't the first advantage I thought of." The gray eyes that gazed down at Megan held a slightly naughty twinkle, and she knew he was thinking about making love to her again. It felt good, knowing he wanted her—even though she knew things might well be different later on. Cal had always been a man with an agenda. He may have put that agenda aside for now, but sooner or later it would resurface. When that happened, it would be as if this romantic interlude had never taken place.

Was she falling in love with him? Was that the reason her brain kept flashing those red warning lights? Cal Jeffords was a compelling man, but Megan knew he didn't hold her blameless for Nick's crime and subsequent suicide. Revenge might not be far from the top of his list. She'd be a fool to lower her guard—but meanwhile she was having such a wonderful time. It was like being Cinderella at the ball—but with the constant awareness that the clock was ticking toward midnight.

By the time they finished their coffee, it was time to meet Harris and Gideon for a quick predeparture breakfast. Cal helped the driver load the last of their gear into the vehicle, and they were off.

They were headed north, toward the Kenyan border where the vast Serengeti Plain spanned the two countries. In the dry season the game herds migrated north in search of water and food. At the start of the long rains, they swept southward by the hundreds of thousands, to graze on the abundant fresh grass and raise their young. It was this grand spectacle that Harris had promised to show them.

As the Land Rover sped along the narrow ribbon of paved road, Cal stole a glance at Megan. She was seated with her arm resting on the back of the seat, the breeze fluttering the green scarf at her throat. He took a moment to feast his eyes on her. True to their understanding, she gave no sign that anything had changed between them. But he couldn't forget that last night she'd been his—quivering above him, her head thrown back, while he exploded deep inside her. Right now, all he could think about was having her again, and soon.

He'd set out to seduce her, and now he'd succeeded, but with more complications than he could've imagined in his wildest dreams. Her beauty was a given. But it was her blend of courage and vulnerability that had hit him with the impact of a ten-ton truck.

She was Nick's widow. Cold reasoning told him he couldn't dismiss her link to the stolen money. But last night she'd given herself to him with all her woman's passion. She'd reached out and trusted him to lead her back from the edge of hell. How could he even think of using that trust to get the answers he wanted? But then, again, how could he not? He'd spent two years searching and had even come to Africa to learn the truth—he wasn't going home without it.

A bump in the road jarred him back to the present. The landscape had opened up into rolling hills, carpeted with pale green shoots of sprouting grass. On a flat rise, a cluster of round huts came into view, with mud walls and artfully thatched, conical roofs. Rangy-looking cattle, watched over by young boys, grazed on the slopes.

"Maasai," Harris explained for Megan's benefit. "They're all over these parts with their cattle and goats, living pretty much like they have for hundreds of years. Back in the old days, do-gooders tried to civilize them. But the rascals didn't take to civilizing. They wanted to keep their spears and their cows and their old ways. They still do."

The Land Rover had come up on a herd of goats, grazing in a hollow where the runoff from the road had nourished the grass. The young boy guarding them showed spindly legs below his crimson togalike garment. He grinned and waved as they passed.

Megan called out *"Jambo,"* laughing as she returned the wave. It was plain to see that she adored children. What a shame she'd never had any of her own. That miscarriage she'd suffered must've been devastating.

"What a beautiful boy," she said.

"Oh, they're a handsome lot, all right," Harris snorted. "And vain as all get-out, especially the so-called warriors. The women do the work, the boys herd the stock, and aside from making babies, the men haven't much to do but strut around with their spears and look pretty."

"Is it still true that a young Maasai has to kill a lion with a spear before he can be called a man?" Cal asked.

Harris guffawed. "Lions are protected these days. But knowing the Maasai, I wouldn't be surprised if it still happens. Years ago I showed up in time to save one of the young fools. His spear had snapped. The lion was about to rip him apart when I stepped in. That's how *this* happened." He nodded toward his pinned-up sleeve.

Megan shot Cal a mischievous glance, rolling her eyes skyward. A smile teased her kissable mouth. She looked luscious enough to devour on the spot. He could hardly wait to get her alone.

He was in over his head—and he knew it.

By the time they arrived at the campsite, it was late in the day. Clouds were rumbling across the vast expanse of sky, threatening a downpour.

Megan had half expected they'd be pitching camp on their own. She should have known better. Harris's competent safari staff had everything set up and waiting for them, including a savory dinner of saffron rice, vegetables and chicken cooked over an open fire.

Set on high ground, safe from flooding, there were tents for staff and guests along with sheltered cooking and eating areas. Megan was astonished to discover that the tent she shared with Cal featured an adjoining bathroom with a flush toilet and a primitive but functional shower.

"Magic!" Harris laughed at her surprise. "We can't have clients wandering out to the loo in the dark, can we? They might not make it back."

After the long, bumpy ride in the Land Rover, it was heavenly to sit in the open front of the dining tent and watch the rain drip off the canvas. The day had been spectacular. They'd seen elephants, giraffes, ostriches and a pride of lions feasting on the zebra they'd killed. White-headed vultures and marabou storks had flocked around them, waiting their turn at the leavings. In this place of raw, cruel beauty, nothing went to waste.

Megan had watched breathless as a cheetah streaked after a gazelle and brought it down in a single bound. Two cubs, hiding in the grass, had scampered out to join their mother at the feast. Death was brutal on the Serengeti, but it nourished new life.

As the darkness deepened, they sat in folding chairs, watching the rain and listening to the sounds of the awakening night—the distant roar of a lion, the titter of a hyena, the cry of a bird and the drone of insects in the grass. Harris sipped his bourbon, lantern light deepening the hollows under his eyes. He looked old and tired, Megan thought. Maybe the life of a safari guide was becoming too strenuous for him.

"Cal already knows this," he said to Megan, "but I need to make it clear for you. Once you go into your tent for the night, you zip the flap and don't open it till you hear the boys in the morning. No traipsing around in the dark, hear? You never know what's going to be out there."

Megan laughed. "Not to worry. No power on earth could drag me out of that tent in the middle of the night."

"Speaking of the tent…" Cal set down his glass, stood and stretched. "I'm ready to turn in. You should get some rest, too, Harris. It's been a long day." He glanced at Megan. Taking her cue, she rose. It had been a tiring day for her, too. But if Cal had lovemaking on his mind, she was on board. Just looking at him was enough to make her ache.

Harris remained in his chair. He really did look tired, Megan thought. Feeling a surge of affection, she bent and kissed the weathered cheek. "Do get some sleep, Harris," she murmured. "We don't want to wear you out tomorrow."

"Thanks for thinking of an old man." Patting her hand, he glanced up at Cal. "You take care of this girl, hear? She's a good one."

"She is, and I'll do that." Switching on a flashlight and opening a handy umbrella, Cal ushered her toward their tent. The storm had subsided to a steady drizzle. Exotic animal sounds, like the track from an old Tarzan movie, filled the night.

"Will it really be dangerous out here," she asked, "or was Harris just trying to scare me?"

"You can take him at his word. The staff will keep a fire going to scare off anything big. But that won't be much help if you walk outside and step on a snake."

Megan shuddered. "That's enough. You've convinced me to behave."

"Behave? You?" Cal teased. "We'll see about that."

They'd reached the sheltered entrance to their tent. Cal laid the umbrella on a chair and checked the interior with the flashlight beam. "All clear," he said. "Come on in."

Megan stepped into the tent and bent to close the long zipper that secured the flap. When she straightened and turned around, Cal was standing in the narrow space between the cots. In the dim glow of the flashlight, his eyes held a glint of pure, unbridled lust.

"I've been waiting all day to get my hands on you," he growled, opening his arms and moving toward her.

Megan met him partway. He crushed her close, his kiss flaming through her like the tail of a meteor. They tore at each other's clothes, buttons popping, belts and shoes thudding. Megan left her slacks wadded on the floor. Still in her bra and panties, she hooked his hips with one leg, bringing his erection into hard contact with her aching sex. Wild with need, she ground against him through his briefs, heightening the hot sweetness until her head fell back and she came with a little shudder, ready for more. She had never felt so free.

"What a little wanton you've turned out to be. Who knew?" He chuckled under his breath as he unhooked her bra and tossed it on the cot. His hand slid inside her panties, fingers stroking her, riding on her slickness. "Damn it, but I want you. All I can think about right now is being inside you!"

"Would you believe it's all I can think about…too?" She shed her panties. Her hand tugged at his briefs, pulling them down to free his bulging erection. The cots were narrow, but that was of little concern as he lowered her onto the nearest one and slipped on protection before he mounted her and drove in hard. Megan flung her legs around his hips, pulling him deeper inside her. She loved the way his length and thickness filled every inch of her. She loved the feel of him, gliding silkily along her sensitive inner surfaces, igniting a trail of sparks that soared through her body. She met his thrusts, heightening the dizzy spiral of sensations that carried her with him, mounting upward to release in a shattering burst.

For a moment he lay still. His breath was warm against her shoulder as he exhaled, chuckled and rolled off the cot.

"Did we break anything?" he teased, grinning down at her.

"Are you asking about me or the bed?" Megan sat up and ran a hand through her damp hair. She felt gloriously spent. "For the record, I believe we're both intact."

He bent and brushed a kiss across her mouth. "You're amazing," he said.

"So you tell me," she responded with a little laugh. "Sometimes I even amaze myself."

They lay awake in the darkness, veiled by mosquito netting and separated by the narrow space between their cots. Outside the tent, the sounds of the African night blended in a symphony of primal nature.

Wrapped in contentment, Megan stretched her legs beneath the blankets. The day had been splendid, the night even more so. She didn't want this time to end. But she knew better than to talk about the future. Here, with the outside world far away, she and Cal had found something memorable. But days from now, she knew, only the memory would remain.

"I wish I could record those sounds outside and take them with me," she said. "The rain, the animals…they'd lull me to sleep anywhere, even in Darfur."

A leaden silence hung between them before he spoke. "You can't mean to say you're still planning to go back!"

"Why not?" Even as she said the words, Megan could feel her resolve crumbling. But she held fast. "I'm feeling so much better now. And those people need me. I can't just turn my back and walk away."

He sat up, a dark silhouette through the mosquito netting that draped his cot. "I'm not asking you to turn your

back. I'm asking you to take more time off. Make sure
you're strong enough."

"Is that all?" The words slipped out before Megan could
stop them. Her heart sank. The last thing she wanted was
to question Cal's motives like a whiny, insecure female
fishing for a commitment.

"No, it isn't all," he said. "The past few days have been
wonderful. I care about you, Megan. I want to see where
you and I are headed before I let you go anywhere. Is that
so hard to accept?"

Megan's throat had gone dry. Only as Cal's words sank
in did she realize how she'd been yearning to hear them.
She *wanted* him to care for her. She *wanted* more time with
him. But believing those words could get her heart broken. Cal had come to Africa seeking one thing—justice.
And he was the sort of man who'd do anything to get what
he wanted. That included playing her any way he could.

She found her voice. "I didn't realize we were headed
anywhere. What about the money you suspect I took? Isn't
that why you came after me?"

He hesitated, as if weighing his reply. "In part—at first.
But knowing you as I do now, I can't believe you're hiding anything. You're as transparent as fine crystal, Megan.
That's one of the things that I…" He fumbled for the right
words. "One of the things I find so compelling about you.
And right now I'm here because of *you,* not the damned
money."

Megan's heart leaped. She'd wanted to hear those words
from him. And now she wanted to believe they were true.
But were they? Or was he still manipulating her?

With a weary sigh he lay down again. The cot creaked
as he adjusted his tall frame. "So what's it to be? Will you
give me more time before you vanish out of my life again?"

Megan gazed up into the darkness, her emotions churning. She wanted this man in more ways than she could name. But did she want him enough to risk heartbreak or betrayal?

"I can't make that decision tonight," she said. "Give me a few days to think about it—maybe until we're headed back to Arusha. All right?"

"All right," he grumbled. "But you can expect some lobbying on my part. I'm not one to take no for an answer."

"I know." Torn, she blinked away a secret tear. "Now, let's get some sleep. Harris will be rousting us out early tomorrow."

He mumbled a reply, already drifting. Megan closed her eyes and soon fell into a dreamless sleep.

It was barely dawn when a commotion outside the tent shocked her awake. Megan sat bolt upright. She could hear the sound of shouts and running feet.

Cal was awake, too. "Stay inside," he said. "I'll see what's happening."

He was pulling on his pants when Gideon's frantic voice came through the closed tent flap. "Open up! We need you!"

"What's wrong?" Cal yanked the zipper down. Gideon's face was ashen.

"Hurry! It's Mr. Harris! I think he's had a heart attack!"

Twelve

Still in her pajamas, Megan raced outside. Harris lay gray-faced and unconscious on the canvas apron in front of his tent. Megan dropped to her knees beside him. He wasn't breathing. No time to check for a pulse. It had to be a heart attack. Willing herself not to panic, she placed her hands at the base of Harris's sternum, shifted her weight above him and fell into the rhythmic compressions of CPR. Her nurse's training had taught her to keep a cool head, but a voice inside her was screaming. This old man had grown dear to her. She couldn't lose him.

Why hadn't she paid more attention to him last night? He'd looked ill even then. If she'd checked him, she might have been able to do something sooner.

Gideon hovered over her, visibly shaken. "He came outside and fell. Is he going to die?"

"Not if I can help it." Megan kept the rhythm steady. "When did this happen?"

"Just before I called you. He has been like a father to me…" Gideon's voice broke.

Megan didn't look up. "Radio the airport in Arusha," she said. "Tell somebody to send a plane with medical equipment. Hurry!"

"No, not Arusha. I know who to call." Gideon raced for the Land Rover, which was equipped with a radio.

Cal had been standing back to give her room. Now he knelt beside her. "I can do this. Let me take over while you make sure the message gets through."

"Thanks." Megan let his hands slip under hers, keeping the rhythm unbroken. That done, she clambered to her feet and raced after Gideon. By the time she reached the vehicle, he was already on the radio, speaking in terse English to a voice that could barely be heard through the crackling static. Ending the call, he turned back to Megan.

"Flying Doctors. We have a contract with them. They can be here in half an hour and take him to Nairobi. Can you keep him alive that long?"

"We can only try." Megan raced back to where she'd left Cal with Harris and gave him the news. She'd heard of the air ambulance company that served much of East Africa, but in her haste to get help she'd forgotten. Thank heaven Gideon had thought to call them.

"That's some hope at least." Cal's strong hands kept up their pumping on Harris's chest. "Go get some clothes on. We can spell each other till the plane gets here." His gaze met Megan's, and she saw the fear that neither of them would voice. There was no way of knowing whether CPR could keep Harris alive. By the time the plane arrived, it could be too late to save him.

Rushing into the tent, she yanked on her clothes and shoved her feet into her boots. As an afterthought, she flung some essentials into her day pack and shoved her passport, with its multiple-entry Kenyan visa, into her pocket. If there was room in the plane, she wanted to be ready to go along. Harris would need someone there who knew him, and as a nurse, she was the logical choice. She would ask Gideon to find Harris's passport, as well. It would at least give the distraught man something to do.

She was closing her pack when she heard Cal's voice calling her. Stumbling over her boot laces, she raced out of the tent. Her heart dropped as she saw that he'd stopped the chest compressions. But then she noticed the relief that glazed his face.

"I'm getting a pulse," he said. "He seems to be coming around."

"Oh, thank God!" Megan dropped to Harris's near side. She saw at once that his color was improving. A touch along the side of his throat confirmed a thready heartbeat. "Water," she called out. "And bring a pillow and blanket!"

Someone handed her a plastic water bottle. Twisting off the cap, Megan wet her hand and smoothed it over Harris's face. He gasped, taking in precious oxygen. His eyelids fluttered open. His mouth worked to form words.

"What the hell…?" he muttered.

"Hush." Megan laid a finger on his parchment-dry lips. "You've had a heart attack, Harris. Lie still. The plane's on its way."

"Feel like I've been kicked by a damned elephant…" He struggled vainly to sit up.

"Stay put, *mzee*." Cal's hands on his shoulders held him gently in place. "You almost checked out on us. We want to keep you around."

Someone handed Megan the bedding she'd asked for. She tucked the blanket around Harris and slid the pillow under his head. He still looked as frail as a snowflake. The plane would be sure to carry oxygen and a defibrillator;

but until it arrived, the old hunter could go back into cardiac arrest at any time. All they could do was keep him quiet and hope for the best.

Lifting his head, she held the water bottle to his lips. "Just enough to wet your mouth," she cautioned. "And then I'm going to give you an aspirin to chew."

"Water and aspirin!" He swore in protest. "Hell, give me a swig of bourbon and let me up. I'll be as good as new!"

Megan exchanged worried looks with Cal. The old man's spunk was definitely back. But that didn't mean the danger was any less grave. In fact, he could put himself in danger if he refused to settle down. While she held his sunburned hands, her eyes gazed anxiously at the sky. Nairobi, the capital of Kenya, was only about fifty air miles away—closer than Arusha. Gideon had promised that the doctors would arrive in half an hour, but she hadn't thought to check her watch. How much longer did they have to wait?

The minutes crawled past. In a blessedly short time, they heard the drone of a small aircraft. Megan breathed a prayer of thanks as the single-engine Cessna landed on a level strip of ground below the camp. Within minutes Harris was hooked up to oxygen, strapped to a stretcher and on his way to the plane.

Megan, who'd been given the OK to come along, followed with her day pack slung on her shoulder. With one backward glance at Cal, she swung into the plane and took the last empty seat. There'd been no time to say goodbye. She would likely see him again in Nairobi, but their interlude in this African paradise was over. Whatever happened between them now would happen amid the stresses and uncertainties of the real world.

Cal watched the departing plane until it vanished into the sunrise. Harris was in capable hands, he told himself. Kenyatta Hospital in Nairobi was modern and well equipped, its doctors as competent as any in Africa. As for Megan, it had been the right decision for her to go. But there was a cold hollow inside him where her warmth had been. He hadn't planned on her being torn from him so soon—or so abruptly, without so much as a chance to say goodbye. Only now that she was gone did he realize how empty he felt without her.

He would see her at the hospital, of course, but under strained conditions. They would both be concerned about Harris and focused on his needs. There'd be little opportunity for them to be alone or to make any decisions about their budding relationship.

Budding? Was that what it was? He'd scarcely spent a week with Megan, but now that she was gone he felt damned near lost without her. What was that supposed to mean?

But that thought would have to wait. Right now he had other urgent concerns on his mind.

The plan was for Cal and Gideon to load the personal gear in the Land Rover, drive back to Arusha and make the flight from there to Nairobi in Cal's corporate jet. It was the course of action that made the most sense. With Megan gone, Cal had no more reason to stay in Arusha. And Gideon was the closest thing to family the old man had. In Nairobi, he could look after Harris's needs and see him home after his release from the hospital.

Cal would see that Gideon had plenty of money for his lodging, meals and transportation. He would also make sure there'd be no problem with Harris's medical expenses. He could afford it, and it was at least one way he could help.

Nairobi might also be his last chance to arrive at an understanding with Megan. Things had been good between them last night. But she still seemed set on returning to Darfur. He'd told her he wanted more time together, but even though she'd agreed to consider the idea, they no longer had the luxury of the rest of their safari to decide what would come next. If he was going to convince her to give him a real chance, he'd have to move very fast. Maybe he needed to open up and tell her how he really felt. Otherwise he could lose her for good—and he wasn't ready to let that happen.

"Hello, sweetheart." Harris was sitting partway up, an oxygen line hooked to his nose. Above the bed, monitors attached to his body flickered and beeped.

"Hello, you old rogue." Megan stepped to his bedside and brushed a kiss across his forehead. His color was much improved, and his eyes had recovered a bit of their twinkle, but he was far from out of the woods. A few hours ago the doctors had performed an angioplasty to clear out the clogged artery that had caused his heart attack. The attending physician had told her his chances for recovery were good, but only if he took better care of his health.

"Where's Cal?" he asked her.

"Cal and Gideon are driving to Arusha and flying from there. Unless they've been delayed, they should be here by tonight."

"Gideon's coming? Good."

"He wanted to be here. He said you were like a father to him."

"The rascal would only say that if he thought I was dying." Harris snorted dismissively, but something in his voice told Megan the old man had been touched.

"The doctor's going to come in to lecture you soon," Megan said, taking a seat next to the bed. "If you don't want to end up back in the hospital, you're going to have to make some changes. No more smoking. Cut way back on alcohol and red meat—"

"Oh, bother! Will he say I have to give up all those women who are chasing me, too?"

"You're incorrigible."

"And you're the sweetest thing to come into my life since I don't know when." His hand brushed Megan's cheek. "If I was thirty years younger and if Cal hadn't already staked his claim on you—"

"Staked his claim? Maybe he should ask me first."

"He will if you stick around. I've noticed the way he looks at you. The man's so lovesick he can barely lace his boots. Hellfire, girl, I do believe you're blushing."

"I haven't blushed since I was fifteen years old." But Megan's face did feel unsettlingly warm. Was Harris right about Cal? Surely the old man was teasing her. How could she let herself believe that? "Let's talk about something else," she said.

He looked thoughtful. "Well, I guess I could thank you for saving my life."

"I can't take credit for that. It was Cal who did most of the CPR and Gideon who called the plane."

"But you're the one who stayed with me and talked me into hanging on. So just for you, I've a confession to make." His pale blue eyes twinkled mysteriously. "I've been filling your pretty head with tall tales about how I lost my arm. If you promise to keep it a secret, I'll tell you the real story."

"You mean it wasn't a jealous husband or a rhino or a lion? This, I need to hear. Certainly I'll keep your secret." Megan leaned closer to the bed. "I promise."

"It was back in England," he said. "My family was dirt poor, with six mouths to feed. I was fifteen when I quit school to work in a coal mine. The place was a black hell-hole. But it was the only job to be had for a boy like me.

One day a slab of coal fell out of the ceiling and crushed my arm. The flesh and bone were too far gone to heal, and there was no money for a doctor. When gangrene set in, the local butcher got me drunk and cut off the arm to save my life."

"Oh…" Megan gazed at him in dismay. No wonder Harris made up those fanciful stories about losing his arm. The real story was too sad to share with clients. "What did you do, Harris? How did you survive?"

"I'd always been good with a gun. It took some practice, but I learned to shoot one-armed with my father's old army rifle. To feed the family, I started poaching deer and grouse off the local estate. Got caught, of course. Barely escaped with my hide. Stowed aboard a freighter and ended up in Africa. No papers—but it was easier to get by in those days."

"That's quite a story, Harris." Cal stood in the doorway, looking rumpled and weary in the clothes he'd pulled on that morning. "I've always wondered about it myself. Trust Megan to charm the truth out of you."

The old hunter smiled, but it was plain to see that so much talking had tired him. Megan watched Cal as he crossed the room toward her. They'd been apart for only a few hours, but now that he was here she realized how much she'd missed him.

"Harris swore me to secrecy," she said. "Since you were listening, you have to swear, too. Not a word."

"Consider it done. My lips are sealed." Cal's hand brushed across her shoulder as he moved to the head of the bed. She felt his touch through her shirt and along her skin like the passing of a warm breeze. After the long, stressful day, the need to be in his arms was compelling enough to hurt.

The look he gave Harris betrayed how worried he'd been. "You gave us quite a scare, old friend," he said.

"Oh, I'll be fine." Harris winked. "Just might have to cut back on my bad habits, that's all. Where's Gideon? Didn't he come?"

"Gideon's down in the cafeteria grabbing a sandwich. He wants to sit with you tonight, so I suggested he eat first. Meanwhile, I hope you won't mind if I take Megan back to the hotel for some dinner and a good night's rest. We can stay till Gideon gets here."

Harris waved them away. "Go on. I'll be fine. There's this good-looking nurse on duty. If I'm alone when she comes in, maybe I can get somewhere with her."

Cal shook his head. "Just don't overdo it, you old rascal! We'll see you later."

Megan rose, blew Harris a farewell kiss and allowed Cal to escort her out of the room. His hand rested lightly on the small of her back as they walked through the maze of hallways and took the elevator to the hospital lobby. "I booked us a room at the Crowne Plaza." He named one of the city's premier luxury hotels. "Your things are there, and we have reservations in the dining room. I'm guessing you'll be hungry."

"Starved. But I'll settle for something quick in the coffee shop. I look a fright, and I'm too tired to get cleaned up for dinner."

The Crowne Plaza was an easy drive from Kenyatta Hospital, but the cab took time to weave its way through the tangle of evening traffic. Too tired to talk, Megan stared out the cab windows at the busy streets. She was no stranger to the big, bustling city of Nairobi. It was the jumping-off point for the refugee camps in northern Kenya and the Sudan. If she decided to go back to Darfur from here, it shouldn't be too difficult to find transportation.

But when it came to that decision, her heart was still torn. She was needed in Darfur. And going back might help her face her buried fears. But she'd found something warm and thrilling with Cal—something she realized she'd been searching for all her life. If there was a chance it might last, she'd be tempted to stay. But she'd known Cal too long not to have doubts. Was he really capable of a long-term relationship—with anyone, much less her—or was he still just a man with an agenda?

The taxi was slowing down, turning left into the hotel driveway. Other times in Nairobi, Megan had ridden local buses and stayed at one of the cheap boardinghouses frequented by volunteers like her. Now as the cab pulled up to the elegant, ultramodern complex, she felt as if she'd stumbled into a different world. The old Megan would have been right at home here. But that woman was gone forever. She was a different person now.

But when he looked at her, which woman did Cal see?

The hotel coffee shop was too noisy for serious conversation. Cal studied Megan across the table as she finished the last of her chicken and rice and sipped her mineral water. He'd planned a romantic evening in a setting where he could lay his heart on the line. But he should have known it wasn't the best idea. Megan had been rousted out of bed by Harris's heart attack, flown with him in the plane and remained at the hospital for the rest of the day. Stress showed in every line and shadow of her face. What she needed tonight was rest, not romance.

They rode the elevator up to their room, having conversed mostly about Harris, the flight, his surgery and recovery. "You look worn out," Cal said as she surveyed the room with its king-size bed. "Your duffel's on that bench by the wall. The bathroom's all yours."

"Wonderful. I could really use a shower." She rummaged in her bag, pulled out a few things and then vanished into the bathroom. Minutes later the shower came on.

Cal had retrieved his laptop from the plane. The device was functional here in the hotel, and he needed to catch up on his messages. He scrolled through his in-box, marking some for reply, deleting others. What he'd hoped to see was some word from Harlan Crandall about his search for the missing funds. Knowing where the money had gone might at least give him some closure, so he could move ahead with Megan. But there was nothing.

Impatient, he pecked out a message to Crandall asking for an update. By the time he'd finished, the shower had turned off. A moment later, Megan emerged in a cloud of steam. Wrapped in one of the hotel's oversized terry robes, she was damp, glowing and so beautiful it stopped his breath.

"Better?" he asked, finding his voice.

"Better. It's been a long day and I'm done in." She began rubbing her hair dry with a towel, fluffing and curling it with her fingers. The sight of her stirred Cal to a pleasant arousal. Although he'd planned to let her rest, the thought of Megan's fresh, naked body in his arms was giving him different ideas. But he'd had a long day, too, and he didn't exactly smell like a rose garden. He needed a shower before he shared her bed.

With a murmured excuse, he walked into the bathroom, stripped down, turned on the water and lathered his body. The shower took about ten minutes, drying off a few more. With his hips wrapped in a towel, he stepped out of the bathroom.

His anticipation sagged. Megan was curled under the covers on the far side of the bed, deep in slumber.

* * *

Megan stirred and opened her eyes. The last thing she remembered was lying awake, waiting for Cal to finish his shower and join her—for lovemaking, serious talk or whatever was meant to happen. But she'd been so sleepy, she had no memory of his even coming to bed.

Now it was full daylight, and Cal was nowhere to be seen. Only his bag on the luggage stand gave any indication that he hadn't gone for good. Sitting up, she found a note penned on hotel stationery and tucked under the clock on the nightstand.

Good morning, sleepyhead. I didn't have the heart to wake you before I left for the hospital. Since Gideon didn't call me in the night, I'm guessing Harris is fine. If he's not, you'll hear. I'll check back with you later. Meanwhile, please relax and order some breakfast. C.

Megan glanced at the clock. It was almost 9:00 a.m. How could she have slept so late? Flinging aside the covers, she sprang to her feet, then realized her mistake. Lying down for so long and getting up so fast had left her slightly dizzy. Tottering toward a chair, she banged her knee on a small side table. She managed to right the table before it fell, but as it tilted, an object crashed to the floor.

Megan bent to pick it up and recognized Cal's laptop. *Oh, no!* What if she'd broken it?

Worried, she gave the device an experimental shake. Nothing sounded loose, but she noticed that the screen had come on. Maybe Cal had left it in sleep mode—not that she had enough technical savvy to be certain. It appeared he'd been checking his email earlier. His in-box was still open on the screen.

Something popped up on the screen, drawing her eye automatically. It was a "new email" notification letting him know a message had arrived, from someone named

Harlan Crandall. Megan would have dismissed it as none of her business—but then she saw the subject line.

Re: Update on missing foundation funds

Her pulse lurched. The right thing would be to ignore the message. But this concerned *her,* and might even have some bearing on her relationship with Cal. She couldn't *not* look at it.

Racked with guilt for snooping, she highlighted the message and clicked it open.

Dear Mr. Jeffords:

You asked for an update on my investigation. I fear I have little to report. I've traced Mr. Rafferty's activities during the weeks before his suicide, but aside from some large bank withdrawals, I've found nothing that might lead us to the money.

What have you been able to learn from Mr. Rafferty's widow? If we can put our findings together, maybe some new pieces of this puzzle will emerge.

Yours truly,

Harlan Crandall

As Megan laid the laptop back on the table, a strange numbness crept over her. So Cal's motive hadn't changed. He'd pretended to care about her, but all he'd really wanted was to track down the money and prove her guilt. His tenderness, his loving patience—it had all been an act to win her trust.

At least she knew. And she knew what she had to do.

Willing herself to move, not think, she emptied her duffel on the bed and began repacking the contents for a long, rough trip.

Thirteen

Cal's gut clenched as he reread the note Megan had left in the hotel room. It was penned in a shaky script—his only clue to her anguished state of mind.

Dear Cal,
By the time you read this I'll be on my way back to Darfur. Now that my decision is made, there's no point in staying, or in drawn-out goodbyes. And there's no point in explaining why I decided to leave. I think you already know.

Yes, he did know. He'd just seen Crandall's message on his laptop and realized it had been opened and read. Lord, he could just imagine what Megan thought of him now.

Don't bother coming after me. I've told you the truth all along—I endorsed the checks and gave them to Nick, and that's all I know. You won't learn anything

new by tracking me down again, and you won't find
the money. I truly believe Nick spent it all. If he
hadn't, he'd have given it back when he was caught.

Please give my best to Harris and Gideon. Tell
them if I get back to Arusha I'll pay them a visit.
Whatever your motives may have been, Cal, I can't
leave without thanking you. You did some good
things for me. But now it's time for me to go back
to where I'm needed. I'm strong enough now. I'll
be fine.

There was no closing or signature, as if Megan had
put so much emotion into the message that she'd been too
drained to finish it.

Cal's first impulse was to go after—find her, drag her
back by force if need be and convince her she was wrong
about him.

Convince her, damn it, that he was in love with her!

But he knew it wouldn't work. Even if he could track
Megan down, forcing her to come back wouldn't be an act
of love. It would be an act of control. Megan had made
her choice. If he loved her, he would respect that choice—
even though letting her go was like ripping out his heart.

He would go home to San Francisco, Cal resolved.
There, he would do whatever it took to find out what Nick
had done with the stolen funds. The answer had to be
somewhere—and when he found it, he would take the
evidence and lay it at Megan's feet. Once he could prove
her innocence, all the civil suits would go away. It would
be safe for her to come home. Maybe then she would forgive him.

Meanwhile, as she faced danger in a savage land, he could only pray that the heavenly powers would keep her safe.

Darfur, two months later

Megan filled her mug with hot black coffee and seated herself at the empty table in the volunteer kitchen. It was early dawn, the sun not yet risen behind the barren hills. But outside the infirmary, the camp was already stirring to life. Through the open window she could hear the crow of a rooster, the cry of a baby and the chatter of women going for water. The familiar scent of baking *kisra,* a Sudanese bread made from ground sorghum, drifted on the air.

Two months after her return to the camp, it was as if she'd never left. Some of the volunteers had moved on, including the doctor who'd diagnosed her rape and filled out the report. But the refugees were mostly the ones she remembered. In a way it was almost like coming home.

The long days kept her blessedly busy. It was only at night that she had time to think about Cal. The man had schemed to win her trust and get information. He had used her shamelessly, and she had let him. She knew she ought to put him out of her mind. But as she lay on her cot in the darkness, the hunger to be in his arms was a soul-deep pain that never left.

"You're up bright and early." Sam Watson, the new doctor, wandered in and filled his coffee cup. He was African-American, middle-aged, with a wife and college-age children back in New Jersey. Megan had warmed at once to his friendly manner.

"This is my favorite part of the day," Megan said. "The only time it's calm around here."

"I understand. Can I get you something before I sit

down? Some eggs? Some nice fried Spam?" He lifted the cover off the electric fry pan where the Sudanese cook had left breakfast to warm.

Megan shook her head. "Coffee's fine."

He filled his plate and sat down across from her. The smell of fried meat triggered a curdling sensation in her stomach.

"You've been off your feed lately." He stirred a packet of sugar into his coffee. "Everything all right?"

"Fine." She forced a smile, clenching her teeth against a rising wave of nausea.

"You're sure? You look a little green this morning. I'd be happy to check you out before we open for business."

"I'm fine. Just need some…air." Abandoning her coffee cup, she rose and stumbled out the back door. The morning breeze was still cool. She gulped its freshness into her lungs.

It couldn't be. It just couldn't be.

But she remembered now that she'd had her last period in Arusha—a week before Cal showed up. That had been more than two months ago.

No, it couldn't be. They'd used protection.

But now she remembered seeing the wrapper on the pack of condoms—a local brand, not known for reliability. Oh, Lord, she should have warned him. But at the time, that had been the last thing on her mind.

"Megan?"

She turned to find the doctor standing behind her.

"I'll be fine, Sam. Just give me a minute."

"I've got something else to give you," he said. "Found a stash of them in the supply closet. Something tells me you might need one of these."

He handed her a small, cellophane-wrapped box. Megan's stomach flip-flopped as she saw the label.

It was a home pregnancy test.

* * *

Megan lay on her cot, staring up into the darkness. One hand rested lovingly on her belly, where the precious new life was growing.

Her baby. Cal's baby. The wonder of it sent a thrill through her body. Two weeks after discovering her pregnancy, she was still getting used to the idea. Only one thing was certain. She wanted this child with all her heart, and she would do anything to keep her little one safe.

When, if ever, would she inform Cal? She supposed he had a right to know. But after the way he'd used her in an effort to glean information, did she want him in her life... or in their child's life?

Cal *would* be in her life, she knew, probably trying to control every aspect of his child's existence—and hers.

She'd learned that Cal could be a genuinely caring person, but his version of caring usually meant taking over. She could do without the Cal Jeffords Master-of-the-Universe brand of caring. But did she have the right to raise her child without a father—and without the advantages that such a father could provide?

So many decisions to make. However, as much as it weighed on her, the question of Cal was far removed from her present world. For now, there were more urgent matters to deal with.

Given her history of miscarriage, Sam had wisely insisted that she be evacuated on the next available plane, which would be arriving with mail and supplies the day after tomorrow. For the near future she could be posted to Arusha, where there was a small modern hospital and ready transportation out of the country. Sooner or later, Megan knew, she would have to face going back to America, where she had no home, no family, no job, few friends who'd remained loyal to her and a stack of legal charges waiting for her. When the time came, involving Cal and his lawyers might be her only choice if she wanted to spend the last stages of her pregnancy anywhere other than inside a courtroom. But for now she wanted to stay in Africa.

She'd asked Sam to keep her pregnancy out of his report, citing simply "health reasons" for her transfer. He'd agreed to her request without demanding the reason.

The hour was late and she'd worked a long day. As she closed her eyes, she could feel herself beginning to drift. Soon she was deep in dreamless sleep.

"Miss Megan! Wake up!" The whisper penetrated the fog of Megan's slumber. She could feel a small hand shaking her shoulder. "Miss Megan...it's me."

Megan opened her eyes. A delicate face, surrounded by the folds of a head scarf, peered down at her. *No! She had to be dreaming!*

"It's me, Miss Megan. It's Saida!"

Still groggy, Megan rolled onto one elbow. "You can't be alive," she muttered. "I saw the Janjaweed—"

"Yes, they took me. For many days they kept me with them. But no more. Now I need you to come."

Megan sat up and switched on the flashlight she kept next to her cot. Yes, it was Saida. But a very different Saida from the innocent girl who'd sneaked out of camp to meet a boy. There was a grim purpose to the set of her mouth, a glint of steel in the lovely doe eyes that had seen too much. Slung over her shoulder by a leather strap was an AK-47 automatic rifle.

"I need you to come," she repeated. "My friend is hurt. I need you to save her."

"You need the doctor. Let me get him."

"No. Not a man. Only you."

None of this was making sense. "Where is your friend? Can't you bring her here?"

Saida shook her head. "Too far. Our camp is in the mountains. I have horses outside. If we ride hard, we can be there by sunrise."

"Saida, I'm going to have a baby," Megan protested. "I can't ride hard."

"We will have to take more time, then." The girlish voice had taken on an edge. "But my friend has been shot. I must bring you or she will die. I made a promise."

Only then did Megan realize what was at stake. Saida had made a desperate vow, and she had a weapon. Megan's choice was to go willingly, as a friend, or be taken at gunpoint. If she tried to warn Sam he might try to stop her, and somebody could get hurt.

"All right." She rose from the bed. "Give me a few minutes to get dressed and gather some medical supplies."

Saida pulled the blanket off Megan's bed and draped it over her arm. "I'll be out back with the horses. Can I trust you?"

"You can trust me," Megan replied, meaning it. She and Saida had shared a hellish experience—the girl's far worse, even, than her own. For good or for ill, the horror of that night had bonded them for life.

As she pulled on her clothes, she glanced at the clock. It was 1:20, no more than five hours before sunrise. At least the camp must not be far away. But if they took more time, as Saida had said, the sun would be well above the horizon before they arrived.

In the supply closet, she dropped bandages, disinfectant, forceps, a scalpel, antibiotics and other needs into a pillowcase. A hastily scrawled note told Sam she'd gone to the aid of a patient in the nearby mountains, and that she'd gone willingly. She could only hope Saida would bring her back before the plane arrived tomorrow afternoon to fly her out of Darfur.

172 A SINFUL SEDUCTION

Saida had said her friend was shot. Megan had assisted with treating gunshot wounds, so she knew what needed to be done. But this time she'd be flying blind. She had no idea how badly Saida's friend was hurt, what complications the injury involved, or what would happen if she couldn't save her.

She found Saida waiting with two horses. The girl had folded the blanket and slipped it under Megan's saddle for a more cushioned ride—a gesture that reassured Megan of her good intentions. Still, she sat on the horse gingerly, ever mindful of her unborn baby.

They rode out of the camp in silent single file. Only when they were far out of hearing did Saida pull back, allowing them to ride abreast.

"I saw what they did to you that night," the girl said. "The Janjaweed made me watch before they took me away. I promised to go with them and do whatever they wanted if they left you alive."

Tears burned Megan's eyes as the words sank in. The idea that her life had been saved by the courage of this fifteen-year-old brutalized child clenched around her heart. Speechless for the moment, she reached across the distance between them and squeezed the thin shoulder.

"Thank you," she whispered, finding her voice. "I didn't know."

"When Gamal died it was as if I died, too. For a long time I didn't care what happened to me."

"How did you get away?"

The beat of silence was broken only by the sound of plodding hooves and the distant yelp of a jackal. In the east, the stars had begun to fade against the purple sky. When Saida spoke again her words were a taut whisper. "I was rescued by a band of women who had escaped the Janjaweed. Now we fight to save others."

Megan stared at her young friend, stunned by the revelation. While she had retreated into nightmares, little Saida, who'd suffered far worse, had used her pain to become a warrior. Falcon fierce, falcon proud—what a lesson in resilience. Never again, Megan vowed, would she allow herself to become the prisoner of her own fear.

Saida glanced at Megan's still-slender body. "Your baby is not Janjaweed?"

"No."

"Where is the father?"

"In America, as far as I know. We are…separated." The words triggered an unexpected ache. Megan glanced down at her hands, fighting the emotions that threatened to unleash a rush of tears. Hearing the despair in Saida's voice when she spoke of her lost love had Megan questioning the decision she'd made back in Nairobi. Should she have given Cal more of a chance? She'd been hurt and shocked by his apparent betrayal…but she hadn't shown much greater faith in him. Had her leaving been justified, or had it been triggered by hurt pride? Would she have made a different decision if she'd known she was carrying Cal's child?

"You loved him." It wasn't a question.

"Yes, I loved him." And she loved him still, Megan realized. She loved Cal, but she'd fled from him at the first flicker of distrust, giving him no chance to explain himself. Her fear had taken over yet again—the fear of being hurt the way Nick had hurt her.

What a fool she'd been—and now it was too late. Cal Jeffords was a proud man, not inclined to give second chances. Once he learned she was pregnant she could expect him to take an interest in their child, but he would never trust her again.

The way had narrowed, forcing them to ride single file

once more. With Saida in the lead, they wound through the barren hills, picking their way over loose rock slides and following windswept ridges. As sunrise slashed the sky with crimson, a sense of unease crept over her. She owed Saida her life, and she'd had no choice except to come; but she was riding into an explosive situation where anything could happen. She and her baby could already be in mortal danger.

If she could reach out to Cal now, half a world away, what would she say? Would she tell him she was sorry, or would it be enough just to tell him she loved him?

But what difference would it make? Cal was a proud man, and she'd walked out on him without even saying goodbye—just as his mother had. He would never forgive her.

Geneva, Switzerland

The three-day Conference on World Hunger had given Cal the chance to make some useful connections, but little else. During the long rhetoric-filled meetings, he'd found his mind wandering—always to Megan.

Almost three months had passed since that morning in Nairobi, when he'd come back to the hotel to find her gone; and every time he thought of it, he still felt as if he'd been kicked in the gut. He'd been ready to open up to her, to lay his heart on the line. But Megan had completely blindsided him.

The worst of it was, he couldn't say he blamed her.

He'd resolved to leave her alone until he found proof of what Nick had done. That search had proved a dead end, even for Harlan Crandall. But what did it matter? She'd never asked him to clear her name—she'd just asked him to trust her. And he hadn't. Instead, he'd let a stupid misunderstanding drive her away. He couldn't blame her if she never wanted to see him again.

Now, with the conference over, he leaned back in the cab and closed his tired eyes. He'd dared to hope that, given time, Megan would come around and contact him. The volunteer roster indicated she was still in Darfur, but he'd heard nothing from her. Maybe it was just because she'd washed her hands of him. But he couldn't ditch the feeling that something was amiss. When he'd checked with the travel coordinator, he'd learned that she was being evacuated to Arusha for health reasons. Had she caught some sickness in the camps? Had her nightmares and panic attacks returned? The more he thought about her, the more concerned he became.

The corporate jet was waiting at the airport, fueled and ready to fly him home to San Francisco. Cal thought about the long, dreary flight and lonely return. He thought about Africa and worried about Megan.

He made his decision.

By the morning of the next day, Halima, Megan's sixteen-year-old patient, was alert and wanting breakfast. Two days ago, she'd been shot in the thigh during a skirmish with the Janjaweed. The bullet had gone deep, barely missing the bone. Without medical treatment she would have suffered a lingering death from infection. Megan had removed the slug, cleaned the wound and dosed the stoic girl with antibiotics. Thank heaven she'd been able to save this one.

Megan had sat with the girl most of the night, on a worn rug in an open-sided tent. When she rose at dawn to stretch her legs, she was so sore-muscled she could barely stand. Wincing with each step, she tottered into the open.

The little band of female guerillas had set up their camp

in a brushy mountain glade, near a spring. Megan counted fifteen of them—all young, some no older than Saida. The toughened faces below their head scarves bore invisible scars of what they'd endured. All were armed with knives and AK-47 rifles.

Saida had explained to her how they lived, raiding weapons, horses and supplies from ambushed Janjaweed and accepting gifts of food from grateful refugees. Some of the rescued girls eventually went home to their families. Others like Saida, who had no families, chose to stay with the little band.

"Come with me." Saida was beside her, taking her arm. "I'll get you something to eat and a place to rest. The others can tend to Halima now."

Crouching by the coals of the fire, she uncovered two iron pots. Taking a piece of *kisra* from one, she wrapped it around a scoop of seasoned meat, most likely goat, and thrust it toward Megan. The spicy smell made Megan's stomach roil, but she forced herself to eat it. She was going to need her strength.

"Now that Halima's doing better, I'm hoping we can start back," she said. "I'm due to fly out on the supply plane this afternoon."

But Saida shook her head. "We can't leave till it gets dark. The Janjaweed have eyes everywhere. If they saw us leave here by daylight, they could follow our trail back to this camp."

Megan's heart sank. "So unless the plane is late, I'm going to miss it."

"Yes. I'm sorry." Saida reached out and took her hand. "I understand you need a safe place for your baby. And I can tell you want to be with your baby's father again. But wherever you are, this man you love, if he is worthy of you, he will find you and make you his."

Megan squeezed the thin, brown fingers. If only she could believe those words were true. But when she'd walked out on Cal, she'd closed a door that would never be open to her again.

Fourteen

Cal had hoped to take off for Africa at once, but storms delayed his flight from Geneva till the next morning. It was late that night when the Gulfstream touched down in Nairobi, once more in a heavy downpour.

After a few restless hours in a nearby hotel, he was up by dawn and back at the airport, looking for a small plane to take him to the Darfur camp, where the jet couldn't safely land. The twice-monthly flight that carried medical supplies and mail for the volunteers had gone and returned earlier that day. When found and questioned, the pilot, who knew Megan, said she'd been at the site on earlier trips, but this time he hadn't seen her.

Cal's vague sense of foreboding had burgeoned into a gnawing dread. He could try to call, he supposed, or radio, or however the hell one was supposed to communicate with that place. But he knew that nothing would satisfy

him short of going to the refugee camp in person. He had
to find Megan, or at least find out what had become of her.

By the time he'd arranged to commandeer the supply plane and pay for a second flight, another storm had
moved in, drenching Nairobi in gray sheets of rain. With
the flight put off till morning, Cal paced his hotel room,
glaring out at the deluge that was keeping him from the
woman he loved.

Why had he let her go? He'd told himself that she had
the right to make her own choices. But if something had
happened to Megan because he hadn't found her in time,
he would never forgive himself.

If he found her—no, *when* he found her—and if she'd
have him, he would never let her go again.

The ride through the hills was taking even longer than
Megan had expected. She and Saida had mounted up after
dark and wound their way down the treacherous path to
the open plain below. Ever mindful of the danger to her
unborn baby, she'd clung to the saddle, silently praying as
the trail skimmed sharp ledges in the dark. There was no
chance of catching the supply plane now. By the time they
reached the refugee camp, it would be long gone. But now
she was just hoping they'd reach the camp safely, without
any attacks in the night.

With dawn streaking the sky, Saida reined to a halt.
Her girlish body stiffened in the saddle as she listened.
Megan could hear nothing except the wind, but she saw
Saida's mouth tighten. "Janjaweed," the girl said. "Not far,
and they're coming fast. We will have to go another way,
longer but safer. Follow me and be quiet."

Megan followed Saida's horse up and over a steep ridge.
Somewhere behind them she could picture the Janjaweed,
arrogant as red-turbaned kings on their swift-moving cam-

els. Saida had her AK-47, but a single girl with a rifle would be no match for the Devil Riders.

Once more Megan said a silent prayer for their safety. She wanted to live. She wanted to hold her baby in her arms. And she wanted another chance to see Cal again.

Would he forgive her for leaving? Or was it too late to mend what she'd broken?

As soon as Cal stepped out of the plane, his worst fears were confirmed. He recognized Dr. Sam Watson from his personnel photo. Tall and balding, his face a study in sleepless concern, he was waiting next to the graveled runway. Megan, who would surely have come out to meet the plane, was nowhere to be seen.

"Megan's gone missing," the doctor said after a hurried introduction. "She left a note, but I've been worried sick, about her—especially since she's pregnant."

"She's...*pregnant?*" Cal's throat clenched around the word.

"Coming up on three months. You look even more surprised than she did." The doctor gave Cal a knowing look. "Would it be presumptuous of me to ask if you're the father?"

The father. Still in shock, Cal forced himself to breathe. This was no time to weigh the implications of what he'd heard. All that mattered now was that Megan was missing in a dangerous place, and she was carrying his child.

"Tell me everything you know," he demanded. "Whatever's happened, I'm not leaving Darfur without her."

Sam was staring past him, into the distance. "You may not have to. Look."

Turning, Cal followed his gaze. Beyond the far end of the runway two mounted figures had come into sight, one small and dressed in native robes, the other taller, wearing a khaki shirt, her light brown curls blowing in the wind.

As she and Saida approached the clinic, the first thing Megan noticed was the plane, which should have departed yesterday. Then she saw the tall, broad-shouldered figure on the landing strip next to Sam Watson.

Her heart slammed. She'd ached to see Cal again, but now that he was here she was suddenly afraid. Had he found more "evidence" against her back home? Was he here to make her pay, as he'd threatened to do at the funeral?

At the end of the runway, Megan slid out of the saddle. Part of her wanted to run to him, but she was sore from riding and dreading the first words he might say to her. She kept her pace to a measured walk while she struggled to build her courage.

Cal was striding toward her, but not running. He seemed to be holding himself back. When they met in the middle of the airstrip, he faced her with his arms at his sides.

Megan forced herself to meet his gaze. He looked exhausted, she thought. The shadows under his eyes had deepened since she'd last seen him.

"Why didn't you let me know about the baby, Megan?" he demanded.

"I only just found out myself."

"Did you ever plan to tell me?"

"Of course I did." She could feel herself beginning to crumble. Her eyes were beginning to well. "This baby is your child, too. How could I not tell you?" A tear escaped to trickle down her cheek.

Something seemed to shatter in him. "Oh, damn it, Megan!" he muttered, and caught her close.

For a long moment she simply let him hold her. Only now did she realize how much she'd wanted to be in his arms.

"Are you all right?" His stubbled chin scraped her forehead as he spoke.

"I've never been more all right in my life." Her arms went around him.

"And our baby?"

"Fine," she whispered. "I should have warned you about those condoms."

"Then I suppose it's time we made an honest woman of you."

Was it a proposal or a joke? For now, Megan decided to let the remark pass. "Forgive me for leaving," she murmured. "I was so upset, I jumped to conclusions. I shouldn't have gone without giving us a chance to talk."

"And I should never have let you go." His arms tightened around her. "But maybe this was meant to happen. Maybe this was what it took, for two stubborn souls like us to work things out and find each other. I'll confess it was the money at first. But then it wasn't. It was you. All you."

"So you never found out what Nick did with the money?"

"No, and I don't give a damn. It's in the past, over and done with."

His kiss was deep and heartfelt. Megan's response sent quivers to the tips of her toes.

She nestled closer, resting her head in the hollow of his shoulder. "About what you told me a minute ago, when you said it was time to make an honest woman of me…"

He drew her closer with a raw laugh. "More than that. I love you, Megan, and I want a life with you and our child—maybe even our children. I'm prepared to marry you the minute I can get you in front of a preacher."

"You mean that?" She gave him an impish look.

"Absolutely." His arms tightened around her.

"You're sure?"

"Hell, yes, I'm sure. Why?"

"Because there's something you might not know about Sam Watson. He's not just a doctor. He's also an ordained minister."

Epilogue

They were married the next day. The ceremony had been brief and simple, performed by Sam and witnessed by Saida, a few of the volunteers and the pilot of the plane. Even with no flowers, no music, no gown and no ring as yet, it had been everything Megan could have wished for—tender, romantic and meaningful.

They'd taken the supply plane back to Nairobi. From there they'd boarded Cal's jet for America, with a side trip to Arusha.

Harris had been so delighted by their news of the baby and the wedding that Megan had almost feared another attack. Surprisingly, the old man had followed his doctor's orders. He'd cut back on his drinking and his work, handling the business end of his company while Gideon replaced him as head guide. And he'd hinted, with a sly wink, that he was dating a sexy widow.

Ironically, on the way home, Cal had received an email

from Harlan Crandall. A Las Vegas casino owner had recognized a photo of Nick as the compulsive gambler who, under a different name, had lost millions at the gaming tables. Nick had also bet heavily on horse races and sports events, losing a good deal more than he won. Megan had been dismayed by the discovery of her late husband's secret life. But the fact that he'd gambled away the money was proof enough that Nick had been the sole embezzler, and that the money was truly gone.

In the two years that had passed since that time, Megan hadn't been back to Africa. With an active toddler son to look after and another baby on the way, she was busy with the family she'd wanted so much. But she'd left a piece of her heart with the refugees of Darfur. Here at home, she'd become an advocate for their cause, helping Cal set up a branch of the foundation to educate their young people.

Tonight she stood at the darkened window of her San Francisco home, watching the rain that streamed in a silver curtain off the overhanging roof. The sound of rain always brought back memories of her time in Africa. Tonight, because of the precious piece of paper in her hand, those memories were especially poignant.

"What's that you've got?" Cal had come up behind her. His hands slid around her waist to cradle the happy roundness of her belly. His lips brushed the nape of her neck.

"It's a letter," she said. "From Saida."

She didn't need to tell him what the letter meant. The last time they'd heard from the girl was a year ago, when she'd been struggling with the decision to leave Darfur and go to school in Nairobi. Her little band of warriors had been shrinking. Two of the girls, sadly, had died. Others had left for a different life—marriage, babies, work, a few for school. Passionate and loyal, Saida had been one of the last holdouts. But finally even she had abandoned the mountain camp to help her people another way, by getting an education.

"How's she doing?" Cal pulled his wife closer, rocking her gently against him.

"Wonderfully, it seems. She loves school, and she's getting excellent marks. She says she wants to become a doctor."

"She's a bright girl. She just might make it." Cal trailed a line of kisses down Megan's shoulder.

"I was thinking." Megan closed her eyes, savoring his closeness. "When she's ready for college, we could sponsor her and bring here, to San Francisco."

"Saida at Berkeley?" Cal chuckled. "Now there's a scary thought. I hope she's not still packing that AK-47."

"Stop it, you big tease! She'd do fine, and you know it!" Turning, Megan planted a playful kiss on his mouth.

Cal deepened the kiss with an intimate flick of his tongue. "Isn't it about our bedtime?" he murmured.

She snuggled against him. "You know, I was just thinking the same thing."

Laughing, he swept her into his arms and carried her off to bed, leaving Saida's letter alone with the rain.

* * * * *

SECRETS OF A SHY SOCIALITE

BY
WENDY S. MARCUS

Secrets Of A Shy Socialite is dedicated to Mary Ritter and Stella Turk: two vibrant, courageous and strong women whom I am honored to call my friends.

With special thanks to:

My wonderful editor, Flo Nicoll, for believing in me and always helping me find my way when I veer off track.

My supportive husband, for calling from work at the end of each day to ask what he should pick up for dinner.

My three loving children, for making me proud of the wonderful people they are growing up to be. I am truly blessed.

CHAPTER ONE

IF THERE was an easy way to explain why she'd impersonated her identical twin sister, lured a man into bed under semi-false pretenses, then left town without a word to anyone, and not come off sounding like an insincere, inconsiderate, immoral hussy, it required more brain power and finesse than Jena Piermont had at her disposal.

"You've been home for two weeks," Jaci, Jena's twin, said, leaning back on the sofa and lifting her fuzzy-slippered feet onto the coffee table. "I think I've been pretty patient, but it's time for answers."

Past time. Where had she been? Why did she leave? How long would she be staying? And the biggie: whose genetic contribution was partly responsible for her adorable six-week-old twin baby girls? Jaci didn't know enough to ask about the impersonation part of Jena's explanation dilemma. Soon enough.

"I'm almost done." Jena arranged the baked brie and slices of crusty French baguette on two large plates and added them to the tray holding the crudité and *pâté de foie gras*. Never let it be said that Jena Piermont, of the Scarsdale, New York, Piermonts, was not a consummate hostess. Even while hosting her own fall from grace.

Now, to reveal the truth before the other invitees arrived at their little pow-wow. Unfortunately the news she most wanted to share, to discuss with her sister and get her advice on—the real reason she'd returned to town and would be staying for a few weeks—had to remain secret. If everything went as planned, fingers crossed, she could pull it off without Jaci ever finding out.

Jena swallowed then used a napkin to blot the unladylike clamminess from her palms. Grace under pressure. She inhaled a fortifying breath, lifted the tray and carried it to the coffee table. "Move your feet." She arranged the delectable treats beside the sparkling water and bottled beer.

Justin liked his beer.

"Stop," Jaci said. "You always do this when you get nervous. Flit around, straightening up, preparing snacks."

Jena dropped the pillow she'd been in the process of plumping and rearranging on the loveseat.

"Just sit down." Jaci patted the sofa beside her. "Tell me why you've been so quiet lately. What has you so upset? Before the guys get here."

The guys. Jena considered excusing herself and running to the bathroom to vomit. But that would waste precious time. So she sat. She could do this, would do this. "I love you," she reminded Jaci.

"I love you, too," Jaci said, studying her. "Why do you look like you've got an olive stuck in your throat?"

Because that's how she felt. Okay. No sense putting it off any longer. Tonight was the night. "Justin is the father," Jena blurted out, her gaze fixed on her lap. "Of the twins," she clarified—as if clarification was needed.

Usually talkative Jaci sat mute.

Jena peered over at her. "Say something," she prompted.

"I'm...surprised. That's all." Jaci shifted on the couch to face her. "I knew you had a crush on him in high school."

Not really a crush. More like a fascination-attraction-day/night dreamy type thing for the totally wrong type of boy. A silent plea for rescue from a mundane existence cluttered with more responsibilities than any teenager should be burdened with. An illicit mental visit to the dark side where the expectations and judgment of others meant nothing and Jena could indulge in the forbidden. Break the rules. Go wild. Have imaginary sex.

"And I'd thought maybe you were considering him as a husband candidate to meet the terms of our trust," Jaci went on.

Never. Okay. Maybe once, or a few times during random episodes of pregnancy-induced psychosis when out-of-control hormones caused gross mutations to the brain cells responsible for rational thought. Moments of weakness when Jena had actually entertained the possibility of Justin protecting her from the machinations of her brother, providing a home for her and their daughters, and taking care of the three of them.

But Justin didn't want her, and Jena refused to be any man's second best, which didn't much matter right now, anyway, since getting married no longer occupied the top spot on her list of priorities. Staying alive for her daughters did.

"I had no idea you two were..." Jaci began. "I mean, I haven't seen you together in years. Neither of you mentioned that you...kept in touch."

They didn't, not technically, unless stalking him on

social networking sites counted. Some childhood habits—like an unhealthy interest in all things Justin—
were hard to break. Jena picked at a chipped fingernail
she kept forgetting to file down, preoccupied with caring for the twins and worrying about the future and Jaci
being attacked… "It was one night." She couldn't look
at her sister. "We met up at Oliver's." A favorite restau-
rant/bar where Justin and Jaci often hung out. And now
for the worst of it. "He thought I was you."

"What?" Jaci screeched. "You did *not* just say Justin
took you to bed thinking you were me."

She couldn't change what'd happened or the outcome. All she could do was own up to it. She looked
Jaci in the eye. "It was the anniversary of Mom's death.
I'd had a horrible fight with Jerald." Their pompous,
older half-brother who'd been aggressively trying to
manipulate them into marrying any one of a dozen of
his equally pompous business associates. "I had to get
out of the house." A.k.a. the Piermont Estate where she
and Jerald each had a wing. "We'd spoken earlier and
you were still so depressed over Ian returning to Iraq.
I decided to surprise you with dinner." And that's how
it'd started, with a kind gesture to cheer her sister.

"I ordered a glass of wine while I waited for the
takeout and noticed Justin sitting across the bar. Alone.
With a couple of empty, upside down shot glasses lined
up in front of him." Normally she would have simply
blended into the crowd and stared at him from afar, attraction battling better judgment. But, "One of the bar-
tenders noticed me and called out, 'Jaci, take him home
before I toss him out of here.'" Boy had Justin perked
up at the mention of Jaci's name. "At the time, it didn't

seem to matter who he thought I was, as long as I got him home safely."

"You mean to tell me," Jaci crossed her arms over her chest and stared at Jena, "during the ride in the Piermont limo, the walk from the parking lot up to the fifth floor, and while you were stripping off each other's clothes it never crossed your mind that maybe you should clue him in to your real identity?"

Of course it had. But close proximity to Justin had caused an arousal spike that forced it away and relegated it to the spot where she stored all the unwelcome thoughts and memories she'd accumulated through the years, corralled deep in the recesses of her brain. Instead she'd allowed herself to enjoy his company and the freedom that came with pretending to be Jaci who balked at the rules and did and said what she wanted, when she wanted. Just like Justin.

For the first time in her life, Jena didn't overanalyze, didn't weigh the pros and cons or think about what a person of good moral character would do. Instead she'd focused on what she'd wanted, what she'd needed more than anything at that specific moment in time—comfort, a caring touch, a brief sojourn from real life—without a care for the consequences. And look where it'd gotten her. "I'm sorry."

"It makes no sense." Jaci said, pulling a pillow onto her lap and playing with the fringe. "Justin and I don't have that kind of relationship. We're friends. We've *never…*" She grimaced. "I have to admit I'm a little weirded out by the whole thing."

"If it helps, I made the first move." An orchestrated meeting of their lips. Jena leaned forward to try to catch Jaci's attention. "He tried to stop me." A half-hearted,

'We shouldn't,' milliseconds before he'd yanked her close and kissed her with the unbridled passion of a man releasing years of pent up attraction and lust.

Jaci smiled. "You little tigress. I didn't know you had it in you."

It'd been a quite a shocker to Jena, too.

Someone knocked on the door. Jena jumped.

"Quick," Jaci said. "Why did you take off?"

"The next morning Justin went nuts, carrying on about what a mistake it'd been. Angry at himself for letting it happen, for ruining your friendship. Guilty because you were Ian's girl and he didn't poach." Jena shivered at the memory of Justin in a rage, which was why she'd chosen to tell him about the twins with Jaci close by. "I knew I had to tell him. And I did."

Him sitting on the side of the bed elbows on his thighs, his head in his hands, completely comfortable with his nakedness. Her standing in the doorway to the bedroom, fully dressed. "I said, 'You didn't have sex with Jaci, you had it with me. Jena.' Rather than a whew or a yippee, he'd tilted his miserable face up, oh so slowly, and simply said, 'Oh, God. That's even worse.'"

"Oh, honey. I'm sorry." Jaci reached for her hand and squeezed.

"Wait, it gets better," Jena said. "Then he'd slapped his hand over his mouth and with a muffled, 'I think I'm going to be sick,' he ran past me and threw up in the bathroom." Intimacy with Jena had nauseated him to the point of regurgitation.

Another knock. Louder.

"Be right there," Jaci yelled.

"So I left."

"Why didn't you come to me?"

Jena looked away. "I was humiliated and disgusted with myself. How could I face you? I'm so ashamed."

"Hey," Jaci said. "Look at me." When Jena did she asked, "Where did you go?"

Jena saw understanding in Jaci's eyes and felt hope that they'd get past this. "Home." Where she'd given the guard at the gate strict instructions not to let anyone up the drive. As if Justin would have wasted his time coming after her. Within three hours she'd made the necessary arrangements, packed and was being chauffeured to the airport. "South Carolina. Marta's there." Their old nanny. "When Jerald sent her away she'd said she'd always be there for us." And boy had Jena appreciated Marta's calm reassurance when faced with an unexpected pregnancy complicated by yet another painful lump in her right breast, her caring support while dealing with the fear of diagnostic testing adversely affecting her unborn babies through the results of yet another needle biopsy, and her knowledgeable guidance leading up to the birth of the twins through surviving those first few sleep-deprived weeks.

"I'm so glad," Jaci stood, pulled Jena up to her feet and hugged her. "But why didn't you tell me? All this time I'd been so worried you were alone and struggling."

Jena shrugged. "If you knew, there'd have been no keeping you away. You have so many people depending on you. The residents of the Women's Crisis Center." Which Jaci had founded. "Your patients." Through the community health agency where she worked. "I couldn't take you away from all the good you do simply because of the mess I'd made of my life."

"I love you, Jena. And while I'd prefer it if you have

sex as yourself and not me, I will always love you." She stepped back and looked into Jena's eyes. "There's nothing you could ever do to change that."

"Thank you." Jena held back tears. Barely.

Another knock and an, "Open the door, Jaci," Ian demanded. "Are you okay?"

Jaci wiped the corner of her eye with a knuckle. "He's such a worrywart." But she smiled when she said it.

"Justin's with him," Jena reminded her. "He doesn't know I'm back." And since she was staying with Jaci, who lived in the same luxury high-rise, she'd rarely left the condo in order to keep it that way. The one time interaction had been unavoidable, at the benefit for the Women's Crisis Center, she'd pretended to be Jaci and he hadn't given her a second look.

Jaci raised her eyebrows and sucked in a breath between her teeth. "Oh, boy."

"You got that right." Girding herself to face the men, well, one of the men, waiting in the hallway, Jena walked to open the door.

And there he stood. Justin Rangore. *Magnificent.*

Tall. Dark-haired. Broad-shouldered. Muscled in all the right places. The perfectly maintained goatee he'd had since the eleventh grade. She fought off a tremble of delight at the tingly memory of him rubbing it against her neck and nipples and…lower. God help her.

"He made it sound like you were a mess," Justin said, sliding a roughened finger from her temple, down her cheek to her chin. "But you look beautiful as always."

No. Jaci was the beautiful one, the perfect one. Even though they were identical to the point only a handful of people could tell them apart—two of them, their parents, dead—whenever Jena looked in the mirror imperfections and inadequacies overshadowed pretty.

The same old ache in her chest flared anew. He didn't recognize her, never recognized her. Once again he'd failed to look deep enough to see the unique individual, separate from her popular, outgoing, life-of-the-party look alike. More than a privileged Piermont, a member of the social elite in a town fixated on status. More than the quiet, studious, rule-follower and people-pleaser others saw her to be. Jena. A woman, who deserved to be loved and respected and noticed for who she was. Not as philanthropic or wonderful as Jaci, but kind and caring and loyal in her own right.

Ian, Jaci's fiancé of twenty-four hours, who had no problem telling the two of them apart, stood beside Justin, shaking his head in disappointment. "She looks beautiful because she's not the one exposed to pepper spray in an elevator yesterday, you ignoramus." Ian walked toward her, placed a hand on her shoulder and squeezed in support. "Hey there, future sister-in-law," he said and slid past her into Jaci's condo.

"Jena?" Justin asked, baffled, searching her face for some identifier for confirmation.

How she'd longed to hear him utter her name that night, in the dark, in the heat of passion. Instead he'd tortured her with each, *"Damn, Jaci, you feel so good."* Punished her with, *"You are so special, Jaci. Do you have any idea how special you are?"*

"Hi, Justin," she said. "Come on in." She turned to the side to make room for him. "Let's get this over with."

He took one long-legged step forward and stared

down at her. "We need to talk," he said quietly, stating the obvious.

He stood too close, his deep brown eyes serious, his expression solemn, his scent making her weak, making her crave... "That's why you're here." She backed into the condo, needed space, air. "To talk." To have the conversation she should have initiated during her first week back in town. But appointments with doctors, hospitals and attorneys, taking care of the twins, and ensuring their futures had taken precedence.

He leaned in close. "Alone."

So he could berate her for what she'd done? He couldn't make her feel worse than she already did. To ask her to keep the circumstances of what'd happened between them a secret? Too late. "Jaci knows," Jena said.

Justin stared down at Jena's deceptively beautiful face. If only she had the personality to match. Shoulder length blonde curls, her complexion flawless, her eyes a striking blue. So much like Jaci's but different. Softer, yet guarded. Funny, he couldn't remember ever getting close enough to notice the difference before. Jena usually hung in the background. Quiet. Boring. A goodie-goodie, judgmental, rich-bitch snob. Not at all his type.

But something had changed in the ten or so months she'd been gone. She stood taller, more confident. Attractive. Alluring.

The words 'Jaci knows' brought him back to the conversation.

Crap. If Jaci knew that meant Ian knew, or would know soon. Ian would pound him senseless for sure. Justin wouldn't fight back because he deserved it and, under the circumstances, would do the exact same thing if a friend he trusted took a woman he cared about to bed. Strangely, rather than apprehension at what was sure to escalate into a full blown physical altercation with one of his best—and strongest—friends, he felt relief.

But that didn't mean he wouldn't try to deter Ian with an explanation. "It's not what you think." Justin walked into Jaci's condo. Jena closed the door behind him.

Jaci gave him a wary, perplexed look. He'd avoided revealing the truth for that exact reason. She was his best female friend. Hell, his only female friend. And they'd been getting into trouble together and looking out for one another since junior high school. He loved her. Like a sister. "I can explain."

Ian went on guard. "Explain what?" he asked.

"Come on." Jaci took Ian by the hand and tugged him toward the bedroom.

"Wait." Justin stood firm. It was time to come clean. "I slept with Jena."

Uninterested, Ian turned to follow Jaci.

"At the time I'd thought she was Jaci," Justin admitted.

Ian jerked to a stop.

"And there's no way you would have slept with plain, boring, inexperienced Jena otherwise," Jena snapped. "Am I right?" She crossed her arms over her chest and glared at him.

He'd deal with her in a minute. "Jaci was so upset when you ran out on her," he spoke to Ian who turned around to face him. "Moping around. She didn't want to do anything, go anywhere. I hadn't seen her that depressed since right after her dad died and her mom was injured. That was your fault, not mine." He pointed at Ian.

"So you thought you'd cheer her up with some naked fun while I was off fighting a war?" To someone who didn't know Ian, he'd seem eerily calm. But Justin could tell when he was about to blow.

How to explain… "I'd come off a lousy shift. A woman and her seven-year-old daughter, missing for thirty-six hours. Found dead. Brutalized." Tossed in a Dumpster like yesterday's trash. Three years on the police force, patrolling the most dangerous crime ridden area in Westchester County, and that day had made him question his decision to forgo a cushy job in his father's investment company to attend the police academy.

"Oh, Justin." Jena set her palm on the bare skin of his arm. "I had no idea."

Her touch, soft, gentle and feminine, moved him in a way Jaci's never had. But there'd been a few times… "Jaci is my friend," Justin said. "Your girlfriend."

"My fiancée."

"Right." Justin snapped. "Still getting used to that." And wondering how it would affect his friendship with Jaci, if they still had one after tonight. "Anyway. My point is. I don't lust after Jaci. Hell, she's like a sister to me." Their relationship platonic…ninety-nine percent of the time. "But there were a few times back in high school…" When something had shifted, when physical attraction flared between them for a few minutes and they'd given in to its demands. After each encounter Jaci had insisted they never speak of it again, that they pick up the next day as if nothing had happened or risk the ruin of a friendship they both valued.

At the narrowing of Ian's eyes and the clenching of

his fists, Justin thought better of continuing on in that vein. "In my crap state of mind I let alcohol skew my thinking. I needed a distraction. She needed comfort. Or so I'd thought." He glanced at Jena.

"I *did*." Jena looked up at him. "That night would have been my mom's fifty-third birthday." She paused. "What do you mean there were a few times during high school? Times when you were physically attracted to Jaci? Like when?"

"I'd rather not—"

"I'd sure like to know," Jaci said, staring at him.

"Me, too," Ian added, straightening up to his full height.

Of course Justin's cell phone didn't ring. No emergency to run off to. No reason he could think of to turn and leave and never address this topic again.

"Like sophomore year?" Jena asked. "Under the bleachers at the Mt. Vernon Scarsdale men's varsity basketball home game?"

Jaci had dropped her purse. It'd been hot in the gym. Stuffy. Her tee had molded to her full breasts. Her scent had affected him. It'd been the first time being in close proximity to Jaci had elicited a physical response. The first time she'd looked up at him with longing. The first time he'd kissed her.

"I wasn't at that game," Jaci said, looking back and forth between him and Jena.

"It was me," Jena said quietly, not looking at him.

Jaci's holier than thou, prude of a sister? Impossible. "Junior year. The gazebo at the Parks's Fourth of July barbeque," Justin said, remembering a friendly hug after a win at horseshoes that had morphed into a frantic, heated groping session where he'd touched her bare

breasts for the first time. And though he'd touched dozens of breasts before them, the smooth, rounded, silki-
ness of Jaci's, capped off by the hardest, most aroused
nipples he'd ever felt, left a lasting impression.

"Me," Jena said, looking at the ground.

That'd been ice-water-in-her-veins Jena hot and
breathless and begging for more in response to his
touch? No way. "Down by the lake," he went on. "The
bonfire after senior skip day." Where they'd paired off
out of sight and explored each other's partially clothed
bodies to the point of orgasm.

Jena inhaled a deep breath then exhaled and looked
up at him apologetically. "Me."

Holy crap.

"Jena Piermont. You little slut," Jaci teased with a
smile.

"You used to ask me to pretend to be you an awful lot
back then and I got pretty good at it," Jena said to Jaci.

She'd managed to fool him, that's for sure.

"To take a trigonometry test or give an oral presen-
tation," Jena said. "To make an appearance at a party
while you went off I don't know where with I don't
know who." Jena looked up at him. "I used to fake mi-
graines and lock myself in my room, then climb down
the trellis outside my window."

"No wonder I had such a bad reputation," Jaci said.
Amused.

"You had a bad reputation because of your big mouth,
your wild spirit and your lack of respect for authority.
Not because you deserved it," Justin clarified.

"And not because of me," Jena added. "It only happened with Justin."

For some reason that pleased him.

"And it's not going to happen again," Ian asserted himself into the conversation, his eyes focused in on Jena accented with a raised eyebrow. "No more switching places." He moved his gaze to Jaci. "For any reason," he emphasized.

"No," Jena said, shaking her head. Contrite. "Never again. I promise."

Jaci, however, chose not to commit. "Let's go." She took Ian by the hand, again, and tugged him toward the bedroom, again. "They need to talk."

This time Ian allowed himself to be pulled away.

Well that had gone better than expected. Justin felt lighter. Freer. Except now he had to deal with Jena. A girl he'd despised in high school, who, apparently, was the very same girl with whom he'd shared some of the more special boy-girl moments of his teenage years. With Jena, not Jaci.

Jena who used to look down her snobby nose at him.

Jena, who'd enticed him into bed by pretending to be her sister.

"But I made snacks," Jena called after Ian and Jaci, seeming nervous, her confidence slipping.

"I could sure use one of those beers." Lined up on the coffee table. His favorite brand.

Jena rushed to open one and held it out to him.

Ian closed the door to Jaci's bedroom, leaving Justin and Jena alone. He took a swig of brew. Cold. Refreshing.

They stood there in awkward silence.

Justin smiled. "You're no better than all those girls you criticized back in high school, whose reputations you disparaged for dating me."

"Dating you?" she asked, looking him straight in

the eyes. "Don't you mean rubbing up against you and sucking face with you in the hallway of our high school or bragging about giving you oral sex in the boys' locker room and going all the way with you on school grounds?"

Good times.

"I refuse to lump myself in with those girls. But I'm sorry." She fidgeted with a button on her blouse. "I was wrong to let you to believe I was Jaci. It was dishonest and repugnant and I ran away like a coward afterwards." She shook her head. "I am mortified by my behavior."

"And so you should be." Fancy that, Princess Jena Piermont capable of apologizing and offering a convincing show of remorse. "But I think repugnant is taking it a bit far." Because he'd enjoyed every minute of their time together, until the dawn of a new day brought with it insight and hindsight. And a hellacious hangover he would not soon forget.

Now for two issues that had been burning his gut for months. First, "Please tell me you were a virgin." As horrible as it was to think he'd taken her virginity without the care of a knowing, sober bed-partner, the alternative was even worse. That he'd unknowingly been too rough and hurt her. Either way the evidence had stained his sheet.

"I'd rather not—"

"Please," he took her by the arm, gentle but firm, and turned her to face him. He didn't like her, hated the upper class lifestyle she embraced and the elitist, unlikable people she called friends, but she didn't deserve… "The thought that I might have hurt you…" tore him up.

"You didn't," she assured him. "A little pinch from it being my first time, that's all."

"Was it…?" Good. He cursed himself for not remembering every vivid detail.

"It was fine," she said quietly. Shyly.

Justin cringed at her bland choice of adjective. Fine, as in acceptable? Adequate? Nothing special?

"Until the next morning."

When he'd totally lost it. "Yeah, about that. I woke up and noticed the condom from the night before draped over the trashcan beside the bed. With a big slice down the side." And his heart had stopped. "I don't know if it happened before, during or after, but on top of thinking I'd ruined my friendships with Jaci and Ian, I realized there was a chance she, well, you, could get pregnant." He took another swig of beer. "I panicked." How could he have been so carless? So unaware?

"Especially once you'd found out you may have gotten *me* pregnant and not Jaci," Jena said. "If I remember correctly your exact words were, 'Oh, God. That's even worse.'"

Had he really said that out loud? From the hurt look in her eyes, yup, he had. Dammit. "Because we have nothing in common. We don't even like each other. But bottom line," after years of being treated like an afterthought and an inconvenience by his father, his only parent for as long as he could remember, Justin had decided, "I don't want kids. With any woman. Or marriage." He didn't do relationships. Never could manage to give a woman what she needed outside of the bedroom. Too emotionally detached, according to numerous women who'd expected more than he was capable of giving, too self-centered to share his life with another person. Like father like son, apparently. "I like my life the way it is." Women around when he wanted them, gone when he didn't. Doing what he wanted when he wanted, on his own terms, without negotiation, explanation or altercation. "But I handled the possibility that our night together may have had long-term consequences poorly. I'm sorry. You deserved better."

She looked on the verge of tears.

Some unfamiliar instinct urged him to take her into his arms to comfort her.

He resisted.

"Hey. No tears," he said, trying to keep things upbeat. "It all worked out. Wherever you took off to has obviously been good for you. You look great. And no consequences." Now what? He should leave. Except he didn't want to, was still coming to terms with the fact he and Jena had shared some magical moments back in high school. Jena, not Jaci as he'd originally thought, which explained why, after each encounter, she'd so adamantly insisted it never be repeated or spoken of again.

At the sound of a baby crying in the hallway, Jena glanced at her watch and stiffened. "There's…"

The baby's cry grew louder. Someone knocked at the door. "I'd hoped to have a few more minutes to ease into this," Jena said nervously on her way to open the door.

Mandy, the wife of one of Ian's army buddies who'd been killed in Iraq, stood there holding a tiny, red-faced, screaming infant while a second tiny, red-faced, infant squalled from a stroller, and her toddler cried in a kid carrier on her back.

"I'm so sorry," Mandy said. "I know you said seven o'clock, but Abbie's hysterical and we couldn't calm her down. Then she set off Annie. And now Maddie."

Jena reached for the baby in Mandy's arms and a heavy weight of doom settled on Justin's shoulders. No.

"This little consequence's name is Abbie," Jena said brightly holding up the baby dressed in pink. "That one is named Annie." She motioned with her elbow to the stroller where Mandy was unstrapping the baby dressed in yellow. "This is why I asked Ian to bring you down tonight. Now that you know, you can go."

What? Justin opened his mouth to reply, but no words came out. He stood there idly, unable to move, watching Jena, her expression worried as she paced, patting the baby's back, trying to calm her.

Girls. Annie named for Jena's mother. Abbie, for his grandmother? Who'd done her best to impart a mother's love and wisdom, and fill in the gaps left by a disinterested father too busy for his own son. Maybe if she'd lived past his eighth birthday, Justin wouldn't have followed in his father's pleasure seeking footsteps, avoiding attachments and commitments with women.

Twins.

His.

There'd be fathers toasting, high-fiving, and laughing to the point of tears all around the tri-state area when the news got out. *I can't wait for the day someone like you shows up at your door to take out your daughter. I hope he's as careless with her heart as you've been with...* " Justin couldn't remember the daughter's name. One of dozens of silly girls who'd hung on his every word, offered themselves to him then got their feelings hurt when he didn't reciprocate their professed caring and love.

What goes around comes around.

Justin wanted to run, to close himself in the quiet of his condo, alone to think. But he would not be dismissed like one of her servants. "I'll go when I'm good and ready to go."

"Right," she snapped. "Because you only do what you want when you want with a total disregard for what another person might want."

Maybe so, but she was far from perfect, too. "Unless someone resorts to deceit to get me to do otherwise." He glared at her.

Unaffected by his retort or his scathing look she fired back, "And you're so easy to trick because you're so darn shallow you only see what you want to see, a pretty face and a pair of breasts."

Jaci ran out of the back bedroom, followed by Ian. "What happened?" Jaci asked, taking the baby in yellow from Mandy while Ian lifted Maddie out of her carrier and handed her to her mom.

"Something's got Abbie all worked up and she got the other two crying," Jena explained.

Ian walked over to Justin. "You okay?"

"You knew about the babies and didn't tell me?" Justin asked, finding it hard to breath. No warning? No chance to adjust or digest? To figure out how to respond? What the hell to do?

"Jena wanted to tell you herself."

"How long have you known?" The screaming echoed in his ears. Dread knotted in his gut. Life as he knew it was over.

"Since the benefit for Jaci's crisis center."

Almost two weeks. "Jena was at the benefit?" Justin had run security for the event. How could he have overlooked her?

"You really need to work on telling the two of them apart," Ian said. "It's not all that difficult." After a moment Ian added, "Time to man up and help Jena with your daughters."

Daughters.

Justin didn't want daughters. Didn't want to be a father. Did not want his life to be contorted into something unrecognizable.

CHAPTER TWO

JENA missed Marta something fierce. She bounced
Abbie gently while patting her tiny back. Knowing
her old nanny had been a few doors down the hall had
eased many of Jena's new mother insecurities and fears.
Of course the girls had been perfect angels then. Text-
book infants.

Nothing like this. Abbie arched her back and let out
an unusually shrill cry.

"It's going to be okay, sweetie girl," she whispered
against the baby's cheek, hoping hearing the words
would make *her* believe them. It didn't work. Jena's
heart pounded. *Don't panic. You're a nurse. You can
handle this.*

"When did she last eat?" Jena asked Mandy, starting
with the most basic reason the twins cried.

"Mrs. Calvin and I fed them about an hour and a
half ago."

Moving on to diaper, Jena walked down the hall
and set Abbie on the changing table where she writhed
and kicked her tiny legs making it difficult to unsnap
her outfit.

Diaper dry. Shoot.

Jena stripped off Abbie's clothes and examined her
naked body for signs of irritation or anything out of the

ordinary. Aside from a red face, the only unusual thing identified during her careful head to toe assessment was a firm, maybe a bit distended, belly.

Please be gas.

"Jaci told me to give you this." Justin walked into the room and handed her a bottle. He stared down at Abbie, still looking a bit shell-shocked.

"I'm sorry you found out like this," Jena said, fastening a new diaper. "I'd planned to give you some warning before—"

A milky-looking fountain spurted from Abbie's mouth. Jena flipped her onto her side and rubbed her back. "Hand me a cloth."

Justin did. "Is she okay?"

"I don't know." Worry seeped into her voice. But maybe after spewing out the contents of her tiny tummy Abbie would feel better.

Wishful thinking, because she sucked in a breath and started to cough and sputter.

"She's choking," Justin so helpfully pointed out, pushing Jena closer to all out panic.

No. *Think like a nurse.* She sat Abbie on the changing table, and, supporting her chin leaned her forward and patted her back.

Airway clear, Abbie's screams turned even more intense, desperate for her mommy to do something to help her. But what?

Helpless tears filled Jena's eyes as she struggled to dress her squirming infant in a soft cotton sleeper. She picked her up and tried to give her the bottle while she hurried back into the living room. Abbie clamped her lips closed and turned her head, refusing the nipple. "How long has she been like this?" Jena asked Mandy.

"A good forty-five minutes before I brought her back. Mrs. Calvin and I tried everything we could think of to calm her."

If Mrs. Calvin, Jaci's upstairs neighbor who'd raised five children and had been helping out with the twins since Jena's return, couldn't solve the problem, Jena had little confidence she'd be able to.

"She said sometimes babies just need to cry," Mandy said.

But not like this. For close to an hour. And what if Jena weren't here to see to the needs of her daughter? Would Abbie's unknown caregiver allow her to cry, alone in her room, for hours and hours, totally unconcerned with her discomfort and distress, thinking 'sometimes babies just need to cry'? Jena's heart twisted uncomfortably. As soon as this was over she'd make a note regarding how she'd like this situation handled in the future, should she not be around to deal with it, knowing there was no guarantee her wishes would be followed. She swallowed a lump of despair.

"We need to get her to a doctor," Justin said in his police voice, taking charge.

"I'll watch Annie," Jaci offered.

"It's probably just gas," Jena said, hoping that was true.

"But you don't know for sure," Justin pointed out.

"No." Jena fought for composure. "I've never quite mastered the ability to read minds," she said, maintaining an even tone. "Even if I had, I imagine reading an infant's mind must be pretty darn difficult considering they haven't yet acquired the skills necessary to communicate."

Justin raised an eyebrow. "So quiet Jena has some bite, and sarcasm is your weapon of choice."

Yup. But she didn't usually speak it out loud. "I don't have a pediatrician in the area yet, which doesn't matter since the office would most likely be closed now, anyway. And Abbie hasn't had all her vaccinations," Jena said. "I can't take her into an emergency room crowded with sick people."

Jena paced and rocked and patted. Abbie screamed. What to do? What to do? A pressure behind her forehead made her eyeballs feel on the verge bulging out of their sockets. An emergency room visit. The absolute worst case scenario. No insurance. Maxed out credit cards. They couldn't turn her away for inability to pay, could they? The humiliation. But this wasn't about her and her stupid choices. This was about Abbie.

"I know a pediatric urgent care center," Justin said. "Twenty minutes away." Perfect. Maybe the car ride would put Abbie to sleep and they wouldn't need to go inside. "I'll need a ride." Jena threw it out there to no one in particular. Pathetic rich girl chauffeured from place to place all her life, she'd never bothered to learn to drive. And at age twenty-four she couldn't even drive her daughter to seek medical treatment.

"I'll take you," Justin said. Before she could tell him she'd rather go with Jaci, or Ian, or Mandy, or anyone but him, he added, "Come on," and headed for the door.

Like a mother of twins could simply run out of the condo on a moment's notice.

Men.

"I have to—"

"Here's a car seat." Ian walked out of the second

bedroom she temporarily shared with the girls. Not all men were as clueless as Justin.

"Diaper bag restocked and ready," Jaci said, holding it out to Justin, who, rather than reaching for it so they could get underway, stared at it like Jaci was trying to pass him a severed limb.

So sorry she hadn't purchased a diaper bag worthy of a macho cop. "I like pink," Jena said, snatching the bag and slinging the strap over her shoulder. "Does the car seat meet with your approval or should I carry that, too?" She shifted Abbie and wrapped her in a baby blanket. Jaci slipped a little pink hat on Abbie's head and gave her a kiss.

"Lord help me," Justin said, taking the car seat from Ian. "I've never seen this side of her. She's got a mouth like Jaci."

Not quite. But Jena smiled, welcomed the comparison, because Jaci stood up for herself. Jaci didn't let people take advantage of her. Jaci could handle anything.

Justin made the twenty minute trip to the pediatric urgent care center in less than fifteen minutes. Apparently speeding, passing on double yellow lines, and ignoring red lights were perks of the police profession. If not for the seatbelt that kept her lower body anchored on the back seat of his SUV, Jena had no doubt she would have been tossed around like a forgotten soccer ball. During the harrowing ordeal she held on to Abbie's car seat which was strapped in beside her, her attempts to sooth her daughter and ignore Justin's aggressiveness behind the wheel both futile.

Abbie's unrelenting crying filled the car, echoed in her head, vibrated through her body.

Justin slowed down—thank you—and turned into the parking lot of a darkened, somewhat rundown strip mall in a not-so-nice part of town. "Why are you pulling in here?" He parked in front of the one lit storefront. The Pediatric Urgent Care Center. "It doesn't look..." Professional. Clean. Safe.

While Jena pondered a way to nicely say, "There is no way I am taking my daughter into that dump," Justin hopped out of the SUV, opened her door, and stuck his head inside. "Now there's the Jena I know. Do you want to take her out of the carrier or bring in the whole thing?"

The Jena he knew? She unstrapped Abbie, removed her from the car seat and cuddled her close as she climbed out. "What's that supposed to mean?" she asked. But she knew. The kids at school mistook quiet, smart and wealthy for snobby, snobby and snobby.

But this had nothing to do with being a snob and everything to do with being a concerned mother who wanted her daughter examined by a qualified practitioner in a well-equipped, high quality medical setting.

Justin set his large hand on her low back and applied a gentle pressure to get her moving toward the glass door. "You don't know me at all," Jena said. Not exactly his fault. No one did. Because in living life to avoid conflict and cater to the needs, wants, and expectations of others, Jena tended to smother her true personality, thoughts and desires beneath her need to keep everyone who mattered to her happy. Well, no more.

"You're right," Justin responded as he opened the door. "I don't know you. But whose fault is that?"

Touché.

The inside of the facility had a much nicer, more

professional feel than the outside. In fact it looked and smelled like a real hospital. Jena's stress level eased a bit. Abbie's screams caught everyone's attention and the ten or so people in the waiting room to the right and the older woman at the registration desk straight ahead all stared at them.

"Hey, handsome," the woman behind the desk said, looking past Jena to Justin with a warm smile. "What are you bringing us tonight? Out of uniform?"

"Hi, Gayle," Justin said. "This is my…" Justin stopped. "Uh…my…"

Gayle lowered her head and peered up at him over the top rim of her eyeglasses.

Jena wanted to help him out but found herself at a loss regarding how to best describe their relationship. Was she his friend? Not really. In truth they barely knew each other. His lover? Did one drunken sexual encounter make them lovers? A woman he hardly knew who just happened to be the mother of the children he didn't know about and doesn't want? Bingo!

Jena decided to go with friend. "I'm a friend of Justin's." She reached out her hand to shake Gayle's and sat down in the chair facing her desk. "This is my daughter, Abbie." She removed the hat. "She's six weeks old and has been screaming like this for going on an hour and a half. She doesn't feel like she has a fever but her abdomen is mildly distended and firm. She's refusing her bottle and," she glanced up at Justin, "we felt it best she be examined by a doctor to make sure nothing serious is going on."

Gayle typed on her computer keyboard. "Insurance card."

"I…don't have insurance," Jena admitted, leaning

in to whisper. "But if you'd agree to a payment plan I promise to pay off the entire bill."

Gayle's expression all but branded Jena a liar. Then she shifted her disapproving gaze up to Justin no longer happy to see him.

"She's my daughter," he said boldly. "I'll make sure the bill is paid."

Gayle couldn't have looked more shocked if someone had slapped her across the face with a fish. But she regrouped and handed Jena a clipboard with papers to be filled out and a pen. If only a pitying look hadn't accompanied them.

Jena lowered her eyes and let out a breath. Her face burned with the heat of embarrassment. She hated being in this position. "Thank you," she said quietly. Then balancing Abbie against her chest with her left hand, she completed the necessary paperwork with her right.

After reviewing the forms Gayle studied Jena's face. "You're one of the Piermont twins?" she asked, with reverse snobbery.

Why, because Jena hadn't had time to put herself together for public viewing? Because a Piermont shouldn't need a payment plan? Because she didn't belong in their little urgent care center? Or with Justin?

"Not a word," Justin cautioned Gayle.

Like a man who didn't want people knowing he was in any way associated with her. Or that he'd fathered a baby. Two babies. Well, who needed him? "You found me out," Jena said with a forced laugh. She sat up a bit straighter and lifted her chin. She could do regal better than just about anyone when she needed to. "See. No worries you won't get paid. I'm a millionairess." With no currently available millions.

"Shshsh," she whispered to Abbie, hugging her close. "You're going to be fine." She and her sister and their mother would all be fine. After Abbie stopped crying, after Jena's surgery and after she found a way to meet the terms of her trust fund.

A payment plan. Justin followed Jena down the long hallway to one of the exam rooms reserved specifically for infants. It absolutely defied logic that Jena Piermont, whose family made The Forbes 400, a listing of the richest people in America, year after year, requested a payment plan for a bill that, at the most, might reach two hundred dollars. And she had no insurance? Doctor and hospital bills for her treatment during pregnancy and the delivery of two babies must have been considerable. But enough to drain her multi-million-dollar bank account?

No. More likely she'd squandered it on fancy clothes, fancy food, and a fancy lifestyle she obviously couldn't afford.

"Thanks, Mary," he said to the nurse manager who'd walked them to the room.

"I hear congratulations are in order," she whispered as he walked past her through the doorway.

"Tell Gayle not to expect any more specialty coffee deliveries while I'm out on patrol."

Mary smiled.

"If you wanted to keep Abbie and me your dirty little secret," Jena snapped, "why did you bring us someplace where you obviously know people?" She laid Abbie down on the paper-lined exam table and began to undress her.

Because he'd been thinking of his daughter, of getting her the best and quickest medical care available. Since he visited the urgent care center regularly in the course of his work and provided their evening security guards through his side business, he knew they'd take him in immediately. And despite Gayle's big mouth among the staff, he trusted their discretion when it came to outsiders.

Mary placed a disposable liner on the baby scale and Jena picked up Abbie and placed her on the scale like a pro. Justin took the first opportunity to really examine the baby he'd helped to create. Ten tiny fingers opening then closing into fists. Ten tiny toes attached to the most adorable little feet. A round head with baby-fine wisps of blonde hair. An innie belly button. A cutie pie.

Jena reported an uneventful pregnancy. Justin was happy to hear that. She took the thermometer probe from Mary, placed the tip in Abbie's armpit and held her arm to her side.

"You a nurse?" Mary asked Jena. Who nodded.

As far as he knew the only nursing she'd done was taking care of her mother who'd been physically and mentally disabled as a result of a traumatic brain injury. When she'd died a few years ago, Jena took on the role of social secretary to her jerk of a brother.

"But right now I'm more nervous first-time mom than nurse," Jena continued. "So don't assume I know anything."

"Got it," Mary said. "I have two of my own." The thermometer beeped.

"No fever," Mary said. "Any allergies?"

"Not that I know of." Jena picked up Abbie, held her naked body to her chest, and covered her with a pink knit baby blanket. While swaying from side to

side she rattled off brand of formula, feeding amounts/
frequency/tolerance, and bowel habits. All stuff a father
should know, so Justin paid close attention.

"I'll get Dr. Morloni in here as soon as I can," Mary
said.

"Thanks." Justin opened the door for her. "Not that
I'm not happy to see you, but what are you doing here
so late?"

"Denise quit. At least tonight I have help. Tomorrow and Sunday I'm on all alone. You know any nurses
looking for work?"

"What hours?" Jena asked.

"Four p.m. to twelve a.m. Why? You interested?"

"If I can work off my bill for this visit," Jena answered.

At the same time Justin blurted out, "No she is not
interested. She's the mother of six-week-old twins. She
needs to be home to take care of them."

For a split second Jena flashed Jaci's defiant don't-
you-dare-tell-me-what-to-do look and he waited for her
temper to flare.

Mary looked up at him. "Oh, boy."

She must have seen it too.

But Jena's expression quickly turned neutral and
rather than yell, she remained composed and calmly
said, "My decision to work or not to work is one in
which you have no say. And whether I care for the twins
myself or arrange for someone to care for them in my
absence, I won't ever request or expect any assistance
from you. So rest assured. My returning to town and
returning to work will in no way impact your life. Feel
free to carry on as if we don't exist."

Wow. A few well-chosen words really could sting as much as a slap across the face.

"You're an idiot," Mary said to him. Jena got a smile and a, "We'll talk before you leave, hon. Look," she pointed at Abbie who lay fast asleep in her mother's arms.

Jena cupped Abbie's head, closed her eyes and let out a relieved breath.

"Sit," Mary whispered. "Might as well have the doctor take a quick look since you're already here."

"I'm afraid if I move she'll start to cry again." Jena gave Mary a beautiful smile that up until that point he would have bet a week's wages she wasn't capable of.

Once alone Justin spoke quietly, so as not to wake Abbie. "I didn't mean to come off like you needed to stay with the babies twenty-four seven because I don't want anything to do with them." It was more about his daughters not being shuffled around between caregivers like he'd been. About them being able to sleep in their own beds and wake up in familiar surroundings. About them having a space that belonged to them where they felt safe and loved and welcome. "I don't know the first thing about how to care for them. But I'll do what I can to help." Although children had never been part of his plan for the future, now that he had them, he would damn well do a better job at fathering than his father had.

"Wow. You're full of surprises." Jena gave him a small half-smile. "I thought for sure you'd demand a paternity test to try to prove they weren't yours."

He laughed. Tried to keep quiet but couldn't help himself. "Honey, if you were intentionally trying to trap a guy into marriage, you'd have shot a hell of a lot higher than me."

Seems he couldn't say anything right tonight because she sucked in an affronted breath and took on a look of total outrage at his comment. "I would never, ever do such a thing."

"Shshsh," he reminded her to keep her voice down.

"What a horrible thing to imply," she whispered as loud as one could whisper.

"Women do it all the time." Just happened to one of his buddies down at the precinct, as a matter of fact.

"Well this one doesn't."

Of course she didn't. Protection had been his responsibility and he'd blown it. "No. You don't have to. You're beautiful and rich." What she lacked in personality she more than made up for in sex appeal. "Guys must be lining up to marry you."

In what he recognized as another attempt at not letting him know what she was thinking, she looked away, but not before he caught a glimpse of sadness. "And that's the only reason men would want to marry me, because of my looks and my money."

Damn it. "That's not what I meant."

His phone rang. He looked at the screen, noting the caller and the time."I have to take this." He turned to face the wall and accepted the call. "I'm sorry," he said to his pal Ryan. "I got tied up." And forgot all about their Friday night poker game. He never missed that game, looked forward to hanging out with the guys. Already Jena and the babies were screwing with his life.

"Damn it, man," Ryan said. "It was your turn to bring the beer."

Jena spoke up from behind him, "You know I don't think you're supposed to use a cell phone in here."

Ryan heard her. "No way, dude. Tell me you did not blow us off for some woman. First rule of poker night—"

"I know, I know. Never let a woman interfere with the game," Justin finished for him. Then he lowered his voice and added, "What about two women?" After all, Abbie was there, too.

"You go, bro," Ryan said, like Justin knew he would. "Call me later with the brag bits."

Not likely.

He ended the call and turned around to find Jena glaring at him. "Very nice," Jena said her words weighted down with sarcasm. "Don't think I don't know what you were inferring. And in the presence of your child."

Who was all of six weeks old.

The doc knocked and walked in.

Thank you.

"Hello, Justin." He shook Justin's hand. "And who do we have here?"

"My daughter." It came out a little easier that time. "She's six weeks old." Although he couldn't take credit for anything more than having strong, determined swimmers, he actually felt kind of proud to have fathered such a perfect baby. Two of them, since he assumed Annie was identical.

"If she grows up to look anything like her mother you'd better keep a loaded shotgun handy at all times."

For sure. And he'd aim it at any man who looked at the twins like Dr. Charmer—the staff's nickname for him—was looking at Jena. A ripple of possessive-

ness surprised him and he imagined aiming that shotgun at Dr. C.

Jena smiled sweetly, totally taken in by the man's
spiel. "There are actually two of them. Abbie's twin
sister is at home with my twin sister."

"Twin girls." He patted Justin on the shoulder. "Better you than me." He turned to Jena. "What brought
you here tonight?"

As Jena recounted Abbie's medical history and the
events leading up to their visit, Justin watched her, determined to learn the differences between her and Jaci.
Right away he noted Jena was softer, more feminine and
well-spoken. Proper. And, apparently easily taken in by
a handsome, sweet-talking male as she hung dreamily on every word Dr. Charmer uttered. "It's none of
your business what's going on between us," Justin inter-
vened, feeling unusually territorial. Jena was the mother
of his children. And he'd be damned if he would stand
by and watch her fall prey to some hound dog doctor,
or allow any other male a spot in his daughters' lives.
They were his.

Life had just gotten infinitely more complicated.

"Just making small talk," Dr. Charmer said finally
getting down to the exam. If nothing else, the nurses
all agreed he was an excellent doctor with a superior—
albeit a bit flirty—bedside manner.

Abbie did not like Dr. Charmer's stethoscope in contact with her skin or his fingers pressing on her belly
or having a scope shoved in her ears and she screamed
in protest.

Granted, Justin was no doctor, but based on what he
could see and hear: Lungs: healthy. Vocal cords: working fine Temper: check plus.

Tough stuff, like her namesake, and his Grandma Abbie would have loved her at first glance. Justin had a sudden urge to hold his daughter and protect her from the man upsetting her, like a dad should.

Probably better to wait until she had some clothes on.

"She looks good," Dr. Charmer said. "You can get her dressed."

"Would you hand me the diaper bag?" Jena asked Justin.

He placed it on the head of the exam table.

Jena took out what she needed.

"Her ears look fine," Dr. Charmer said. "Her lungs are clear. She has good bowel sounds. No abdominal tenderness. No visible injuries. She's moving her extremities freely. If I had to guess, I'd say she had a bout of gas. If it happens again, it may be colic. Talk to your pediatrician."

"Can you recommend a good one?" Jena asked. "I've done some inquiring but haven't decided who to use. Two more weeks and the girls will need their next round of immunizations."

"You know in addition to urgent care cases we handle routine pediatrics by appointment, if you're interested."

She wouldn't be. The urgent care center wasn't near upscale enough for Jena.

"That'd be great," she said with a smile brighter than any he'd ever seen on Jaci. "Would it be okay if I requested you?"

No. Dr. Blake was a much better choice. Portly, married, Dr. Blake.

"I'd be insulted if you didn't."

He was going to be a lot more than insulted when Justin got finished with him.

What the heck was happening? Jena was the quiet one. The mousey one. The stuck up one. People didn't like her. Yet Mary did. And Dr. Charmer did—to the point Justin felt it necessary to attend every pediatric appointment from today on to prevent Jena from falling victim to his charm.

With Abbie diapered and dressed, Jena struggled to hold her and pour water into a bottle.

"I can hold her," Justin offered.

"It's okay," Jena said, taking a can of formula out of the diaper bag.

"I want to." She was his daughter and a good father would want to hold her.

Jena looked up at him. "Thank you," she said. "For not questioning if I was sure they were yours. For taking this much better than I'd thought you would."

Frankly he still felt sort of numb. But one thing he knew for certain, he'd do right by his girls.

Jena placed Abbie in his arms. So small. Delicate. He felt awkward, his hands too rough, too big.

"Hold her head." Jena positioned his hands where they needed to be then measured the formula powder and dumped it into the bottle. "I need a microwave."

"Down the hall to the right, third door on your left will be the staff break room."

Alone with his crying daughter for the first time the responsibility of parenthood hit him. What did he know about being a father? To girls, no less. About feeding them and dressing them and getting them to stop crying? Absolutely nothing. He swayed and rubbed Abbie's back the same way he'd watched Jena do it. "Daddy's got you while mommy's heating up your bottle."

Daddy and mommy. One of each. How he'd wished for a real mommy of his own when he'd been little. Grandma Abbie had tried. But she'd been old and tired. To be honest, he'd wished for a real daddy of his own, too. One who showed an interest in his kid by visiting his classroom on career day and attending baseball practices and games. One who took his kid out to dinner and enjoyed spending time with him instead of constantly looking for places to dump him so he could entertain women too numerous to remember any one in particular without interruption.

Jena returned. "Mary said they don't have anyone waiting for the room so we can take as long as we like."

He looked at the bottle and saw his hand reaching for it.

"You don't have to— "

Something strange happened. The man who had never before felt an inclination to hold or feed or have any contact with a baby said, "I want to," be the one to get his daughter to stop crying, which feeding her at this moment would hopefully do.

"Okay. Sit down." He did and Jena repositioned Abbie in his arms. "Keep her head elevated." He touched the nipple to Abbie's lips and she latched onto it like she hadn't eaten in weeks.

They both stared at their daughter, her eyes closed, the slurping of her contentedly sucking the only sound in the quiet room. It was a moment he'd never forget. And an opportunity to ask a question that'd been gnawing away at him since the morning he'd learned he'd slept with Jena not Jaci. "Why did you do it?" He looked up at Jena who'd taken a seat on the exam table. "Why did you have sex with me knowing I thought you were Jaci?"

Jena hopped off the exam table and walked over to the small sink. Her back to him she said, "I had a bit of a...fascination with you back in high school."

The surprises of the evening just kept on coming.

She opened a drawer and looked inside. "I joined the astronomy club because of it." She glanced over her shoulder and smiled. "So daddy would buy me a high-powered telescope."

She closed one drawer and opened another. "Did you know with the assistance of said high-powered tele-scope it was possible to see from the walk-in attic in the new wing of our house directly down the hill into your bedroom at your dad's house?"

He smiled. No he did not know that. "So you and Jaci—"

She whipped around. "Not Jaci. Only me. She didn't know. I swear."

Did she think he was mad? Actually, it kind of turned him on to think of her watching him in his bedroom.

She played with a Band-Aid wrapper. "You did a lot more studying than you let on in school."

Because no one gave his dad a free ride so he shouldn't expect one. Funny how that memory pre-sented itself in his dad's booming voice.

"You need to burp her." Jena came over, spread a cloth on his shoulder and showed him what to do. He breathed in her scent, similar to Jaci but more floral and fresh. He made a mental note of the difference.

"I did a lot more than study in that room and you know it." He watched her reaction to that statement and sure enough she started to look away, but not before he caught the tinge of deep pink on her pale cheeks. "You voyeur," he teased.

She didn't apologize or try to explain. "You looked gentle, like you truly cared for each one of them. Sometimes you lit candles."

Whatever it took to get the girl of the moment into his bed.

"Before we'd met up at the bar, I'd had a terrible fight with my brother over him pressuring me to marry a man I didn't know and had heard terrible things about."

Abbie must have sensed his tension because she started to fret. Or maybe it was the burp that followed that'd riled her up. "Good, girl," Jena said. "Now you can give her some more of the bottle." He got Abbie set up to finish the bottle on his own. And felt a bit proud of that, as stupid as it may seem.

"Anyway," Jena went on. "When the bartender told me to take you home the first thing that popped into my mind wasn't 'Ooooh goodie, now's my chance to get him into bed.' I wanted to get you home safely. And I figured I'd have a better chance of you coming with me thinking I was Jaci than knowing I was Jena."

She had that right. "You made the first move," Justin pointed out. For what reason he had no idea, just he felt it needed to be said.

"I know." She did not look at all repentant. "In your condo, you and me alone, I remembered how good it'd felt to have your hands on me down at the lake. I wanted that again. I wanted more. With you. I didn't want to lose my virginity to a man I had no feelings for, one who would only be marrying me for my trust fund. I wanted to share the experience with you."

Because she'd seen him treat other women gently. Yet he'd been too drunk to notice her inexperience or have a care with her untried body or even protect her. If Abbie wasn't in his arms he'd have banged his head against the wall until he achieved a level of pain he deserved. Or went unconscious. Whichever came first.

"Anyway," she shrugged. "It's done. And the next time will be better because I'll know what to expect and hopefully the man I'm with will be telling *me* how special *I* am and how good *I* feel."

Justin had spent so much time wondering why she'd done the switcheroo he'd never considered what it must have been like for her. "I'm sorry."

"Oh, it's not your fault," Jena said.

Then her words registered. "Next time it will be better." "When you say 'next time it will be better' does that mean you haven't been with anyone since me?"

Jena plucked a wooden tongue depressor from a canister on the counter by the sink and tapped it on her palm. "Turns out morning and evening sickness, exhaustion and maneuvering around with a big, fat pregnant belly didn't put me in much of a mood to go looking for love. Therefore, as of this moment, you remain my one and only," she said.

It shouldn't matter, but he kind of liked being her one and only.

CHAPTER THREE

JENA ended her call to Jaci and looked over at Justin in the driver's seat. He'd been quiet since they'd left the urgent care center. Introspective. "Jaci said Annie's sound asleep."

Justin stared straight ahead at the road. "Mm mm."

"Since Abbie's sound asleep, too, I was wondering if you'd do me a favor?"

He glanced her way. "Depends on what it is."

"I need to stop by the house." Since Mary had hired her on the spot and she'd be starting work the next afternoon, "I need to pick up the nursing uniforms I wore while taking care of my mom." Since she'd given back the maternity ones she'd borrowed down in South Carolina.

"Is it even legal for you to start work so quick?" he asked. "Mary could not have checked your references at eight o'clock on a Friday night. Do you even have experience in pediatrics?"

"Wow. Someone's grumpy." But he did turn in the direction of the estate.

"Abbie screamed for hours tonight," he continued. "What's going to happen if she does it again tomorrow night? And her mother isn't there to take care of her?"

"It's not like I plan to leave her home alone, for heav-

en's sake. Have a little faith in me, will you? Before I
accepted the job I called Jaci to make sure she was willing to watch the girls. And if there's a problem she'll
bring them to the urgent care center, like we did tonight,
and I'll be waiting, with a doctor, to take care of them."

"If you need money—"

This wasn't about money as much as it was about cre-
ating the need for Jaci to take care of the twins, without
Jena around, for more than an hour or two. An opportunity to put Jena's mind at ease, to confirm that Jaci
was, in fact, the right person to entrust with her precious
girls. Just in case... And Jena was running out of time.

But, "If I need money I'll work for it, thank you very
much." And get paid for it, in an actual paycheck which
she would put in her personal bank account which she
had sole control over. "And for your information, Mary
most certainly did check my references on a Friday
night. I gave her the home numbers for the doctor who
visited mom at home while I cared for her, for six years,
and for the family practice MD I worked part time for
while I was down in South Carolina. Both gave me very
high recommendations because even though you seem
to think very little of me, I am a hard worker and an
excellent nurse." Now he'd gone and made *her* crabby.
She stared out the window at the darkened street where
she used to ride her bike as a child.

Justin turned up the long drive, slowing when the
guard walked out of his little guardhouse. "You think
there's still a picture of me with orders to shoot on
sight?" he joked.

"Let's hope not."

Thank goodness she recognized the man on duty.
Justin lowered his window. The guard scowled. Jena

leaned toward him so he could see her. Her hand in contact with Justin's muscled thigh—for support, her back resting against Justin's chest—for balance, her nose inhaling Justin's arousing male scent—for the pure enjoyment of it... Oh, right, "Hi, Mitch. It's me. Jena."

He smiled. "Welcome home, Miss. Is Mr. Piermont expecting you?"

Shoot. "He's home? On a Friday night?" She considered asking Justin to turn around.

Mitch nodded. "I'll have to announce you."

She gave him her sweetest smile. "Would you mind announcing me after we're through the gate?"

He hesitated then smiled back. "Only for you, Miss." It paid to be nice and generous to one's employees.

Justin started to drive. "Why do you have to be announced in your own house? Why have you been staying with Jaci? What aren't you telling me?"

The stately white mansion and grand columns looked spectacular all lit up at night. And to the right, mom's pride and joy, bed after bed of colorful perennials, accented by huge, expertly carved and maintained topiaries, spotlighted, still magnificent, the highlight of the perfectly manicured grounds. So many happy childhood memories. Until her mother's breast cancer had invaded their perfect lives. Chemotherapy. Radiation. Hair loss. Weakness. Nausea. Vomiting. Bilateral mastectomies.

Mom and dad's relationship changed after that. Mom changed. Life changed.

The heat of Justin's large, warm hand on her thigh brought her back to the present. "You okay?"

She nodded. "Reminiscing." To avoid thinking about Jerald's temper. While he'd never raised a hand to Jena in anger, he had to Jaci. Many times, because she stood up to him. Defied him. Like Jena had done, for the first time, when she'd left town, and again at Jaci's benefit two weeks ago.

They hadn't spoken since.

Justin steered around the final curve, the headlights illuminating Jerald, standing on the front porch, waiting for her.

Bringing Justin had been a mistake bound to make the entire situation worse. Jena covered his hand with hers. "Please stay in the car."

"Your hand is like ice." He slammed on the brakes about twenty feet from the porch and turned to face her. "What's going on?"

"I'm not one of his favorite people at the moment." And Jerald in a rage was a frightening sight indeed. "Maybe I should come back tomorrow." When Jerald was at work.

An abrupt knock on the window made her jump. Heart pounding she turned to see Jerald looking back at her. He tried to open her door. Thank goodness it was locked.

Justin lowered her window halfway.

"It's about time you came to your senses," Jerald said, trying the door again. "This house is where you and your daughters belong. I had the room next to yours made into a nursery."

A total turnaround from his "I'm through with both of you" declaration to her and Jaci as he'd stormed off after their last encounter. Jerald could be so nice and accommodating. In order to achieve his desired objective, she reminded herself, which in this case was to get Jena back into the family home, back under his control so he could continue his quest to barter her future and her fortune for the benefit of Piermont Enterprises.

"Rather presumptuous of you, Jerry," Justin said, calling Jerald by the nickname he hated.

At the sound of Justin's voice Jerald went rigid. Slowly he bent to look through her window into the driver's seat.

Justin gave him a goofy smile and waved.

"What the hell is he doing here?" Jerald yelled.

Friendly welcome over.

Abbie let out an unhappy whine at the noise.

Jena unlocked the door and got out. "Keep your voice down," she said to Jerald, pulling him away from the open window.

"Yeah, keep your voice down," Justin added, getting out of the car. "My daughter is sleeping."

"You promised to stay in the car," Jena reminded him.

"I did not," Justin said. "So how've you been, Jerry?" he asked, enraging Jerald further.

"You and your spawn are not welcome on my property," Jerald blustered. "Leave now or I'll call security and have you forcibly removed." He put his arm around Jena and held her to his side.

"Stop it." Jena twisted away. "She's my daughter, too, and has just as much right to be here as I do. This is the Piermont estate. It's on Piermont property. And whether you're happy with me or not, I'm still a Piermont."

"Him?" Jerald said, sounding like the remnants of something foul coated his tongue. "That degenerate is the twins' father? Have you completely lost your mind? He ruined your sister's reputation."

Technically, Jaci had ruined her own reputation back in high school.

"Here I thought I was the last to know the girls were mine," Justin said, amused.

"Be quiet." Jena glared at him, hoping he got the full effect of her displeasure despite her being in the shadows.

"It wasn't enough to corrupt Jaci and destroy her chances for a respectable marriage. You had to go after Jena, too," Jerald accused. Then he turned to Jena, softened his tone and said, "Honey, I warned you about men like him, men who will do anything to snag themselves a Piermont," pretending to be a concerned big brother.

"It's not like that," Jena defended Justin, praying he didn't share the circumstances of their night together. The humiliation of Jerald knowing would be too much.

"Don't be a fool, Jena," Jerald said. "What happened to your insisting you wouldn't marry without love?"

That'd been her silly hope, an unrealistic dream.

"Men like him don't know how to love," Jerald went on. "He'll tell you what you want to hear to get what he wants. He'll marry you but he won't be faithful."

"Hey, wait a minute," Justin piped up.

"He'll sneak around," Jerald said. "But the wife always finds out. You have a soft heart, Jena. He'll hurt you. You'll be miserable married to a man like him."

"You can save your arguments," she said to Jerald. "He doesn't want to marry me."

"I'm standing right here, you know," Justin said. "And I'm capable of speaking for myself."

"So speak," Jerald challenged. "Profess your undying love. Make an offer of marriage. Go ahead. We're waiting."

Jerald should consider himself lucky Jena didn't see anything within reach she could use to clobber him over the head. Justin wanting to marry her, no matter how misguided his reasoning, would only further complicate her already complicated life.

Thank goodness Justin had the good sense to keep quiet.

"Just as I thought," Jerald said and turned to Jena. "I've been in contact with Thomas Rosendale's father. You remember Thomas?"

Her lab partner in AP Physics. Graduated second in their class. "I thought he was gay."

Jerald hopped right over the question of Thomas's sexual preference and said, "He needs a wife. He's up for partner in a prominent law firm on Madison Avenue. He owns a three bedroom on the Upper East Side. He's very successful and polite. He'd make a good husband. His father assured me Thomas would do his best to make you happy, and he'll adopt the twins and raise them as if they were his own."

"Over my dead body," Justin yelled.

"That can be arranged," Jerald taunted. "What do you say?" he asked Jena. "Will you at least think about it? Please?"

"No she will not think about it," Justin snapped.

Only because she had other more pressing matters to deal with first. But, "Please?" She looked Jerald in the eyes. "For years you have been trying to force the most horrible men on me," she said. "You accepted invitations, on my behalf, for dates I did *not* want to go on, with men you should have been protecting me from rather than pushing me to be seen with in public. When that didn't work to marry me off you used your position as my business manager to deny me access to my money. When I left you stopped paying my credit card bills and cancelled my company health insurance in an effort to make me come home. The hospital where the girls were born is threatening to put me into collection, for heaven's sake. And after all that, I finally get a please? Why are you asking so nicely? What's so special about Thomas? What's in it for you?"

"I didn't know you were pregnant," Jerald said. "If you'd have called me—"

"You could have called *me,*" Justin said. "You *should* have called me. You don't need to bow down to your brother and marry when you don't want to. I have money saved up. When we get home—"

Jerald let out a condescending laugh. "How sweet. He has some money saved up," he mocked.

"Stop it," Jena said. It *was* sweet.

"She doesn't need whatever paltry sum you've amassed working as a minimum wage security guard. This is rich." Jerald laughed again. "He's pretending he has no idea how much you're worth once you marry."

"What's he talking about?" Justin asked.

"You mean you really don't know?" Jena asked. "Jaci didn't tell you? Ian didn't mention it?"

"You've been home with my twin daughters for two weeks, living in the same building as me and I just found out about it tonight," Justin said. "I think it's safe to say Jaci and Ian don't feel it necessary to keep me in their loop."

"Don't believe him," Jerald spat. "He knows. It's not a secret. Why else do you think he slept with you? What'd he feed you, some lie about a broken condom? Did he even wear one?"

Justin charged around the car.

Jerald went into some ridiculous martial arts pose as if that would effectively ward off an attack by a six-foot-tall enraged cop.

Abbie cried out.

Justin stopped.

Jena ran the few steps to the car and opened the rear door. "It's okay," she whispered. Please don't start crying again. "Mommy's right here." Abbie blinked and stretched but closed her eyes and went back to sleep.

Thank you.

"Bring her inside," Jerald said, opening the rear door opposite her. "Where's the other one?"

"Home with Jaci. We're not staying. I'm here to pick up some of my things." She turned to Justin. "Watch Abbie, I'll be out in a few minutes."

"We'll come with you," he offered.

"No." It'd be quicker if she went herself, so she turned and ran up the marble steps into the grand foyer.

"You're not worthy of her," Jerald told Justin after Jena disappeared into the house.

No, he wasn't, but he and Jena shared two infant daughters. And tonight he'd learned enough about her to peak his interest, to make him curious about the girl who'd spied on him with a high-powered telescope, who'd crushed on him from afar and the woman who'd chosen him as her first lover, who'd given birth to his babies without asking for or expecting anything from him. The millionairess socialite who'd been manipulated and controlled by her brother for years, yet had the inner strength to escape him despite being cut off from her funds and having to take a part time job in a doctor's office, while pregnant with twins, to support herself.

"How much will it cost me to get rid of you?" Jerald asked.

"I'm not for sale, Jerry."

"All men like you have a price." He scrunched his face like a troll. "Name it."

Justin closed the car door as quietly as he could so their conversation wouldn't disturb Abbie. "You seem hell bent on lumping me in with some unsavory fellows, Jerry." He kept his tone light but made it a point to insert "Jerry" in as often as possible to piss off the pompous ass. "But I'm in a league all my own."

"Because you're so vile and disreputable no one wants to sink low enough in society's regard to join you."

Justin crossed his arms and nodded. "Not bad, Jerry. Sounds like someone's developed himself a sense of humor over the past few years." About damn time.

"Stay away from her."

"No can do." Justin walked over to Jerry, acting all casual and carefree like the bum Jerry thought him to be. "You see now that she's back I'm thinking one night in the sack wasn't near enough. And I plan to use my status as her babies' daddy to my full advantage." Jerry wasn't the only one who could taunt. "And a great big FYI,"—for your information. "My little security business is something I do on the side." To earn enough money to keep him in his luxury high rise. "My full time gig is police officer."

From Jerry's surprise he had no idea.

Good. "That's right," Justin said nonchalantly, kicking the toe of his boot against a clump of something lodged in the thick grass. "I've taken an oath to uphold the law." Which is the only reason Jerry wasn't lying in a bloody ball for the crap he'd put Jena through. "And first thing Monday morning I plan to make use of every investigative and legal resource at my disposal to find out what laws you've broken by denying your sister access to her money."

Jerry didn't flinch. But he swallowed.

Play time over. Now to seal the deal. "Notice I'm planning to hold off until Monday." He leaned in and lowered his voice. "Because I think this weekend is all the time I'll need to come to Jena's rescue and ease her financial burden. How do you think she'll show her appreciation? Huh, Jerry?" He elbowed Jerry in his stiff side then rubbed his palms together conniving style. "Maybe she'll give me the opportunity to knock her up with another set of twins. You think?" Take that you overbearing, condescending jerk.

Footsteps sounded behind them. Jena ran down the stairs, a stuffed medium-sized duffel bag in one hand and a cloth carryall in the other. "I'm done."

"Let me take that for you." Justin grabbed the duffel, which turned out to be heavier than it looked, a bit surprised she hadn't sought out a servant to carry it for her. With a few short hours in her presence, Justin had come the realization he'd made a few glaringly incorrect assumptions about Jaci's homebody, except when out in high society, not as shy as he'd thought twin.

"Hold on a minute," Jerry said. "I need to give you something." He speed-walked toward the porch. "Don't leave," he yelled over his shoulder.

Atta boy. Go fetch Jena the info needed to access her accounts so they could put all this talk of marriage and

Thomas what's-his-name behind them, so she wouldn't be in a position where she needed to take the job at the urgent care center and could stay home to take care of the twins. Where she belonged.

Jena looked up at him? "What was that about?"

Justin shrugged. "No idea." He carried her bag to the car and placed it on the backseat next to Abbie.

No sooner did he close the door then he spied Jerald, hurrying back in their direction, too high class to full out sprint, but moving as fast as possible without officially lowering himself to the point of actual running. "Here." He handed Jena an accordion file folder, panting from his exertion, although he tried to cover it up with an elegant cough. "It's all in here." He patted the folder now in Jena's hands. "Your most recent bank statements, your checkbook, and a snapshot of your investment portfolio from August. You may not remember, but you signed signature cards when you turned eighteen so you can write your own checks."

Jena clutched the folder to her chest, looking overwhelmed, relieved, and on the verge of tears. "Thank you," she said quietly.

"I'm happy to go over it with you and answer any questions," Jerry said actually pulling off a caring tone. But the only things he cared about were his company's bottom line and himself.

"Let's go." Justin put his arm around Jena's shoulders and guided her to the car. Before getting in she looked over at Jerry and said, "I'll think about Thomas."

Oh no she wouldn't.

"Thank you," Jerry said. "Come back any time, Jena." He glared at Justin. "You and my nieces are always welcome."

The ride back to the condo was a quiet one and Justin used the time to think. And come to the conclusion, if Jerry acted as Jena's business manager, paying all her bills and managing her money, there was the possibility she didn't know how to do either on her own, which would explain the uneasy tension emanating from her side of the car.

Jena spent the trip staring out the window, maintaining a tight grip on her financial data like someone might try to wrestle it from her at any moment. Which was kind of disconcerting since the only other person in the car capable of wrestling was him.

He parked in a guest spot close to the front door, turned off his SUV and shifted in his seat to face her. "You okay?"

She just sat there, gazing out the window, looking lost and in no apparent hurry to exit, her demeanor not that of someone he'd identify as okay. But she nodded in response to his question.

"I'm not sure if you're aware," he said. "But in addition to my undergraduate degree in criminal justice, I minored in finance. And I worked at my dad's investment firm every summer from the time I turned sixteen until I graduated college. I'd be happy to take a look at everything Jerry gave you and help you make sense of it," he offered, half on edge, waiting to see if she'd lash out at being insulted by him thinking she didn't know how to manage her money when she did.

Instead of a reply, she reached up to dab at the corner of her eye with her knuckle and Justin wanted to pull her into his arms and tell her everything would be okay. That she could count on him to help her and take care of her.

Whoa. That came out of nowhere. But there was something about her, a naiveté long worn off in the women he dated, that made him want to be the man to teach her and tend to her, placing him in unfamiliar territory.

"Thank you," she said, so softly he almost didn't hear her. She inhaled a deep breath, let it out then turned to look at him. Light from the outside fixtures reflected in her watery eyes. "It's not that I'm dumb or lazy. It's the way I grew up," Jena explained, lowering the folder to her lap.

"While Jaci fought for independence I was content to be taken care of. I chose to blindly trust Jerald to manage my money. I chose to leave rather than fight him for control. But I have worked from the age of thirteen, managing the house and as a nurse for my mom, even while I went to college. After she passed away, I took on the role of Jerald's social secretary full time. Yet I never received a formal paycheck. Jerald made sure there was cash in the safe in his office, and I took what I needed when I needed it. My credit card bills came to the house and he paid them when he paid all the other bills. If I had to go somewhere there was always a car and driver waiting to take me."

She looked down and fiddled with the elastic band holding the folder together. "And now I'm a twenty-four-year old mother of two who can plan a dinner party for fourteen with two hours' notice, coordinate an exquisite gala for five hundred on a strict budget, and manage a staff of thirty-six, half of whom only speak Spanish, but I can't drive, I have no idea how much money I have aside from the two hundred thirty-six dollars in the envelope in my dresser drawer, and I don't know the first thing about paying bills or writing checks."

Justin reached out to take her cool hand into his. He squeezed it. "I promise you, by the end of the weekend, you will have your bills sorted and paid, you will know how much money you have in the bank and in your investment accounts, and you will know how to write a check."

She peered up at him from the corner of her eyes. "And the driving?"

He smiled. "If we can't find the study guide for a driver's permit test online, I'll pick one up from the DMV"—Department of Motor Vehicles—"on Monday. As soon as you pass the test, I will personally teach you how to drive and you can use my SUV to take your road test."

She dropped her precious papers to the floor, lunged her upper body across the center console, and wrapped her arms around his neck. "Thank you," she kissed his cheek. "So much." She kissed him again.

Then they were kissing for real. Because he'd turned his head, intent on catching her lips with his. Success.

For a split second she stiffened and he thought she might pull away. Then she melted against him, opened for him, and before he knew what he was doing he'd dragged the rest of her onto his lap like some hormone-crazed teenager looking to get lucky in daddy's Dodge.

His eyes may still be working on identifying the differences between Jena and Jaci, but his body sure recognized Jena, and at that moment, was most interested in rekindling their naked acquaintance.

They came up for air, both breathing heavy. "I'm sorry." He wasn't. "I shouldn't have—"

"It's okay." She started to move away. He let her go but was not at all happy about it. "I guess I made the first move." She patted down her hair and readjusted her blouse. "Again."

He smiled. "Next time it's my turn to make the first move." In a room with a bed, when the babies were sound asleep and Ian was somewhere else and there was no chance they'd be interrupted. Then he'd wipe "fine" from her memory and replace it with amazing, unforgettable, stupendous. Never to be topped by any other man.

She looked away, like she often did when she didn't want him to know what she was thinking. "Can we not tell Jaci how inept I am at managing my life?" she changed the subject. "I'd rather she not know."

"You're not inept you're inexperienced." He reached out, gently took her chin in his hand, and turned her head to face him. "By Monday that will no longer be the case, because I have the next two mornings off, and I plan to spend them teaching you." Hopefully about more than her finances. "And on account of the major secrets your loving sister and my alleged best friend have kept from me, I'm kind of looking forward to having some secrets to keep from them. You got anymore?"

She nodded. "You know the rich, gooey, chocolate cake Jaci delivers to you on your birthday?"

"Of course I do." With milk chocolate ganache frosting, layers of the best buttercream mixture he'd ever tasted, and dark chocolate shavings on top. His mouth watered. "Every year since I turned fifteen."

Jena smiled sadly and nodded. "They weren't from Jaci, they were from me. And she didn't buy them at a bakery, I made them."

"You?" No way. That cake was pastry chef quality. "From scratch? Come on."

"I spent a lot of time at home. I made friends with the staff. They taught me things."

She stared back at him, confident, seeming to dare him to question her. Well wudda you know? "That explains why Jaci missed my last birthday. That little liar. I'm going to—"

She smacked the base of her palm to her forehead. "I forgot your birthday. I can't believe it. I'm so sorry."

He reached out to move a curl that'd fallen down close to her eye. "I'm guessing you had a lot going on at the time." Since she would have been around eight months pregnant.

She nodded.

He leaned back in his seat. "It's been quite an evening," he said, letting out a huge breath, feeling weighted down by all the revelations of the past few hours.

She stretched. "I'm exhausted." She angled her watch to catch a ray of light. "Annie should be up for a bottle soon. Then hopefully I can sleep for a few uninterrupted hours so I'm bright and cheery for my new job tomorrow."

"Wait a minute," Justin said. "You have your money back. You don't *need* to work."

"Maybe not, but I like working as a nurse. And I promised Mary I'd help her out this weekend. She needs me."

"Your daughters need you, too," Justin pointed out. If given the choice, didn't women *want* to stay home to take care of their babies?

"Relax," Jena said. "It's sixteen hours. It'll be good

for me to have some time away from the girls, to use my skills, and engage in professional conversation. I'm not in a position to commit to more hours right now. And if I come to an agreement with Thomas, I'll be moving into the city in the next two months anyway."

Thomas. They were back to her considering a marriage to Thomas. "What is this fixation with marriage? You. Jaci. Your brother. I don't get it."

"Keep your voice down," Jena whispered.

He froze, waited to see if he'd woken Abbie, and said a private thank you for blessed quiet.

"When my father died," Jena said, keeping her voice low, "Jaci and my inheritances went into a trust. To be distributed on our twenty-fifth birthday."

November twenty-eighth. In two and a half months.

"Typical of my dad, controlling tyrant that he was, he placed stipulations on the money." She looked up at him. "To receive it, Jaci and I have to be married and living with our respective spouses by our twenty-fifth birthday. To be sure we don't enter into a sham of a marriage, the payments are to be broken up over five years at five million dollars per year for each of us. If one of us doesn't marry by the age of twenty-five, we forfeit our portion of the trust and the money will be donated to charities designated by my father before his death. If we divorce or separate during the five year period, we forfeit any monies not yet paid."

Even dead that evil, arrogant menace managed to exert his power. "Twenty-five million dollars is a strong incentive to marry."

Jena nodded. "It's my daughters' legacy, their future. And I will do whatever it takes to see they get it."

"Even marry a gay guy?" slipped out before he could stop it.

"Trust me when I tell you, he is a million times better than most of the other men Jerald's tried to pair me off with."

The opportunistic bloodsucker. "What's his interest, anyway?"

"Fathers come to Jerald looking to make a good match for their wayward sons. Men come to him looking for a quick infusion of cash our trust would provide to bolster their failing business endeavors and dwindling bank accounts. Both promise Jerald favors or contracts or something that he wants." She shrugged and turned to look out the window. "Not exactly how I'd hoped to meet my future husband," she said sadly.

Damn it. "It's only for five years, right?" An idea started to form. A way to keep her from marrying someone else, to protect her from her brother and have her for himself, temporarily, to ensure his daughters' financial future and make sure he would be the one and only daddy in their lives.

She nodded, staring into the night.

"Hell, five years isn't all that long. I'll marry you."

CHAPTER FOUR

"I NEED a nurse out here," Gayle called out. Again. One hour into her first shift and Jena had been called to patient sign-in to triage more than a dozen patients. Thank goodness Jaci had dropped her off two hours early to meet with Mary, review policies and procedures, and familiarize herself with the facility before she'd officially started work.

"I'm on my way," Jena called out, freshening the paper liner on the exam table in room four and stuffing it and a disposable gown into the trashcan.

"Everything okay?" Mary, who was supposed to be supervising her closely, asked as she hurried in the opposite direction down the hallway.

"Fine. How's that little boy?" A three-year-old found unresponsive for an undetermined period of time, and rather than call an ambulance the older brother had scooped him up and run, barefoot, through a major intersection, to the urgent care center.

Mary shook her head and gave Jena a look that said "not good." Out loud she said, "We're doing all we can for him. Paramedics are finally on their way to transport him to the hospital." Forty-five minutes after they'd placed the call thanks to a train derailment with multiple casualties.

Jena entered the lobby to find a woman carrying a small child, holding a bloodied cloth over the left side of the toddler's face, the woman's blouse and the little girl's pink overalls stained red. "What happened?" she asked, taking a pair of latex gloves from her pocket and slipping them on.

"I turned my back for a minute." The mother started to cry. "I don't care if that coffee table has been in my mother-in-law's family for years. When I get home I am tossing it into the street."

"Let me take a look, sweetie," Jena said to the little girl, pushing aside a mass of black curls and lifting the cloth to take a peek at the injury, a rather large laceration to the left eyebrow area. But the cloth had adhered to the wound and Jena would need to moisten the area with saline to get a better look. "It seems to have stopped bleeding. Gayle will take your information and we'll get you into a room."

"My daughter has been waiting for almost an hour," a big brute of man bellowed from the standing-room-only waiting area. His nine-year-old daughter, who sat quietly, in no apparent distress, watching cartoons on the television, had fallen from her bike, while wearing a helmet, and denied hitting her head. No visible head trauma. Right wrist swelling and pain. Minor scrapes and bruises to the extremities. Stable.

"I'm sorry for the wait."

"That's what you said half an hour ago." He stood up and stormed toward her.

"Is there a problem here?" a deep voice asked from behind her. Justin's voice. Jena had never been so happy to hear it.

"Yeah there's a problem." The man didn't back down.

Justin came to a stop beside her, khaki pants covering his long legs, a navy blue polo shirt with Rangore Security embroidered in red letters on the left breast pocket, clinging to his muscled chest. His bare arms thick and powerful. His light scent enough to attract, to make her crave closeness.

Justin didn't suffer the paunch of an overindulgent lifestyle or the pallid, diminished physique of a seventy hour week white-collar workaholic. He was an imposing specimen of man, the personification of macho alpha male, the standard to which she compared all potential marriageable males. The reason she found some otherwise decent men lacking.

"Well look at you," Gayle's voice intruded. "What did we do to deserve the head honcho tonight?"

Jena didn't have time to question Justin's unexpected arrival or wait for an answer to Gayle's question because she heard a siren. "We have a critically ill patient in the back," she told Justin. "I think that's our ambulance." She looked out the glass front door. Shoot. "Whose red car is that?" Parked perpendicular to the entrance, blocking the ramp.

"Mine," the woman carrying the bloodied little girl said.

Justin held out his hand. "Either you move it or I will."

The woman handed Justin her keys. On his way out he did something to the double doors to make both remain open.

"I'm guessing if it were your child in respiratory distress you'd want the doctor to give her his full attention," Jena said to the irate father. "Even if that meant people had to wait while he did."

The man returned to his seat.

"We're doing the best we can," she told the patients and family members waiting. "I've spoken with each of you and as soon as the doctor is ready you'll be called in, the most acute cases first, then by order of arrival."

For as long as they took to get there, the paramedics were in and out in under ten minutes. After they'd gone, Jena, Mary, and Dr. Morloni met in the hallway. Jena held up her pad. "I'm not quite comfortable with the laptops yet. But this is what we've got waiting and the order I think they need to be seen."

Mary leaned in to look at her notes.

"Three-year-old, audible wheeze. Color within normal limits. No fever. Increased respiratory effort. Nine-month-old. One hundred and three point seven temperature. Mild lethargy. Two toddler lacerations, one eyebrow vs. coffee table, the other thumb vs. steak knife. Nine-year-old fall from bike with right wrist pain and swelling, wearing a helmet, no signs or symptoms of head injury and a very impatient father. Then the rest by order of arrival, three sore throats requesting strep tests. Two ear pain and pressure with fevers. Two seventeen-year-olds one with back the other with shoulder pain. A six-year-old with a pea or peas obstructing his left nostril, right nostril clear, no respiratory distress. And a four-year-old who may have swallowed a coin or coins from a bowl of change, no reports of GI distress."

Jena looked between the two of them. "To speed things up I've documented vital signs, chief complaints and past medical histories on each of them in the computer. I put the audible wheeze in room one to keep him calm and the nine-month-old fever in room two to get him out of the crowded waiting room."

"You done good," Dr. Morloni said. "We're back in business." Laptop in hand, he turned and walked in the direction of room one.

"These two." Mary pointed to the two seventeen-year-olds on Jena's list. "Did they come in with their parents?"

"An older gentleman who claims to be guardian to both."

"Insurance?"

"You'll have to check with Gayle, but I think he planned to pay cash."

Mary shook her head. "Point them out to Justin." When Jena looked up at her in question Mary added, "Local drug dealers send teenagers in to get prescriptions for narcotic pain medication which they turn around and sell on the streets."

"That's terrible."

Mary looked her in the eye. "Prepare to see a lot worse."

"May I ask a question?" Jena asked. "Unrelated to the patient population?"

"Fire away."

"What's Justin doing here?"

Mary smiled. "We contract with his company for evening security. This plaza is busy during the day, but we're all alone after five p.m." She removed her hairband and redid her pony tail. "Being able to advertise we have security on site at night helps us attract quality staff and expands our patient catchment area into the neighboring middle class towns."

"Does *he* usually work here?"

"On occasion, as his schedule at the police station allows. But I was told Steve would be on duty this weekend." She smiled. "I'm guessing the change has something to do with you."

Jena didn't know whether to be flattered that he'd shown up to spend time with her or insulted that he'd come to keep an eye on her because he didn't think her capable.

"Hey," Mary said, moving her head around to catch Jena's attention. "Dr. Morloni's right. You did a great job holding things together."

Jena smiled. "Thanks. Honestly, I enjoyed every crazy minute of it." For weeks her life revolved around caring for the twins. Jena loved being a mom. But her temporary job, which entailed three of her favorite activities, organizing, prioritizing, and nursing, energized and revitalized her.

After filling the rooms and walking the wrist injury to X-ray, Jena found Justin in the lobby. "May I speak with you?"

He followed her into the hallway.

"There are two teenagers in the waiting area, sitting with an older gentleman," she informed him, keeping her voice hushed.

"I noticed them."

"Both are here with complaints of pain and Mary asked me to point them out to you. Something about a drug dealer sending kids in to get prescriptions for narcotics."

"They fit the profile." Justin ran his fingers over his goatee. "Let Mary handle them."

Absolutely not. "I so appreciate your confidence in my skill as a nurse and my ability to handle this job." She turned to leave.

He caught her by the arm, his large hand strong, yet

gentle. "These are street kids," he whispered forcefully. "They're more dangerous than they look. Working in rural South Carolina give you a lot of experience dealing with patients who'd have no problem pulling a knife on you to get what they want?"

So he'd been pumping Jaci for more information about where she'd been. And no, it hadn't. A sudden chill made her twitch. But that did not lessen her resolve to do the job she'd come here to do. "If taking care of street kids, as you call them, is part of my job responsibilities, then best I learn how to deal with them. And if keeping me safe is part of your job responsibilities, best you focus on that rather than worrying about my past work experience."

"You're as stubborn as your sister."

Not quite, but she liked that he thought so.

"Okay," he acquiesced. "Take them in one at a time, and not until the doctor's ready for them. Make sure I'm in the lobby and I see you walk each one in."

She nodded her understanding.

"Anything makes you uncomfortable, you call me."

She looked up and saw his concern. "I will." Instead of feeling flattered or insulted by his presence her first night at work, she felt appreciative, realizing he'd come to keep her safe. "Thank you," she said, "for being here." Because it provided her a level of comfort she may not have had otherwise.

He skimmed his index finger down the side of her face. "You can be real sweet sometimes."

She winked, "When it suits me," and returned to work.

The next two hours went by in a blur of activity, but Jena still made time to call home twice to check on the girls, who were fine. Mary insisted on accompanying her for the discharge of each of the teens, which turned out to be a good thing as one in particular started arguing and begging when Dr. Morloni a.k.a. Dr. Charmer, informed the patient his exam was negative and recommended over the counter non-steroidal anti-inflammatory medication for pain management.

The boy's desperation clawed at Jena's heart, to be so young and possibly involved in the illegal drug trade. What would happen to him when the dealer found out he'd been unsuccessful?

"I tried," Justin said when he returned from escorting the boys and their "guardian" to Gayle to pay then to the parking lot to leave. "I gave each of them the chance to come clean, to give up the name of the drug dealer who put them up to coming in for narcotics prescriptions in return for police protection."

Great. Maybe...

He shook his head. "They laughed and shared their thoughts on police and their protection. I won't pollute your ears with the specifics. Suffice it to say they weren't interested."

Stupid. Maybe if they'd had access to a quality kids club with positive role models to look out for them when they were younger, or vocational training programs to funnel them into legal, well-paying jobs. Jena made a mental note to research what programs and services were available to the youth of the area. Jaci had championed women in crisis. Maybe with some of the money from her trust Jena could do the same for children.

"Hey." With a finger under her chin Justin nudged her face up to look at him. "You can't help people who don't want to be helped."

"Says the jaded cop."

"Not jaded as much as realistic." He smiled. "Your brother was right. You *do* have a soft heart."

"They're kids," Jena pointed out.

"In this area, childhood ends a lot younger than seventeen. Come on." He put his arm around her shoulders and guided her down the hall. "I heard Mary tell you to eat your dinner."

In the break room, Jena washed her hands in the small sink and Justin collected their bagged meals from the mini-fridge. Then Justin washed his hands and Jena poured two cups of coffee which she carried to the round four-person table in the corner.

In the process of unwrapping his deli sandwich Justin said, "Last night I promised you would have your bills sorted and paid, you would understand your investments and know how much money you had, and you'd be writing checks by Monday. That's not going to happen if tomorrow you refuse my calls and pretend you're not home when I knock on your door like you did today." He bit into half of what looked like a twelve inch Italian combo sub.

So he'd figured out the truth. Well, Jena had another bit of truth for him. "I'm not going to marry you," she blurted out. There. She said it. No more thinking about his degrading non-proposal. "*Hell, five years isn't all that long. I'll marry you.*" Or how much his I-can-put-up-with-anything-for-five-years attitude bothered her. Like she was a nuisance. Someone to be tolerated.

Justin took his time chewing and didn't respond until after he swallowed. "Funny, I don't recall requiring marriage to help you with your finances." He casually reached for a creamer from the basket in the center of the table, poured it into his coffee and stirred. "But since you brought up the topic, why not?"

"You really want to get into this?" She entwined her fingers on the table. "Here. Now."

"No time like the present, don't you think?" He took another bite of his sandwich.

Jena had lost her appetite. This was her opportunity to tell him, to dispel any notion of them getting married. To reveal the truth. Soon she would no longer be an exact replica of Jaci and the only part of her he desired—her body—would be altered, her full womanly curves gone forever. Unless…no. She'd made her decision, would not change her mind. She opened her mouth. Closed it. Could not find the words, where to start, how to explain. She needed more time. Only she didn't have time. So she settled on, "It would never work," and busied herself by adding two creamers and a packet of sugar to her coffee so she didn't have to look at him.

"Why wouldn't it work?" He stuffed more food into his mouth.

So many reasons. For starters, "because each time we were intimate I'd know you'd rather be with my sister. That I'll never be anything more to you than a poor substitute for the woman you really want."

He choked.

Good.

"That's not true."

"You feel so good Jaci," Jena repeated the words he'd uttered over and over when they'd been in bed together. "Do you have any idea how special you are?"

"That's not fair." He placed his sandwich on the paper wrapper. "I said those things because I *thought* I was in bed with Jaci. Because you'd led me to *believe* I was in bed with Jaci."

"Which gave you the opportunity to pour out your true feelings."

"I was drunk."

"A drunk man's words are a sober man's thoughts."

"This is nuts." He slapped his hand on the table. "You won't marry me, the father of your daughters, because of a bit of wisdom you found inside a fortune cookie?"

"I won't marry you because you don't want to marry me." She pushed away from the table. "I won't marry you because making you a daily part of my daughters' lives, knowing you plan to desert all of us in five years is cruel." She stood. "I won't marry you because Jerald's right." She scooped up her uneaten dinner and turned to leave. "I'd be miserable married to a man like you." A man she would love who could never love her, one focused on physical beauty and incapable of monogamy. At least if she married Thomas terms could be negotiated, time frames agreed to, her heart protected. And her body wouldn't matter.

"Wait." Justin made it to the door before she could open it. "I *do* want to marry you."

"Why?" she asked, her blue eyes challenging him.

Because it was the right thing to do. The honorable thing. But from the look on her face he was pretty sure neither answer would satisfy her.

"Because I'm rich?" she asked. "Because if you marry me, you'll be rich too?"

No.

Before he could expand his no from an instantaneous mental reaction to an actual verbal response she said,

"Because I'm pretty?" She grazed her fingers down his chest enticingly. "Because you want my body night after night?"

Oh, yeah. He liked that idea. He turned them so her back was to the door and pressed his body to hers. "I don't need your money," he whispered in her ear. "And maybe five years will turn into ten or twenty or a life-time." He kissed down the side of her neck. "We won't know until we give marriage a try. But no matter what happens between us, I will never desert my daughters."

He kissed back up to her ear. "While we're figuring it all out, sex night after night sounds real good to me." He brought his hand to her breast. "And trust me." He caressed until he felt the tight bud of her nipple through her bra and blouse. "I'll make you feel so good so often you won't have time to be miserable."

He moved his lips to hers. Kissed her, tasted her, wanted more of her. "You have the most amazing breasts." He explored their supple fullness with both hands.

She pushed him away. "And what if I didn't?" she snapped, straightening her clothes. "What if I didn't have amazing breasts? What if my body repulsed you?"

She wasn't making any sense. "But it doesn't. It's perfect. I love your body. I want your body." Any man who swung toward heterosexual would want her body.

At that last thought, an unfamiliar, possessive, mine, mine, mine all mine popped into Justin's head.

Jena shoved him.

"What?"

"I am more than a pair of breasts." She had tears in her eyes. And he'd put them there. An odd, uncomfort-able pressure settled in his chest.

She reached for the door.

He grabbed her hand. "What's wrong?" How had complimenting her body taken such a wrong turn?

"I can't do this," she said. "Please." She looked up at him. "I need to get back to work."

The aftermath of whatever the hell happened between them in the break room helped Justin recognize yet another difference between Jena and Jaci. The silent treatment. For better or for worse, Jaci put her emotions out there for all to see. In stark contrast to her sister, when something upset Jena, she went quiet. Of course she was too well-mannered to completely ignore him, but her interactions turned brief, coolly polite, and only when necessary.

She didn't want to marry him? Fine. He'd tried to do the right thing. She'd turned him down. Done. Pressure off. He could still parent without the hassle of marriage. Even better.

Jena smiled warmly at an unkempt woman in the waiting area, helped her with her diaper bag and, while accompanying her and a small child to an exam room, chatted like they were old friends. Comfortable. Genuine.

When she passed by Justin he may as well have been a cobweb for all the attention she paid him. They'd reverted back to high school.

Except now he couldn't help noticing *her*. Long blonde curls restrained in a tight bun, her luscious curves hidden beneath a boxy scrub top, and her face devoid of trendy, high-fashion makeup, she looked nothing like socialite Jena Piermont from the society pages of newspapers and magazines. She looked better. Real.

Desirable.

And he had a hankering for the genuine version of Jena.

Dr. Charmer passed her in the hallway and smiled.

Justin imagined the satisfying crack of dislocating the jaw attached to that smile with one powerful punch.

Which made no sense. Because Justin didn't do jealousy. Except, apparently where Jena, the mother of his twins was concerned, he did.

Lord help him.

A married couple returned to the desk to check out with Gayle. The man guided his wife with a gentle hand at her mid-back while holding their sleeping baby in a car seat. He'd watched them and listened to them since they'd arrived. They were about the same age as he and Jena, their baby a couple of months older than the twins. The woman had been nervous, worried about the child's fever and bright red cheeks. The man held her hand or sat with his arm around her while she rested her head on his shoulder.

The guy probably had a better role model growing up than Justin had. He didn't know how to be the type of man Jena wanted. The type of man she deserved. That didn't stop a small part of him from wondering what if?

Thank goodness work saved him from his thoughts. "You folks all set?" he asked as they stood. "I'll escort you out."

The man opened the car door for his wife then walked to the other side of the car and placed the car seat in its base.

"How long have you been married?" Justin asked.

"A few weeks," the man replied.

So they'd had the baby first, too.

"Thank you," the man said and got into the car. Before he started the engine, he leaned over to kiss his wife. She smiled at her husband like he was the most special man in the world.

He imagined Jena giving him a look like that and went all warm inside. Until he remembered women like Jena didn't give men like him looks like that. Because he didn't do love, sucked at demonstrating affection, and while she was looking for long term he'd never managed to stay with the same woman longer than one month. Twenty-two days to be exact. And the last three he'd spent ignoring her phone calls until she officially broke it off.

Back inside his cell phone buzzed. He checked the number—Jaci—and walked out of Gayle's hearing. "What's wrong?"

"Hello to you, too," Jaci said. "The girls are fine, sleeping like little angels."

He relaxed.

"Ian just told me you scheduled yourself to work at the urgent care center tonight. Very interesting," she teased.

"What do you want?" he asked.

"To know how Jena's doing. We haven't heard from her in over an hour." Despite the non-stop pace of patient after patient with little to no downtime in between, Jena had managed to check on the twins. Caring. Concerned. A good mother. Unlike his who'd chosen the lure of the Las Vegas stage over caring for a toddler. Without so much as a phone call or birthday card since.

"She's fine." He watched Jena move from one exam room to the next. Purposeful. Confident. Impressive. "Just busy."

"Ian also tells me you'll be giving her a ride home tonight to save him a trip out?"

"Yup." Justin picked up an abandoned tiny sneaker, lying on its side at the base of a potted plant and put it on the corner of Gayle's desk.

"I don't know," Jaci said. "She was pretty quiet today and didn't want to see you when you stopped by. Did something happen between the two of you last night?"

Interesting. So Jena hadn't shared his offer of marriage with her sister.

"Is she okay with you bringing her home?" Jaci asked.

She'd have to be since she'd have no other option. "Yup."

"Can you put her on? I'd like to hear it from her."

"Nope, she's in with a patient." That wasn't a lie.

"Have her call me."

"Sure thing." That was. "But don't worry if she doesn't. It's crazy here tonight."

The next time Jena went to breeze by him without a word he reached out to stop her. "Jaci called."

She stiffened and flashed him a worried glance.

"The babies are fine. She wanted you to know since they're asleep she's going to sleep," he lied.

"Thank you," she said without looking at him and continued on her way.

A few minutes before close, upon returning from investigating a disturbance behind the building, Justin met up with a worried Gayle hurrying toward him. "One of those boys you escorted out of here earlier came back."

Justin sped up.

"He said something to Jena and the fool girl followed him outside," Gayle said.

Justin broke into a run.

"I told her to wait for you," Gayle said as he passed her on his way to the entrance.

"If I'm not back in one minute call the police." Justin shot out into the dark. "Jena," he yelled.

Nothing.

"Jena," he yelled again, louder, so anyone within a mile radius would hear him.

Nothing.

So he listened. Cars driving past. A horn honked in the distance. Then quiet. A muffled… He turned to the right. Followed the sound to the far end of the parking lot where the spaces designated for the urgent care staff were located, noting it seemed darker and more shadowed than it had earlier. "If you hurt her I'll kill you," he called out. Even unarmed—because the urgent care center management did not want their security guards to carry weapons of any type with children around—he could do it. And would.

He looked up to see the corner parking lot light out.

How convenient.

He ran.

"Jena."

"I'm he—"

Someone cut off her response.

Not smart.

Justin followed her voice. Quietly. He crept between two cars to the grassy edge of the parking lot and saw her shadowed form, on the ground with someone on their knees behind her, a hand covering her mouth.

An uneasy feeling ran a chilly sprint up his spine.

Two teens accompanied by an elderly man had entered the care center earlier. He scanned the area and behind him for the other two.

Jena began to struggle.

The person behind her jerked an arm around her throat.

Justin's body tightened with rage. He would not allow that miscreant to hurt her, or worse, would not even entertain the possibility of his daughters growing up without their mom. And fueled by an emotion powerful enough to make him ignore proper police procedure and the good instincts that'd kept him safe over the years, Justin sprang to action. "Release her this second if you want to live." He showed himself and stalked toward the attacker who didn't move. "I can make it quick or I can make you die an excruciatingly slow and painful death."

Jena tried to fight, twisting, gasping...

"Don't—" Something struck the side of his head. A pipe? A bat? He held in a shout of pain. His vision blurred. Unable to stand he dropped and rolled onto his side, fought to remain conscious.

"Don't hurt him," Jena cried out. "What do you want?"

Money. Drugs. Her. Unacceptable. Justin struggled onto his knees, willed his head to stop spinning.

"Stay down," a male voice yelled.

Another male voice, this one sounding panicked said, "Let's go."

Jena crawled over to him. "Are you okay?" She gently touched the side of his head. "You're bleeding," she cried out.

He put his arm around her, would not let them touch her.

The two men loomed over them.

"I told you this wouldn't work," one of the men said.
"If we show up—"

Justin chose their moment of conflict and inattention to jump—well stumble—to his feet and fight. His right fist connected with a nose, his elbow with a cheek. A siren sounded in the distance. Thank goodness because Justin felt seconds from collapsing to the ground.

The siren grew louder.

The men ran off. But Justin would make sure they were found.

He swayed. Jena caught him, maneuvered him up against the side of a minivan, and pressed her body to his to keep him upright.

"What the hell were you thinking?" he yelled and made his headache even worse in the process.

"He said when they showed up without the prescriptions the drug dealer beat up his friend and he was scared to come in for treatment because you'd banned them from ever coming back. I'm so sorry." She hugged him.

Damn she felt good. He reached down, grabbed her butt and pulled her hips flush with his.

She tilted her head up to him. "On account of you likely have a head injury I'm going to overlook this little display."

"I want you, Jena." He tried to nuzzle her ear, the movement throwing him off balance, tilting him forward.

"Now I know you're not thinking clearly," she joked, throwing her entire weight against him—which he liked a lot. "Stop moving around or I'm going to drop you."

A car screeched into the parking lot. A siren echoed in his head. Loud. Make it stop. He clutched his hands over his ears. Lights blinded him. A car door slammed. He groaned but knew enough to reach for his badge in his front pocket and held it up. "Officer Justin Rangore. MVPD. Two men. One lured Jena into the parking lot."

"One pretended to be injured. But once outside they tried to convince me to get them narcotics," Jena explained. "Justin was working security. He came out to find me and they hit him in the head. He needs to go to the Emergency Room."

"They fled on foot," Justin added. "Heading north."

The officer conveyed the information into the radio affixed to her shoulder. "That's a pretty nasty cut," she noted.

Yeah. Cut. He wanted to cut with the chit chat and take Jena to bed.

Someone said something, sounded far away.

"Stay with me." Jena's voice broke through the haze.

"I want to. I really do." Again. At his place. In his bed. All night long. If he could just get rid of the pain in his head. "Let's go home."

Of course she didn't let him go home until after he'd had an X-ray, a CT scan, a tetanus shot, and twelve stitches. None of which were all that bad since Jena stayed with him, holding his hand, talking quietly, the sweet melody of her voice relaxing him.

The best part of the entire night was the neurologist informing Jena and Ian that Justin had a concussion and would need to be woken up hourly until morning, and Jena insisting since she was responsible for his injury she be the one to do it.

After driving them home, Ian walked Justin up to his condo while Jena went to check on the twins, give Jaci an update and change out of her uniform.

Into something clingy and skimpy would be his preference.

"You going to be okay?" Ian asked. He'd been unusually quiet at the hospital, on the ride home, and in the elevator.

Justin plopped onto the couch. "Yeah. I promise I won't die." As soon as the words left his mouth Justin wanted to suck them back in. "Hey. I'm sorry." Because Ian had lost four of his buddies in the explosion that'd left him with a permanent limp. Damn war. "I didn't mean—"

"I know," Ian said. "You need help getting changed?"

"If I do I don't want it from you."

Ian smiled. "I guess that blow to the head hasn't affected your sex drive any."

If anything it'd made it even more powerful. Or maybe that'd been hours of close proximity to Jena.

"Take it easy on her," Ian warned. "Jaci's worried about Jena, says she hasn't been herself since her return."

Justin liked the changes.

"She's been preoccupied, quiet and secretive," Ian went on. "Jaci thinks it has something to do with Jerry the jerk."

"I'm taking care of it," was all he'd share. "Tell Jaci not to worry."

Ian stiffened, looking ready for battle. "What's going on?"

Justin yawned. "I'm taking care of it," he repeated, feeling himself drifting off to sleep.

Jena's voice woke him. "Help me get him up."

Justin smiled.

But those weren't Jena's dainty hands pushing into his armpits and lifting him to a standing position.

"Let's get him undressed," she said.

"Yeah. Let's," Justin said, liking the idea of getting naked with Jena. "I can walk." He twisted out of Ian's hold. "Three's a crowd. Good night, Ian." He lifted his shirt over his head, forgetting about his stiches. "Yowza," he yelled out when his collar rubbed along his sensitive suture line.

"Be careful." Jena took him by the arm. "Come on. I'll get you cleaned up and ready for bed."

"Call if you need me," Ian said, from behind them.

"I will," Jena said at the same time Justin said, "We won't." He had everything under control. Except for the dizziness. He leaned on Jena for balance. And the throbbing ache in his head. No chance a little headache, okay, a big headache, was going to keep him from having Jena. Again. Lots of agains.

CHAPTER FIVE

JENA led Justin into the bathroom, knowing his shirt was stained with blood and would have to be removed at some point, wishing he hadn't chosen to expose so much of his delectable body before she'd had a chance to fully prepare herself to combat the overwhelming desire to touch it. She closed the lid to the toilet. "Sit." He was a bit unsteady on his feet so she guided him down, which put his enticingly bare chest in full view, close enough to kiss.

Stop that, she chided herself for unprofessional thoughts. She was here as a nurse, nothing more.

Smooth skin covered exquisitely defined muscles. A dusting of hair up high and a line from his navel down…

He undid the top button of his slacks. "You like what you see?"

She most certainly did. What healthy, heterosexual woman wouldn't? "You've seen one you've seen them all," she said, belittling the fact men's naked bodies varied greatly in their aesthetic qualities. And Justin's earned a check plus in each box on her What I Like Most About Men's Bodies wish list.

He cleared his throat. "You going to clean up my head or is there another reason you brought me in here?"

He smiled a flirty all-you-have-to-do-is-ask smile, at least that's how she chose to interpret it.

"How are you feeling?" Jena asked to remind herself he'd been struck in the head a few hours earlier, had been diagnosed with a concussion and received twelve stiches. Only a callous, self-centered woman would entertain sexual thoughts while providing care to a man who'd been injured trying to protect her, a man who was in no shape, neurologically or physically, to engage in the totally inappropriate acts circulating through her mind.

Bad Jena.

"I'm a little tired." He smiled again. "But up for anything."

Okay. Conversation not helping. So she focused on his suture line instead. The ER doc had done a nice job of bringing the wound edges together, the stitches relatively equidistant and coated with antibiotic ointment. "I want to clean some of this blood out of your hair. Where are your washcloths?"

"Under the sink."

Jena retrieved a few and got to work. After a minute or two Justin sighed. "You have a very gentle touch."

She smiled. "Thank you."

"I didn't think I'd like this as much as I do," he said.

She looked down at him. "Like what?"

He opened his eyes. "You taking care of me."

She liked it, too.

At some point while she'd been concentrating on her task, rinsing and re-wetting the cloth, he'd shifted so now she stood between his spread thighs, his face pointed straight ahead at her breasts. She could almost feel his heated gaze. Her nipples went tingly and hard, the sensation divine. And one she would soon miss mightily. She fought back sorrow, needed to focus on the big picture. Life.

"You're killing me," he said.

Lost in thought she'd been too rough. "I'm sorry." She stopped rubbing his head and went to step back.

He palmed her waist and pulled her close, dropped his forehead to rest just above her belly. "You smell so good, look so good. I want to touch you, undress you. Take those tight, aroused nipples into my mouth."

Heaven help her she wanted the same things, especially to feel his mouth on her nipples. One last time.

"You have no idea what being this close to you is doing to me."

Oh yes she did, because it was doing the same to her.

"What would you do if I touched you? Would you let me?"

Yes.

As if he'd heard her mental response he set a gentle hand on her right breast, ran his thumb across its peak which sent a jolt of pure potent arousal raging through her system. Wonderful yet worrisome. Without sensitive, responsive nipples, would she ever again feel this overwhelmingly extraordinary desire for a man?

"You okay?" he asked.

"I'm fine." Not really. "But I think that whack to the head dislodged your impulse control." The condition apparently contagious as Jena had a few impulses on the verge of slipping outside of her control, too. The impulse to lift her shirt, grab him by the ears and direct his mouth to where she wanted it. The impulse to press her lips to his, to slip her tongue into his mouth and taste him, devour him. The impulse to straddle his lap and rub herself shamelessly along the length of the erection gaining prominence behind his zipper. Seems he was physically capable after all. But…

Think nurse-patient relationship. Nothing more. "Your head is clean enough." She tossed the washcloth into the sink. Distance would really help this situation. And sleep. "Where's your acetaminophen?"

He didn't answer.

She tried to step away. He held her close, not on board with the distance part of her plan. "Come on," she said.

Nothing.

"Justin?"

"Don't move," he said. A moment later he added, "I think I'm going to be sick."

And he was. Good thing she hadn't listened when he'd told her not to move. "That's two for two." When he was finished she handed him a clean dampened cloth to wash his face. "Two times in your condo during which you've had your hands on my body. Two times you drop to your knees and heave up the contents of your stomach as a result. Is it my perfume? My shampoo? Me?"

He sat on the floor, his back against the wall, looking miserable. "First time," he held up his index finger, "hangover. Second time," he added his middle finger, "concussion. It's not you."

Although tonight's injury and subsequent GI distress could be directly attributed to her stupidity in running out into the parking lot alone with someone Justin had told her to be cautious of.

He reached for the towel bar and started to pull himself up. "You think I like you seeing me at my worst?"

She rushed to help him. "Let me help you." She

tugged on his arm. But really he did most of the work himself. "You still nauseous?" If he vomited again she'd be on the phone, calling the doctor.

"I'm fine," he said not looking or sounding fine. "Let's go to bed."

Time to firm up the sleeping arrangements. "During your little impromptu nap a few minutes ago Ian said I could sleep in his bed."

"Did he have a big smile on his face when he said it?"

Come to think of it, yes.

"You're sleeping with *me*." He grabbed her hand and led her to his cave. Very me man you woman you do what man say.

A big apology to feminists worldwide, but she kind of liked it. Although, "It's a bad idea, Justin. We can't—"

"You promised the ER doc you'd keep an eye on me through the night."

Yes, she had.

"How are you going to do that when you're in another room?"

"I'll set the alarm on my phone. I'll come in to wake you every hour."

"Not good enough." He dragged her into his room without turning on the light. "The more I argue, the more my head hurts."

"Let me get you some—" Before she could name a pain reliever he said, "You're all I need."

How could a women argue with that?

He released her hand, unzipped his pants and let them fall to the floor. "Would you undo my shoes?"

Of course. That's the reason she was here. To take care of him. Caring for others is what Jena did best.

Naked except for a pair of cotton boxer briefs—

the room too dark for her to see anything more than the basic outline of his body, darn it all—he lifted the covers and slid into the middle of his queen-sized bed where he laid down on his side, held up the covers, and waited for her.

She removed her phone from the pocket of her lounge pants, pressed the buttons necessary to set the alarm for one hour, and placed it on the bedside table. Just for tonight. She climbed in beside him. Because of his head injury. She turned on her side facing away from him. Definitely not because she wanted to be there just as much as he wanted her there.

He cuddled in behind her, like he'd done the last time she'd spent the night in his bed, his chin resting on the top of her head, his anterior in full contact with her posterior and his powerful arm draped over her ribs with his hand cupping her breast.

"Thank you," he said on a deep sigh.

No. Thank *you*. Jena closed her eyes and savored the feel of him. Just. For. Tonight. Her body relaxed, indulged in a closeness that would never be repeated.

Jena woke to darkness, her phone alarm going off. She lifted it to check the time—four o'clock—and stop the ringing. She listened for the twins, thrilled to hear nothing but quiet, thankful the noise hadn't set them off. So warm. She closed her eyes.

Someone moved behind her.

She sucked in a breath.

"What?" a male voice asked, pulling her close.

Justin. It all came back. His head wound. Stiches. A concussion. Hourly neurological checks. "What's your name?" she asked.

"Do you often wake up unsure who you're in bed with?" he mumbled, teasing her. Back to normal.

"You'd think with the wild, party-girl lifestyle I lead, I'd be used to it by now," she quipped.

He squeezed her. "Wise ass."

Only with him, probably because so many of their interactions over the years had occurred while she'd been pretending to be Jaci whose personality lent itself to sarcasm and playfulness. "I was checking to see your level of orientation or if I need to drag you back to the hospital."

"My name is Justin Rangore," he whispered.

"Now here's a toughie," she said, "Who am I?"

He rocked his hips. Something firm poked her butt cheek. "You are the lovely, and when I say lovely I mean alluring, sensual, and charming *Jena* Piermont."

His emphasis on "Jena" made her smile and delighted her beyond measure. She reset her alarm to go off in an hour. "Back to sleep," she said a bit surprised when he didn't balk and continue putting the moves on her and actually seemed to drift right back into slumber.

The next three times Jena's alarm startled her back to consciousness she could barely stay awake long enough to gently shake Justin, determine him to be oriented to person, place and time, and reset her alarm before falling back into an exhausted sleep.

"Hey, beautiful." A man's soft voice interrupted a delicious dream. Lips, she assumed his, pressed a kiss to the tip of her nose. "Rise and shine."

Lying on her side, Jena opened her eyes to sunshine and Justin's face less than an inch away. She slapped her hand over her mouth.

"Relax," he said so at ease with their position. "Two morning breaths cancel each other out."

"Are you speaking from your vast experience waking up in bed with women," she asked from behind her hand, "Or saying the first thing that came to mind to keep me from leaving the bed to gargle with mouthwash?"

"Yes." He smiled.

"How do you feel?" she asked.

He took the hand covering her mouth, slid it down his naked chest, to an impressive morning erection. "You tell me."

Oh my. Great. He felt great. Awesome. "Well, that's a pretty big indication you no longer need me around to take care of you." She started to roll away but came to an abrupt stop on her back, when Justin pounced on top of her, pinning her hips beneath his.

"But I do." He rested his upper body on his elbows and leaned down to kiss her cheek. "Don't go."

Somehow her knees parted and he settled in between them, his groin flush with hers, the pressure of his arousal…right there. She wanted to lift her hips. Needed…

He pushed some hair off of her forehead and stared deeply into her eyes. "Stay with me, Jena."

Jena. Stay with me, Jena. Not Jaci.

She shouldn't. Sex would only make her eventual choice of husband, and doing what was best for her and her daughters, more difficult. She glanced at the clock anyway. The girls would be up soon. Jena had never been separated from them for as long as they'd been apart over the last twenty-four hours. She ached to see their smiling faces and kiss their baby-scented skin. And it was too much to expect Jaci—

"Please," he said, the need in his voice, the rich, sensual timbre made her woman parts tingle. "I want to show you something." And Lord help her, Jena wanted to see it, feel it and experience it.

He rocked his hips. Slowly. Forward. Then back. The length of his erection providing an intimate massage that drove words like "stop" and "no" from cognition, leaving only synonyms of "yes", "more", and "faster" accessible for use.

"What?" On impulse she skimmed her hands down the soft skin covering his lateral ribs to his waist. "What do you want to show me?"

"How good I make love when I'm sober." He kept his voice quiet, seductive, as he lowered his mouth to her ear and whispered, "When I take my time, and my sole focus is your pleasure."

Jena couldn't contain a sensual shiver.

The little demonstration of "sole focus on her pleasure" that followed proved him a proficient and talented sexual multi-tasker.

Aroused Jena, the one listening to her stimulated, needy body crying out for one last sexual hurrah battled Rational Jena, the cautious, responsible one wedged in her head, over the pros and cons of crossing her ankles behind his butt, opening for him and exerting some control over the speed, depth and direction of his frustratingly languid pelvic activity.

Rational Jena won out. This time. But with each caress of her breast, each glide of his palm over her nipple, each slide of his erection along her swollen, moistening sex Aroused Jena was gaining strength.

"That's very altruistic of you," she teased. And very tempting. If she married Thomas goodbye sex life hello abstinence. Even if she held out in search of an understanding heterosexual male who could accept her treatment decisions—as if one would be easy to find within the next two months—from the research she'd done, after surgery she expected changes in the sensation, look and feel of her breasts that would impact both her and her partner in any future intimate relationship. This could be her last opportunity to enjoy the delicious tingle of aroused nipples, of a man's hands caressing her breasts and his mouth… "But don't you mean how good you are at sex?" Because making love would require, well…love. Or at least some degree of mutual affection.

He kissed the sensitive cove at the base of her ear. Oh so gentle. His hips maintained their unhurried rhythm. Forward. Then back. Over and over. His fingers teased. "How about I spend the next couple of hours demonstrating the difference?" He kissed along the line of her jaw to her chin. He touched his lips to hers. So tender, nothing like the mashing, passionate kisses she now associated with sex.

Sex. Not making love.

When he lifted his head she said, "We already had sex."

"Honey, I'm not proud to admit it, but what we had was a sloppy, drunken version of sex I want to eradicate from your memory." He started to slide down her body.

"Hey," she said. "I haven't agreed to anything." Yet.

He pushed up her cotton tee. "But you will." He set his mouth to her breast, swirled his tongue around her nipple, sucked and Oh. My. Goodness. Without conscious thought, "Yes," shot from her mouth like a cork from an agitated bottle of bubbly.

He moved to her other breast. The feel of his triumphant grin against her skin gave her pause. This is what Justin did. Seduce. Convince. Use whatever means necessary to get what he wanted. Being treated like just another conquest didn't sit right, regardless of how much she wanted him, so she forced out a, "Stop," and pushed him away.

He lifted his head and looked at her, confused. Surprised.

"Annie and Abbie will be up soon," she said. "I have to go."

She expected him to bargain or cajole.

He didn't.

He did, however, move up her body, slowly, setting his moist tongue to her neck for the last part of his journey up to whisper in her ear, "Tonight, then. After work." He blew out a hot, shaky breath. "Baby, tonight. What I'm going to do to you."

Jena swallowed, gulped actually, as an excited, adventurous, illicit anticipatory longing started to bubble deep within her.

"You look tired," Jena said, walking over to where Justin stood in the lobby of the urgent care center with his back resting up against the wall.

It was kind of sweet that she kept checking on him. "Because someone kept waking me up last night."

"Which is why tonight you need a good night's sleep," she tried, not for the first time, to get out of going back to his place.

She took him by the hand. "Justin is taking a quick

break, Gayle," she said then led him down the hall. "Come."

That was the plan. For both of them. Multiple times.

"I cannot believe you don't trust me enough to work without you watching over me like an overprotective parent," Jena complained. "You should be home in bed."

"Which is where I'd be right now if you'd agreed to stay there with me when I'd asked," he pointed out.

As she walked she chirped about headaches and blurred vision. Warning signs. Forgetfulness. Potential for delayed subdural hematoma. Permanent brain damage and dysfunction. Death.

While he chose to focus on his urge to release the thick curls restrained in her tight bun and muss them up for a wild, untamed look. But then they'd cover the smooth kissable, lickable skin at the back of her neck. His mouth actually watered at the thought. He moved his gaze lower, to the enticing sway of her hips and glimpses of the rounded perfectness of her butt each time her long top shifted.

Beyond her enticing physical attributes Justin found he actually enjoyed spending time with her which was a good thing since they'd spent so many hours in each other's presence over the past two days. Like the better part of his morning and early afternoon in Jena's bedroom, playing with the twins and learning to care for them. And while they slept, reviewing her financial statements, and teaching her to read them and pay her bills.

To date it'd been the longest period of time he'd ever spent in a room occupied by a bed and a woman without getting naked. And yet he'd still enjoyed himself, finding Jena a captivating mix of contrasts. Innocent yet sexy. Caring yet guarded. Insecure yet confident.

"Honestly," she said, jolting him back to the conversation. "I promised I wouldn't leave the building until Ian came to get me."

Like to protect her was the only reason he'd shown up at work. No, his motives way more self-serving, Justin had loaded up on acetaminophen so he could stay close to take advantage of every opportunity to entice her and remind her where they were headed at the end of her shift. To his bed where he would prove his attraction to *her* and not Jaci. Where he would make Jena crave him as much as he craved her. Where he would drive thoughts of Thomas and Dr. Charmer and a relationship with any other man right out of her head.

But she needed to get married. To someone. The mere thought of Jena tending to another man's wounds while dressed in her clingy pajamas, or cuddling up to another man in bed, caused his chest to tighten. As did thinking of binding himself to a woman, of disappointing her, and upsetting her over and over for five long years.

"I feel fine." Except for a residual nagging headache.

She pulled him into an empty exam room. "Sit." She pointed to a chair.

"Yes, ma'am." But only because he hoped maybe she'd come in close to check his stiches so he could— Yes! She walked toward the chair. He spread his knees in welcome and she moved between them.

Oh yeah.

He inhaled. "You smell so good." He set his hands at the backs of her knees, lightly. Testing. When she didn't

Feel so good."

She ignored him. "Your incision line looks fine. Any headache?"

"No," he lied. Nothing would interfere with his plans for tonight.

"Blurred vision?"

He slid his hands up, under her scrub top to bare warm skin. "Nope."

She tried to step back.

He held her in place. "You didn't ask about my lips. They hurt." He looked up at her with what he hoped was a convincing sad expression. "I think a quick kiss would make them feel better."

She pushed on his shoulders, a half-hearted display if ever there was one. "Stop it." Her smile belied her tone of annoyance.

"After you kiss me." Obviously she needed more of an enticement so, holding her with one hand at her back, he moved his other hand around front, to her right breast, her nipple hard beneath his palm. "Breasts are my favorite part of the female anatomy. And yours are perfection." The nicest he'd seen, touched and tasted. No lie. Considering the number of women he'd been with over the years that was saying something. "I love that you don't wear a padded bra." So he could feel her arousal and revel in her response to his touch.

She let out a breath. "We can't."

He noticed she didn't make any attempt to flee. Gotcha.

He moved his other hand around so he could caress both of her lovely breasts at the same time, lavishing attention on the rounded fullness of her perfect Cs, watching the movement of her scrub top as he maneuvered underneath it, wishing he could see his hands on her fair skin.

"My goodness you're making this hard."

"Well *you're* making *this* hard." He reached for her hand and lowered it to his growing erection.

Major miscalculation.

She jerked her hand away like she'd received an electric shock. "This is so wrong." She glanced at the door then at his crotch. "So unprofessional." She stepped back. He let her go. "What if Mary came in with a patient?"

"She wouldn't open a closed door without knocking first." But Jena was right. He'd gone too far. "Later." He stared up at her. "Promise me."

She thought about it. "Okay," she agreed, backing away from him. "Tonight." She turned to leave, mumbling something that sounded like, "One last time."

After the door closed Justin leaned back and shut his eyes. Last time? Silly girl. They were just getting started.

For the rest of their shift Jena didn't look him in the eye. But she looked at other parts of him. And the pink blush that erupted on her cheeks when he caught her staring got him hotter than the most overt sexual advances. "What's going on in that head of yours?" he asked.

"Wouldn't you like to know?" She hurried off.

Why yes he would like to know, as a matter of fact. What made one of the richest girls in town focus her telescope on him? Choose him as her first lover? Trust him to help her with her finances? Look at him with lust in her eyes and treat him with caring when she could have her pick of men? Better men, wealthy, cultured men more suited to circulating in her upper class circles.

A car screeched to a stop outside. Justin went on alert. A man jumped out of the driver seat, yanked on the rear passenger door, and pulled out a young child wearing blue pajamas. Justin held open the heavy glass door for him.

"My son," the man said, panting, his eyes wild. "He's having trouble breathing."

Justin looked down at the sleeping child cradled in the man's arms. Maybe two or three years old, his nose red, his eyes puffy, his lashes clumped with tears.

"Okay. Not right now," he said "But a few minutes ago he was crying and coughing, a strange barky cough that scared the hell out of me. He couldn't catch his breath. My wife is away on a business trip. I called the pediatrician who said it sounded like croup. What the hell is croup? And what kind of kook doctor diagnoses a child over the telephone?" The man shifted the boy so his head rested on his shoulder. "Drive to urgent care with the windows open, he told me."

"Seems to have worked," Justin commented, after filling in at the urgent care center dozens of times, very familiar with croup and this exact scenario.

Beyond listening, the man continued on as if Justin hadn't spoken. "If the coughing stops and Joshua calms down turn around and go back home, he told me. So the crying and coughing and gasping for breath can start up again in an hour? I don't think so. My son needs treatment. Right now. I want him examined by a doctor," the man demanded.

"That's why we're here," Justin replied. "Please sign in with Gayle." Justin directed the man to the registration desk. "I'll get a nurse to come out." Because he wasn't a medical professional and would rather Mary or Jena decide if the little boy needed to be taken right in.

He found Jena in the supply room carrying a pack of disposable diapers and a case of formula. "Where're these going?" He took them from her. "There's a little boy out front I'd like you to take a look at. Possible croup. The man with him is pretty upset."

"Exam room four," she said without argument. "Then they're ready to go."

An hour later, ten minutes to close, after a visit with a doctor and lots of instruction and reassurance from Jena, Justin accompanied Joshua and his dad out to the parking lot.

"Sorry about before," the man said.

"No need to apologize," Justin replied.

The man unlocked the car, opened the rear passenger door, and tucked Joshua into his car seat. When he emerged he asked, "You have kids?"

As of two days ago, "Yeah. Two little girls. Twins." He noticed he stood a bit taller, feeling rather proud about it.

"This parenthood gig is one crazy ride." The man shook his head.

Justin had no doubt it would be once he secured his spot on the parental rollercoaster beside Jena.

Who sure took her time cleaning up and restocking for the next day.

By half past twelve even Mary had had enough. "Come on, Jena," she called down the hallway. "I've got to get home. Max is waiting up for me." She turned to Justin. "With candles burning and lotion warming."

"Thanks for the visual but that's more information than I need to know."

"Tough. Do you think I want to go home and have sex? My son wakes up at sunrise. I won't get home until close to one in the morning. I need to sleep," Mary complained. "But I fear I inadvertently strayed into the path of those horny vibes pulsing back and forth between you and Jena. Heck, even Dr. Morloni set up a late night rendezvous. Did you see how fast he bolted out of here?"

Come to think of it, yes he had.

"Sorry. I'm ready," Jena said, walking toward them while slipping on her lavender sweater.

"Me, too," Mary said brightly.

"Me, three," Justin added, controlled, squelching a, "Halleluiah let's go home and get us laid", restraining the urge to grab Jena by the hand and make a mad dash to his SUV.

"Have fun, you two," Mary said with a sly smile and a wink as she slid into the front seat of her car.

"Oh, no," Jena said after Mary slammed her door shut. She grabbed his arm, pulling him to a stop and looking up, her expression lost in the darkness but concern evident in her tone. "Do you think she knows?"

"Knows what?" He played dumb, didn't want her distracted by unnecessary embarrassment.

"That we're going back to your place to… To…"

He found her prim inability to speak the words for what they were headed to do, amusing. Refreshing. So different from his usual women. "Get naked? Have sex? Renew our intimate acquaintance? Get it on? Make love?" he teased.

She smacked his chest. "I'm serious."

"Me, too." He tucked her hand in the crook of his

arm and headed to his SUV. "This parking lot at night is not a place to hang around talking." No matter how entertaining he found the topic of conversation.

Subject effectively changed, he slid his free hand into his pants pocket to grip the tactical folding knife he'd placed there before work. Only a fool with a death wish would try to jump him tonight.

On the walk into the condo complex Jena admitted, "I'm a little nervous."

Justin stopped.

"Now that you're sober," she said not looking at him. "And you know I'm not Jaci, what if you find me…lacking? Disappointing? What if you can't…?"

"Whoa!" He held up both hands. "Stop with the crazy talk." Justin Rangore had never as in N*E*V*E*R*E*V*E*R* been unable to get it up for a woman.

But this wasn't only about him. He hadn't missed the genuine concern in Jena's voice. Thankful for the benefit of standing under a large outdoor lighting fixture, he looked down into the beautiful blue eyes looking up at him, worried, vulnerable, searching for reassurance.

And he gave it to her. "Honey." He took her cold hands in his. "I have been craving you since this morning, fantasizing about you, counting the minutes until I could be with you. There is no way you could disappoint me."

"Sometimes," she turned her head away. "When we want something so much we dream about it and yearn for it and fantasize what it'll be like, we set unrealistically high expectations for how amazing it'll be. And when it isn't, the disappointment is so much worse than never having it at all."

Pow! A verbal uppercut to the diaphragm. Quite painful, actually. *He'd* disappointed *her*, had been in too much of a rush. An experienced woman knew how to find her pleasure. Had the confidence to ask for it and convey her likes and wants. An inexperienced woman needed to be shown her options, taught the possibilities, and encouraged to vocalize her desires.

The teacherly aspect turned out to be a pretty big turn on, as was her honesty and trusting him enough to share her concern. It made him determined to do better. To prove his attraction to *her*. To give her the spectacular night of loving she deserved. A night to remember. Always. No matter what happened in the morning.

He pulled her close, lifted her chin, and set his lips to hers. "Neither one of us will be disappointed tonight." He kissed her again. "I promise."

He stepped back and held out his hand, palm up in invitation. And waited.

With a small smile she placed her hand in his. Trusting him. Believing in him. No gesture ever meant more.

In the lobby Brandon, the concierge, waved and called out, "Hi, Jaci. Hi, Justin."

Without hesitation Jena smiled and waved. "Hi, Brandon. How's your mom feeling?"

"Much better," he said. "Thanks for asking."

Justin saw the man every day and had never once discussed his mother. He doubted Jaci had either. "Why didn't you correct him?"

Jena pushed the up arrow at the elevators and shrugged. "It's easier not to. I'm the shy twin. The quiet twin. The smart and obedient twin. Jaci's fun and friendly and popular. I don't mind people thinking I'm her." She glanced up with sad eyes. "Usually."

Then she looked down at her feet. "Anyway, I'm tired of always being the good twin."

In the elevator Justin said, "I bet if you'd give people the chance to get to know you they'd find you're friendly and they'd like you, too." He pushed her up against the metallic coated wall. "Take me for instance." He bent to tongue her ear. "I like you."

She trembled.

"I like you, too," she said quietly.

He picked her up at the back of her thighs, wrapping her legs around his hips so he could rub his hardon between her legs, to show her how much he liked her. "And if you're looking to let your bad girl out for a little play time, you have come to the right place."

He rocked his hips.

She let out a breath and dropped her forehead to his shoulder. "Lord help me, being bad feels so good."

"Baby you ain't seen nothing yet."

CHAPTER SIX

WITH a ping the elevator doors opened. And rather than put her down, Justin took a step. Like he planned to exit with her wrapped around him like a tree-hugging coconut-picker. With a total disregard for who might see them. "Put me down." She tried to wiggle free, wasted energy when a man as strong as Justin wasn't on board with the put-me-down plan. "Seriously," she said. "My burgeoning bad girl isn't ready for public displays." And probably never would bc.

He loosened his arms just enough for her to shimmy down over that very prominent, very hard, very male, very dream-worthy part of him. "Behind-closed-doors-bad-girl works for me, too," he said with a wink. Then he walked out of the elevator, looked back over his shoulder, and flashed her a cocky but oh-so-sexy follow-me-for-a-good-time smile. So handsome and confident.

And follow him she did, but not before the elevator doors started to close. Shoot. She darted in between them and, not wanting to come off overly eager or desperate to feel his hands on her, even though she was, she walked at a moderate pace until she reached his side. He set his heavy arm across her shoulders and pulled her close.

An act of possession? Protection? Preventing escape?

It didn't matter. She liked it.

Inside his condo, without even taking the time to turn on the lights, he slammed the door closed and gave her More—with a capital M. Again he lifted her feet from the floor. Again he pressed her back to the wall and positioned his hips between her wide open thighs, pressing and rubbing where she wanted pressing and rubbing the most. Only he added a wet, aggressive, breath-stealing, tongue-probing, passion-inducing kiss that had her twisting her fingers in his hair, pulling his mouth even closer, and grinding against him like some uninhibited, lust-crazed, sex fiend.

Apparently her inner bad girl didn't require much coaxing to come out in Justin's presence.

He pulled back, breathing heavy. "My, God, Jena. You feel so good. I'm having a hard time controlling myself."

My, God, Jena. You feel so good. Jena. Not Jaci. Justin admitted having a hard time controlling himself because of Jena. The only thing that could have improved that moment was if she'd had the wherewithal to record his statement for future listening pleasure.

He rested his forehead on hers. "If we don't slow it down I'm going to take you right here, right now. Just. Like. This." He punctuated each of his final three words with a delicious thrust of his hips. More promise than threat.

She wanted to yell, "Do it! Let passion take over. Give in to your urgent need to take me hard and fast like you'll die if you don't." Like she'd seen time after time in the romantic movies she watched in the quiet loneliness of her bedroom, wishing to be the recipient of rip-your-clothes-off, got-to-have-you-now, can't-wait-

the-time-it'd-take-to-get-to-the-bedroom desire at least
once in her life. And since this particular moment in
time might turn out to be her last chance to experience
it, Jena quietly said, "That'd be okay."

He let out a breath. "I am barely holding it together,
Jena. Don't tease."

"I'm not." She needed him. So bad. Tonight. Now.

He leaned down to her ear and whispered, "Tell me
what you want."

"This."

He chuckled. "In detail. I want to make tonight special for you. Tell me what you want." He blew out a puff
of hot air and tongued the inner rim of her ear, setting
off waves of lust throughout her body. At the same time
he set his hand on her breast, teasing her nipple into a
tight, aroused peak. Between her legs, the entrance to
her body throbbed with its yearning to be filled by him.

"Please," she begged.

"Please, what?" he asked seductively, his lips tickling
her ear as he spoke, his hand moving to her other breast.

"Please, don't make me ask. You know what I want.
What I need." Normally, Jena would have left it at that
and whatever happened, happened. However, seemed
her bad girl wasn't taking any chances and Jena found
herself turning toward his ear, and, with the same hot
puff of breath he gave her, demanding, in the most de-
mure voice she could muster, "Now strip me naked and
give it to me." As if someone else had taken control of
her body her hips rocked along his erection in three
long slow strokes. "Just. Like. This."

Through the thin fabric of her scrub pants and lace
panties his hard heat warmed and aroused her. Bring
her higher. Making her ache. "I need—"

"I know what you need, honey."

Evidently somewhere between direction and perception some pertinent information got lost because he lowered her to a standing position which was not at all what she needed. Yet her words of protest got sucked down her throat on a gasp of surprise when he tugged off her sweater, lifted her scrub top in one smooth motion, and unhooked her bra with ease before pulling it off and flinging it aside. Then he matched her half-naked by yanking his shirt off.

That's more like it. She lunged forward and wrapped her arms around him. Bare breasts to naked chest, loving the feel of him, focusing in on every detail, every sensation, making a memory that would have to last a lifetime.

"I'm liking your bad girl," he said, his hands at work untying her drawstring.

"Me, too." She kissed his shoulder, licked and sucked his skin into her mouth. "Seems she only comes out for you."

"Good." Her pants slid to the floor. "Let's keep it that way." Justin followed them down, taking her panties with him. Seconds later she stood naked, except for a pair of socks, darkness the only thing keeping her from total mortification. Her body had changed since their last time together, and not for the better.

Justin stood.

Yes.

The light in the entryway came on.

No.

"Turn it off," she cried, hunching forward, trying to cover her abdomen with her hands. She didn't want him to see...

"I don't want us to be two anonymous people making out in the dark. I want to see you. Watch you—"

No. "Turn it off," she yelled, trying to swivel away from him. She wanted the dark, the covert encounter, even though her current blemishes were nothing compared to the metamorphosis to come.

"Hey." He took her by the shoulders and held her in place. Gentle but firm. "What's wrong?" He lowered his gaze to her hands.

Don't. "I have to go." She never should have come, would never measure up to the women Justin favored. Slim. Beautiful. Perfect.

"Talk to me," he said. So calm. Concerned.

"Only if you turn off the light."

He looked at her like she was an absolute crazy person, justifiably so. But finally did.

Only she no longer took comfort in the darkness because now she wanted to leave and couldn't see her clothes.

"The light is off," he pointed out. "And it occurs to me you gave birth to two babies six weeks ago and I don't know if you had surgery or delivered them via the regular route. Or if you're all healed and we should even be doing this."

"If I wasn't healed, I wouldn't be here," she said.

He stood quietly, offering no response.

"I'm naked and I'm cold and would rather have this conversation with some clothes on." Or not at all worked.

"Not a chance." He picked her up, his body warming hers on contact. When she didn't immediately wrap her legs around his waist—which took quite a bit of restraint, mind you—he took one leg and then the other and did it for her. Then, in the limited light from a cloudy night, he carried her to the couch.

"The doctor told you no heavy lifting." Which had completely slipped her mind the two times he'd hoisted her up against a wall and held her there. Bad nurse.

"Nice try."

He sat down with her facing him, her thighs spread across his lap, pulled her chest to his, and covered them both with a knit blanket. "Now talk."

"I delivered both girls vaginally and my doctor told me I could resume sexual activity at six weeks."

"Good." He thrust his hips up.

"I *could*," she emphasized. "Not I *should* or I *had to*. And upon further consideration I've decided to wait." She tried to slide off of him. No chance of that happening. But in her wide open state, with him still impressively firm, her attempts provided some much welcome stimulation which ramped up her heretofore waning arousal. Yum! She started to rock in earnest. "My goodness, I like this position."

"Me, too." He pushed down on her butt while he moved beneath her, skilled at massaging the exact right spot. "Just think. All I have to do is unzip my pants, slip on a condom and I could be inside you. Ten seconds tops."

Worked for her. End of conversation about her body. A night of fabulous sex with Justin sober and at the top of his game. A night to indulge and be thankful for this last randy rendezvous with all her parts present and in full working order. She fought the urge to shave off precious seconds by telling him to forget the condom she was on birth control—because never again would she leave her protection to someone else. But the condom was the right choice for reasons other than preventing pregnancy and even with her good sense hazy with lust, she knew that. "Do it." She reached between them to help.

He clasped her hands in his. "After you explain your vampire-like exposed to sunlight routine when I turned on the light."

Party pooper. "Here I was just starting to enjoy myself again." And she could tell he was, too. So, taking advantage of his arousal, she rubbed her breasts from side to side across his chest making sure to shift her body over his erection at the same time. "Sex now. Talk later." Much. And if he happened to fall asleep before the talking, and she happened to slip away in the dead of night to go take care of her babies? Oh well.

"Talk now." He stayed her hips "Sex every hour on the hour until we're too exhausted to move, later."

A tempting offer. A wonderful, stupendous, amazingly excellent offer. Except for the talk now. "You're so eager to know? You can't wait until morning? You want to ruin absolutely everything?"

He didn't respond. Didn't move.

She sat up. "Fine. My body. It's not the same as the last time we were together."

He sat in silence. Waiting. Darn stubborn man.

She let out a breath. Might as well get it over with so she could get home and get some sleep before the twins woke up. "I've got stretch marks, okay? Ugly red stretch marks from the pregnancy. They're a total turn off and I had hoped to get through this night without you seeing them." She pushed off his chest and started to climb off his lap. "You happy now?"

"Wait." He palmed her hips and held her in place.

"I decide what turns me on and what turns me off. Not you."

"Trust me, you like pretty and they are not pretty. Now let me go."

He shifted on the couch, leaned to the side, and holy cow—turned on a lamp.

"Are you kidding me?" She wrapped the blanket fully around her. "Is today opposite day? I say one thing you do another? Rather juvenile if you ask me. As is not taking another person's feelings into account and being plain old mean."

He looked up at her. Serious. Thoughtful. "I think you giving birth to my daughters is a beautiful thing. I think you are a beautiful woman. And a few marks on your skin aren't going to change my mind."

Gonad-guided guy focused on external beauty and women as a recreational activity that he was, she doubted that.

He reached for the edges of the blanket she had clutched tightly in her fists. "Please," he said in such a way she relaxed her hold and allowed him to open the sides of the blanket, giving him a full view of her torso.

To Jena's surprise he showed no immediate reaction as he studied her. She knew what he saw, loose skin around her navel and numerous dark pink squiggly lines at the base of her belly spreading out toward her hips. "They look tender," he said. "Do they hurt?"

"Only my body image," she replied and for some reason felt the need to explain. "The nurse at the doctor's office said they'll fade in time. But I fear my bikini days are over."

He ran a finger down a particularly large, offensive

looking one. "You've been through so much, changes to your body and your life, because of me."

Okay. That was not at all the reaction she'd expected. She studied him back, the strange look on his face. Far from the revulsion she'd expected. More wonder, mixed with concern and was she totally out of her mind to think maybe a bit of caring?

"I wouldn't change a thing," Jena said. Meaning it. "I love the girls. I love being a mother." And she was kind of looking forward to being a wife, cooking for her man, whoever he turned out to be, managing their home and their lives, planning her daughters' futures.

"I still think you're beautiful, Jena," he said, looking up at her, sounding so sincere.

Lying rather convincingly. "Keep talking that blarney and I won't be able to trust anything that comes out of your mouth."

"Okay. You're right," he said with a dramatic sigh. "They're hideous. I can't stand to look at them." He shielded his eyes.

"Hey." She slapped his shoulder. "That's not nice."

He let out an exaggerated huff of frustration. "I can't win. I tell you you're beautiful, you say I'm full of blarney—a word I haven't heard used in casual conversation since Timmy Oswald and I played pirate back in elementary school, by the way. I tell you you're hideous and you tell me I'm not nice. And physically assault me."

"I did not—"

"Is there any pleasing you?" He slid both hands up to her breasts and squeezed her nipples between the V of two fingers while staring down at her sex. He licked his lips and said, "I think I know a way."

The blood drained from Jena's upper body, pooling in hot, pulsing need between her legs. "I hope it involves you finally removing your pants."

He smiled. "Among other things."

Her teenage fantasy about to play out in real heart-pounding, breath-gasping, pleasure-finding life. Starring Jena and Justin as themselves.

"But first," he said. "Kiss me, Jena. Then I'm all yours. Tell me what you want. Show me. Ask me. Anything."

Anything...

I still think you're beautiful, Jena. Kiss me, Jena. Justin made it a point to use her name often and planned to keep repeating it. So there'd be no question. No doubt. So she'd know for certain his every word was intended for her alone.

Jena pressed her lips to his in what turned out to be so much more than the lusty, desirous prelude to sex he'd expected. Starting off slow, with gentle touches moving along his lip line, she cupped his cheeks between her soft palms, before taking the kiss deeper. And not in a physical way. But with a fervor he hadn't expected. Unrestrained affection. A bonding. A sealing of fates and futures.

Yet rather than putting a stop to the surge of intense feelings flowing at him to give her the 'Don't make this out to be more than it is' speech, Justin hugged her close and kissed her back, upping the ferocity. Taking what she offered and giving her more in return. For the first time allowing himself to feel an emotional connection. To the girl who'd watched him from her mansion up on the hill. The woman who'd chosen him as her first and only lover. The mother of his children.

When they finally broke for air Jena said, "I don't want sex."

Disappointment threatened to suffocate him.

"I want you to make love to me."

Can do.

She slowed them down with another soul-searing, yearning-filled, delicately passionate kiss. "Like you would to a woman you really care about. Someone who matters."

Wait a minute. He went rigid. She mattered.

"If you can't... I mean don't want to—" She misunderstood.

"No. It's just—"

"Don't ruin the mood." She kissed him. "It's okay." She moved her fingers to the button of his pants and he let her. While he came to terms with the fact he did care about her. For so many reasons. Like their clandestine encounters in high school. The cakes she made for him. The way she cared for Jaci, his daughters, her patients, and him after he'd been injured.

That he cared for her, too, was the only explanation for the level of fear he'd felt at the thought of her alone in that parking lot, not knowing what those thugs planned to do, were doing to her, and the degree of anger he'd experienced when he'd seen a man slip his arm around her neck in a chokehold. Both disturbing, and so much more powerful than a police officer typically felt for a victim or random acquaintance in a similar situation. And then there was the painful ache that'd tightened his insides at the thought of him and his girls having to live life without her...

"You okay?" she asked.

"Yeah." Considering in the course of the last forty-eight hours his past as he knew it, his present as he lived it, and his future as he'd envisioned it, had all been altered by the woman in his arms.

"Then how about a little help here?" She tugged at the waistband of his pants. "If there's a way to get these off while I'm sitting on your lap I haven't been able to figure it out. The way I see it, either you need to clue me in to the disrobing secret or let go of me so I can move around a little."

That's when he realized he had his arms clamped around her in a bear hug someone three times her size wouldn't have been able to escape. "Sorry." He released her.

"Now that's more like it." In a move sexier than the most seasoned seductress had in her arsenal of allure, Jena slid off his lap, taking his pants and briefs with her. He lifted his butt, grabbing his wallet out of his back pocket and placing it on the arm of the sofa.

She came to a stop, kneeling on the floor at his feet, her lovely, naked body between his now bare thighs. In the light of the lamp she looked him over. "*You're* the one who's beautiful," she said.

At his erection her eyes went wide. Then her tongue made an appearance, glossing her lips and Justin almost lost it. "Not that I wouldn't love for you to do what you're thinking." He reached for his wallet. "But tonight is for you." Mostly.

She smiled. "I like the sound of that."

"Baby, you're going to like what comes next even better." He took out a condom and held it up. "How about we do this together to make sure it's in good working order?"

She nodded.

He ripped open the wrapper and handed her the ring of latex.

She took it while admitting, "I've never done this before."

He liked being the one to share her firsts. He also liked the eager interest in her eyes as she stared at his proud member, standing full and tall. For her.

"Like this." He took her hands and set the condom on the tip. Together they rolled it on. No visible rips or deformities. "Looks good."

"Yessiree, it does," she said. "Now can we *finally* get to the good stuff?"

Oh yeah. He leaned forward and lifted her high enough to get an eyeful of magnificent breasts. "Straddle me." She did, resting her knees on the sofa beside his hips. He shifted them and, using both hands on her bottom, spread her wide and directed her down until the head of his erection slid ever-so-slightly into the slick heat of her opening. Teasing. Tempting. Torturing.

She moaned. "That feels so good."

Yes. It. Did. He said a quick prayer to the God of endurance. "This is only the beginning." He leaned forward and gave her lovely nipples some attention while taking quick, shallow dips inside of her.

"More," she said, her hands gripping the sides of his head below his stiches, holding him close.

He lowered her while pushing up into her moist heat. *Stay in control.* Up then out. *So damn good.* Advancing a bit further each time. *Keep it slow.* Deeper. *Atta girl, take it all.* Until fully surrounded. *Amazing.* "My,

God, you feel good, Jena." He fought the powerful urge
to pound into her, hard and fast, to bring them both to
climax. No more talking. No more waiting. Satisfaction. Now.

But that's not what she wanted. At least it's not what
she'd asked for. *"...make love to me. Like you would to
a woman you really care about. Someone who matters."*
And to do that he'd need to stay in control.

"Hang on," Justin said, wrapping her arms around
his shoulders. And with them still joined together he
pushed up off the couch and cradled her butt in his
hands. "I've got you."

"Now what?" she asked.

He started to walk.

"Oh." She wiggled her bottom. "I like this, too."

And suddenly five years of marriage—to Jena—
didn't seem all that daunting. Hell, neither did ten or
twenty. Balancing her on one hand, he flicked on the
lamp by the bed.

"You scared of the dark?" she asked. Teasing. "Your
electric bill must be astronomical."

"Ha. Ha." He lowered them to the bed. "Next time
we'll do it by candlelight, flashlight, or sans light. Your
call. But for right now I can't wait one more minute." He
set her on her back, went up on his elbows and looked
into her eyes. "To watch you come. Keep your feet
crossed behind my back." He pulled out and sank deep.

She inhaled and arched her spine as her eyes rolled
back in her head.

"You like that." He did it again.

She nodded. "A lot."

"Good." He lowered his mouth to hers and kissed her
deeply. Pressure began to build. *Too soon.* He swiveled

his hips. She moaned. *Good.* He fondled her nipple. She turned her head and groaned. *Better.* "Tell me what you want," he said.

"This," she answered rocking to meet his thrusts. "You."

"I want you, too, Jena." And not just for tonight. "Only you."

Her eyes shot open.

He stared into them. "You matter," he said. "To me." She tightened her inner muscles and squeezed him so tight he lost focus. And it was his turn to close his eyes and take the pleasure she offered. No. Jena first.

He forced his eyes open to find her smiling. "Kegel exercises."

"I'm a fan." He scooted up, made sure each long, deep thrust slid along the epicenter of her arousal, effectively wiping the smile from face, and increased his pace. "You're beautiful, Jena…smart…sexy." He took a moment to try to catch his breath. "We're so good together." In sync. "I—"

"Justin," she cried out.

"Come for me." He reveled in her panting and high-pitched moans.

"Hold me," she cried, reaching for him.

He dropped down, hugging, kissing, and loving her, finding his satisfaction mere seconds after she did. Then he rolled onto his side, taking her with him, to ride out a sweet new life-changing contented bliss in her arms.

The next morning Justin woke to a warm, naked Jena curled up against his side, her head on his upper arm, her leg slung over his thigh. He smiled. A cuddler. And for once he didn't mind. Didn't think about how he could slip away without waking his lover or what excuse he'd use to get rid of her. Quite the opposite, he spent some time enjoying the feel of her, thinking that making it a regular thing, a permanent thing, wouldn't be so bad.

He waited for the dread that typically accompanied thoughts of being stuck with one woman on a long term basis, the resentment and defiance that typically accompanied him feeling forced to do something he didn't want to do, and felt only a happy contentment with the idea of marriage to Jena, with sleeping beside her night after night, living with her and taking care of her and their daughters, his family.

Now all he had to do was convince Jena to marry him.

He glanced at the clock, knowing, good mother that she was, Jena would want to get home before the girls woke up. That gave him about twenty minutes, fifteen to work off his morning arousal and five to bring up the topic of marriage while she was suspended in the afterglow of orgasm.

Carefully, he turned to face her, easing his thigh deeper between her legs, palming her butt, pulling her close which set his growing erection against her belly. He caressed her leg and hip up her side to cup her breast.

She stretched.

"Morning, beautiful," he whispered.

With her eyes still closed she gave him a sleepy smile and rotated her pelvis. "Three times wasn't enough?"

The bed. The shower. The kitchen table after their three a.m. refueling.

"I'm afraid not." It didn't feel like he'd ever get his fill of her. "What do you say?" He turned to his back pulling her on top of him. "We haven't done it like this yet." And she'd sure liked being on top on the couch.

She pushed up on her arms to look at the clock then reached into the bedside drawer where he kept his condoms. Pulling one out she smiled and said, "I think I'd like to try out a quickie."

Compatibility in the bedroom.

They were off to a good start.

Within seconds she had him sheathed and lined up and was sinking down on top of him. "Lean forward and open your legs wider. Up and down." He guided her hips. "Take a little at a time. That's it."

How could she still be so tight after last night? And having twins?

Jena set her hands on his chest and took him deep. "I like this."

He liked her honesty, among other things. "Me, too." He gave up the battle to lie quietly and let her take her pleasure. "Now get moving." He arched his back and drove into her. "Quickie means quick."

She rode him hard and fast, rocking, repositioning, experimenting.

Justin shifted beneath her varying the depth and direction of his thrusts until—

"Oh," she cried out her eyes wide.

Found it.

Holding her steady to maintain their exact position he directed her to, "Lean back and put your hands on my knees."

She did. And he massaged her G-spot over and over.

"My goodness," she said. "That's…"

Yes indeed. He didn't slow down until Jena cried out, flooding him with her pleasure. Justin bent up his knees to keep her from falling, giving him just enough time to grab her arms and pull her forward, where he held her tightly to his chest as he found his own release.

After a few minutes Jena stirred. "That was…" she started.

Indescribably amazing. "Yeah."

"So much better than I'd ever thought possible," she finished.

Providing him with the perfect segue. "I agree." He twirled a finger in one of her unruly curls. "Us together is so much better than I ever thought possible." He hugged her. "You're funny and sweet and caring and beautiful and sexy. And while I doubt I'm the type of guy you ever pictured yourself marrying, I will try my hardest to be a good husband to you and father to our girls. So what do you say? Will you marry me?"

She didn't respond.

"I'll get a ring. A nice one," he said. She just laid there. Limp. Heck, she didn't even seem to be breathing. "Hey." He shook her shoulders. Far from the excited "yes" he'd hoped for, she'd gone catatonic.

"Is this about my stupid 'five years isn't so long' comment? Because that came out all wrong."

Nothing.

Making love to her, making her feel special and cared for hadn't been enough. Justin felt his recently reconfigured plans for the future slipping out of reach. In a last ditch attempt to convince her he broke into a desperate babble. "I know there are no guarantees but we like each other." He looked down at the top of her head. "At least I like you. And I think you like me. And we both want what's best for our daughters. And we're good in the sack so that's a start, right?"

She lifted her head and looked at him with dead eyes. "What if I wasn't beautiful and sexy. And what if we weren't good in the sack? Would you still want to marry me?"

And they were back to that. Damn women and their ability to twist around everything a guy said. He answered one way he was a liar, another way he'd prove her point.

"I didn't think so," she said, pushing off of him and with an evil squint of her eyes, daring him to try and stop her.

"Give a guy a chance to speak, will you?"

She stopped at the side of the bed. Just sat there staring in the direction of his bedroom door, giving him a view of her back.

"You keep asking me questions I don't have the answers to," Justin said, angling his pillows against the headboard. This was a conversation he needed to sit up for. "Do you want me to lie to make you happy? Should I say I will always find you pretty? That I will always love your body no matter what? That from today until the day I die I will never ever find another woman as sexy you?"

She dropped her head to look down at her lap but didn't say a word.

"I can't predict the future, Jena. All I can do is be completely honest in telling you I want to marry you. And I give you my solemn vow to try my hardest, to respect you and take care of you and the girls for at least five years so you meet the terms of your trust."

She stiffened.

He rushed to add, "Does that mean I'm planning to run out and start divorce proceedings the second your fifth check clears? No. Does it mean we're going to live out our entire lives in wedded bliss? I hope so, but I just don't know. What newly married couple does?"

"Did you know my mother died of cancer?" Jena asked.

Finally she spoke. Totally off topic but he'd run with it. "No. I thought she died from pneumonia."

"Secondary to metastatic lung cancer that spread from her breast. I'd been so busy providing her day to day care after the traumatic brain injury, I had no idea the cancer had returned."

Justin had a vague recollection of Jaci mentioning her mother's breast cancer in passing maybe back in seventh or eighth grade.

"From the time of her first diagnosis mom and dad's relationship changed. Cancer wasn't pretty. Cancer showed weakness. Imperfection. Mom tried to maintain life as we knew it but dad started spending more and more time at the office. Chemotherapy made her sick, surgery made her sore and radiation therapy made her too tired to do much of anything."

Justin listened but had no idea where she was headed or what her mother had to do with them getting married.

"At the age of thirteen I took over managing the house and the staff and taking care of mom."

While Jaci spent hours after school and on weekends hanging out with him and their friends.

"When her beautiful blond hair started falling out clump by clump I helped her find ways to hide it. I accompanied her to treatments and held the basin while she vomited and retched. I saw my father, who'd once loved her dearly, look at her with distaste and regret. I watched helplessly as my vibrant, loving mom retreated inside of herself, trying to hide from the sickness and fear, growing more and more depressed as her life spiraled out of control. I gave up my teens to take care of her, and while I wouldn't have had it any other way, I refuse to put my daughters in the same position."

Wait a minute. Justin moved to sit beside her on the bed. "Are you trying to tell me you have breast cancer like your mother?" At the age of twenty-four? Were they doomed to months instead of years? Would he have to raise their daughters without her?

CHAPTER SEVEN

"No. Goodness, no," Jena said, feeling very naked and self-conscious with him sitting next to her.

"Thank God." He sounded relieved.

Unfortunately the story didn't end there. "But I tested positive for the BRCA2, commonly referred to as the breast cancer gene, mutation, which means I have an increased lifetime risk of developing breast and/or ovarian cancer accompanied by an increased risk of developing those cancers at an early age." Before menopause.

She stood and walked toward the door, trying not to think about him watching her naked butt jiggle.

"Hey. We're in the middle of a conversation here. Where are you going?"

"To get my clothes." She came to her turquoise lace bra hanging off the back of a black leather recliner chair first and slipped it on.

"I'm trying real hard to understand, but I think I'm going to need some clarification, small male brain and all." Justin strolled into the living room wearing a pair of navy boxer briefs and nothing else, his body absolute perfection, a total distraction. "What exactly does your mom having cancer and you taking care of her have to do with us getting married?"

Did he honestly miss the part about her having a significantly increased risk of developing the disease, too? Jena pulled up her matching lace panties, stepped into last night's scrub pants and glanced at the clock on the microwave in Justin's kitchen. "I have time for the short version." She tied the string at her waist.

Justin sat down on the couch, leaned back calm as can be and crossed his ankle over his knee. "Go."

Jena picked up her scrub top.

"You know I think I'd enjoy what you're about to tell me a lot more if you kept that off." He smiled.

She pulled it over her head. "I found the first painful lump in my breast at age twenty."

His smile vanished.

"Since that first lump I've found two more for a total of three in four years. The most recent five months ago."

"Jena." He sat up, Mr. Relaxation transformed into Mr. Concern. "I had no idea."

She cocked her head. "You know this will go a lot quicker if you save all comments and questions to the end." Please just let her say what had to be said without making her discuss every detail.

"Sorry," he said, leaning back. "Go on."

"That's three painful lumps, three rounds of repeat diagnostic testing, and three needle biopsies, the second one followed by a small lumpectomy, which were all negative, thank goodness." She bent over to slip on a sock.

"But each time, from finding the lump until I got back the final laboratory report, I spent day and night in a state of panic. What if it's cancer? What stage is it? What are my treatment options? My prognosis? My life expectancy?" She slipped on the other sock. "This last time was particularly rough." Being pregnant with twins, away from home, and unable to visit her regular doctors.

"I can't even imagine," he said quietly, more to himself than her, so she let it slide.

"I'm a mother now. A single mother responsible for two babies. What happens to them if I get sick and can't care for them? What happens if I die?" And per usual, whenever she thought of her daughters growing up without her, Jena's chest burned with sadness and a lump of despair balled in her throat.

"I—" Justin started.

"No." Jena held up a finger and cut him off. Because for the purposes of her decision making, the issue was not who would care for the twins, only that if she did not take action to decrease her risk of developing cancer, it might not be her wiping their tears, kissing them goodnight, or cuddling with them before bed. It most likely would not be her talking to them about boys or shopping for their prom dresses or planning their weddings. And no matter how loving her replacement might be, the overwhelmingly distressing fact that it would be someone other than Jena left her heartbroken.

"I can't live with the threat of cancer looming," she went on. "Feeling like I'm on death row, my days on earth numbered, not worrying about *if* it will strike but *when*. I need to take control of my life. For me. For my daughters." She slipped her feet into her clogs, walked to the recliner, and sat down facing Justin. "I've researched my situation and learned about genetic testing. I spent hours with a geneticist—which is largely responsible for maxing out my credit cards—discussing the risks and possible outcomes of testing, addressing why I wanted the test, what I planned to do with the information, and convincing her I wouldn't allow a positive result to negatively affect my life and my relationships."

"Yet you *are* letting it negatively affect *our* relationship," Justin pointed out.

Maybe, but to protect them both. "Well we didn't have a relationship at the time. And it's not affecting our relationship in the way you think." How to explain... "People handle the results of their genetic testing differently. I've decided to take a proactive approach. I have two first degree relatives—my mother and her sister—who were both diagnosed with breast cancer before menopause. My aunt found her first lump around age twenty-five. Stage three. She died before her thirtieth birthday."

Justin looked stunned.

Try sharing genetics with a woman first diagnosed at the age Jena would be turning in two and a half months.

"My mom didn't make it to fifty, granted she had other contributing factors. As for me, at a young age I've been diagnosed with dense breasts, another risk factor for developing breast cancer, and I've tested positive for a harmful genetic mutation. Yet instead of feeling doomed, I feel empowered."

His mouth opened but nothing came out.

So she kept the conversation going. "Because based on my research and evaluation of my cancer risk and the results of my genetic testing I can make a rational, educated, informed decision on how I want to proceed. *Before* cancer invades my life. I'm in control." Jena took a deep fortifying breath in preparation for the next part. "Which is why I've decided to undergo bilateral prophylactic mastectomies with immediate reconstruction and, at some date in the future, after I decide for certain

I don't want any more children, but no later than age thirty-five, a total abdominal hysterectomy."

Justin stared at her blankly. Information overload. Understandable. Been there.

"Prophylactic?" he asked.

"As in preventative or protective. Removing the breast tissue will significantly *reduce* my risk of developing breast cancer."

"Does it eliminate the risk?"

"No." She shook her head. "Because it's impossible to remove all the breast tissue."

"So." He stood. "Just so I'm sure I understand." He crossed one arm over his waist, rested the elbow of the other on his wrist, and traced his goatee in a downward motion with his index finger and thumb. "You're planning to have two major elective—am I correct in assuming they're elective?" He looked down at her for confirmation.

She nodded

"Two major *elective* surgeries that will disfigure your body and put you at risk for any number of surgical complications, because there's a chance that you *may*, at some point in the future, develop cancer." He moved both hands to his hips. "And you honestly think *you're* in control not the threat of cancer?"

"I can do without your sarcasm, thank you very much." Jena stood, too. "I knew you wouldn't understand and that you'd completely miss the point and focus in on the breast surgery and nothing else. Because heaven forbid the woman you marry didn't have big, beautiful, *real* breasts. They're your favorite part of the female anatomy, after all. And that, in a nutshell, is why no, I won't marry you. Bottom line, it's my body, and I decide how I will take care of it. You," she pointed, "don't get a say."

She turned to leave but stopped short to look over her shoulder and add, "And for the record, deciding to have surgery to significantly decrease my high risk of developing cancer gives me a control I wouldn't have once the cancer cells invade my body. No chemotherapy. No radiation therapy. No living with the threat of dying," she ticked each one off on her index, middle then ring finger, "day after day for months while waiting to see if the treatments were effective. You don't know what it's like." Tears leaked out of her eyes and ran down her cheeks as she remembered her mother's torturous battle against the disease. "As long as I have the choice, I choose life. And if choosing life means I have to live it without a pair of breasts and a uterus, then so be it." Jena continued on to the door, had to leave or she'd collapse to the ground exhausted by this journey, trying to be strong and independent but feeling so very alone.

"What about Jaci?" Justin asked quietly, stopping Jena dead in her tracks. "What does she think about all this? What's she going to do?"

Jena whipped her head around. "She doesn't know and you can't tell her. Promise me you won't tell her."

"You mean you have the deadly cancer gene and you haven't told your identical twin sister who likely has it, too?" he chastised.

Like Jena would willfully, and with a total disregard for her sister's wellbeing, withhold potentially lifesaving information. "It's a genetic mutation and she knows I went for testing but asked me not to share the result. And I respect that. She knows her risk is the same as mine and she's chosen regular cancer screening for early detection."

"Which makes perfect sense." Justin threw his hands up in the air.

"For her," Jena stressed. "She hasn't had three cancer scares in four years. She's not a mother. Maybe when she has children she'll change her mind, maybe she won't. It's *her* choice. And when our girls turn eighteen, I plan to be around to discuss their choices, as a living example that a strong family history of breast cancer and positive genetic testing isn't a death sentence, as a role model for taking control and seeking options. I will help them get the most up-to-date medical and treatment information. Then I'll support their decision regarding how they want to proceed." So they didn't have to go it alone like she had.

"If you wanted to keep the surgery quiet, why come home? Why not do it in South Carolina or anywhere but here?"

Because she needed to give Jaci time to get accustomed to caring for her nieces and make sure she'd be comfortable with the role of guardian. And she needed to be close by in case something went wrong with the surgery so Jaci could assume the responsibility immediately. "Some of the best doctors and hospitals in the world are within an hour of here. My doctor, who I trust implicitly, is here." Jena turned to pick up her sweater. "Now if you'll excuse me."

"No," Justin said. "I won't excuse you." He joined her in the entryway, crossed his arms over his chest and leaned his shoulder against the door, looking like he had no intention of moving any time soon. "So far you've been doing the majority of the talking and now I'd like a turn."

Jena took her watch out of her pocket and checked the time.

"Jaci and or Mandy will take care of the twins if they wake up. Now answer me this," he said. "What happens to *our* daughters if something goes horribly wrong during your surgery and you don't survive? Don't look at me like that. You're a nurse, you know all about complications and surgical risks. Don't tell me they hadn't crossed your mind."

Of course they had. The risks and benefits of going through with the surgeries had been clogging her mind for months. Day and night. "I've had legal documents drawn up, signed and witnessed in the presence of my attorney. If I should become incapacitated, Jaci has my power of attorney and can make decisions on my behalf. If I should…," thinking about it was bad enough but saying it out loud, actually hearing the words was excruciatingly difficult, she cleared her throat, "die, everything I have goes to the girls and the girls go to Jaci who's agreed if anything happens to me she'll adopt them and love them, provide for them, and raise them as close to how I would want them raised as she can manage." Although she didn't know it, Jena had left a guide of very detailed instructions with her attorney.

"Unacceptable," Justin yelled.

"You have no say," Jena yelled back.

"Now that's where you're wrong." He lowered his voice and narrowed his eyes. "I may not have a say in how you treat your body, but I most certainly have a say in the lives of *my* daughters, and I refuse to allow you to put me in a position where I have to fight someone for custody."

Jena grabbed the kitchen counter for support. "I didn't think you'd—"

He leaned in, angry, crowding her. Jena took a step back. "Because apparently *you* don't know *me* all that well, either. I'm not the boy you knew in high school. I'm a responsible adult, and I am determined to do what's best for *our* daughters, which is why you *will* marry me and you'll do it *before* your surgery."

"But—"

"This isn't about you or me, Jena. This is about doing what's best for Abbie and Annie. It's about them settling in here and getting comfortable with me, and me learning to take care of them before, God forbid something happens to you, so they'll have the stability of familiar surroundings and at least one parent in their lives."

Justin made sense, and she'd be lying if she didn't admit a teeny tiny part of her may have, in private and without her permission, hoped for this very outcome. But, "There's no way—"

"You need to get married. I want to marry you. Why are you making this so difficult? Do you find me so objectionable—?"

"If you'd let me finish," Jena interrupted him. "Regardless of what either of us wants, there's no way we'll be able to get married before my surgery."

Justin stood totally still. Watched her. Understanding dawned. "It's already scheduled. How? You just got your money back. You have no insurance. And how did you plan to sneak off and have the surgery without Jaci finding out?"

"The Piermont name carries a lot of clout here in

Westchester County," Jena explained. "I met with my doctors, their staff, and representatives from the hospital who agreed to wait for payment of their exorbitant private pay rates until my birthday."

"Rather confident you'd find a husband," Justin pointed out.

Jena shared the harsh, disgusting truth. "Money can buy almost anything." Even a man willing to marry a fake-boobed mother of two. "Anyway, as for keeping it from Jaci, while working for Jerald, I've planned parties and coordinated rooms at all the major hotels in the area. And I handled all the scheduling of my mother's care. A quick couple of phone calls and I had a two room suite courtesy of the Piermont Enterprises account." She smiled. Her rat of a brother owed her. "And a nurse to stay with me and the girls for two weeks."

"What'd you tell Jaci?"

Nothing yet. She hated lying to her sister. It was too hard to think of saying good bye, telling her everything that needed to be said in case...

As if he understood her anguish he didn't wait for an answer. "When?"

"Wednesday." In two days.

Justin pulled out a chair from under the kitchen table and sat down. "So soon."

Two. Days.

Jena made the short distance between the counter and the kitchen table on numb legs, pulled out a chair and inelegantly plopped onto it. After weeks of fending off their attacks, doubt and indecision fought through her thin protective layer of certainty that surgery ASAP was the right path to take. Instead of being proactive was she actually being over-reactive? But the same ar-

gument against waiting waged a counter attack. Aunt
Lynnie's breast cancer was diagnosed at stage III at age
twenty-five, which Jena would turn in too short a time.
Were the deadly mutant cells already multiplying inside
her body? Was she already too late? Was she going to
ruin her physical appearance and her sex life and her
chance at a real marriage, real love, only to be stricken
down by the disease anyway?

Justin eyed her with concern. "We're going to get
through this," he said. So sure. So Confident.

Jena wanted to place her palms on some part of his
body to draw on his strength to replenish her depleted
reserves. She looked up at him. "We?" She wasn't his
problem. This wasn't his concern. Jena would handle it
on her own, like she handled everything else.

He placed his hand, palm up, on the table, stared into
her eyes and waited.

She needed to touch him, feel him, absorb his certainty of a positive outcome, so she placed her hand
in his larger one which he tightened around her. For
some reason the gesture gave her hope, made her feel
safe and protected.

"My mom left when I was two," Justin said, looking at the table as if remembering. "When I was old
enough to understand, Grandma Abbie told me it was
because my dad didn't take care of my mom the way
she needed to be taken care of. I remember telling her
when I grew up I'd do such a good job of taking care of
my wife she'd never leave me. And I'd take such good
care of my kids they'd love me forever. Grandma Abbie
smiled," and so did he at the memory, "patted my head
and called me a good boy." He shifted his gaze to their

joined hands, loosened his grip, and ran his thumb back and forth over the backs of her fingers.

"Then Grandma Abbie died, leaving me alone with my dad for so many years, and I forgot my promise to her. As I grew I started following dad's egocentric example, becoming more and more like him each year. Oh I'd tell myself I was a better person. A better man. That given the chance I would be a better husband and father. Then, like on some subconscious level I thought myself incapable, I never let any woman get close enough for anything resembling a relationship so I wouldn't fail." He looked up.

"Then you came along and gave me two beautiful daughters who each share a part of us. Never have I wanted to do the right thing as much as I do now. You're my chance, Jena." He added his other hand hers in both of his. "To prove I'm a better man than my dad. To prove I'm worthy of being a husband and a father. That I'm capable of taking care of a family the right way. The way I'd promised my Grandma Abbie I would. The way you and the girls deserve. Let me, Jena. Give me that chance. Marry me."

Jena's eyes watered at his heartfelt words. She wanted so much to say yes. But the thought of Justin looking at her with the distaste and regret she'd seen in her father's eyes when he'd looked at his wife's post-surgical body kept her quiet.

"Say something," Justin prompted.

She couldn't.

"You okay?" he asked, squeezing her hand.

No. She was so far from okay she doubted they were even in the same time zone. "I need time to think." She yanked her hand from his and stood. "And you need to get ready for work." She hurried toward the door. "We can talk about this later." And she ran from his condo like the coward she was.

Later that night, after a hellacious shift on his day job, and a stop at a jewelry store after his ten hour day, Justin returned home to his quiet condo hungry, dirty and exhausted, yet determined to convince Jena to marry him despite the niggling apprehension that'd cropped up during the day. He threw his keys on the counter noticing one of Jena's amazing chocolate cakes sitting on an elegant crystal plate at the center of his kitchen table. He picked up the card beside it and read the inscription out loud, "Sorry I missed your birthday. Hope it was happy. If you're hungry when you get home I made you a meatloaf. It's in the refrigerator. Jena."

Not the "Yes I'll marry you" he'd hoped for, but thoughtful and appreciated. With all she had going on she'd taken time out of her day to cook for him. Because, he'd realized over the past couple of days, that's what Jena did. She took care of others. And while he considered himself fortunate to be on the receiving end of her caring, he couldn't help but wonder who took care of her?

Fifteen minutes later, showered and changed, Justin sat down to dinner and an ice cold beer. He took a forkful of actual home-cooked meal into his mouth, closed his eyes, and almost wept with joy. Man she could cook!

His hesitation toward marriage eased a bit. Hoping to alleviate it further—believing knowledge is power— Justin pushed his plate to the side and reached for his laptop, needing to learn about Jena's genetic condition, the surgical procedure she would be undergoing and the

care she'd need afterward. And while he was at it, he
hoped gain some understanding as to what would drive
a perfectly healthy young woman to undergo a drastic
body-altering surgery that carved off a female's most
prominent, identifiable and let's be honest, arousable
attributes of her sexual identity.

Once booted up he typed in keyword: breast cancer gene. Over the next three hours he added BRCA2,
mother with breast cancer, dense breasts cancer risk,
treatment breast cancer, survival rates breast cancer,
and prophylactic bilateral mastectomies to his search.

He scanned dozens of articles, both technical medical pieces and detailed personal accountings from
women, some Jena's age, a few in various stages of
dealing with cancer others recovering from prophylactic bilateral mastectomies. And blogs. With pictures.
He could have done without the pictures. Yet some unknown force had compelled him to look.

By the time he shut down his computer Justin had
a newfound understanding of Jena's plight and accep-
tance of her plan. But thanks to the pictures, he also
had a newfound concern over whether he actually possessed the strength of character necessary to give Jena
what she would need to help her through recovery and
dealing with the altered body image he'd read about.
He shook his head to scatter the images now plaguing
him. Scarred, unnatural, irregularly shaped mounds.
Without nipples.

Suddenly Jena's willingness to marry a gay man
made sense, to avoid rejection from a straight man. A
man like Justin.

Would he still be attracted to her after surgery?
Would his body respond to her in the same way it did

now? God help him, what if he wasn't? What if it didn't? What if he couldn't?

Idiot. He smacked both palms on the table, the burn bringing his focus where it belonged. This wasn't about sex and it wasn't about him. It was about Jena, the mother of his daughters, an integral member of their four person family unit. And the tremendous respect he had for her strength in making what had to be an excruciatingly difficult decision meant to prolong her life in the face of a well-documented, very real, and significantly elevated risk of developing cancer.

A decision he'd belittled by making it about breast removal, when it was really about so much more. Selfish jerk.

Her words haunted him. *As long as I have the choice, I choose life. And if choosing life means I have to live it without a pair of breasts and a uterus, then so be it.* And, *I am more than a pair of breasts.*

Yes she was. Jena Piermont was a dedicated, loving mother, an amazingly strong, courageous woman who he'd be lucky and honored to have as a wife. And he couldn't wait until morning to tell her. He picked up his cell phone to check the time. Ten thirty-one. He didn't want to wake her or the babies. So he dialed Ian.

"Hey," he said when Ian answered. "What's going on down there?"

"Well, Jaci's out of her mind with worry about Jena. She's been pacing back and forth and talking to herself for the past half hour."

"Who's on the phone?" Jaci asked in the background. "Is that Justin? Give me the phone."

"Good luck," Ian said. Then Jaci came on. "Justin

Rangore you had better tell me what's going on with my sister or our friendship is over."

"Hi, Jaci."

"Don't you 'Hi, Jaci' me all friendly like nothing's wrong. Jena's gone quiet. She barely said two words since Ian and I got home from work. From the looks of my condo and my refrigerator she's been cooking and cleaning all day, typical upset Jena behavior. She served us this elaborate feast for dinner then disappeared into her room without eating a bite. Something's going on and I know you know what it is."

Yeah, he did. And as much as he'd like to confide in Jaci and or Ian, his two closest friends, he couldn't. "I'm coming down," Justin said, disconnecting the call before Jaci could protest. Then he retrieved the engagement ring he'd bought for Jena—because even if they couldn't marry before her surgery, at least they could be officially engaged. And his emergency key to Jaci's condo—in case she went all angry and refused to open the door. And one, no, three condoms—because he was a guy and guys always remained hopeful, and therefore, should always be prepared.

Too impatient to wait for the elevator he took the stairs down. To find Ian casually leaning with his back to the hallway wall beside Jaci's door, waiting for him. "I'm supposed to stop you from coming in," he said half-joking when Justin reached him.

"You going to try?" If he wanted a fight Justin would give him one.

"Nah." He held up two fingers. "On two conditions."

"Name them."

"One, you look me in the eyes and promise me that

you talking to Jena right now is going to make things better and not worse."

Justin looked him in the eyes. "I promise." At least he hoped.

"Two, you give me some bit of information to relay to Jaci so she'll calm down enough for me to get her into bed." Ian smiled. "I'll take it from there."

Justin reached into his pocket, took out the velvet ring box he'd stashed there, and opened the lid to expose the two-carat emerald cut diamond ring, the sales lady assured him Jena would love, inside. She damn well better for all it cost him. "Tell Jaci, I'm here to propose to Jena." And to let Jena know he supported her decision to opt for surgery and would stand by her and take care of her and the girls. His family. That she wasn't alone.

Ian held out his hand to shake Justin's. "Congratulations, man." Their hands clasped together, Ian jerked Justin forward and they bumped shoulders in a male sort of hug.

"I need a favor," Justin said when they parted. "You okay with moving out so I can move Jena and the girls upstairs with me tomorrow?'"

Ian smiled. "What's your rush?"

If only Justin could tell him. "You okay with that or not? You're sleeping down here every night anyway."

"Tomorrow night work?" Ian asked as he slowly pushed open the door.

"The earlier the better."

Ian looked back. "Keep it down," he whispered. "Mandy and Maddie are asleep in the living room. Jena's door is closed. Not sure what she's doing but there's no noise coming from her room so I'm guessing the twins are asleep."

By the light over the kitchen sink, Justin followed Ian into the condo and down the hall to Jena's room. He knocked lightly. She didn't answer. He tried the doorknob. Unlocked. So he turned it and as quiet as he could so he didn't wake the twins, pushed into the dark room. "Jena?" he whispered.

A lamp lit up in the far corner of the crowded room revealing two cribs end to end along one wall, a changing table and bureau along another. A laundry basket of folded pink and yellow baby clothes sat on the floor. Two car seats lay stacked one on top of the other in a corner. Two baby swings. Two lay on the floor and play with the dangling thingies things. And hardly any room to move.

"Justin?" Jena whispered. "Is something wrong?"

Their cramped living area for one thing. "Where did all this stuff come from?"

"I wanted to make the condo look nice for Ian and Jaci so I moved all of Abbie and Annie's stuff in here so everyone would stop tripping over it."

She sat up in the bed her hair a mess, her eyes puffy and rimmed in red, the tip of her nose a dark pink and asked, "What are you doing here?"

"I've spent the last couple of hours on the computer doing research, which is why I'm down here so late. Sorry about that, by the way."

"No problem," she said, looking at him. Wary. "What did you research?"

"The breast cancer gene. Breast cancer in general. Prophylactic bilateral mastectomies."

She threw her pretty, bare legs over the side of the bed. "If you came down here to try to talk me out of—"

He sat down beside her. "I came down to tell you I am humbled by your courage."

She stared at him with watery blue eyes.

"I can't imagine what it must be like to be in your situation, and if I were, I don't know if I'd have the balls to do what you're planning to do." He took her small hands into his, brought them to his lips and kissed her knuckles. "There's no one I would rather have as a role model for our daughters than you. They need you. *We* need you. And selfish man that I am, I want you to take advantage of whatever treatment will enable you to remain here on earth with us for as long as possible."

Tears spilled out of the corners of both of her eyes.

"You were right," he said, feeling somewhat choked up himself. "You are so much more than a pair of breasts. You're the mother of my children, a woman I care about, a woman who matters to me."

She reached for a tissue and dabbed at her nose. "Thank you. But—"

"No buts." Justin stood, pulled the ring box from his pocket and went down on one knee. "I don't know what the future will bring." He flipped open the lid and tilted the sparkly diamond in her direction. "I *do* know that I want you, me, Abbie and Annie to be a family, a real, traditional family that lives together and takes care of one another. Not to be a complete cornball, but in sickness and in health, in good times and in bad." He looked up at her and tilted his head. "You want me to keep going?"

She gave him a small, almost shy smile and shook her head.

"So what do you say, Jena? Will you marry me?"

The smile faded.

"Before you answer there's something I think you should know," he started out, hoping to make a point. "It's not easy keeping this physique in tip top shape. And with me being a family man and all I doubt I'll have much time to get to the gym." He stuck out his belly and patted it. "Based on tonight's sampling of your culinary skills, I'm thinking there's a real good chance if you marry me you may be taking on a future three-hundred-pounder. You willing to marry me knowing that in the months and years to come my body may look totally different than it looks right now?"

More tears leaked out of her eyes. But she gifted him with a small nod.

"Are you willing to marry me, *knowing* that my body *will* soon look and feel different than it does right now?" she asked in a soft voice.

He stared into her eyes. "Yes." He removed the ring from the box and held it out to her. "Jena Piermont, will you do me the honor of becoming my wife."

While she thought about it Justin's heart proved it is actually possible for a heart to beat against a ribcage. Or at least feel that way.

"I'll accept your ring," she said slowly, looking down at him. "I'll agree to get engaged on one condition."

"Anything."

"If, after my surgery, you find me…unattractive…"

"I won't," he said, meaning it, wanting it, praying he could manage it.

She looked away. "And you don't want to…"

"Jena," he said. "Look at me." She turned her head slowly. "Let's get through the surgery first. The rest we'll deal with as it comes up."

"But I want you to promise to be honest with me. To

talk to me about what you're thinking and feeling. And if you change your mind about marrying me it's okay."

"I won't change my mind," he tried to reassure her.

But she went on like he hadn't even spoken. "I couldn't bear you being unhappy, or turning your back on me in bed, or looking at me with revulsion and regret."

Her distress affected him, made him desperate to comfort her. "I promise to be honest with you. But I won't—"

She placed to fingers on his lips to quiet him. "Thank you. That's all I needed to hear." Then she held out her hand and he slid the engagement ring onto her finger.

She lifted her hand up to the light. "This is the most beautiful ring I've ever seen." He doubted that. "I love it." Whew. "It fits perfectly. How did you…?"

"I held the hand of every woman in the store until I found one that fit like yours."

Justin's cell phone went off. He grabbed it to silence the ringtone and looked at the screen. "It's your sister." He held the phone out to Jena.

"She knows?"

"I had to come clean to Ian about my intentions or he threatened not to let me in. But she doesn't know your answer. And since she'll probably come barging in here any minute if you don't tell her…"

Jena took the phone. "Hi, Jaci. Yes, Justin proposed." She smiled. "Yes, I said yes." Jaci screamed loud enough to startle one of the babies. "Shshsh," Jena said. Then she looked up at him, uncertain and said into the phone, "I don't know. Definitely by our birthday."

Justin leaned forward. "But we're moving in together tomorrow." Because his future wife needed him to take care of her and their daughters. He said a quick prayer that he'd be able to do a decent job of it.

"Perfect," Jena said to Jaci. Then, "Now I've got to go. Justin's pawing at my pajamas."

He wasn't but took that as his cue to start.

One of the babies made some sucking noises. Shoot. "How long do we have until they wake up?" he asked, lifting Jena's silky pink negligée over her head. "Love this, by the way."

Jena removed his shirt. "Probably around fifteen minutes." She grabbed his hand and yanked him onto the bed. "Longer if you keep real quiet and you let me turn off the light," she teased.

"Longer is good." He slid her pink lacy panties down to her ankles while she reached for the lamp. "For the record, I am a huge fan of sexy lingerie."

She pulled him down on top of her and whispered, "So am I."

CHAPTER EIGHT

JENA should have added "Frontal lobotomy" to her enormous list of Things To Do The Day Before Surgery, because adding "Move in with Justin", "Cancel hotel reservation and nurse", and "Change will to make Justin the sole legal guardian of the girls" showed a severe decision-making impairment in need of immediate remediation.

But at least she'd kept so busy she hadn't had time to worry and obsess. Which meant she'd probably be up most of the night.

"One slippery baby fresh from the bath." Jena lifted Abbie from her baby tub and handed her into the pink towel draped over Justin's arms. "You have her?"

"I have her." Justin cuddled Abbie close with one hand and wrapped the towel and hood around her with the other. Careful and gentle. The ideal parent.

Jena spread the yellow towel on the bathmat then lifted Annie out of her tub, wrapped her in the yellow towel, and lifted the squirmy baby into her arms.

"You're sure you're ready to go solo?" she asked on the way to the second bedroom.

"Gotta try sometime."

Except for leaving for a few hours to complete the paperwork necessary to take an emergency two-week leave of absence from work, Justin had been by her side all day. Watching. Learning. Helping. She couldn't have asked for more in a fiancé.

"Be a good girl for daddy," Jena said shaking Abbie's little foot through the towel.

Justin smiled. Seemed he liked being called daddy. Which made Jena smile, too.

"Time to get you ready for bed," he said, placing Abbie on the changing table. "And you and your sister better sleep for a good couple of hours because daddy has special plans for mommy tonight."

Since they only had one changing table, Jena set Annie on the bed. "Oh does he?" she asked, an excited tingle taking up residence deep in her core. There was nothing she'd rather do than spend the night before her surgery in Justin's arms. Every night in his arms.

"What the—?" Justin said. "That is not being good for daddy."

Jena looked at the changing table, watched Justin rush to cover Abbie's privates with her towel and laughed. "You've got to be quick."

"She got everything wet," he complained.

"I'll clean it up when we're done," she said. "Come. Join me on the bed."

He looked over his shoulder. "Why, Jena. I'd love to join you on the bed." He wiggled his eyebrows.

"To finish changing Abbie," she specified.

"Spoilsport."

He grabbed the baby wipes, a diaper, rash cream, and a new set of pink PJs and moved to the bed. "No more funny business," he ordered, setting Abbie on the bed next to Annie.

And in typical fashion, while Annie lay quietly,

Abbie started to squirm. He handed her a rattle. Then he got started, concentrating so intensely, Jena didn't think he even realized he was talking himself through it as he went. "Diaper, tabs in the back. Check. Shoot. Clean with a baby wipe first." He did a very thorough job. "*Then* diaper, tabs in the back. Check. Diaper rash cream. Yuk." He wiped his fingers on the towel. "Cover her up. Check. Secure sticky tabs. Check. Yes!" He lifted his hands over his head in victory. "Job well done."

Jena laughed again. Changing the girls had never been this entertaining.

Justin struggled to insert Abbie's kicking feet into the leg openings of her sleeper. "Minor setback." Out of the corner of her eye she caught him watching her. "You make it look so easy. Some trick of the hands for sure."

Abbie started to cry.

"Shshshsh. We don't want mommy to think daddy's incompetent."

Jena smiled. And fell in love with him, trying so hard to do a good job of taking care of his daughter.

"You're far from incompetent," she reassured him. "I've been doing this a lot longer than you have. And I've learned it's easier to hold the leg like this." She took a firm but gentle hold of Annie's leg over her knee. "Then put the sleeper on over the leg rather than trying to put the leg into the sleeper. Does that make sense?"

Justin followed her lead and had Abbie dressed in under a minute. "Works for flailing arms, too."

That it did.

With both babies dressed they moved to the kitchen where Jena supervised Justin making and heating up bottles like she'd taught him earlier, while she held the girls.

Again he concentrated on doing everything exactly as she'd shown him and spoke out loud as he did it. "Take the plastic insert like this—don't touch the inside. And only use bottled water at room temperature." He lifted the jug and poured a measured amount into each bottle. "I measure the powdered formula carefully according to the instructions on the can." Which he double checked. "And I don't change brands without checking with the doctor first." He looked and Jena and she nodded. "I replace the ring and cap and shake." He did.

"Then I unscrew the ring and remove the nipple before placing the bottle in the microwave." He set the microwave as she'd taught him and pressed start. "After heating, I reattach the ring, shake again to eliminate any hot spots, then squeeze out any remaining air into the sink like this."

Abbie arched her back and screamed her displeasure at the formula not being squirted into her mouth.

"Then, even though my daughters are ravenous and crying loud enough to make the neighbors think we're abusing them, which makes me feel like a terrible parent because I am taking so long, I don't, under any circumstances, feed them until I check the temperature of each bottle by squeezing a small amount of formula on the inside of my wrist, like this." He demonstrated.

"Perfect," Jena said when he'd finished. "Now take your daughter." She handed him Abbie, who had become quite the daddy's girl.

Justin smiled proudly. "I feel like I just aced an important test."

"Care to join me on the couch?" she asked. An innocent enough invitation. But Jena's mind wandered to the last time they'd come together on that couch. Both naked with her straddling his lap.

He looked at her with a teasing grin. "Based on that cute blush of yours, you are so thinking what I'm thinking."

Busted.

"To feed our daughters," she clarified because it seemed they both required clarification.

Jena settled into the couch and gave Annie the bottle. Justin must have given Abbie her bottle at the same time because instant quiet. Ahhhhh. "This is my favorite part of the day," Jena said. The peacefulness of sitting in a darkened room, while holding her sleepily relaxed, contentedly sucking daughter or daughters.

"I can see why," Justin said. "But my goal as your future husband will be to make *our* bedtime your favorite part of the day."

If she survived the surgery. If they continued to share a bed. If he wasn't completely turned off by the post-surgical changes in her body. Quick, change the subject. "It's so nice to have help, so each of our daughters can get the individual cuddling she deserves," she said. "Abbie's a gulper so you need to be diligent about burping her after each ounce. No matter how much she protests."

And boy did she protest. "I think this one's going to be trouble," Justin said trying to hold Abbie still while he patted her back.

"Maybe," Jena said calmly. "And if she is, we'll handle it. But please promise me you won't label her. The troublemaker. The wild one. People used to label Jaci and me as a way of telling us apart. We both hated that. And you know what? For as long as I can remember,

people called Jaci 'The Wild One.' Since we were little girls. And she did, in fact, grow up to be 'The Wild
One.' Was it because she was born that way or was she
simply living up to what people expected of her?"

"If I had my guess I'd say she was born that way. But
I get your point. No labels. Promise."

As the girls drifted off to sleep Jena and Justin sat
side by side in companionable silence, until Jena's
thoughts turned to her surgery and dozens of unpleas-
ant "what if" scenarios. She needed to move around,
to work off some of the accumulating nervous energy
and keep her mind busy. So she stood. "I'm tired and I
still have to clean up."

"Hopefully you're not *too* tired," Justin said as he
stood, too.

She wasn't.

He followed her to the cribs and set Abbie down,
gently, on her side, with a rolled blanket at her back and
a light comforter covering her, exactly as she'd shown
him for their nap earlier.

On his way out, he brushed past her, sliding his
front along her back and his chin along her curls. As
he passed he whispered, "I'll do the kitchen. Then I'll
be waiting for you in our bedroom."

Jena almost melted.

She cleaned up the girls' room and the bathroom
on auto-pilot, having done it so often she barely paid
attention anymore, even in her new environment. Her
thoughts filled with tomorrow and what she had to do
beforehand. Show Justin the notebook where she'd written down the girls' routines, likes and dislikes, and important information/telephone numbers. Add Abbie and
Annie's birth certificates and her updated will. She'd

kept Jaci as her Health Care Proxy, couldn't risk Justin shutting down life support prematurely if he changed his mind and decided he wanted to be rid of her. Oh, and she couldn't forget to put out the letters she'd written, just in case.

With the bathroom clean, Jena clipped up her hair and jumped into the shower, wanted tonight to be perfect. But when she stepped out and caught a glimpse of her naked reflection in the mirror she couldn't look away from the sight of her body with two full, beautiful, real breasts. She cupped them, their weighted fullness heavy in her palms. She ran her thumbs over her dark nipples, felt them tighten and the responding needy twinge that traveled all the way down to between her legs. Always so sensitive, so arousing.

The impending loss burned through her. The finality of it. Complete. Permanent.

Cleaning up the kitchen and lighting the three dozen candles he'd placed around his bedroom took Justin all of ten minutes.

Now what?

He went into the master bathroom to wash up and brush his teeth.

Fifteen minutes down.

He stripped off his clothes and pulled on a pair of black satin boxer shorts.

Sixteen minutes.

How long did it take Jena to get ready for bed? At twenty-five minutes he went looking for her, finding the door to the hall bathroom partially closed. He peered through the crack to see her, staring at her naked torso in the large mirror over the sink, tracing the shape of her exquisite breasts with her fingers, looking sad.

He knocked softly as he pushed open the door.

She didn't flinch or move to cover herself, mesmerized by her reflection. "I'm saying goodbye," she said.

Justin walked up behind her, covered her hands with his, and leaned down to whisper in her ear. "Come to bed so we can say goodbye together."

"In a minute," she said.

Yeah right. She'd already had twenty-five minutes.

"Thank you for today." She looked at him via the mirror. "For taking time off from your job and working so hard to learn the girls' routines and get us settled in. I really appreciate it."

And he appreciated her giving him the opportunity to step up and do the right thing. "You're welcome." He caressed her breasts and now her hands rested on top of his. She closed her eyes and let her head drop back to his collar bone, elongating her neck.

"I've been thinking." He bent to dot a line of kisses down the side of her neck. "I've decided it's time for me to find a new favorite female body part," he said. "Breasts are so yesterday." He moved his hands to her hips, kissed back up her neck and dipped his tongue into the small cove at the base of her ear.

She tilted her head to give him better access and moaned.

"I think this is the spot. The delicate curve of a woman's neck." He kissed his way back down. "*My* woman's neck," he specified.

"Perfect," she said on an aroused sigh.

Perfect indeed.

"Now come," he prompted.

"In a minute, I promise." She moved his hands and gave him a gentle shove toward the door. "I want to make myself pretty for you."

"The clock starts now," he turned her, kissed her lips, and pressed his growing erection against her. "I can't wait much longer."

A few minutes later she stood in the doorway to his, no their, bedroom looking at all the candles and every second he'd waited had been worth it. Speech eluded him. Never in all his days had he seen a vision lovelier than Jena at that moment in time, her loose curls teasing at the thin straps of a pale pink, knee-length silk negligee with a deep, tantalizing V that dipped between her breasts and two sexy side slits that showed off plenty of leg. On her feet she wore a pair of silver stilettoes which matched the silver earrings dangling from her ears. He met her at the door. "You are...stunning."

"The room looks beautiful all lit up with candles."

Especially for her. He knew she'd like it. "*You* look beautiful." And alluring. And his. And he wanted her. Now.

"Thank you," she said. "And thank you for going out of your way to make this night special." She leaned in to kiss his cheek, her silky body pressed to his, her aroused nipples poking his chest. He refused to think about her surgery and changes that may or may not occur in their sex life as a result. Because right now he had his sexy fiancée in his arms and nothing would keep him from making this night off the charts amazing.

He backed her toward the bed. "You smell so good." Fragrant. Floral. Enticing.

"You feel so good." She ran her soft hands up his

chest, over his shoulders then down his arms. "So strong." She set a soft, sweet kiss on his right pectoral.

He pulled her close reveled in the feel of her, thread his fingers through her hair, angled her head so he could plant a lusty kiss on her luscious lips. On contact a potent arousal surged through his system. His body hardened in response. "You drive me wild, Jena Piermont." He kissed her again, slid his tongue into the slick heat of her mouth, over and over until he needed to break for air. "I want to take things slow, to linger and make tonight last, but I don't know if I can."

"I don't want slow right now." She pushed down his boxers which dropped to the floor at his feet. "Save it for next time." She cupped him and he almost finished before he'd started.

He moved her hand, lifted her negligee over her head and followed her down to the bed where he lavished attention on her breasts. Caressed them, kissed them, squeezed and sucked and loved them. And said his goodbyes before moving down to the elastic of her panties. "These have to go." He shimmied down to her ankles with them and slid them over her sexy heels before kissing his way back up. "Open for me." She bent her knees and dropped each to the side so he could get to her inner thighs. Higher.

She moaned and writhed and clutched his head tightly as he tasted and enjoyed her. "Please," she begged. "I need you." She pulled his hair. "Make love to me. Now."

They were of one mind. He crawled on top of her, not taking the time to expose the fancy new sheets he'd bought for her, reached for a condom and rolled it on. He positioned himself for entry. "Are you ready?"

"I feel like I've been waiting for this moment my entire life."

Oddly enough, "Me, too." He nudged her entrance, found her wet and ready, and thrust into her tight, slick heat. She wrapped her arms and legs around him, contracted her muscles, and squeezed him inside and out. Fully ensconced. The sensation wonderful. Astounding. So. Damn. Good. "My, God, Jena. You feel so unbelievably fantastic. I'm afraid if I move I'll—"

She rocked her hips and that was it. Justin thrust into her, over and over, got lost in her depths, went out of his mind with lust. "You feel so good, baby." He kissed her. Felt a connection, more than sex. Caring. He wanted to please her, to make her happy, to make her love him. Pressure started to build. He needed release. But not without her. He slipped a hand between them.

"Oh my heavens that feels good," Jena cried out, panting and rocking into his touch.

Oh my heavens. Only Jena. He smiled.

She dug her fingers into his back, clamped her legs about his butt, and urged him deeper. "Yes."

He fought for control. Needed to wait. "Come on, baby. Come for me." Now. Please.

She tightened around him.

He rode out her orgasm then let go, his release powerfully satisfying. On a scale of one to ten, a twenty-five, with an intensity people dream of, but few are ever lucky enough to achieve.

"Goodness gracious, I love you," Jena said dreamily on a long, contented sigh.

The aftereffects of best-sex-ever talking. But it got Justin thinking of how nice it would be to be loved by Jena. To hold hands and cuddle on the couch, to know

that his safe return home from work mattered to someone and over dinner that same someone was eager to
engage in conversation about his and her day. He rolled
to the side, taking her with him, still joined together,
and held her close. He kissed her forehead, realizing
he wanted her to love him. And he wanted to love her
and for their marriage to be real and happy and not
only for the sake of their children or to gain release of
a trust fund.

CHAPTER NINE

A FEW short hours later, after a night of loving Jena would never forget, it was time to go. She looked around the condo wondering if this was the last time she'd ever see it. Justin's stomach growled. "You're silly for not eating breakfast," she said.

To which he replied, "Like I already told you, if you can't eat I'm not going to eat."

Too sweet.

He pushed the double stroller out the door to head up to Mrs. Calvin's, who'd agreed to watch the girls overnight. Jena popped her head out the door and said, "I'll meet you upstairs. There's one more thing I need to do." She pulled each of the four letters she'd written, just in case, out of her folder. She sorted through them once again to check that they were all there. One for Jaci. One for Abbie. One for Annie. And one for Justin. Each sealed with a lipstick kiss. She kissed each one again for good measure and set them on the kitchen table. "God willing you'll never have to read them."

Justin drove Jena to the hospital where he accompanied her to the plastic surgeon's office to get marked prior to surgery. Then he remained by her side, holding her hand, his presence calming and reassuring, until the nurse denied him access to the surgical suite. He leaned over the railing on the stretcher, kissed her on the lips and whispered. "I am not leaving this hospital without you."

A few minutes later, as the anesthesiologist administered her medication, while she counted back from fifty, Jena thought about Justin's last loving kiss and his emotion-filled expression as he told her, "*I am not leaving this hospital without you*" and felt at peace.

Jena emerged from sedation unable to move but aware of sounds. A monitor beeped out a steady rhythm. People talked, Justin and a male voice she didn't recognize. She tried to open her eyes but couldn't. She swallowed. Her mouth felt dry.

She drifted back to sleep.

The next time she awoke to quiet, lying on a bed. This time she opened her eyes to a darkened hospital room. A big, warm hand held hers. She turned her head. Justin stared back at her. "About time," he said with a smile.

"I made it." She forced a small smile. "Time?" It hurt to talk.

"Nine o'clock at night."

"Water?"

He stood to get a cup and held a straw at her mouth. She took a small sip.

"Abbie and Annie?"

"Mrs. Calvin says they're doing fine. One of her granddaughters came over after school and is spending the night to help her. She said not to worry about a thing and to concentrate on healing."

Jena tried to change her position, felt an uncomfortable pull beneath her armpit, and winced.

"Should I buzz for the nurse?" Justin asked. Worried. "Do you need pain medication?"

"No. Feel strange. Woozy."

He sat down. "The doctor said to expect you to be groggy."

"You don't have to stay," she said.

"I know I don't *have* to. I *want* to stay." He leaned in close. "Maybe you don't remember, but I told you earlier. I'm not leaving this hospital without you."

She thought that'd been a dream. "Okay by me." Jena closed her eyes and drifted back to sleep.

The next afternoon Justin walked beside Jena ready to catch her, amazed she'd made it from the car to the fifth floor unassisted. "I can't believe you refused to stay in the hospital another night," he said. He'd even offered to pay for the room, not that she needed his money.

"I'm fine," she said, but more tight-lipped than the last time she told him. "I need to be home."

"Almost there." Duh. Of course she knew they were almost there.

Justin wanted to help her, to hold her up but he didn't know where it was safe to touch her above the waist. In addition to two dressings over her breasts, held in place by a surgical bra he'd seen glimpses of, Jena had four bulb-type drains he'd been taught to empty, two below each armpit, that she said hurt worse than her surgical incisions.

In the condo, Justin got Jena settled into the recliner chair where she promptly fell asleep.

And for the first time since they'd left the hospital he inhaled deeply then exhaled a relieved breath. They'd made it. He entered the kitchen to microwave water for a cup of coffee and saw some letters on the table. Four of them.

He lifted the one on top labeled "Justin" and opened it.

Dear Justin,
If you're reading this letter I guess my worst fears have been realized and I didn't survive the surgery.

A read-if-I-die letter. He dropped it and hurried over to Jena—to check her breathing—fearing he'd somehow jinxed her by reading a letter she'd intended for post-mortem viewing. The thought made him sick to his stomach. The microwave pinged. He dumped the boiling water down the sink and sat at the table. Stared at the letter. Wondered what she'd want him to know if she wasn't here to tell him. Only she *was* here, thank you, God. And whatever she had to say to him he'd much rather hear coming from her beautiful lips in her melodic voice. He picked up the letter and crumbled it into a ball. But couldn't get himself to throw it out.

Curiosity got the better of him.

He flattened out the wrinkles.

I'm sorry to leave you alone to care for our daughters. You have to know if it were at all within my power to be there with you, I would be. Since I'm not, I thought you should know I have complete confidence in your ability to raise our daughters in a way that would make me proud. Don't be afraid to ask for help if you need it.
In the pages that follow I've left detailed in-

structions for special things I'd like you to do for
the girls each year, little things to help them re-
member me and how much I loved them.

Justin's heart felt raw and he reached for a napkin
to blot his eye. This was crazy. He should be celebrating Jena's survival not reading this letter, but he had to
know how it ended.

In high school, I had a crush on the boy you were,
handsome, fearless, and fun. As an adult, it's only
taken me a few short days to fall in love with the
man you've become, still handsome, fearless and
fun but also kind and gentle, confident and re-
sponsible. Your support and help has meant so
much. Nothing would have made me happier than
to live out my years as your wife. I am so sorry I
didn't get the chance.
 I love you.
Yours Always,
Jena

Justin sat back and clasped his hands behind his
head. Jena loved him. He looked over at her sleeping
form. Never in his life did he ever think it possible that
a smart, proper, discriminating woman like Jena would
ever see him as more than a quick screw. *I love you.*
Yours Always, Jena. She loved him. Always.

And since his hours in the surgical waiting room
consisted of some time spent considering the possibility of a life without Jena—during which his insides felt
like every one of his internal organs had gone rotten—
he was pretty sure he loved her right back. And he'd

make it a point to tell her at the first opportunity. He glanced at the clock on the stove. An hour until dinner.

Time to prove his worth as a family man. He preheated the oven, took out the vegetable lasagna Jena had left in the refrigerator, and put it in to cook. Then he called Mrs. Calvin and went upstairs to retrieve the twins.

They started to cry in the elevator. Maybe he should have taken Mrs. Calvin up on her offer to feed them before he took them home. But in giving a full report on Jena's condition, he'd already spent more time upstairs than he'd planned, and he worried about leaving Jena alone for too long. "Daddy's going to take good care of you," he told them as he wheeled the stroller down the hallway. "You need to quiet down or you'll wake mommy."

Seems they were more concerned with their empty bellies.

He entered the condo ready to apologize for waking Jena, to find the recliner chair empty. "Jena," he called out, maneuvering the stroller inside and closing the door.

No answer.

He walked to the closed door of the hall bathroom. "Jena?" He tried the knob. Locked. "Jena!" He knocked on the door.

"I'm fine," she said, sounding weak.

"Unlock the door."

"Go take care of Abbie and Annie. I don't need any help."

"Call me if you do," he said. Although how the heck would he hear her over their crying daughters?

He rushed to get the bottles made. Had all his supplies lined up and was ready to start when he heard a horrible gassy squirty type noise come from the vicinity of the stroller. Red-faced Annie—dressed in yellow— the guilty party. "This is not a very good time," Justin said as he placed the empty liner-filled bottles on the counter to wheel the girls into their bedroom.

He picked up Annie, holding her away from him so her soiled bottom didn't leak onto him. He set her on the changing table. "Daddy will have you all cleaned up in a minute." He unsnapped her outfit, revealing her cubby legs. Then he undid the diaper and, "My, God!" He closed her back up. But not before a hideous odor wafted up to the pocket of air where his next inhaled breath had come from. He retched. While he may be new to this diaper changing thing, it did not take an expert to see that Annie was not tolerating her formula well and something needed to be done. He eased down the front of the diaper. Slowly. Hoping. Nope. That gagworthy, hold-your-nose-and-close-your-eyes mess had not been his imagination. And it was, in fact, as bad as he'd first thought.

Annie kicked and twisted, and the mess started to spread.

"Whoa. Hold still."

She didn't.

"I can do this," Justin chanted. "I can do this." Had to do this. Like ripping off a Band-Aid. Do it quick. He turned his head, inhaled and removed the diaper. It took eight baby wipes and four gasps of tainted air to get her clean. He set her on a fresh towel, put on a new diaper and changed her into a sleeper. In what had to beat the slowest most toxic diaper change on record.

While Annie had calmed down, Abbie continued

to scream. He couldn't put Annie back in the stroller which she'd defiled, so he set her on the bed. Then got worried she'd roll off. Although he'd never seen her roll, and had no idea when she might start, he refused to risk it. She would not get hurt on his watch.

He put Annie in her crib—which she did not like at all, and ran to check on Jena.

He knocked on the closed bathroom door.

Nothing.

Abbie and Annie continued to scream their displeasure with him not giving them his full attention.

He pressed his ear to the door. "Jena? Are you okay?"

He heard what sounded like sobbing. "Go away." Her words, the way she said them, conveyed absolute misery.

"Open this door or I'm going to kick it in."

A smoke detector went off somewhere in the condo, the noise shrill, and loud enough to drown out Annie and Abbie. Something smelled burnt. Damn it. The lasagna. He ran to the kitchen and opened the oven door releasing a plume of thick black smoke. He turned on the fan over the stove. It did nothing. He checked for flames, seeing none he closed the oven door and turned it off.

He ran back to the bathroom. "Jena!" He pounded on the door.

But the girls were screaming and the smoke alarm blaring and now someone was knocking on his front door. He ran to open it to see his pain-in-the-ass neighbor. "It's okay. Burned dinner." He slammed the door in the man's face.

He climbed on a chair and tried to disable the smoke alarm.

He glanced at the closed bathroom door worried about Jena. Surely, if she was okay she'd have come out to investigate. The siren hurt his ears. The smoke made him cough. And Justin realized he could not handle this alone.

Don't be afraid to ask for help if you need it.

He hopped off the chair and called Jaci then ran to check on the girls to make sure the smoke hadn't affected them. He found a screaming Annie in her crib, her pink cheeks wet with tears, her legs kicking in anger. Abbie had gotten herself all wedged sideways in the stroller, pushing with her legs and jamming her head into the side cushion. And she had a cut under her eye. Tiny but a definite nick. With blood. "Dammit." He unstrapped her lucky she hadn't strangled herself. He was a total screw up. A failure at fatherhood. What the hell had he been thinking taking on care of an incapacitated Jena and two babies by himself?

"Justin," Jaci called out.

"In here."

He heard some banging and the smoke alarm went quiet.

Jaci entered the girls' bedroom followed by Ian who held a broom. Justin handed Abbie to Ian, picked up Annie from the crib and dragged Jaci by her arm to the bathroom. "I'm sorry to do this to you, and Jena will probably hate me forever, but I don't know if she needs a nurse or her sister. All I do know is she needs someone and she certainly isn't opening the door for me." He knocked. "Jaci's here. Open up."

"No," Jena cried out.

"What the hell did you do to her that she locked herself in the bathroom?" Ian asked.

"Shut up." Justin pushed Annie into Ian's other arm. "Go wait in my bedroom and open a window. I'll be in with the bottles in a minute."

Ian didn't move until Jaci said, "Go. The smoke isn't good for them."

"What happened?" Jaci asked, worried.

"She needs to be the one to tell you," Justin said. He leaned close to the door. "Honey, come on. It's me or Jaci. One of us is coming in." Tomorrow he'd remove the lock.

"Jena," Jaci said calmly through the door. "You're scaring me. Please, let me in."

The lock clicked. Thank you. Jaci turned the knob, opened the door and peered inside. She must have gotten the go ahead because she disappeared into the bathroom and closed the door behind her. Justin didn't have time to feel relieved because he still needed to tend to Abbie and Annie. So he headed to aerate the kitchen and make bottles.

Jena sat back down on the closed lid of the toilet, too tired to stand any longer, sore from wriggling out of her zip up sweat jacket and multiple unsuccessful attempts to empty her drains.

Jaci stood with her back to the door, staring down at Jena's surgical bra in shock. "What happened?" It didn't take her long to figure it out. "No," she whispered. Her eyes went wide and filled with tears. "Not cancer." She lifted her fingertips to her mouth. "Not you."

"I'm fine," Jena said, hoping if she said it enough— and avoided mirrors—she'd believe it.

"You don't look fine. You look like a woman who is

post op bilateral mastectomies. You look like you went and had a major surgery without telling me. Why?"

Jena looked down. "You said you didn't want to know the outcome of my genetic testing. I couldn't very well share my decision to undergo prophylactic bilateral mastectomies without explaining why."

"Prophylactic." Jaci clutched her fist to her heart. "Thank, God." She let out a breath. "I may not have wanted to know the results of your testing, but I most certainly would have wanted to know your plans included surgery. I most certainly would have wanted to be there for you, to listen and research and help you formulate the pros and cons list I'm sure you have stashed somewhere."

In her research folder. Jena smiled.

"When did you have it?"

"Yesterday morning."

"Yesterday morning?" Jaci screeched. "What are you doing home from the hospital? With twins? And Justin? Of all the—"

"I made a terrible mistake." Although she'd thought she was all cried out, new tears flooded Jena's eyes. She dropped her forehead into her palm. "I wanted to be home, but I feel awful, I can't manage my drains by myself and I don't want Justin to see me like this."

"Oh, Jen." Jaci leaned down to give her a gentle hug. It felt so good.

"I think I rushed the surgery." She sucked in a stuttery breath. "Maybe if I'd waited." She looked up at her sister. "Maybe this would be easier if I'd given Justin and me more time together to feel more comfortable around each other." Too late now.

"But Aunt Lynnie." Jaci understood.

"I can see daddy's face when he looked at mom after her surgery. Can't bear to see that look from Justin." Now she ached on the inside, too. "Re...re...repulsed by me."

"Jena Piermont you snap out of it, right now." Jaci knelt on the floor by Jena's feet and put her hand on Jena's knee. "Daddy was an inconsiderate jerk. Justin is a good man."

"I love him," Jena cried.

"I know." Jaci rubbed her back.

"He won't ever love me now." She hated that she sounded so pitiful.

"I think you're mistaken," Jaci said. "He's pretty upset out there. If he's not crazy in love with you already, it's only a matter of time. I'm sure of it. Who wouldn't love you? You're perfect."

Not even close.

Jena reached up to touch her breasts. "I'm half the size I was." She pressed. "And I can't feel anything." But an overwhelming, smothering despair. "They feel dead."

"It's so early in your recovery. Maybe some of the sensation will come back."

And maybe her retained nipples would survive and not fall off. And maybe the scarring would be minimal. And maybe in a few weeks, fully clothed, no one would be able to tell the difference. Maybe. Maybe. Maybe.

"Come on," Jaci said. "Let me take a look at you." And just like that, she shifted into nursing mode, assessing Jena's dressings and drains.

"Thank you, for coming," Jena said, feeling calmer. "I hate to be a bother."

"Stop it," Jaci snapped. "You're my sister. My twin.

I love you." Jaci turned to face her, so serious. "You have to know how much I love you. You hurt, I hurt. You're happy, I'm happy. I'd do anything for you, Jena. Anything."

"You're going to make me cry again," Jena said.

Jaci waved her off. "Then forget I mentioned it."

Not likely.

Jaci washed her hands in the sink.

"Jaci?"

"Yeah."

"I love you, too. And I'd do anything for you, too."

Jaci smiled. "You know, to be quite honest, while I'm sorry for the circumstances, it feels damn good to have *you* need me for a change."

Someone knocked on the door. "Everything okay in there?" Justin asked.

Jena tried to hunch so he wouldn't see her. Something pulled. Ow. "Lock the door."

Jaci did. "Jena's okay. We'll be out in a few minutes."

After Jaci emptied her drains, helped her wash up and change into a different cotton zip up running suit, Jena felt much better.

Jena woke up the next morning, after a relatively good night's sleep—thank you pain medicine—still in the recliner, where she felt the most comfortable. Justin, who'd refused to sleep in the bed because he didn't trust her to wake him if she needed him, was asleep on the couch. Jena got up from the chair, basically feeling achy all over, and shuffled to the bathroom.

She closed the door, noticed it no longer had a lock, and opened it. "Really?" she yelled. "That's what you did after I fell asleep?"

"I figured if you could lock yourself in there then

the girls can," Justin said from the couch. "I'm being a proactive parent."

"Ha ha." She closed the door.

"Do you need me to empty your drains?" Justin asked from the other side of the door.

Too close. "Don't come in."

"I promise to honor your privacy. But if there's an emergency I need to get in there. Now do you need me to empty your drains?"

"No." Jena finished up and washed her hands. "Jaci said she'd stop by before work."

"The nurse said I did a good job of it."

She'd only allowed that because they wouldn't discharge her otherwise, and the minutes she'd spent sitting there while he practiced, trying to make sure he couldn't see under the front of her gown, had been the worst of her entire hospital stay.

"I'd prefer Jaci."

"If that's what you want."

He sounded disappointed. Jena opened the door. "I appreciate you wanting to do it, really. I just feel more comfortable with Jaci."

"A nice big good morning kiss would go a long way toward soothing my hurt feelings." He leaned in and puckered his lips.

Had she really hurt his feelings? No. He had to be teasing. She kissed him.

"Now what would you like for breakfast?"

"You don't have to—"

"I want to," Justin insisted.

So sweet. "How about rye toast and tea?"

"Coming right up."

Over the next few days they fell into a nice routine. Each day Jena felt a bit better and tried to do a bit more, always under Justin's watchful eye. He was absolutely wonderful. But other than an occasional peck of a kiss, she kept her distance, feeling unappealing and unfeminine and not even remotely ready for intimacy of any kind.

One night in the recliner extended into six. And even though Jena's pain decreased and her activity increased, she insisted on sleeping in the recliner chair, claiming it was more comfortable for her than the bed. But with each passing day Justin felt more certain it was her way of putting physical distance between them.

When they sat on the couch to watch television he tried to put his arm around her, she asked him not to. Too sore she'd said. Okay. But he tried to hold her hand and she pulled it away. Tried to flirt and couldn't get one blush out of her.

And those sponge baths the nurse mentioned prior to discharge? The ones he'd gotten kind of excited about? Never happened. Because Jena would only let Jaci in the bathroom with her.

Selfish Justin regretted calling Jaci. But desperately-trying-to-do-the-right-thing fiancé and father Justin accepted that Jena preferred having her sister readily available, whether he liked it or not.

One week after her surgery, Justin drove Jena to the doctor's office to have two of the drains removed, hoping to finally get a look at her chest. Only to spend the duration of the visit, at Jena's request, in the waiting room. Jena had denied him entry into the examination room.

Justin felt her growing more distant, more skittish.

Smiling less. Preoccupied. And he knew in his heart if he didn't do something, he would lose her.

Thinking maybe the first step to getting back the old Jena was to get her out of the condo; he took the opportunity of her doctor's appointment to take her to lunch.

"Why are you stopping here?" she asked as he pulled into a parking lot.

"I'm taking you out to lunch. You've been cooped up in the condo for too long."

"I'm not hungry."

"Well I am."

"I don't want to go." She adjusted her shirt. "I still have two drains. Everyone will see."

He turned to face her. "You are wearing a loose blouse with a bulky sweater. I promise you, the drains and any bandages you may or may not still have are not visible."

He got out of the SUV and walked around to open her door. She looked up at him. Hesitant and unsure. He held out his hand. She placed her hand in his. Thank you. And he helped her out of the car. The first thing she did was tilt her beautiful face up to the sun. "That feels nice."

"Grandma Abbie always used to say the fresh air will do you good."

He tucked her hand in the crook of his arm and led her into the small bistro like any other couple out for a lunch date. It felt good.

The waitress seated them along the wall.

"I feel like everyone is staring at my chest," Jena shared, closing the sides of her sweater.

Justin looked around. "I don't see anyone staring at your chest. Do you?"

Jena looked around. "I guess not."

The waitress took their orders.

"I thought you weren't hungry," Justin teased.

"Well it would be impolite of me to sit here and watch you eat," Jena said primly. Then they lapsed into a casual, comfortable conversation. Jena warmed up and he managed to coax a few smiles and one very distinct blush out of her.

And Justin felt hope.

But back in the condo her don't-touch-me walls shot right back up.

That night after they put the girls to bed Jena said, "I'm going to take a shower."

A shower sounded good to him. "Want some company?"

She reacted like he'd asked her to have kinky sex in front of a room full of men, but quickly regained her composure. "Uh, thank you. But no."

Not one to give up easily he tried a different tack. "Do you need help?"

"No. No." She hurried to the guest bathroom. The guest bathroom. Always the guest bathroom. "I'm good. I'll be fine."

He would have yelled for her to call if she needed anything, but the way things were going, he'd likely hear the thud of her unconscious body hitting the shower floor before she'd call for him. He threw the magazine he'd been reading, frustrated as hell, and he sat there, listening for any signs of distress, imagining rivulets of water flowing down her body, and foam—

Something fell—maybe a shampoo bottle—followed by a groan. He jumped up from the couch, ran to the bathroom, and thank you no more door lock, pushed inside. "Are you okay?"

"A little dizzy." She sounded weak. Dazed.

He threw the shower curtain to the side.

"No!" she screamed. "Go away." She hunched forward and covered her chest. But that meant she had to release her hold on the tub grip bar. She swayed.

Justin reached into the shower spray, turned off the water and scooped her up before she fell.

"Don't look at me," she cried, covering her chest.

Not before he'd seen the purple bruising and the strip of something tape-like over her incisions. And the string from a sweatshirt hood she had tied loosely around her neck with the long tubes of her drains threaded through diaper pins to keep the bulbed ends from dangling.

He sat on the toilet settling Jena on his lap.

"Please, don't look at me," she said again, Quiet. Defeated.

Justin had had enough. "You know what? It's too late. I looked. And you want to know what I saw?"

"No," she said miserably.

"I saw the breasts of a woman I care deeply for looking bruised and painful. And you want to know how it made me feel?"

She shook her head, looking down, almost curled into a ball.

"Tough. You were the one who refused to accept my ring unless I promised to talk to you and be honest with you. So here goes. It makes me feel mad as hell. At cancer. And helpless, that I can't take away the pain or speed your healing. And damn determined." Careful of her drains he draped his arms around hers and hugged her. "I feel you pushing me away and I won't let it happen." Tears pooled in his eyes. She was something special. A keeper. He felt it in his heart. "You can push all you want. But I'm not going anywhere."

Jena said nothing.

"Before your surgery you told me you are more than a pair of breasts. Right on. I agree. What about you? Saying the words isn't enough. You have to believe them." He kissed her head. "You are so much more to me. I love you, Jena. And not solely for your beautiful body, but because of who you are. A smart, sweet, thoughtful, caring, courageous woman."

"I don't feel very courageous at the moment." She lifted her head to look at him. "I love you, too," she admitted. And he'd been right. He'd much rather hear the words come from her mouth than read them on a piece of paper—that now resided in the town dump with the other three letters she'd written. "You've taken such good care of me and the girls."

"I got off to a rocky start."

"But you didn't give up." He wouldn't let himself. "And with everything that went on that night, I think I'd have needed to call in reinforcements, too."

"Thank you." He kissed her forehead.

"You're all wet," Jena said.

"That's what happens when I brave a shower to rescue my fiancée."

"My hero." She smiled. And Justin couldn't help but smile, too.

"You smell like baby shampoo."

"That's what the doctor said to use until I'm all healed."

Which is probably why she always used the guest bathroom. Not because she was avoiding their bedroom, but because they kept the baby shampoo in the guest bathroom where she bathed the twins. And maybe so he'd be close by in case she needed him. "It's starting to harden in your hair."

"I guess I'd better finish my shower."

"About that," he said. "Should I be calling the doctor to tell him you almost passed out?"

She looked away. "He, uh, warned me this might happen."

"And you risked cracking your head open on the tub floor rather than asking me to sit in here with you on the off chance an experienced medical professional may be right?"

"I felt absolutely, totally fine before the shower." She looked up at him with her beautiful blue eyes. "I took care of my mother for years. Trust me. I would not have risked a head injury by taking a shower if I felt the least bit unwell. I honestly thought I'd be fine."

"How do you feel now?" he asked.

"Like I'd appreciate it if you'd sit in here with me while I rinse off."

Good, because no way he was leaving.

"But please," she said, starting to stand. "It makes me uncomfortable for you to look at me right now."

He closed his eyes.

She kissed his cheek. "Thank you."

She turned on the shower. He waited until he heard the curtain close before he opened his eyes. "You okay?"

"Fine."

He lifted his wet shirt over his head, then what the hell, stripped off the rest of his clothes and wrapped a towel around his waist. "Now that you're cleared to take showers, does that mean no more sponge baths?

Cause I was kind of really looking forward to giving you a sponge bath."

She laughed. "You have got to be kidding me. After everything you saw just now, all you're thinking about is giving me a sponge bath?"

As a matter of fact, "Yeah."

"You're amazing," she said.

"Back atcha, baby."

"I like it when you call me baby."

"Why, Jena Piermont. Are you flirting with me?"

She turned off the water. "Please hand me a towel and close your eyes."

Obviously, there was still work to be done. He closed his eyes and opened a large bath towel prepared to wrap her up in it. But they'd made some progress tonight. And progress was good.

Post op week two Jena let him take care of her drains, and she returned to their bed, although she slept out of reach and propped up almost as high as if she was in the recliner. At least he could hold her hand as they drifted off to sleep.

On the next Wednesday they returned to the surgeon's office and Jena's remaining drains were removed. That time he was allowed in the exam room but had to stay on the outside of the curtain. At least he could hear the doctor's evaluation and instructions.

Progress.

Within a few days of drain removal things started to return to normal. Jena could move around better and required less assistance caring for the twins. But by far the best part was she resumed sleeping on her side so he could cuddle up behind her at night. An activity he enjoyed much more than smoking cigars, drinking beer, and playing cards with a bunch of guys into the early morning hours. So when Ryan gave him a hard time for cancelling his fourth poker game in a row, Justin told him to find a permanent replacement to fill his spot. Justin had no interest in playing every week. Here and there maybe, but right now he'd much rather spend his time with his fiancée and daughters.

Toward the end of post op week three it was as if the surgery had never happened. Except he had yet to set eyes on his lovely fiancée's undressed post-surgery body, and they had yet to have sex.

Justin didn't push. But he made it known when she was ready so was he.

Nothing.

So in the middle of post op week four, when he returned home from work, color him totally surprised when Jena greeted him at the door, wearing an instant hardon inducing red babydoll negligee with a matching, sheer, robe, complete with a hint of cleavage, and those silver stilettoes he loved.

"Welcome home," she said with a hesitant smile. Shy. Unsure. She fiddled with her feathered hem. "I thought maybe…" She looked away. "If you wanted…" She swallowed. "We could try…"

"You look fantastic, Jena…amazing." Justin's sex-starved body went hard at the sight of her.

She gifted him with a beautiful smile, walked to him and went up on her toes for a kiss. Not the platonic pecks from the last few weeks. But a real tongue in the mouth, I want you naked now, kind of kiss.

As difficult as it was to do, Justin stopped her.

At her hurt expression he explained, "I have been in some terrible areas today and I need to shower. Five minutes. Tops." He kissed her. Then ran for the shower chanting 'Please don't change your mind. Please don't change your mind. Please don't change your mind.'

He finished in three.

"Now." He hurried into the living room, wearing nothing but a pair of briefs. "Where were we?"

She sat on the corner of the couch with her hands crossed in her lap her feet on the floor, looking prim. And nervous. "The girls are spending the night with Jaci."

Finally. Justin joined her on the couch. Night after night, morning after morning, he'd held her close, aroused and wanting, waiting for her to be ready, waiting for this very moment, waiting to prove how inconsequential breasts had become. Because he loved every enticing, alluring, lovable inch of Jena and was raring to show her.

"Come here." He patted his lap.

She looked over at him. "I'm not sure how this will turn out. But we need to get past this first awkward time if there's any hope…" She turned her head. "I want to make you happy, to give you what you need. But…"

"You do make me happy," he said. "Please." He reached for her arm. "What I need right now is to hold you close." To calm her nerves, rouse her passion and build her confidence.

In a show of trust that humbled him, she climbed over to straddle his lap. "Is this okay?"

He was so desperate to have her, hanging by their feet from the ceiling would have been okay. He nodded, placed his hands on her hips and guided her down.

Her eyes went wide with surprise when she settled on top of his erection.

"You feel what you do to me?" he asked, rocking beneath her, feeling her body relax. Good. "I want you just as much now as I did before."

"Kiss me," she said seconds before she set her lips to his.

Soft. Warm. Moist. Tentative. Justin channeled every bit of his love, relief, and hope for the future into the kiss he gave her back, careful not to squeeze her as tight as he wanted for fear he'd hurt her.

When Jena broke away, breathing heavy, looking slightly dazed, she said, "I love the way you kiss me." She touched a finger to her lips. "I didn't think it'd be enough but..." She rocked her hips. Tears formed in her eyes. "That feels so good."

Justin massaged her through her panties, slid his hands up under her satin and lace teddy, down to her butt, pressed her down, swiveled, teetered on the verge of bursting.

She rubbed along his length. He stayed her hips. "Baby you don't want to do that right now. Lift up."

Jena did and he shimmied out of his boxers.

When she sat back down he met her bare sex. What the...? He looked down. When had she removed those sexy red panties?

"They have an opening. For you to..." She blushed.

Justin hoped she'd never stopped blushing for him. He thrust up. Made contact. So damn good.

"I'm on birth control," she said. "And since both our STD panels came out negative..." She sank down, taking him inside of her, naked skin to glorious hot, wet, naked skin. His first time ever and it felt so good Justin wasn't sure he'd survive it.

She leaned forward to whisper in his ear. "I'm not

sure if I mentioned how much I appreciate all your understanding and patience over the past few weeks."

She had.

"Or how lucky I am to have you as my soon-to-be
husband."

Yup. But he didn't mind hearing it again.

"Or how much I love you."

Now that he'd never get tired of hearing. "I love you,
too, Jena."

In a move that far exceeded her experience she jerked
her hips and took him even deeper, making using his
big brain near impossible. He fought to remain focused
on the conversation.

Unsuccessfully.

He gripped her butt, withdrew and surged back in
then pulled her down for a kiss. "Thank you for choosing me as your one and only." He started to lift her
teddy, needing to see all of her, to show her he was okay
with the changes to her body, that they didn't matter.
Because he loved her.

"No," she said, holding it in place. "I'd prefer to leave
it on."

Perfectly fine, as long as she didn't push him away.
"Did I mention my fondness for sexy negligees?" He
caressed the smooth, luxurious wisp of fabric covering her belly.

"I've got dozens of them."

And Justin couldn't wait to see and feel and snuggle
up against every single one of them.

EPILOGUE

Two weeks later

"You look beautiful," Jaci said to Jena.

"So do you," Jena replied. Identical, in fact, from their matching ivory wedding gowns in simple, understated, tasteful, elegance to their updos, makeup and manicures.

"Mom would love that we're getting married here." In her beautiful garden. "Thank you for suggesting it." Insisting actually, just as she'd insisted on waiting to get married until Jena was all healed and ready to participate in a double ceremony. "I feel like she's here with us."

Jaci looked around and smiled. "Me, too."

Jena would forever be indebted to her stubborn sister who'd refused to let her be content with a quickie courthouse wedding.

"Is that harp music I hear?"

Jaci listened. Then smiled. "Surprise!" She bounced on the tippy-toes of her pricy pumps. "I couldn't help myself. I'd seen her at Patsy's wedding last year. I came across her card while looking for a ring I'd misplaced. I called her and she had room in her schedule. It was meant to be."

"You did it," Jena said. While she'd been preoccupied by the twins, Justin and adjusting to her new body and her new life to realize. "Except for the hundreds of guests and mom being here, you've put together my dream wedding." Right down to the harpist. "How did you know?"

Jaci picked at her bouquet. "You only talked about it incessantly when we were teenagers."

"I didn't think you listened."

"Well I did," Jaci said. "Over the years your fantasy kind of became my fantasy, too." She shrugged. "So here we are."

"I love you." Jena hugged her sister. "And I don't care if you wrinkle."

"I love you back." Jaci squeezed her tight. "I want you to be happy."

Jena stepped out of their embrace. "I am." So happy. So in love. So blessed. "And I want you to be happy, too."

"I am." Jaci smiled.

"Well," Jena said. "Neither one of us thought it possible, but we both managed to find great guys who love us as much as we love them. Despite daddy's mandate."

"And Jerry's underhanded maneuvering."

No. Their childhoods weren't perfect. But with each new generation came the opportunity for change. "I won't ever force my girls into marriage. Or allow either one of them to give up their childhood to take on adult responsibilities just to make my life easier."

Jaci set her hand on her flat belly and looked down at it. "And I won't allow my children to ever feel the pain and degradation of physical abuse. I will accept them and love them, faults and all, no matter how wild or badly they behave or how much they act out."

"How could I not have seen it?" Jena said, eying Jaci's protective, loving caress of her abdomen. "You're pregnant!"

Jaci smiled and nodded.

"Oh, Jaci." Jena wrapped her arms around her sister again. "I'm so happy for you. Now our children will be close in age. They'll grow up together and be best friends."

"Which is exactly what I wanted. But please, don't say anything. I'm going to tell Ian tonight."

"Dah-lings, you look mah-velous." Aunt Mill, who'd spared no expense dressing up for the wedding and looked very Hollywood glamorous, walked down the stone pathway to where they stood. Out of hiding from her abusive husband just for the day, Jena and Jaci had decided having Aunt Mill at their ceremony was more important than any other local guests. "It's time to go." She reached them, turned around, and held out an elbow to each of them. "Your young men are getting antsy. I need Jena on the right and Jaci on the left."

Jena looked at Jaci. And Jaci looked and Jena. And with sweet smiles they switched places.

Completely unaware, Aunt Mill led them down the pathway.

"I can feel your mother all around us." Aunt Mill looked up to the clear blue sky and inhaled deeply. "As she was before the cancer and the head injury and she is exuberant."

A fragrant breeze blew past.

They turned a corner and Ian, Justin, and the judge who would be performing the ceremony, came into view.

Marta stood to the right beside Justin, holding Abbie

and Annie. Mandy stood to the left beside Ian, holding Maddie.

Justin, so handsome in his tuxedo, looked back and forth between her and Jaci.

Ian, looking equally handsome, winked at Jena then focused in on his real bride.

Aunt Mill stopped about five feet from the men.

Justin looked at Ian who motioned for him to go first so he walked toward Jaci and Jena's heart squeezed. After all they'd been through together he still couldn't recognize her. He extended his hand palm up in front of Jaci. Jena debated what to do. But at the last possible second, he turned toward Jena and quietly said, "I believe I'm supposed to be marrying you today, Jena, unless you've changed your mind."

Joy fluttered just under her skin. "I haven't." She took his hand and accompanied him to stand before the judge.

A warm, fragrant breeze enveloped her in love and Jena knew, without a doubt, her mom was in attendance.

Abbie started to fuss.

Justin made a move toward Marta then stopped himself.

The judge started to speak.

Abbie started to cry.

"She's not going to stop until you hold her," Jena whispered.

And sure enough Justin took Abbie into his arms and she immediately went quiet.

"Sorry," Justin said.

The judge continued.

Then Annie started to cry.

Jena took her from Marta and she immediately went quiet.

"Sorry," Jena said.

The judge continued.

After they repeated their vows and as the judge said, "You may now kiss your brides," Justin handed Abbie back to Marta and took Annie and handed her to Marta, and over their cries of protest said to Jena, "I love our girls, but some moments aren't meant to be shared." And he took her in his arms and kissed her.

During the small luncheon at Jaci's condo—because Aunt Mill couldn't be seen out in public—that followed, Jena whispered in her husband's ear, "I forgot to tell you, your package arrived this morning while you were at the store." The surprise present he'd ordered for her to wear on their wedding night.

Since Jena preferred to keep her foobs—fake boobs—under wraps, she and Justin had taken up the fun and surprisingly stimulating hobby of searching out enticing negligees and arousing outfits for her to wear to bed.

Justin smiled that smile that never failed to put her in the mood. "I can't wait to see you in it," he whispered back with a quick swipe of his tongue in her ear.

"And I can't wait to see you see me in it." Modeling for Justin turned out to be a highly erotic form of foreplay they both enjoyed, and Jena loved to watch his lust-filled eyes when she performed for him.

Their sex life had changed, but was no less satisfying than it'd been before surgery. Jena couldn't remember what aroused nipples felt like, and she didn't miss them at all.

* * * * *